SLEEPING DRAGONS

OMNIBUS

OPHELIA BELL

Sleeping Dragons Omnibus

Cover Art Designed by Dawné Dominique

This is a work of fiction. Names, places, characters, and events are fictitious in every regard. Any similarities to actual events and persons, living or dead, is purely coincidental. Any trademarks, service marks, product names, or named features are assumed to be the property of their respective owners, and are used only for reference. There is no implied endorsement if any of these terms are used.

Published by Ophelia Bell
UNITED STATES

ISBN-13: 978-1505528480
ISBN-10: 1505528488

ALSO BY OPHELIA BELL

RISING DRAGONS SERIES

Night Fire

Breath of Destiny

Breath of Memory

Breath of Innocence

Breath of Desire

Breath of Love

Breath of Flame and Shadow

Breath of Fate

STANDALONE EROTIC TALES

After You

Out of the Cold

OPHELIA BELL TABOO

Burying His Desires

Blackmailing Benjamin

Spankable

CONTENTS

ANIMUS 1

TABULA RASA 59

GEMINI 103

SHADOWS 173

NEXUS 247

ASCEND 319

SLEEPING DRAGONS

BOOK 1

ANIMUS

OPHELIA BELL

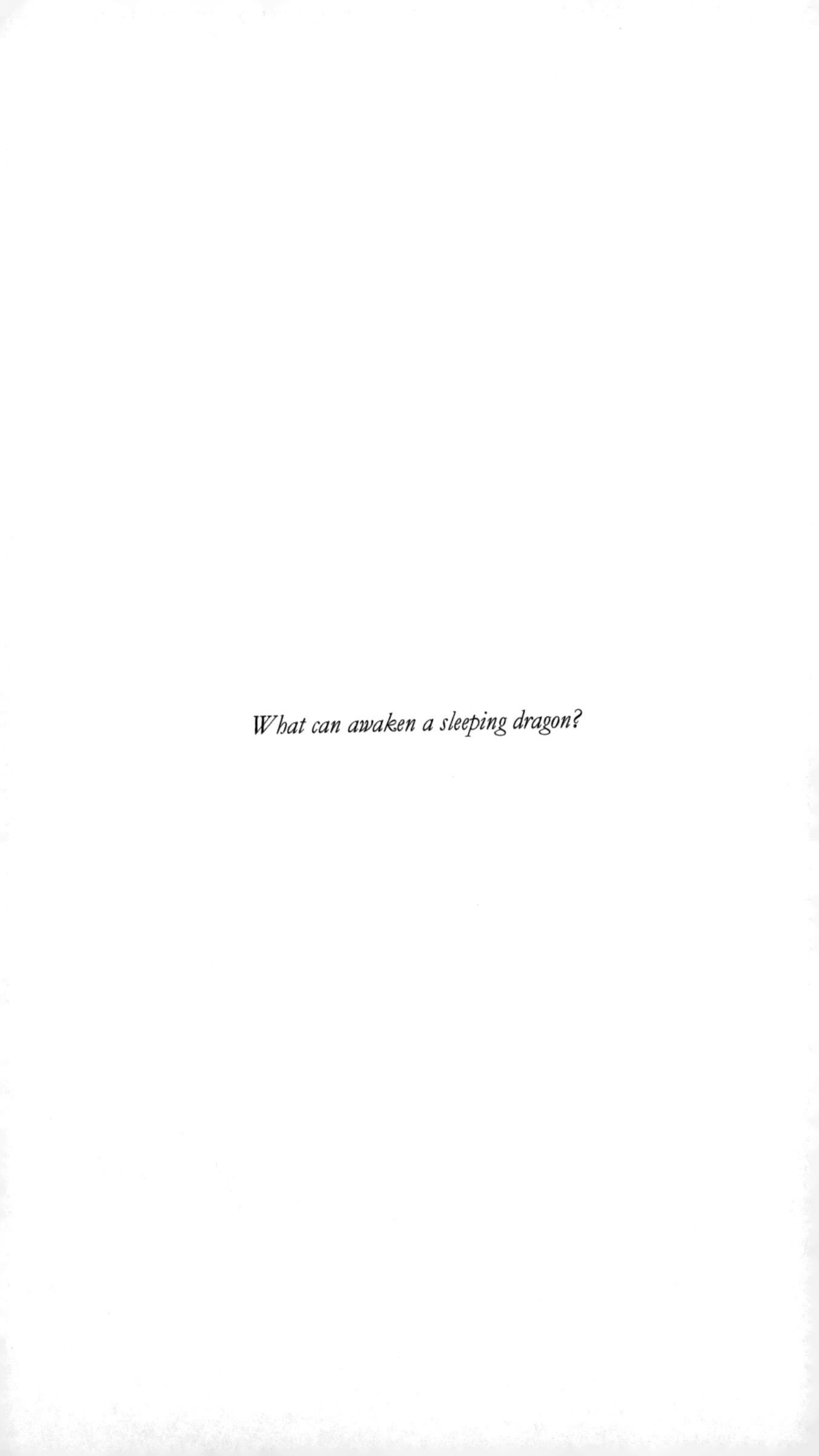

What can awaken a sleeping dragon?

CHAPTER ONE

Erika always got a little damp between the thighs on the cusp of an archaeological find, but this wasn't just any old pile of ancient bones she was about to uncover. Today her entire body thrummed with excitement. If the coordinates were right, this would be the find of the century.

The vine-covered rock wall in front of her was the final barrier. Her heart pounded in anticipation of what she hoped lay beneath. With passionate rips, she yanked the foliage away to display the elaborate, smooth carving of a dragon wound into a disc-shape.

The image sent a thrill through her. *Hot-damn, we found it!* The culmination of her hard years of graduate research rested in the darkness somewhere behind that slab of vine-covered rock. She and her team would be the first to set eyes on it.

In spite of her conviction that they'd finally reached the end of their quest, she glanced back to her geologist for confirmation, itching with impatience.

Eben's eyes widened and he looked up from the handheld GPS unit. "I just sprung wood, baby," he said, echoing her own thoughts. "Fuck yeah! This is it!"

Cheers erupted from the group behind them. They deserved to celebrate after enduring an exhausting trek through the remote reaches of the Sumatran jungle to get here, but the true celebration would have to wait just a little bit longer.

"Yeah, but it's just a wall." She swept her hands over the ridged face of the stone slab in front of her, ripping down more vines as she went. "How do we get inside, assuming there's an inside to get to?"

Eben slunk up behind her, pressing his tall, muscular body against her back. His hands covered hers while they explored the rock face. The arousing scent of his heady musk hit her nose and she inhaled. "Maybe extra hands are necessary," he whispered in her ear. "Those old dwarves could be horny bastards, wanting their stones touched by everyone."

"Dwarves…You've been watching too many movies. But I know someone's a horny bastard," she whispered, shifting her backside against his obvious hard-on.

She let him take control of their exploration of the hard surface before them. Eben had an uncanny ability to suss out the secrets of just about any mineral. He also had a particular skill at sinking his rock-hard shaft into her deeper crevices whenever the mood struck them. It was why she'd been so attracted to him during their undergrad years. Post-graduation, she'd kept him around because he was every bit as ambitious as she was to explore the deeper reaches of the world and all its secrets. It also didn't hurt that the tall, irreverent blond was very easy on the eyes.

"Here," he said, pushing her fingertips into a cleft she hadn't noticed. She grabbed onto the edge of the fissure and followed it down, pressing as she went until she felt it give. She gasped when the entire face in front of them receded at least a foot and began to slowly shift aside with the rough grinding of stone on stone. More cheers sounded behind them as their team looked on.

"We're inside!" she yelled, pulling away from Eben and raising her arms up in triumph.

Cool, dry air rushed out, carrying with it a familiar, pungent aroma. Her skin prickled with gooseflesh at the memories that surfaced in response to that scent as much as from the sudden chill of the air.

She'd been dreaming of this place ever since her dad had hinted at a mythical dragon race, spinning bedtime stories that rivaled those her friends heard from their parents when they were children.

In retrospect, she believed her father had left his research notes out deliberately to entice her. She'd read them over multiple times from age ten onward and fantasized ever since about finding the elusive dragon temple her father had always been searching for. All he'd had were small clues, one of which was the tiny jade carving of a dragon she wore around her neck right now. Another was a jade bottle, empty, yet still holding the lingering, spicy scent of whatever substance it had once contained.

Her father had died wondering, and Erika had vowed afterward that she would find it for him. And here she was, about to cross the threshold with the same familiar smell from her father's old bottle filling her lungs with each breath.

The opening displayed a dark corridor lined with smooth, pale stone. She reached inside and slid her fingertips across the rock. In spite of the cooler air beyond the threshold, the ethereal warmth of the walls sank into her fingertips. Once the door stopped sliding open with a heavy *cachunk*, a series of recessed sconces that lined the corridor began to glow one by one.

"Whoa," Eben said. "Magic?"

"Engineering, most likely. Old school…I bet there's a trigger somewhere in that door pocket that lights these up when the door is opened. Hey, Corey!" she called back behind them. "You'll love these lights. Get up here and document how they work."

The athletic, dark-haired figure of her tech nodded from behind the digital camera he held. "You got it, boss."

She held her eagerness in check for the time being. Instead of giving in to the urge to run inside and begin exploring, she took over camera duty for Corey and let him do his job. He diligently tested the air quality and gave her a swift thumbs-up indicating all was good on that front. The glowing sconces, on the other hand, caused his dark eyebrows to arch high on his tanned brow.

"It's like nothing I've ever seen," he said. "They come pretty close to light bulbs, but we both know better than that. Take a look…" He reached a leather-gloved hand into one of the half-moon-shaped recesses. What he pulled out continued to glow brightly when he held it up before her. Heat radiated off the oblong shape. It was round and bulbous at the lit end, dark and tapered at the end Corey held. The others circled around murmuring in awe while the glow gradually subsided. When it emitted only the brightness of a low-burning ember she reached out a tentative finger to touch it. Heat still lingered in it, but it felt solid, more like a stone than a fragile glass bulb.

"See," Eben said. "*Magic.*"

She rolled her eyes and took the odd stone from Corey, her first artifact from the temple. Corey grinned at what she was sure had to be a giddy expression on her face. She certainly felt like a kid on Christmas morning.

"Ready to conquer the dragon temple?" Corey asked with a quirk of his mouth and a wink. The epitome of professional behavior and honorable to a fault, Corey had always felt like the protective older brother of the group. She eyed him curiously now. Even though he'd traveled with three very attractive, intelligent single women for months, not once had he given any hint of flirting. Until now.

Dismissing his odd behavior as a side effect of the same excitement that afflicted her, she returned the camera to him. She turned back to the doorway and with a deep breath stepped slowly into the wide opening, caressing the pale stone walls as she went. The lights illuminated the translucent stone in a warm glow and she could just make out the beginning of a staircase several yards ahead.

"Jesus, this place is paneled entirely in jade." She paused to study a section of the wall, noting the faint green and gold coloring that threaded through the white stone in amorphous serpentine patterns. Her footsteps echoed in the wide space as she went further in. She reached the end of the corridor and paused to stare down at what appeared to be an endless staircase.

"You guys ready for this?" she asked the group behind her. Of course they were ready, she chided herself. But was *she* ready? So far the place had exceeded her wildest dreams and she was barely in the door. How deep would it go? What kinds of wonders would she find inside? And the biggest question that occupied her mind: Would her father's research be proven true after all? If there really were dragons down there, would they be as intelligent and powerful as her father's notes suggested? Too many questions, but she was a scientist. The only thing to do was…Well, fuck. *Boldly go, dammit! That's what you do!*

As if sensing her hesitance, Eben stepped up beside her and placed a large, warm hand on her shoulder. "Need a hand to hold, babe? This is your discovery. You should be the one to take the first step down. We're all right behind you."

After the first step, the anxiety disappeared and excitement returned. It took a lot of effort to maintain a casual pace, her curiosity making her itch to move faster. A hundred steps into the depths, she began taking steps two at a time, impatient to get to the good part. How deep was this place?

Fifteen minutes later, they finally reached the bottom and were faced with an elaborately decorated door. Onyx and gold shone in the light of a pair of larger sconces that flanked the door, the decorations depicting several dragons that appeared to be tangled in the throes of mating, but not with other dragons. All their partners appeared human. In the center of the carved coil of bodies was a small, circular depression with a starburst pattern of upraised black nubs.

"What kind of crazy sex dungeon did you bring us to, Erika?" Dimitri asked, his words accented with subtle drawn-out syllables that belied his Greek ancestry. He stifled a chuckle. "Not that I'd complain, but that looks kinky even for me."

"Y'know, Dimitri, sometimes I wonder if I didn't pick *the* horniest team on the planet. But maybe you guys are meant to be here. All the lore I've managed to find suggests that dragons have particular sexual appetites. And I suppose this is our first clue that it was accurate."

They paused to take pictures and record more for the ongoing documentary they'd been filming. The door was locked, but they were prepared for this one. Eben pulled out the solid gold disk they'd found a month ago in Myanmar and fitted it into the depression. It fit neatly, the nubs in the door filling in small holes within the disk. Eben twisted it and the door swung open, almost seeming to float on its hinges.

"I've got another hard-on," Eben whispered in her ear. She elbowed him and he laughed, but she had to admit she was turned on in the extreme.

Beyond the door they all paused. Her entire team let out a combined exhalation of awe.

"Yeah, we kick ass don't we?" Erika said.

Eben let out an excited whoop and picked her up, spinning her around. The others cheered and hugged. Once Eben set her down again she took a deep breath and gazed around in wonder.

The chamber beyond the door was immense, with long, curved walls, white and glowing with recessed lights like the corridor they'd just passed through. The entry led down another staircase to the center of an elliptical amphitheater surrounded by tiered stone benches that extended from the floor to the walls. At the far end was a high dais occupied by a throne elaborately carved out of jade, the translucent grass-green of it reflecting the light of a pair of those impossible lights that sat in two shallow alcoves behind it.

"Wow, check those out," Eben said. "Nothing like what we'd imagined they might be."

He pointed toward the pair of large, white dragon guardians that flanked the throne, and Erika's eyes widened at the sight. The guardians each rested on their haunches supported from behind by thick tails. Both sported large, erect phalluses jutting up between their scaled thighs. They'd have made interesting guest seats, that's for certain.

"Yeah," Erika said. "That's almost obscene, isn't it?"

He chuckled. "No more than you shoving my face into your wet pussy and telling me to eat you like a starving man..."

She dug a knuckle into his ribs and glanced around to see who might have heard, but the others were already spread out scouting the room. Not that it was any secret that she and Eben occasionally slept together. That kind of thing was hard to keep quiet when you shared a campsite with five other people for weeks at a stretch. But she knew Camille had a thing for Eben and didn't want to rub the younger woman's face in it unnecessarily. Her relationship with Eben had always been built out of convenience and mutual need. She sensed he had a limit that he would hit long before she hit her own. He'd been her best friend for years, but he wasn't the man she was meant to be with. If that man even existed.

"Look at those doorways behind the dais". She pointed at the pair of double-doors that rested deep on either side of the throne. "What do you think is back there?"

Eben shrugged. "The dungeon? The kitchen? What do dragons eat anyway? Pretty virgin princesses?" He glanced at Camille who was still gaping in awe in the doorway just out of earshot of his joke. "If I were a dragon I'd *love* eating virgins."

Eben grinned at Erika, irritatingly confident that she'd appreciate his sense of humor. He walked down the stairs and crossed the floor in long strides, taking the steps up to the throne two at a time with her following close behind.

"I wonder why the throne is empty," he said. "Usually an elaborate religious display like this would have the object of worship in plain sight."

Erika countered sharply. "You're a geologist, what the hell do you know about religious displays? To me this looks like a place to hold court. Not symbolic. Functional. See the alcoves in the mezzanine?" She pointed at the second tier above them. "I'd bet you anything those lead to more rooms behind the seats, maybe back into the surrounding structure as well. This place is more than just a shrine, it's a compound. People—or dragons—actually lived here." *And maybe they still do.*

"Well, I guess we'll have to wait for the experts to say otherwise, huh?" He raised an eyebrow and crouched in front of one of the draconic figures that flanked the throne. "They look so real, like they could wake up at any second."

"Master artisans, I guess." She walked up to the other statue and stroked the dragon's snout affectionately, trailing her fingertips over its polished white brows and the curling horns that extended backward from its skull. Her fingertips tingled strangely and her nipples hardened against the coarse linen of her shirt.

The stone was so smooth and warm it would have felt like flesh if it had any give to it. It really was a fantastic representation—polished to leave no evidence of the maker's tools anywhere. When she looked over at Eben, he was stroking the prominent stone phallus of the dragon statue in front of him.

"I can't take you anywhere," she said.

"Tell me you don't want to play with it. They're all so... anatomically correct. I always wondered what a dragon's dick looked like. Almost as nice as mine. And it's so *smooth*. Seriously, you need to touch it."

"It's just a reflection of their virility." Her heartbeat sped up. She knew her assessment was accurate from an academic standpoint, but the growing heat between her thighs confused her.

"So erect cocks are only symbolic, is that what you're saying?"

Erika gave him a sidelong glance. "In a statue, yeah. In you, it just means you haven't jerked off in a few hours." She looked pointedly at the huge bulge in his crotch.

"I always have a cock. It's not my fault if you're too big a prude to want to touch it," he muttered.

She scowled back at him knowing he was digging at her for kicking him out of her tent the night before, but she'd been too stressed about their imminent discovery to entertain him. Her plan had been to rub out enough orgasms to send herself into a mini-coma and sleep through the night without the distraction of another body beside her. She'd hoped tonight would be a different story. It was unlike him to take issue with a night apart, but maybe she'd taken advantage of his eagerness to please her one time too many. She knew he'd just as soon go hungry when they were in a tiff, rather than come begging to her for sustenance of the carnal variety.

A hesitant throat cleared nearby and they both glanced up. Camille stood fidgeting slightly, her bright blue eyes locked onto Eben's hand where it still absently stroked the rod of polished stone.

"What is it, Cammy?" Erika asked.

"Uh…um…Do you mind if I start translating?" Camille asked, darting a look at Erika. "Everything is covered with text. Well, almost everything." Camille's attention slid back to Eben's hand on the dragon statue's cock. Erika narrowed her eyes when she caught the wicked smile on Eben's face while he watched Camille blush.

"Have at it," Erika said. "The sooner we find out the secrets of this place the better, right? The boys can set up camp. It's their night, anyway."

Camille nodded and left, clutching and twisting at the end of her long, blond braid, a nervous habit she only seemed to affect when she was around Eben.

"You're such an asshole sometimes," Erika said. "She's got the hots for you and you keep taunting her like that. It's not fair."

He chuckled and let go of the dragon's penis. "I'd love a taste of her, but I have a feeling she's nowhere near as experienced as you. I like women who take the initiative."

"Or men?" she asked, reminded of his excuse after she'd found him entangled with a fellow geology TA named Jared. Eben had been cocky enough to invite her to join them, but she'd been too shocked to take advantage of the opportunity. Later when she questioned him about it, all he'd said was, "He asked."

Eben shrugged. "Depends on the man, but yeah." His expression grew thoughtful as he turned to watch Camille bend over to extract a notebook from her gear. "I don't know, maybe I could teach her something."

Erika let out a long-suffering sigh. "Behave yourself while we're here, alright? I can't have my linguist falling to pieces mid-month because you popped her cherry and she's too in love to keep working."

"Yes, mistress," he said with a gleam in his eye.

CHAPTER TWO

After exploring for a time, they erected their equipment and set up camp in one of the four alcoves that flanked the mezzanine. Each of the alcoves possessed a fire pit that seemed to work the same way as the wall sconces had, and put out a steady amount of heat, sufficient for cooking. They settled into camp to plan their study and catalog their finds.

Kris began cooking dinner. Within moments the entire area was awash in aromatic spices that made Erika's mouth water and distracted her from her planning. She'd only mapped out a fraction of the compound that afternoon. They had mostly encountered a lot of jade corridors lined with locked doors. Tomorrow she would focus on the doors, but now she was distracted by a deeper need. It was like an itch she couldn't scratch. She shoved it aside for the time being to eat dinner, thanking Kris when he brought a steaming bowl of curry and rice to her.

The sculpted Thai made Erika think of a Mongolian warrior sometimes. While she ate the spicy food she imagined him naked on horseback, clad only in scant fur armor, coming to ravage her. The delicate flavors of her dinner made her mouth water more with every bite; the spice on her tongue sent a zing of pleasure straight between her thighs. If he made love as well as he cooked, he'd have her sweating and salivating all night. Her nipples pricked and a sweat broke out on her skin. She found it tough to keep her eyes off Kris now, or any of the men for that matter.

They were all attractive, though Eben had always been the most forward one of the group. Dimitri was soft-spoken, though quick-witted, and flirted in a very subdued manner with everyone. His sweet face and short-cropped blond hair evoked images of Nordic gods. His full lips consuming the delicious food had her mesmerized for a moment. Her heart sped up when his tongue darted out to lick his lips. She shifted her gaze away, replying to their steady banter mindlessly while she watched the rest of her team.

Corey ate quickly in general, but tonight he seemed to savor the meal for a change. He took slow bites in between conversation about their find. The normally prominent lines beside his blue eyes relaxed making him look ten years younger, and oh what a pretty boy he must have been when he was in his mid twenties like the rest of them. Now, he was a very attractive man who'd probably been hurt one too many times if the sad look in his eyes was any indication. He'd always been the most aloof member of the group, but he'd been a more than competent team member during their long trek to get here.

Camille was still giving Eben that puppy-dog look, but appeared more flushed this time, her glance periodically darting to his crotch. Erika eyed Eben's lap and raised an eyebrow. The man still had a hard-on. What the hell was up with him? He'd been a tad oversexed at least as long as they'd known each other, but this was something new. She glanced around at the others to gauge their relative levels of excitement. When she met Hallie's eyes the pretty brunette raised an eyebrow and shot a pointed look at Eben. Erika just rolled her eyes in response and smiled.

Hallie was the reliable one. Open and honest to a fault, not afraid to share her opinion. She had managed to rebuff Eben's periodic advances adeptly. Erika wondered if the woman was gay until they'd actually talked and she expressed that she preferred men who were just a little more mysterious.

"Why not Corey?" Erika had asked.

Hallie had pursed her lips and confided, "He's way too laser-focused on his own agenda. I don't do casual sex and neither does he, from what I can gather. If I'm gonna sleep with a guy I need to know he's doing it because he wants me—not some feminine ideal that I probably wouldn't live up to anyway."

But now Hallie had pulled her long hair up and was fanning her face while she eyed Kris. Kris was the mysterious native, his Asian features a contrast to the other men. He'd spent their weeks-long trek being the ideal guide, regaling them with stories of the jungles they traveled through, protecting them from potential predators, and cooking the best food they'd ever tasted. Yet he'd shared very little about himself. Mysterious didn't begin to cover the large man who was now collecting their dishes to clean up, smiling politely at each of them as he went around the camp. One thing she did note when he collected her bowl was the unmistakable bulge of an erection pressing against the front of his khaki shorts. It caught her eye before she could censor herself. When she met his eyes a second later he just smiled and said, "Still hungry?"

She blinked at him and swallowed. A vivid image of taking his cock in her mouth right there blazed across her mind and her thighs clenched involuntarily. What the hell was happening to her?

"Ah…I'm full." Full was an understatement…she'd love to be full of him. So much that her vaginal muscles ached. God, she wouldn't normally think of it so clinically, but the feeling was akin to an affliction now. No longer just a dull itch, but a very present distraction bordering on discomfort.

"Thanks for another great dinner, Kris. I'll be right back." She stood and wandered into the dimly lit corridor that led from the back of the alcove behind the tiers of the amphitheater seats.

Past the offshoots of a side-corridor that she knew spanned the circumference of the temple was a cozy rear chamber that contained a flowing fountain of the ubiquitous jade, its water spilling into a shallow pool. The entire chamber was lit with the same small globes that had come to life when they opened the outer doors.

She bent over the edge of the pool and splashed water on her heated face, undid a few buttons of her shirt and splashed more on her chest. Something about this place made her too hot. It couldn't just be the excitement of finding it. Ever since they'd opened the doors, she'd grown more and more aroused.

It wasn't unlike her to want sex after a find like this, but she normally had control over her impulses. Here she feared she was completely losing it. There was no logic…no focus to her desires. She found herself gazing longingly at the oblong tip of the fountain that spewed fresh water into the pool and wondered what it might feel like buried inside her.

"You okay?"

The deep voice startled her. "Kris. Yeah…I think so. This place is pretty epic. I guess I'm just a bit overwhelmed by it."

"You don't look okay. Did the magic get to you already? I tried to keep the spice light tonight."

"Magic…what magic? And what spice?"

He looked around like there might be invisible things floating in the air, then smirked at her.

"Dragon magic. It's everywhere. Giving me a hellacious boner, too. Dragons are horny beasts."

"Not Dwarves?" she asked laughing about Eben's earlier joke.

"Nah…Dwarves are a myth. Dragons are real, and they live here." He leaned closer and said in a conspiratorial voice, "And they really love to fuck."

His words made her quiver and she had to close her eyes to get herself under control. When she opened them again, he was kneeling beside the pool and stripping off his shirt. His shoulders rippled in the warm glow of the lights that illuminated the room. He leaned over the edge of the pool bracing both hands at the lip and plunged his entire upper body through the surface, down into the cool water. She watched the expanse of olive skin submerge, the tattoos that twined around his torso nearly obscured. Dragons. No, not plural. One dragon, its head draped across his back, eying her steadily from where it rested on the surface of one bunched shoulder. It coiled around him in a proprietary fashion, its tail twining around his waist. The eyes of the tattoo seemed to follow her.

Kris emerged from the pool and flipped his head back, flinging water behind him. He sat gasping and blinking, his glistening, tattooed torso covered with little rivulets of water. Her mouth watered, and her pussy began to tingle in a way not unlike her tongue had during dinner.

"It won't take long," he said cryptically, swiping a hand down his face and flinging water off into a corner.

"What won't take long?"

"The magic. You don't really need to translate the text for it to happen. It's your destiny as much as it is mine. Now that you're in the current of the magic, it'll take you where it needs you to be."

"And where is that?" she asked, a pang of anxiety dimly present inside her, but not enough to counteract the lust. Why the hell was she humoring him? He was speaking nonsense. Magic? And *dragons*? She needed to get hold of herself for Christ's sake.

He raked fingers through his wet hair and stood up, gesturing down the shadowed corridor. "I'll show you."

"Should I be scared?" she asked with the last shred of logic in her. Goddamn if she wasn't curious enough to let him prove it to her.

He chuckled and let his eyes drift down over her sweaty, dirty trekking shirt that was already half undone. The fabric was soaked through from the water she'd splashed on her chest to counteract the heat that seemed to well up from deep within her. Her nipples were clearly visible, pressing against the weave.

"With tits like yours, no." He took a deep breath through his nose and closed his eyes as if savoring some aroma that lingered in the air. "And a pussy that sweet, definitely not. I'd fuck you now if I were allowed to."

If he were allowed to? "Who the hell are you?"

"Your guide." He grinned and turned to walk away.

"Wait!" she yelled after him, then ran to catch up. "What the fuck about the fucking dragon magic?"

"It's everywhere in here," he replied with an all-encompassing wave of his arm that made the muscles in his broad back flex alluringly. "And it's the strongest it's ever been since they were sent to sleep half a millennium ago. Now it's time for them to awaken and live in the world again. To mate with humans and ensure the magic stays strong."

CHAPTER THREE

Kris led her down a pale corridor that glowed with magic dragon light, or she supposed that's what it was now. She felt a little drugged. Her skin tingled, so sensitive the rub of the material of her shirt over her nipples sent jolts of pleasure through her with every stride. She'd been horny enough upon opening the doorway into this place, but now her normally healthy appetite seemed to be magnified ten-fold. *Magic,* she thought. A little thrill went through her at the memory of some of the stories her father had told her, but she still wasn't quite prepared to believe it.

"I guess magic *might* explain Eben's perma-boner," she joked, trying to dispel her anxiety. It might also explain the personal porn-video that kept running through her mind—the one of Kris nailing her against the warm jade of the temple wall, or bending her over the edge of the pool and fucking her from behind, or countless others she'd imagined just in the span of the last fifteen minutes.

In a moment, they emerged at the back of the main room, outside one of the heavy carved doors that flanked the dais.

"Those doors are locked," she said.

Kris smiled back at her. "Not if you know how to open them." He pushed against the smooth surface of the door. The door swung open just enough for them to slip into the darkness beyond. More sconces lit, illuminating a row of closed doors set deep into the curved wall of the corridor, each one flanked by a pair of majestic white jade dragons similar to the ones that stood guard beside the throne in the main chamber. All of them sported similar erections to the one Eben had so lewdly stroked earlier. Kris paused in front of the first door, one carved out of red and lavender jade.

"This door will kick off the ritual. Then this…" He moved to stand in front of the door beside it, staring up at the shimmering golden carvings. Not gilt, she realized when she looked closely, but more carved jade in a hue that resembled gold. "Then those over there." He skipped the central door, which was larger than the others and a translucent grass-green that matched the throne. He pointed at the two on the far side. One of solid black at the end, then then one next to the green door—a twisting swirl of almost every color in the rainbow.

"The ritual happens in that order," Kris said. "My door…" He walked to the rainbow door. "Is this one, the last one before the Queen."

"Your door?" she asked. She had too many questions. She'd only gotten as far as the first door and stood mesmerized by the carved figures of the dragons on its face.

"Yes, that one is my door. This is your door." He came back and stood close behind her, his breath audible in her ears. Goosebumps rose up on her skin at the caress of his words. She wanted to spin to face him, kiss him savagely, then fall on the floor and fuck him. She spread her fingers thinking to reach back and touch him.

"You can't touch me," he said in a near whisper that tickled at her skin. "I know you want to, but it isn't allowed. Not by human hands. No one has touched me since I was a child."

"What?" she asked, finally turning to face him and staring at him in disbelief. She tried to remember any moment during their trek when he'd touched another member of her team, but he'd always been oddly distant, camping a little further away from the rest. She'd interpreted his attitude as a cultural divide of some kind, but his brash declaration by the pool a moment earlier contradicted that.

"I'm destined for this." His dark eyes met hers, intent and steady. He didn't *look* like a crazy man. Should she believe him?

"What the hell is this, Kris? I hope you understand I'm having a very hard time believing what you're telling me. Dragons? Seriously?"

"I'm the sacrifice that will revive them."

She laughed. "You're crazy. You just need to get laid."

"I'd love to. But you can't help me unless you walk through that door and begin the ritual."

She gave him her best skeptical scientific once-over. "So how did you get that tattoo? Someone had to touch you to give it to you."

"I've had this since I was born."

"You're telling me they gave a newborn baby a tattoo?"

"My mother gave it to me. She was one of them—a dragon—before she died. Two of the monks who helped raise me were also."

"Ohh kayy…I believe *that* about as much as I believe you can't be touched." She narrowed her eyes. His story was so outlandish she couldn't wait to prove he was full of shit.

"I'd love to feel your hands on me, Erika." His voice held a hint of challenge but she didn't move. She couldn't decide how to start.

"I'll help you out," he said. He stripped off his shirt again, and dropped his pants. He stood in front of her, resplendent in his nakedness and glowing in the warm light. Not only did he have the dark coil of the dragon around his sculpted torso, but his strong thighs were tattooed in a dark, scaled pattern all the way up over his hips. His erection was spectacular, too. Long and thick, with a glistening bead already dripping from his tip.

She reached for him but stopped, her knuckles curling in like she'd hit a barrier just an inch away from him, so close the heat of him seemed to sear her skin. She shook her head thinking it was hesitation.

"I'd love to have you suck me, Erika, but it can't happen. Their power is too strong. I'm the sacrifice. I'm too sacred for contact and it's driven me crazy my entire life, but the frustration is nearly over. No matter how hard you try, they won't let you touch me. Not until we walk through that door over there. Before we get there you and your friends need to open the other doors. It's my job to watch you carry out the first four stages of the ritual."

"You're telling me you have some magical dragon curse that won't let you come into contact with another human? And what…that you're destined to be some blood sacrifice to resurrect a mythical race?"

He smiled. "It isn't a curse. I'm a gift to them, and it isn't my blood they want but my lifetime of pent up need. You just need to play your part. Now that the magic is in you, all you need to do is let it carry you."

"So, we do our part and you get laid? What exactly are we putting on the line here?"

"We give up our pleasure to them and they awaken."

"They?" she asked.

"The dragons." He reached out a hand and stroked the wing of one of the guardians that stood sentinel outside the doorway they stood within. "They're asleep, but when this is all over they'll be awake again. And free to live among humans again. To mate with us. To extend their existence for another generation."

The tattoo around his middle seemed to shift in the flickering light. Kris's cock twitched. She slicked her tongue across the smooth inner skin of her lower lip, imagining what he must taste like. She dropped to her knees, intent on proving him wrong, but just knelt poised and fevered at the effort to get closer. Her mind wanted him but her body was commanded by something beyond her.

"Fuck," she muttered. "Fine, if I can't give it to you, I'll give it to myself."

"Don't," he said, crouching in front of her, but she'd already pulled her shirt open and shoved up her tank top to expose her firm, bare breasts. Her nipples were hard as small pebbles. She pinched them between her thumbs and forefingers—her own favorite brand of foreplay. Twin jolts of pleasure shot straight between her thighs. Having his eyes on her, all smoldering and hungry, just made her hotter.

"Don't what? Don't jerk off in front of you? You like looking at me. I know you do."

"I love looking at you, but this won't help."

"It'll help me." She unzipped her shorts and shoved her hand down the front. Her pussy was slick and wet, her clit a hard, thick bundle, swollen and throbbing. Her fingertips swept over it, sending a rush of tingles up through her body. She continued down, sinking into the slick heat between her pussy lips, gathering wetness, then back up to rub with two fingers over her clit in delicious slow circles. She squeezed one breast in her free hand, rubbing her nipple with her thumb while she watched him. His eyes stayed fixed on the movement of her hand underneath her shorts. After a second he swallowed and cleared his throat then met her eyes.

"It won't help."

"It will when I come, and you'll wish you did it to me."

"That's just it. You can't. Now that the magic is in you, your nirvana belongs to them." He glanced to the tightly closed door beside them.

"We'll see about that." The rush was already beginning, her muscles clenching and her body tingling all over, but it dissipated as quickly as it had begun. She rubbed her clit harder, chasing the sensation she was so ready for—she just needed a little bit more to get there. Her jaw clenched in the effort to find it. She sped up her motions and tweaked her nipple harder, grabbed her other breast and teased, but nothing. She was *there*! Why couldn't she come? It had never been hard for her to have an orgasm. If she wanted it all she had to do was this…exactly what she was doing. Usually it was easier and better if someone happened to be fucking her at the same time, though that had never been a requirement.

"Why aren't you touching yourself?" she asked, breathless and pausing to let her tired muscles rest for a moment.

"I can't." He slumped back against the wall behind him and looked down between his thighs at his cock like it was some foreign beast he couldn't quite comprehend.

"What do you mean? You can't touch me and you can't touch yourself either? How do you *bathe*?"

He laughed. "Well, I *can*...technically, but I learned years ago that it did no good. I can't bring myself off. And you won't be able to…ah…*come*…while you're here."

"Let me guess…dragon magic." She settled back against the wall, too exhausted to keep trying even though her pussy screamed for release.

He smiled ruefully. "Yes."

"So you've never had an orgasm? That's tragic."

"I have, but only in my sleep. They send me dreams sometimes. It's how I knew you and your team were the ones I was meant to bring. I dreamed of all of you the week before I met you. Especially of you. Probably because you are the leader."

She stared up at the illuminated carving on the door. The polished red and purple colors beckoned to her and she reached out, tracing her finger over the upraised surface of the carved design. The smooth stone was only slightly cooler under her heated touch and the colors mesmerized her. Jade came in an array of colors, Eben had said, and was also one of the toughest minerals, nearly impervious to breakage, which the pristine quality of these carvings attested to. It had to have taken years to carve it all, and the entire place was decorated entirely in carved jade.

This door included a bas relief image depicting two dragons coiled around what looked like two human figures. It was like looking at a page of the Kama Sutra the way the angles were just a little off, but it was clear enough for her to understand what the image was meant to convey. Two humans, a man and a woman, engaged in passionate coitus with two dragons. Though she had to blink a few times to register the shapes of the dragons. Sometimes they looked like scaled, long-tailed beasts, but if she shifted her eyes the right way, they looked almost human.

"What the hell did you put in our food, anyway?"

"Some spices I cultivated myself known to awaken the senses. Other than that, nothing but the water here. It's been steeping in their magic for hundreds of years. Their need to awaken is very present. This is the time."

He seemed so earnest, but his need wasn't enough to sell her. She stood up and straightened her shirt.

"I think you're playing us somehow. I have no idea how, but I'll figure it out. Put your fucking pants on." *Before I go nuts.*

As she was walking back toward the doorway to the main chamber she heard behind her, "Erika. You can't leave this place until you've completed the ritual. I didn't trap you into this."

"Oh? Then why does it feel like I have no other options?" she shot back over her shoulder.

"I'm more than just a guide, so I know it was always your quest to be here. This is where you belong—where we both belong. You know it's true, deep inside. Just translate some of the text and it'll be clear, I promise."

She paused for a single step and clenched her fists. If he was playing them all for his own ends, she'd figure it out, but he wasn't lying about her quest. Still, Kris's words were too much fantasy for her to reconcile. She'd found it. That was enough. All she needed to do now was catalog the artifacts and transport the pieces suitable for study and display. Then write her dissertation on the entire expedition. After it was published she would reap the rewards and bask in the professional limelight. End of story.

Except deep inside she knew there was so much more to the story than that. Her father had never been after glory, but his research had led her here after all. Maybe there was more for her to find besides artifacts. Maybe Kris was the key to uncovering the deeper secrets of this temple. Before she'd walked through those doors at the surface she would have argued that only science could convince her of the truth. Now, she wasn't so sure. With each step further away from the doorway she'd just left behind, the weaker her hold was on her own convictions until what she wanted had shifted entirely.

She raised her hand up to fondle the small jade figurine at her throat. It was a childhood dream come true. More than that, it was her life's work realized in spectacular fashion. Her entire body buzzed with the understanding that *this* was what she really wanted. To awaken the dragons.

And Erika was used to getting what she wanted.

CHAPTER FOUR

Camille's breath finally steadied and she rested her head back against the solid stone behind her. A narrow band of light seeped in from the crack in the doorway leading to the main chamber, illuminating her boot-clad feet where they rested on the stone.

She could still hear Erika's low voice asking questions and Kris's even replies. When she'd followed Erika to the pool, she'd been sure she would catch the two of them screwing, but what she ended up witnessing was so much more interesting. She couldn't quite process it all. She'd stayed far behind and snuck through the open doorway to the rear corridor behind the dais without them noticing, then stayed in the shadows, listening to them talk. If she tilted her head forward a tiny bit she could see them, and ended up rubbernecking while Kris stripped and challenged Erika to touch him.

Her mind reeled at all the implications, and she was even more eager to get to translating but just needed a breather after watching the two of them together. They hadn't even come close to having sex, but she'd never seen such a tense, sexual exchange. And when Kris had divulged the secret of the temple, she had to test it herself. She pictured Eben's broad hand stroking the dragon's penis and moaned softly while she stroked herself. But the idea that they could all come alive was what thrilled her the most. There had to be hundreds of dragons in here. Most of them were frozen in their native form, but if what Kris said was true, they could all appear like humans.

Her clit throbbed beneath her touch and the familiar surge of sensation made her speed up to reach that crest. Kris was lying, she thought when she got close to the edge. But just before she climaxed, her pleasure hit a wall. Tension pooled deep in her belly, seeking a release but nothing was imminent. She groaned out loud and pulled her hand out of her shorts, smacking it against the stone floor beside her. He was right. As much as she wanted it and as close as she was, there was no way she could make herself come. How, though? Their nirvana belonged to the dragons. What the hell did that mean?

When Camille heard Erika's emphatic arguments coming toward her, she scurried out the door and back to the throne. At least she knew enough now to know what to look for.

With her pen light and notebook, she crouched down and began translating the characters that were etched into the base of the dais. After a few hours and a set of very sore knees, the truth began to emerge. She made the notes and kept going, forcing herself to exhaustion to avoid the very present issue of how horny she was. Keeping her hands busy was the best means of avoiding what she really wanted to do, and if Kris was being honest it wouldn't help anyway.

Camille had always admired Erika's easy attitude about sex and wished she could be that free about it. To not care in the least what people thought to the point it made men's tongues fall out of their mouths when she walked by. That's how all the men in their group seemed to behave around Erika anyway. Even Corey, the dark and broody, seemed to *see* Erika for something more than just 'the boss.' Camille had seen him assess their leader. Maybe not in an overtly sexual way, but the two had talked and Camille had watched Corey's expressions. She knew he respected Erika and found her attractive. Like maybe he wouldn't have joined them at all if he didn't.

She forced herself to think in the native language while she translated. It was a common ancient dialect, so the act was mindless for her. The pencil was an extension of her brain, transcribing the words as she read them. While she transcribed she could happily daydream about other things. Like imagining Eben doing dirty things to her. His hand stroking that dragon's cock had aroused her incredibly, making her eager for the end of supper when she could have some alone time to pleasure herself while thinking of him. Then all this happened, and now she was rubbing her nose on the surface of what was apparently a platform that held the throne of an enigmatic leader of an elusive race. The more she learned the more she had to keep translating.

The ritual was the most interesting thing. In particular, the one facet of it that drove her out of her mind with desire. They needed a virgin, and as far as she knew, she was the only one besides Kris. No, she was sure of it. She knew Eben and Erika weren't virgins…they'd been fucking like bunnies the entire trek. Hallie wasn't, Camille knew because Hallie had shared a pregnancy scare story with them one night. Dimitri was the only guy who might've been, and he'd destroyed that illusion after confessing to having shared a girlfriend once with his twin brother. And Corey…well, you didn't get to be as worldly and experienced as Corey without having sex.

That left her and Kris, and Kris had clearly been destined for a different role in the ritual. And she knew from her personal lack of experience that she was an appropriate subject.

She read and re-read the ritual until it started to sound like a legal document. Most of the ritual components were obvious. They required witnesses, but the virgin component was different. All it said was "…and a virgin's blood to anchor the dragons to the earth." It was very specific to differentiate the 'virgin' from the 'catalyst,' which she understood was the role Kris was meant to fill. He might be a virgin, but he had no free will if his own words were any indication. The virgin had to have free will and choose her own mate at a random point during the ritual.

Odd, the gender was very obvious in the language, too. The virgin was intended to be a female. The very visual presence of erect dragon appendages throughout the stronghold made that detail a little less mysterious. It gave her a lot of options, she supposed. She eyed the statue beside the throne that Eben had been fondling earlier and stood up abruptly. She walked over to it and crouched down again beside the figure. The dragon sat in a position similar to her own, but with an erect spine, all its weight apparently resting on its hefty tail. Its thighs jutted out parallel to the floor and its wings curled up like twin sails behind it.

She reached out a tentative hand, then paused, looking up into the dragon's eyes. They might be alive. If they were, she couldn't just grab him, could she?

"I'm just going to touch you now," she whispered. "I won't hurt you."

She stretched her hand and gripped the solid column of the dragon's phallus. Her palm hit warm stone and it took her a second to register the incongruity of the sensation. It was stone, it should feel cold, but it didn't.

"Oh, you're warm. I wonder what that means."

It meant more research. She released him and turned back to the text beneath her feet. Why were they so warm? And why did she have an uncontrollable urge to climb on and fuck one of them?

She rubbed her eyes and wished for coffee, but didn't want to wake the others to make it. She'd just have to power through. The golden shapes of the characters filled her vision when she knelt down again with her notebook and continued transcribing, looking for some enlightenment about the statues and what she'd learned in the corridor. And trying her damnedest not to think about Eben.

CHAPTER FIVE

Eben rolled over in his sleeping bag and stared into the darkness that filled the cavernous reaches above him. His balls ached and his dick was as hard as it had been when the door on the surface opened, giving them admittance into the depths of this place. He'd tried sleeping, but his mind kept wandering to images of Camille's full, round ass. He rolled over and began stroking himself surreptitiously beneath his covers, trying his best to stay quiet. He fisted his cock and nearly groaned out loud in pleasure after the first stroke. He imagined her blond braid resting along the arch of her spine while she bent on all fours before him, displaying her perfect ass for him. This shouldn't take long. He'd jerk off, then sleep—his standard procedure during his college days—then maybe dream of Camille talking sweet to him.

Except it didn't happen. The ache in his balls just intensified, and he still couldn't come. He hovered on the edge, but no amount of stroking could bring him past it. Something was very wrong with this scenario. He'd never had trouble jerking off.

It had gotten even easier since he'd been screwing Erika. She was so dirty she'd given him a wealth of material to masturbate to. But his fucking dick was apparently on strike tonight, which made no sense. He couldn't sleep like this. Cold showers were out of the question.

Now all he wanted to do was shove his hot cock into something and the urge drove him mad. Frustrated with his inability to orgasm, he threw off his sleeping bag and decided to go exploring to distract himself. There were doorways that they hadn't opened yet. Lots of them. There were the ones behind the throne that he knew Erika was laser focused on. But there were others, too, all locked. Maybe he could find a way to open some of those locked doors and earn a few points with Erika.

Camille's pretty ass waited out there somewhere for him to open, too. He shouldn't go looking for her, but her bedroll was empty so he did anyway. He was worried, he told himself. *I wanted to make sure you were okay,* he heard himself rehearsing in his head. Not *I really want to go down on you.* That was an understatement. He wanted to shove his tongue into every single orifice she possessed. Camille had featured in his fantasies since he'd first met her when Erika assembled their team. But, over the course of the weeks they'd traveled together, he'd become more and more enamored of her—a detail he could never properly articulate to Erika without sounding like a complete pussy. In spite of a generally healthy level of self-confidence around women, he'd been hesitant to approach Camille. Each time he tried, she looked at him like she had earlier that day—like he might just be crazy. He supposed the thing with the dragon cock might have been too much, but damn, she was so beautiful when she blushed like that.

So he kept going back to Erika. Erika wasn't just his oldest friend, she was also the perfect casual fuck buddy. He wondered if Camille would like having her asshole licked the way Erika did. Fuck, he'd love to do that to her. Even though the mere image of making love to her could satisfy him most nights, for some reason tonight he couldn't *stop* imagining her in the naughtiest positions. Not just bent over displaying her perfect ass to him, but sometimes doing that with her thighs spread on either side of his face with her pussy poised above his tongue and her sweet mouth wrapped around his cock, or riding him face-to-face with her full breasts rubbing against his chest. The vivid image of his dick buried hilt-deep in her ass flashed through his head, making his balls ache almost painfully. Maybe he should just find Erika instead. She might at least be good for a blow job if he promised to return the favor.

He got as far as the stone dais and stopped, momentarily dazed by the image before him. Camille lay in the center just before the huge green jade throne, sound asleep. She was on her side, her cheek resting on one arm, and her pretty braid draped over her shoulder. Her top had ridden up, and she clenched one breast in her sleep. Her other breast was bare, the fabric of her tank top shoved up above the pink tip of her hard nipple that just begged to be sucked. Christ, he'd do it if he could without feeling like a complete perv. She was too good for him, so pure and naïve and virginal, but with an ass that could halt time. What he wouldn't give to be able just once to bury his face between those round cheeks and go to town until she screamed his name.

Just a touch, he thought. One touch—she'd never know. His mouth watered and his cock throbbed when he quietly crouched beside her and reached out. The hard pink flesh of her exposed nipple beckoned, the aureole a perfect pebbled circle of vermilion, about the size of a quarter, perched atop the creamy mound of her full breast.

"Eben, I need you."

He jerked his hand back like he'd come too close to a flame and shoved it in his pocket. He stood and turned abruptly in response to the voice behind him.

"Fuck, Erika. You scared the shit out of me." He tried not to look like a guilty fool when he turned to face her. Erika glanced at Camille's half-naked sleeping body and eyed him with apparent suspicion.

"You were about to molest Camille, weren't you? You perverted bastard."

"I…what? No, it's just that…Fuck, I'm horny as hell and you pretty much disappeared tonight." It was as likely an excuse as any.

She stepped quietly across the dais and surveyed Camille where she slept. Once by the other woman's side, she bent and carefully tugged Camille's shirt down to cover her breasts, then gently extracted Camille's notebook from beneath the sleeping woman's cheek.

Her eyes scanned the pages of penciled scrawl quickly. "Holy shit, he wasn't lying. Eben…this place is a lot more important than we thought it was." She looked up into his eyes, her pretty face beseeching. "We have to wake them up."

"What the hell are you talking about? Wake who up?"

Erika laid the notebook back down and grabbed his hand. Her dark eyes were wide and excited. She was more excited than he'd ever seen her. With a brief glance he realized how disheveled she was, but it just served to make her sexier. Women like Erika were so good at wearing their fixations like a badge that just made men like him gravitate toward them. Her hair was a tangled mess, her dirty shirt half undone and wrinkled, her breasts almost spilling out from her low-cut tank top, and her nipples were hard little circles pressing against the fabric.

"Dragons, my dear. They are fucking *real.* That statue you were so crudely fondling earlier? Real. Living but asleep. I've been walking for the last three hours probably, just trying to figure it all out, but this is the answer. *We* are going to wake them up."

"I think lack of sex has made you a crazy woman."

"Sweetie, I'm just as horny as you are, but apparently that's by design. Kris gave me the scoop. We can't orgasm unless we're touching one of them."

"Ah…one of what?"

"One of the dragons."

Images of shoving his cock into a stone hole made him crease his brow with worry. "I'm not fucking a rock."

"I don't know how it works with the female dragons, but we'll figure it out. Maybe all they need are facials."

"Right." He laughed. "And the idea of screwing a reptile turns you on? I admit I'm as kinky as the next guy, but bestiality? Not gonna go there."

"They're not *beasts*. They're mythical creatures who actually aren't so mythical after all. Come on."

"Can't she come too?" he asked, gesturing to Camille. "I'm sure she'd want us to wake her up to see."

"No, honey, this is a two-man job. She's not ready for this, I promise you."

She led him back to their camp, urging him to silence while she found the camera and tripod stashed in Corey's gear.

A moment later they slipped through the now open doors behind the dais and into a shadowed corridor. Kris stood waiting by the first of several recessed doorways, his expression eager.

"Kris, you beautiful man, I changed my mind. Let's do this," Erika said.

Kris nodded and stepped up to the door, placing his hands atop a pair of inlaid characters and reciting a few words in a language Eben didn't recognize. The doors swung open and the room inside blazed to life when all the sconces along its walls lit up simultaneously.

"Wow. This looks like some rich bastard's version of a personal fetish room," Eben said. The first thing he noticed was the wide altar-like platform in the center of the room with the figure of a naked man chained to it. A very aroused naked man carved entirely out of brilliant red jade. When Eben's eyes traveled past the platform to the end of the room they nearly popped out of his head.

A lavender-hued sculpture of a beautiful woman rested upon a small bench. Large wings stretched out behind her, making her resemble a majestic bird of paradise. The figure was shapely, with plump breasts and a lovely face. And she had huge, swirling horns that emerged from the top of her forehead and angled backward. Behind the horns, her wings stretched out in pure lavender jade so translucent that the lights behind her made them glow. Coiling tendrils of hair draped over her shoulders trailing down to a flat stomach that culminated in spread thighs flanking her bare pussy.

His eyes rested between her thighs, trying to imagine how much fun the sculptor must have had while polishing it to such a brilliant shine. And shine it did, as though she were already wet and ready for fucking. Without even thinking he gravitated toward her. The shape of her sculpted breasts was just about as alluring as Camille's had been. He had no qualms about touching this one, though. When his fingertip grazed the smooth purple stone of her nipple, a bolt of lightning seemed to shoot straight through him. He *needed* to fuck her somehow, but how?

"Eben, aren't they beautiful?"

He turned his feverish eyes to Erika. She'd set the camera and tripod in the doorway and now stood naked beside the prone statute on the platform, wearing nothing but the cord of leather around her throat, from which dangled an ancient jade figurine of a dragon. Her auburn hair had been released from its perpetual ponytail and flowed freely around her shoulders. Her nipples were hard, dusky peaks and her breasts rose and fell with excited breaths. He licked his lips at the glisten of wetness visible between her thighs.

Her hand swept from chest to hips over the contours of the chained man, then slid slowly up along the rigid shaft of the statue's cock.

"How does he feel?" Eben asked.

"*Amazing.*"

"Let me watch you fuck him." His beautiful dragon woman wasn't going anywhere. From this angle he could see the taloned feet of the prone man and the hint of scales on his lower legs.

He stood and walked around to the head of the platform and stripped off his shirt, then his pants.

"Do it, Erika. Climb on and fuck him."

"Get me ready first?"

"Seriously? You look so lit up right now you're glowing. Touch yourself. I can already see you're wetter than the jungle outside."

She let one hand slide up her stomach and clutch her breast, squeezing her nipple harshly. The fingers of her other hand skimmed through the coarse, roan-colored hair between her thighs and dipped between her lips. His cock twitched in response to the moan that erupted from her mouth when she began stroking herself.

"See, you look pretty ready to me. Give him your best, baby."

CHAPTER SIX

Erika glanced at the corner where Kris stood as if he could give her some kind of signal that she was on the right track, but he only stood passive and intent while he watched. It had to be torture for him to witness all this and not be able to find his own release until the end. His lips twitched a bit which she took as a positive sign. She climbed onto the platform and straddled the naked statue, positioning herself over the polished jade phallus. Jesus, was she really about to fuck a statue? Her vaginal muscles clenched painfully, a sure signal that she needed this, and if what Kris had told her was true, this was the only way for her to find a release. She was already flushed with need and Eben looked even worse off.

"He wants you, can't you see it?" Eben said.

She laughed, but the jade man's face seemed to be looking up at her with needful longing. Like she was teasing him by not fucking him right now. He was pretty, with wide-set eyes, a square jaw, and full, kissable lips. If he'd been a living man she'd have been instantly attracted to him. She impulsively bent over and kissed him. His lips were almost as warm as flesh, and just as smooth even though they were hard, polished stone. Up close she was startled to realize that his skin had an odd geometric texture. Scales, she realized, though the pattern was faint. And he had horns protruding from his hairline, almost completely obscured by the carved waves of his hair. Not carved, *frozen*, if what Kris said was true.

"You're already in love, aren't you?" Eben asked, stepping closer and drifting his fingertips across the red stone of the man's face. "I don't blame you. He's…otherworldly. And you need to fuck him now."

"Damn, you can be an asshole sometimes. You want to see me fuck this cock, huh?"

"Yeah, baby."

She poised herself over the huge erection that jutted up between the thighs of the statue and pressed down slightly.

"How does it feel?"

"Shut up."

Eben leaned over the end of the platform and laid his own kiss on the lips of the figure.

"You're in love with him, too," she said, breathless at the zing of sensation the velvety-smooth stone between her thighs evoked even with just the tip of it penetrating her.

"I just want to see if he can make you come as hard as I do," Eben said. "Considering he's inanimate."

She sank down further, unsure whether she could take the entire length of the jade cock into her, but when her hips rested on the statue's hard thighs and his thick tip pressed into her deeper recesses she had her answer.

"Tell me how it feels," Eben said. He was leaning over the end of the platform, his hand clutching at the head of the statue. He gripped his cock in his hand, clearly wanting to stroke it but hesitating for reasons she was all too aware of herself.

"Incredible." She couldn't think of any other words. All she knew was that she needed to keep fucking. She pumped up and down, each stroke hitting her in just the right places. Every single one…the shallow little sensitive spot that she could reach herself when she jerked off, and the deeper spots that almost paralyzed her with how good they felt.

Eben continued stroking his cock in front of her. He looked so desperate for an orgasm she felt sorry for him, but within a second he groaned and his cock erupted in a stream of creamy white cum that covered the statue's face. Her own orgasm was a knife's edge away, and when she watched Eben come she surrendered. She slammed herself down on the cock she'd been riding and succumbed to the waves of pleasure. Her pussy clenched on the stone and she cried out, crazed with the exquisite sensation of release. The statue beneath her warmed perceptibly and an answering pulse throbbed between her thighs.

Something was wrong. The air vibrated with a loud, guttural sound. Her body shifted up, but she was barely conscious in the aftershocks of her orgasm. She heard the sound of chains breaking. Taloned claws raked her back making her cry out at the sharp pain that seared her skin, but it was nothing to the pleasure still rocketing through her. The cock inside her expanded in girth and a long tongue swept itself across her breasts leaving her nipples tingling. When she opened her eyes the shimmering visage of a dragon greeted her briefly before coalescing into the very human-looking face of the man she'd been fucking. Still was fucking. He gasped and embraced her, thrusting his cock so deep she grew dizzy.

"I'm awake," he murmured. "And you…are *mine.*"

He held her close and nuzzled at her breasts. "You are a joy to wake up to. So tasty." She froze, clutching her hands in his mane of red hair. His skin had become the hue and texture of normal skin, but his eyes and hair remained the same blood red as the stone he'd apparently been sculpted from.

"You're not going to eat me, are you?"

He chuckled and latched onto one of her breasts, sinking his teeth in slightly but not breaking skin. He kept steadily thrusting up into her.

"I might *eat* you, but no…we don't dine on humans. You're much more fun to fuck." His voice was deep and resonant, the timbre teasing at her eardrums with every word, caressing the depths of her mind as thoroughly as his cock caressed her pussy walls.

"Do you have a name?" she managed to gasp out between panting breaths. She'd come again very soon now that he was reciprocating.

"I have many names. You awakened me, it's your choice."

"Ah." It was increasingly difficult to focus, but she had to know. "You don't have your own name?"

"I do. My name is Gevaerentethessis. Humans tend to not like long names though, so you pick one, my love."

"Geva?" she panted.

"Yes, I like it. Your friend is about to die from need."

"My friend?"

"Yes, the one who so graciously ejaculated on my face earlier."

"Oh God, sorry about that."

Geva licked his lips but otherwise ignored the splatter of cum that graced his cheeks. "No need to apologize. He tastes young and healthy. But very needful. Is he for my mistress?"

"I guess he is," she said, wiping the remnants of Eben's orgasm off Geva's cheeks. "Eben?" She glanced over Geva's shoulder. In spite of an epic orgasm, Eben looked shellshocked and still aroused.

"Your turn, sweetie." She looked over her shoulder at the purple jade figure on the seat behind them.

Eben walked in a near-dazed state and knelt in between the statue's spread thighs. He always was so attentive that way, Erika thought. He loved going down on women.

"He looks competent," Geva whispered in her ear. The hot breath sent a pleasant tingle down her body that settled right in her clit.

"He is. *Very*."

"Would you like to watch while I fuck you?"

Oh, did she. She let him turn her around and position her on her hands and knees where she could see Eben begin to service the statue of the female dragon.

"I hurt you," he said and she felt the sting of his fingertip graze over the edge of the wounds he'd laid into her back when he'd climaxed.

"Just a little. I don't mind."

"Let me fix it."

The air shifted around her and a huge shadow loomed above her. She glanced back to see a large red dragon, its velvety snout gusting warm clouds of red steam along her back. The sensation made her shiver, but the scratches stung less and less.

"That feels nice," she said. Geva's forked tongue flicked out from his snout and she shivered as it tickled over her skin. The warm, velvety wetness of it slipped around and teased at her breasts, then snaked back and explored between her thighs. The forked tip of it stroked between her pussy lips, tasting her until she moaned. She stared back over her shoulder at the thick column of flesh that protruded from between his massive, scaled thighs. It was half again as big as it had been when he was human, but she craved every inch of it now.

"You like the way I taste?" she asked and was startled to hear the very intelligible response in a deep, gravelly voice.

"You taste alive. You taste beautiful. Hmmm, I could taste you for eternity." His heavy claws tightened slightly around her hips and her exposure to him aroused her further.

"Will you fuck me like this?"

"My dragon form is too much for human women."

"Please. I can see you want me. I can take it."

"Oh, I do. If you desire this form, I will go slowly." The beauty of him had her mesmerized even more in his true form.

His wings stretched out behind him, quivering in his apparent need to take her. His glowing red eyes flashed with lust.

He nuzzled her behind and flicked his tongue in a tickling trail along her spine while moving closer. Soon the scorching heat of his thick tip pressed against her entrance.

"Oh, yes! Do it!" she cried out, pushing back, inviting him in deeper. His rumbling response vibrated through her entire body, amplifying her desire. The stretch of her pussy walls made her groan when he began pushing into her. When he was fully encompassed within her he paused and bent his long head down over her shoulder, teasing his tongue over her breasts again. This was so surreal, but it all felt so right. Geva began moving carefully at first. He fucked her with long, languid strokes, filling her up while she watched Eben attentively lick the jade pussy of the female dragon.

"Worship her pussy well and you will be rewarded," Geva said, directing the statement at Eben. "You can fuck her to life that way."

The words seemed to make no sense to Erika, as full as she was with Geva's cock, but Eben apparently understood and licked with increased fervor. He groaned in elation a few moments later then rose up on his knees. Eben looked like he was about to fuck the statue, though all Erika could see was his tight, muscular backside and the clench of it when he thrust into the statue like she was actually real.

Through her fevered haze of ecstasy she asked, "Geva, what did he just do?"

"He woke her up. That part of her, anyway. The rest will come. Now, I need to make you come."

All it took was the rumble of his deep voice and a series of solid thrusts that reached the deepest parts of her. Soon Erika's eyes fluttered closed and her body spasmed in an earth-shattering orgasm. His thick cock pulsed red-hot inside her, then receded, his entire shape dwindling back to human again and pulling her back with him. He embraced her and she rolled over, looking into his red-hued eyes.

"I just fucked a dragon, didn't I?"

"Yes. And you will again. You are too tasty to let go of easily."

"What about Eben?"

"She seems to like him," he said.

Erika glanced down to the bench where the other dragon had been. Now Eben was seated with a pretty violet-haired woman riding him. After a few minutes the purple-haired beauty yelled out a resonant cry and her wings unfurled then embraced them both in a violet cocoon. Erika could just barely hear Eben's familiar orgasmic yell as his hands clenched at the dragon-woman's bottom, yanking her down hard on his cock while he came.

"Who is she to you?"

"My mistress. Or she was in the last cycle. I misbehaved. She was my jailor of a sort, but my penance has been done now that you have awoken me."

"So what happens next?"

"Now, we make love some more. Every climax feeds the Queen's well. Soon we awaken the twins. And I do hope you brought a virgin with you. She's the secret ingredient. The magic will tell her what to do all on its own."

"A virgin?" she asked, but became distracted when he shifted down her torso and his tongue elongated and slipped between her thighs. He toyed with her clit until she couldn't think straight.

"How do you do that?" she asked when coherent thought returned to her.

"I can transform any of my body parts at will into the shape I desire. My natural form is this…" His body shimmered and a second later he was a resplendent red dragon, four times the size of a man. Then his tail disappeared and his legs became human along with his torso. All that was left was the dragon head atop the very beautiful muscular shape of a man with a huge hard-on.

"Show me your human face again. I like that face."

He smiled at her when the face appeared again. "I like this face, too. But my human tongue is not as functional as my dragon tongue."

"No, your dragon tongue is definitely much more…ah… functional."

"I thought you'd prefer that one," he said, grinning at her with perfect white teeth. God, he was pretty. He even had dimples. If she'd seen him on the street she'd have done a double-take, thinking, "Who summoned a Viking?" what with his long red hair and ample muscles. When he'd been stone it was hard to imagine his personality, but now she warmed to him. She wanted to know his life story, but first she really just wanted to fuck him again. She glanced at Eben and saw him in a tender conversation with the dragon-woman, who was now curled up on his lap nuzzling at his cheek. The woman really did like him. Her wings were still extended and drifted through the air in a lazy rhythm, sending pleasant gusts across Erika's skin.

"I want to make you come again." Erika heard the words while watching Eben mouth the very same ones to the dragon girl on his lap. It took her a second to realize that the words she'd heard had come from Geva, not Eben. She extracted herself from her fascination with Eben's love tryst to pay attention to the far more fascinating creature in front of her.

"I could fuck you all night, but I have work to do," she said. "We need to awaken the twins. How do we do that?"

Geva grinned. "If the guide has followed the laws of the ritual, you will have brought enough humans to complete all the phases."

"Yes, there are seven of us, counting Kris."

"Then we just need to fuck until the next phase begins on its own, so you choose. Work, or…um…*work*?"

"Kris can't just go lay hands on the doors and make them open like he did with this one?"

"Kris has a very specific role to fill here," Geva said. His glance into the shadowed corner reminded her that they'd had an audience all along.

Kris nodded. "I can only open the first door. The others will only open when each phase is due to begin, but it won't take long."

"How does fucking you help open the doors anyway?" she asked Geva. She climbed onto his lap and slipped his erection inside her again, sighing with the fullness of the sensation.

"Every door has a key, my love."

SLEEPING DRAGONS

BOOK 2

TABULA RASA

OPHELIA BELL

Waking up is hard.

CHAPTER ONE

In Camille's dreams, she was never the shy, bookish girl who got tongue-tied in the presence of a beautiful man. No, in her dreams she was the pursuer, dominant over her desires, the mistress of her own fantasies. The subject of those fantasies in recent weeks had been one man—lovely Eben—who had destroyed all her past fantasies in a single afternoon, just by being *him*.

While in the real world he barely spoke to her, in the dream realm he became her supplicant. There, he would kneel before her, begging for the honor of pleasuring her. Out of his mouth would spill the most deliciously dirty words. The power she held over him in the dark of night made her giddy with delight.

After hours working to translate the text etched around the jade throne in the ancient dragon temple, Camille had succumbed to exhaustion. She now dreamed she sat naked upon that very throne, flanked by the jade dragon statues. The setting was unlike past dreams, but the situation familiar enough for her fantasy to play out as it always did. Eben stood before her, naked. Her gaze traveled hungrily up his strong legs, over muscular thighs and narrow hips. His cock stood proudly erect and appeared massive to her inexperienced eyes, yet it didn't frighten her.

Camille's gaze lingered there, and she licked her lips, imagining the taste of the moisture that glistened like a tiny jewel clinging to his tip. Would he be salty or sweet? Still, there was so much more to him than his virile manhood. Her gaze moved higher, over his taut stomach, rippling with the evidence of a body well kept, over tight curves of pectorals and long, powerful arms dangling from wide, strong shoulders. So many moments had she caught herself staring at the way his muscles flexed when he would move—to lift his heavy trekking pack to his shoulders each morning. More recently, the image that came to mind was the bunching of his thick forearm when he stroked the column of the dragon statue's huge phallus the day before, when they'd first explored the room at the heart of the dragon temple.

Eben's face was what really incited her desire. The wide-set blue eyes that seemed to undress her on the rare occasions she managed to capture his attention, a perfect nose above his bow-shaped mouth—a mouth just made for doing those things he promised in her dreams.

Since the first day they'd met, two months earlier, her infatuation had grown with every stolen glance. While he rarely spoke to her, sometimes she would catch him looking, and each night her dreams would grow more intense until she woke in a sweat, her heart pounding and the flesh between her thighs craving contact.

But during her waking hours, she was far too reserved to follow through.

Words came more easily within the sanctuary of her subconscious. All she had to do was speak and he was kneeling at her feet.

"My sweet Eben. Tell me what you want to do to me."

He leaned forward and tilted his head to rest one rough cheek against her inner thigh, tickling her sensitive skin lightly with his short stubble. His gaze rested at her core, the intensity of his desire burning in his eyes, causing her own flesh to tingle and grow warm without a single caress.

The corner of his lips brushed her skin when he started speaking. "I want to kiss those pretty lips, so deep there can be no doubt how much I want you." His face tilted higher, gaze lingering on her plump, pink-tipped breasts. "I want to suck those perfect rosebuds until they're so hard and tender you beg me to fuck you."

With each word, he moved incrementally closer between her thighs, and now his lips barely brushed against her slick pussy. She had to fight the urge to tilt her hips closer to his mouth as the words gusted against her tender flesh. She held her breath, waiting, vibrating with desire in anticipation of what he would say next.

"And I want to bury my cock inside you so deep I touch your soul."

True to his word, Eben nestled his face in the cleft between her thighs, fastening his lips against her slick folds. The wet heat of his mouth always startled her at first, hotter even than the flesh he latched onto. But shortly she lost herself in the sensations. He plunged his tongue deep inside her, sliding it in and back out in a languid thrust. The licks grew slower and longer with each pass, slipping up higher and swirling around and around her clit that already throbbed thickly with arousal.

Each curling tease of his tongue sent little jolts of pleasure through her body, bringing her nearly to the edge before he stopped. She braced herself for the next step and wasn't disappointed. Rising higher on his knees, he latched on to one nipple, sucking until she gasped and arched her back. He worshiped the other in kind, swirling his tongue around her areola once before pulling the pink tip between his lips. When both nipples were thoroughly attended and aching from his attention, he took her face between his large hands, gazing deeply into her eyes.

"Take me in, baby. Let me fuck your tight, virgin pussy."

She spread her legs wider, inviting his thick shaft into her. The sharp pain of tearing flesh came first, followed by the exquisite pressure of him filling her. Her virginity was ever present, undeniable even in these nocturnal interludes, so she used it as an anchor. It made the dream seem all the more real.

It never took long after that. He would fuck her soundly, whispering all the most suggestive things he planned to do to her, and within a few minutes they would both be crying out each other's names while they came.

Camille would awaken, replete and glowing with satisfaction. She would spend the rest of the day in a happy buzz, not fazed in the least by the petty annoyances of their expedition, or even Eben's generally circumspect attitude toward her.

Except this dream changed. When they were at that cusp and her impending climax began to grip her, an unfamiliar voice spoke through Eben's lips, the words exuding a power that tickled inside her eardrums.

"It is not yet time, my flower. To have him you must awaken one of mine first. You must give your virgin gift to my brood to get your heart's desire."

She awakened with a frustrated groan. Not time yet? Then she remembered her revelation earlier that evening. The ritual would keep any human in the temple from finding sexual satisfaction unless they were offering it to a dragon. *What did they call it? Their Nirvana?*

Apparently the Queen had reprimanded her in her dreams just now. Camille wasn't sure if she should feel special or not, knowing they needed her in particular to ensure the ritual's completion.

Right now, she was just incredibly frustrated, her body tingling still with Eben's imagined touch. It may have been the lack of release, but she wanted him so badly she could taste it.

During their journey, she'd tried to come up with ways to seduce him. Each day she'd tried to find moments when he would be alone. She would start to go to him, just to talk, but always ended up paralyzed by indecision and anxiety over taking that first step. Still, she knew she wanted him to be her first.

The difficulty was compounded by the fact that he and Erika had slept together nearly every night of their trip and didn't do a whole lot in the way of disguising the fact.

But not every night, Camille reminded herself. *Not the night before we arrived here.* That gave her a shred of hope, as did the subtle looks she sometimes caught him throwing her way.

She would just have to find him. There was a ritual to carry out. A sex ritual if she'd interpreted the etchings around the throne correctly. She imagined convincing him to assist with her part of it. *Help me find a dragon to—* To what? Give her virginity to? That thought brought her up short. If she were going to be part of the ritual, Eben wouldn't be her first after all. But to have him there with her, even just watching—the thought drove her back to the camp to find him.

But his sleeping bag was empty. As were Erika and Kris's. No! Tonight of all nights she needed him, and he was with *Erika* again?

"Camille?" Hallie's groggy voice spoke in the dim light. "Y'okay? W'assup sweetie?"

She realized she must've cursed out loud. "Nothing. Just burning some midnight oil to translate. Go back to sleep, Hal."

Her friend rolled back over in her sleeping bag. Camille felt a little guilty for not at least letting Hallie know what was going on. The other woman had been her closest friend in the group since Erika had brought them all together with the promise of adventure and academic renown. Hallie had even encouraged her to pursue Eben in spite of the obvious connection he and Erika had. *It's just a casual thing between those two, sweetie,* Hallie had said. *I see the way he looks at you.* Except now that Camille finally had the courage to chase him, she couldn't even find him.

The sleeping bodies of Dimitri and Corey didn't budge when she stole past them back into the corridor to search for Eben. She hoped he wasn't actually with Erika for once.

She navigated the darkened reaches of the maze that was the underground compound they had discovered. None of the multitude of intricately carved jade doors that lined the corridor walls gave entry. She tried them all until she finally came back to the beginning, frustrated. She stared at the huge, dark door that led to the passage behind the throne where the five doors of the ritual were concealed. Eben wouldn't have gone to those doors first, would he? He couldn't know about the ritual. But if Erika had found him, perhaps…perhaps they'd already begun.

Her chest tightened with rage and hurt. To think he was embarking on the beginning of this ritual with Erika and not with her—even if he and Erika weren't in love—somehow made their relationship something beyond Camille's reach. What if he'd left her behind without a backward glance?

"Dammit!" She angrily wiped a stray tear from her eye. Hoping she was mistaken, she pushed through the heavy door and quietly slipped into the shadows of the corridor beyond. Within several yards, the light from an open doorway spilled out across the pale stone of the floor before her. The most startling thing was the series of sounds that accompanied it. A chorus of urgent noises met her ears—the moans and whispers of people in the throes of ecstasy.

Consumed equally by jealousy and eager curiosity, she crept closer, keeping to the shadows just outside the door. She paused, hidden behind one of the large guardian statues that flanked all the doorways in this place. The carved white dragon kept her concealed and still gave her a perfect vantage to see everything happening in the room.

She stifled a gasp at the sight that was both disturbing and arousing. Erika was on her hands and knees on a low altar. Behind her crouched a large creature the likes of which Camille had only seen in storybooks, its red scales glimmering like translucent jewels in the glowing lights. Long, red claws delicately gripped Erika's naked hips as it plunged its thick, smooth penis in and out of her. His cock looked so big he had to be uncomfortable for Erika, but she writhed and moaned and pushed back against the dragon's cock with obvious, enthusiastic enjoyment. Camille couldn't pull her eyes away from the sight. Heat coalesced between Camille's thighs while she watched, throbbing in time with every thrust.

After a moment, the dragon's wings extended, blocking Camille's view of everything but where his hips were joined with Erika's, and he bucked against the woman's ass as he climaxed with a low, velvety roar.

Camille thought her eyes were deceiving her when the dragon shimmered and shrank down to the size and shape of a large man, pulling Erika back into a tender embrace and nuzzling soft words Camille couldn't hear. She was comforted by the fact that the large red-haired man was decidedly not Eben, but where was Eben?

A motion at the far end of the room caught her eye. She drew her hand to her mouth to suppress a cry of astonishment. In an almost perfect reflection of her dream, Eben knelt, naked, between the thighs of a rigid statue of a beautiful woman. The figure was so much more than a woman, though. She had shimmering lavender skin that hinted at a scaled texture and majestic horns extending from her forehead, coiling back behind her. Sprouting from her back like sails were a pair massive wings.

Before Camille's eyes, the lavender dragon-woman shimmered as though the light had changed, but there had been no shift in the ambient lights of the room. Camille heard Eben groan as he latched his lips onto one bare, stone breast. In the most surreal of motions, his hips seemed to sink against the statue like he'd just shoved his cock in deep. Camille's pussy clenched and she groaned in empathetic ecstasy, wishing so hard that she were the object of his attention just now.

Her skin prickled beneath her clothing while she watched. Too hot…it was too hot in this dark corridor. She closed her eyes and rested her cheek against the cooler stone of the statue she hid behind. The sounds of passion that rolled over her only made her temperature rise.

She swiped a hand over her sweat-drenched neck and down her chest, gasping when her palm brushed over her breast, causing one nipple to stand erect. Experimentally she teased the other nipple and her eyes fluttered closed in response to the pleasant tingle that resulted.

She opened her eyes again to see Eben's head still bent to the statue's breast, sucking on the dark purple jade of its nipple.

She shoved her tank top up and tweaked her own nipples trying to mimic what it might feel like to have his tongue on her. Oh God, her head spun with the pleasure of it. Stronger heat tingled between her thighs, but she knew it wasn't sweat making her wet down there.

She hastily stripped off her tank top and pressed her bare breasts against the silky smooth jade of the statue in an effort to cool herself off. The cool stone rubbed pleasantly against her nipples, relieving more of her tension but leaving behind a deeper need.

Eben let out a surprised grunt. He glanced between himself and the statue of the dragon-woman who now glowed with a subtle light that emanated from deep within, growing stronger with each thrust of Eben's cock. His hand disappeared between them and Camille could see his shoulder flexing with the hidden motions of his hand between the dragon-woman's thighs.

The visuals that image incited were too much for her to bear. She was beyond modesty now. It was just her and the silent statue of the guardian in front of her. She unzipped her shorts and slipped a hand into her panties. The fabric was sticky wet from her arousal, and her pussy tingled in anticipation of her touch.

She leaned against the statue and braced one knee on its heavy, smooth thigh, spreading herself open. Oh, she'd never been so wet before. Her clit had never felt so much like a swollen bundle of nerves, ready to burst with a single touch. She believed she could have come with the slightest pressure just then, but knew it couldn't happen. Not after the ending of her dream. *You must awaken one of mine,* the voice resounded in her head, and for the first time she was feverish enough to want to make it happen. But how?

She clenched her eyes in frustration, suppressing all the worst curse words she could think of but would never actually say out loud. When she opened her eyes, the remedy to her need stood proudly before her in the form of the polished white jade cock that jutted up between the guardian dragon's thighs.

All the guardian dragons were posed identically, like loyal dogs, resting back on their haunches, arms upraised and wings unfurled. If it weren't for the presence of their large phalluses, they'd have made comfortable seats with their thighs perfectly parallel to the ground and their arms outstretched above them. It occurred to her perhaps they were meant to serve a different purpose. *Her* purpose.

She stood, now practically within the embrace of this guardian, and the feel of its polished skin against hers suddenly felt a lot more intimate than it had a moment earlier. Her face flushed savagely. He could be alive, she remembered, and here she'd been wantonly rubbing her body all over him. But that's precisely what she should be doing, wasn't it?

She gripped the base of the dragon statue's erection to test it. Her hand didn't quite close around its girth, but it was smooth and soft, polished to a high shine and perfectly proportionate to what she'd always imagined Eben might look and feel like, only much, much bigger—so big she was a little terrified.

With a fascinated gaze, she let her hand slide slowly up the shaft to the tapered tip, then back down. Her palm tingled the entire length of him. He was a little warm, particularly at the base, though the smooth, twin globes of his testicles were cooler to her hot touch. The smoothness of him encouraged her to stroke again and wonder if Eben had the same texture or if he would be softer, more pliant, and would he have a slight curve, too.

She glanced quickly into the room again. The sights inside caused another surge of heat to rise between her thighs. Erika now rested astride the red-maned man, and Eben's pretty, lavender dragon had fully awoken. She was riding him as he sat on the bench, his hands tightly clenching her ass while he plunged his cock into her.

Camille pushed her shorts down over her hips and stepped out of them, eying the penis of her statue with some trepidation. Was she crazy to try this? What would Eben or the others think if they knew? Then Eben's murmurs from inside the room hit her ears.

"*You like my hard cock deep inside your pussy, don't you baby?*" The dragon-woman let out a hum of appreciation in response.

The sound of Eben's voice reminded Camille of her dream, and a violent flutter of need erupted deep in her belly, making her close her eyes and moan softly. When she opened them again she focused with determination on the statue in front of her.

"This is going to hurt," Camille said as though the dragon could hear her. Her voice shook a little, but she wanted this. She *needed* this. She climbed up onto his thighs and braced her hands on his shoulders.

Leaning forward slightly, she raised her hips and positioned herself above the head of the jade cock. Each brush of the stone against her skin, from her breasts against his chest to her slick folds against the solid tip of his cock, was enough to make her shudder with increased desire. When she pressed down, her lips spread wide and she pivoted her hips in a tight circle, sliding her clit around the tapered head. Little pulses of pleasure shot through her as she did so, making her moan softly.

"You feel nice." She looked into the dragon's stony eyes beneath his horned brow and imagined she could see a flicker of recognition there. "Are you ready for my virgin pussy to wake you up?" She giggled nervously at her attempt at dirty talk, but it somehow made things easier. Finally she angled her hips so that his tip pressed directly against her hot, clenching opening and began to press down slowly.

She stopped when she hit painful resistance. *Pretend you're ripping off a Band-Aid, silly. Just get it done.*

With that thought, she gritted her teeth and plunged her hips downward, seating herself entirely onto the dragon's massive erection with a loud cry. She immediately bit her lip and blinked away the tears that sprung to her eyes in response to the sting of her hymen breaking and the thick shaft stretching her wide open. She glanced into the room, but the others were being far too uninhibited in their own fun to have heard her little outburst.

In an attempt to distract herself from the pain, she leaned against the dragon's chest and grazed her nipples over the smooth stone again. At the same time, she began rubbing her clit gently with one finger, the zing of pleasure making the ache in her pussy all but disappear. Bracing her knees on the statue's thighs, she rose up slowly, her eyes fluttering at the slick friction of the smooth polished cock as all its contours rubbed against her sensitive inner flesh. She could even feel the thick ridge on the underside that led to the rounded flare of its head.

"Oh, wow, you do feel good," she murmured, sinking back down again. The pressure of the dragon's thick length inside her caused a pleasant buzz of sensation with each stroke, up then back down, as slowly as she could.

After the third stroke the pain was completely forgotten, replaced by urgent need to find her peak. She sensed that this time when she came it would be nothing like the times she'd toyed with herself to orgasm. No, she was filled so completely by the hard, smooth stone, she almost forgot she was fucking an inanimate object.

A fresh sheen of sweat broke out over her entire body and she panted out little whimpers against the dragon's chest. The temperature beneath her palms seemed to rise with each thrust of her hips. The cock deep inside her had more give against her needful thrusts, but she had no frame of reference to consider why.

She turned her head to face the open doorway just visible beyond the edge of the dragon's wing that still shielded her from view. A shiver of pleasure ran through her at the sight of Eben, standing now, his beautiful cock erect and about to be serviced by the pretty dragon-woman on her knees before him. Oh, to taste him like that. Then her eyes flitted to Erika who now lay back, her chest arched up and her pussy being thoroughly attended to by the red-haired dragon-man with a tongue that looked impossibly long and agile.

"I wonder, do you have a tongue like that?" she whispered to her serene and silent lover. Impulsively she brushed her lips across the end of his carved and slightly open snout, teasing her tongue between the smooth jade of his lips. He tasted of earth and sex, and a tiny jolt hit her tongue like she'd just touched it to the end of a battery.

The sharp sensation set off a chain reaction through her body. The tingling began in her core and her pussy began to clench in steady spasms. It came on so suddenly it surprised her. She clutched at the dragon's shoulders, gasping for breath, but unable to stop moving her hips—it felt so good. Then it overtook her like a wildfire, consuming her from head to toe.

She arched her back and cried out, rising up and slamming down again and again just to prolong the pleasure. The dragon's shoulders gave beneath her fingertips and his wings shuddered. His eyes flashed bright silver; a gust of white smoke rushed from his mouth followed by a low, curious growl.

With his first solid thrust back, she screamed in unbridled ecstasy, and everything went black.

CHAPTER TWO

In spite of the spectacular blow job he was enjoying, Eben's attention immediately shifted to the sound of the scream from outside the door. He placed a hand against the dragon Issa's cheek, but she'd already slipped her sweet, violet lips off his cock and turned her head to face the direction of the noise.

"The virgin has awakened a guardian," she whispered, her eyes growing wide.

"What?" Eben asked. He looked toward the doorway. Erika and Geva were equally distracted by the sound, Geva already striding toward the door.

A second later the figure of a huge, muscular man filled the doorway. He had white hair flowing to his shoulders, interrupted by two huge horns that jutted up from his brow. Intense, silver eyes surveyed the room from beneath heavy, white eyebrows. He held the slack form of an unconscious, naked woman in his arms.

"What the fuck?" Eben muttered. Was he another dragon come to life? He must be, considering those horns and his unworldly eyes. When Eben spied the long, golden length of Camille's braid trailing over the man's arm, cold rage coursed through him. Before he could think, he was running for the man, ready to pummel him to pieces, no matter how much bigger he was.

"Let her go!" Heedless of his nakedness he swung a hard punch that squarely met the man's jaw. In spite of the strength behind the punch, it had no effect aside from numbing Eben's arm to the elbow.

"Eben, no!" Erika shrieked. Three sets of hands soon held him back.

"Eben," Issa's softer voice said. "Let him speak. She awakened him, he couldn't have forced her. The virgin always makes her own choice during the ritual, and she made hers. Much sooner than is common, but still, it was meant to happen." Looking at the towering dragon-man who held Camille's unconscious body she said gently, "Roka, is this the virgin?"

The large, pale man nodded his horned head solemnly but didn't speak.

Eben clenched his fists ready to swing again, but thought better of it. "She doesn't belong to you, you bastard," he bit out through clenched teeth. "What the fuck did you do to her?"

The pale eyes narrowed on him, assessing him and contemplating. He looked like he was about to speak but held his response in check.

"She chose you, didn't she, Roka?" Issa said, ignoring Eben's outburst. "That means you have unlimited leave to speak now."

The man studied Issa from beneath a creased brow. His lips pursed and his frown deepened. After a pregnant moment he took a breath. In a deep, growling voice he said, "Her nirvana awakened me, but she fell unconscious before the awakening was complete. I am worried for her."

He turned his gaze to Eben, his low voice steady and calm. "This woman has a mild affliction. If you care about her, human, you will let me heal her affliction. I will give her to you now as a show of trust until you decide."

Eben nodded and held out his arms. When the larger man transferred Camille to him, Eben immediately carried her to the altar in the center of the room and sat with her cradled in his lap.

"Cammy, wake up." He caressed her cheek, noting how flushed and warm she was to his touch. "Someone bring her some water!" he called out to the room. Unsure what else to do, he bent and whispered in her ear. "Camille, it's Eben. Please wake up, baby."

He gazed at her unconscious face, regretting that he'd never tried to talk to her in depth, to nurture some kind of connection. He'd been such a fool.

He wasn't oblivious to the way she'd looked at him since meeting her months ago, but had always preferred a woman to make the first move, something she never seemed too keen on doing. Over the course of their journey, he'd watched her covertly, curious to see if she would come out of her shell. When she finally did, it was only when she believed he wasn't looking. During those rare moments, he would catch her in uninhibited discussion with one of the others and marvel at how beautiful she was. Unfortunately she always clammed up as soon as she caught him watching. Her pretty blushes as a result had begun to incite a kind of desire even Erika had never been able to draw from him.

A couple weeks into their expedition he'd finally decided to do something about it, yet she'd somehow inadvertently turned the tables on him. He found himself at a complete loss as to how to approach her, yet wanted her more than ever.

The idea of her being with another man enraged him after all the nights he'd spent fantasizing about being with her.

He looked up when the large figure of Roka knelt in front of him. "Leave her alone!" he yelled, shooting the other man a heated glare.

Issa sat beside Eben and laid a gentle hand on his arm. "Eben, he can help, but you need to help him, too. The part of the ritual to awaken him is incomplete."

"He looks awake enough to me. He can go fuck himself."

Roka snorted. "If only it were that easy. But that's not how it works. She chose me; she awakened me with her nirvana. But if I don't find my own with her I will sleep again and the ritual is rendered null."

Erika piped up. "Null? You mean we'd have to start over?"

"Not entirely," Issa said. "But you would need a fresh virgin. If you have one it should be no issue, but either way Roka will sleep for another cycle for having failed in this one." She gave Roka a mournful look and traced her lavender fingertips over one of his horns.

Eben darted his eyes between the two dragons, trying to comprehend what they were saying. He turned and looked plaintively at Kris who still stood in the corner, every bit as much a sentinel as all the statues that littered this place. Kris only nodded slightly and said, "She speaks the truth."

The body in Eben's arms shifted and a soft, groggy voice said, "Eben?"

"Camille? Oh, thank fuck. Are you alright?"

"What's going on? Where am I? Did…did it work?"

He glanced at Roka, who now sat back on his haunches watching silently. Eben met the man's eyes and swallowed tightly before looking back down at Camille's pretty, flushed face. "If you mean did you manage to wake one of them, yes. I'm impressed." And, in truth, he was impressed. The knowledge that she'd taken it upon herself to do something so overtly sexual changed his perception of her drastically, and in a way that aroused him to no end.

"I did? Where…where is he?" she asked bashfully. Eben raised his eyes to Roka.

Camille turned her head. "What's your name?" she asked.

"Rokaurasaelaethessis. They call me Roka, my love."

She shifted and the slight movement reminded Eben how very naked and soft she was cradled in his arms.

"You can call me Camille. After all, we did just…um…*fuck*. If we're being super technical, I kind of raped you."

Roka nodded. "Yes, we did, Camille. And no, you didn't rape me. I was born willing, as are all dragons. But something happened to you before my awakening was completed. Are you alright? My only care is for your well-being."

Camille's eyes widened and she sat up abruptly in Eben's lap. It took all his concentration to focus on her words and not the insanely fantastic feel of her lush bottom against his swelling erection. Her complete lack of modesty under the circumstances surprised him, too.

"You didn't finish? Oh no! I remember what the text says. You have to finish! The ritual depends on it!"

Roka nodded and met Eben's eyes, the gesture indicating some deference to his feelings at least. Eben slid his hand possessively around Camille's waist, wanting nothing more than to touch her now, to lay her down and spread her open and have her, and damn the ritual. With the barest glance, Roka rose and walked away.

Eben grimaced at the pang of guilt he felt and called out. "How much time do you have before it's too late?"

"Once the ritual is begun it must be completed within the span of a day. I have only a few hours."

Would it be enough time for Eben to get used to the idea of watching Camille fuck this other man? He couldn't decide if he'd hate it or enjoy it.

Eben looked down at Camille again. Her brow was creased and she gnawed distractedly at her lower lip. He followed her gaze to where Erika was seated on a polished jade chaise along one wall, resting in intimate connection with Geva. The red dragon-man seemed to be telling her quiet stories while he caressed her from head to toe.

"Erika's done with me," he said. "I was never enough for her."

"Are you sad?" She looked into his eyes without judgment or accusation—only curiosity.

"No. I'm …Christ, Camille, ever since I met you I haven't been able to think of anything else. You're all I want. I just hope you want me, too."

Her eyes widened at his confession, and her mouth made a soft little O shape that just made him want to kiss her. She shot another look at Erika. "But…all those nights? I mean, Erika's so much more…experienced. How could I measure up to her?"

"I'm not exactly a delicate kind of man, you know, but I'd love to help you *be* experienced."

She shifted around to straddle his legs, completely shameless about how very naked they both were. This new version of her dazed him. She gripped his jaw in both hands and kissed him, long and slow, and so sweetly. She was a study in contradiction now, kissing him like that after having done something incredibly erotic that he wished like hell he could have witnessed, and apparently willing to do even more with the dragon she'd awakened. The thought of getting to see her in action again decided the issue for him. It made his cock throb in anticipation.

"Oh, Eben, I want it all. I want to be *dirty*. Consider me a blank slate just waiting for you to teach me everything."

He held her closer, reveling in the way her curves pressed against him in all the right places. She tilted her head with a sigh when he nuzzled at her neck.

"Do you mean everything?" he murmured against her skin. "Because there's another man over there who you left hanging." Eben raised his eyes to look past her. Roka still waited on a bench across the room, watching them with an expression of overt desire.

She followed his gaze and whispered, "Do you mean…*both of you?*"

He only quirked a corner of his mouth suggestively, and noted that Roka had to have heard her based on the other man's body tensing and his eyes flashing expectantly.

A bright flush rose up Camille's chest and colored her cheeks. The way her breathing seemed to quicken made him wonder if all that blushing during their expedition hadn't been out of shyness after all. Maybe it was because she'd been turned on whenever she looked at him.

"You're excited about getting to fuck him again, aren't you?"

She clenched her eyes shut and after a second nodded. "How…how does this work, with two of you?"

Eben shrugged slightly, imagining all the potential configurations. "We'll just have to see what happens. I want you to myself for a few minutes first, if that's alright?"

CHAPTER THREE

Camille relaxed in Eben's arms when he lowered his head and kissed her. Oh how delicious his kiss tasted, better than she had imagined. His tongue teased and caressed, prodding deeper, then pulling back. His hand grazed over her hip and up her side to cup her bare breast. The electric sensation of his thumb against her nipple made her inhale sharply.

He laughed. "I love seeing you turned on like this. Fuck, you're beautiful." His hand pulled back and hovered over her skin, but it was the look in his eyes that made her quiver before he touched her again. His eyes intently followed his caress upon the curve of her breast. He traced the underside, skimmed across to her other breast and up over the top, seemingly mesmerized by both pale mounds. With a bolder motion, he skimmed around again, but brushed her nipples on the second pass. The brief contact made her clit twinge and her heart speed up.

"Oh? Why did you never tell me so before?" she murmured, sliding her palms over his shoulder, rejoicing in the feel of him tight against her and apparently in no hurry to let her go. As eager as she was to move things along, she was enjoying his caresses too much to rush.

"I always thought it," he said, apparently distracted by the texture of her nipple against his palm. "I imagined your face while Erika fucked me most nights. She was good, but never as perfect as you."

She gaped at him. "You thought of me when you were… with her?" she asked, slipping her fingertips up into the hair at the base of his skull and beginning to pant a little in response to his touch.

If she weren't so astounded she'd have thought the flush that rose up to color his cheeks was cute. But this was a revelation.

"Camille…I told you I've wanted you since the first time I saw you. I meant it. That first day in that bar in Boston. I probably seemed rude, but I couldn't stand up because I had such a hard-on after you walked through the door." As if to agree with his point, his hard cock twitched perceptibly between them.

"But…why? Why didn't you ever tell me?" she asked. Confusion tangled within her stomach. All those nights fantasizing about being with him, having to listen to him with someone else through the thin fabric of their tents. She was torn between wanting to punch him and drag him down to the floor, begging him to make love to her.

His brow creased above his closed eyelids and he seemed hesitant to meet her gaze again. He shook his head a tiny bit and let out a little sigh. "I misunderstood you, I guess. At first I figured you were just too shy. Boy did you prove me wrong. You just climbed right on that dragon cock didn't you?" He opened his eyes and gave her a challenging smirk.

She punched him softly. "Yeah, but this place…there's something…" *Magical*, she thought, but her logical mind rebelled against articulating it. As if somehow it made more sense for her physical need to overwhelm her to the degree that she'd pleasure herself on a statue. Who then *magically* came to life? Who was she kidding? Knowing what all the text etched in the floor around the throne meant didn't make it any easier to grasp.

"Something in the air that makes you horny as shit. I know."

She nodded, grateful that Eben seemed to have the same mental block. "Yes! Exactly. And I was so turned on watching you with the purple dragon-lady. And Erika with the red one… wow, those two."

Eben chuckled. "Yeah, they were spectacular together."

"What about your dragon?" she asked, suddenly concerned about the dragon-woman who she'd summarily displaced. She hadn't seen the woman since regaining consciousness.

As if hearing her question the female dragon seemed to materialize beside them. "Hello, Camille. You may call me Issa. I'm free now, thanks to your lovely man." Issa ran her fingers through Eben's thick, blond hair and give him a sensuous kiss.

When she pulled back she smiled with pure, white teeth framed by a pair of luscious purple lips. "Don't fret on my account. Just promise me you'll treasure him. He is such a prize. Besides, I can't bear to part two lovers, so I've agreed to let Roka have you both. He will treat you well."

When she finished speaking, Issa bent and rested her lips against Camille's. A smooth, sweet tongue gently parted her lips and Camille responded instinctively, slipping her hand behind Issa's neck to hold her closer. The dragon let out a contented hum and deepened their kiss. Camille responded, sitting up straighter in Eben's lap. The kiss had her so tangled up in sensuous abandon she interpreted the caress moving up her inner thigh as being part of it. Eben's low groan hit her ears at the same second fingertips parted her pussy and began stroking.

She gasped against Issa's lips and the dragon-woman pulled away, gazing at her appreciatively. "I may regret letting the Guardian have you both. Perhaps he will share sometimes if you two are amenable." Then with a gust of wind and dragon wings she disappeared again, landing across the room where Geva and Erika were tangled up with each other.

"You liked kissing her," Eben said.

She only nodded, too aroused for words under his soft stroking.

"How long were you out there watching us?" he asked.

"I don't even know." Heat rose up her chest and her face flushed remembering the rush of sensation just before she blacked out.

He nuzzled against her ear. "I want you to stay awake when I make you come. No checking out, alright?" He dipped his head to look into her eyes. She nodded. There was no denying his blue-eyed stare and especially no denying the gentle massaging of his fingers over her clit. Her eyes fluttered closed when one of his fingers ventured deeper, sliding inside the wet heat of her and caressing secret places she'd never been aware of until tonight.

"Camille, you are so tight and wet. I can't wait to feel you ride my cock like you did his. I also can't wait to show you all the other things we can do. Maybe with him. Or even with Issa if you like her as much. Would you like that, baby?"

Camille bit her lip and moaned in pleasure before glancing at Roka. He was attractive, strong and solid, and very, very large. Her pussy clenched around Eben's fingers in reflex when her eyes rested on Roka's still painfully erect cock. She remembered the polished jade shaft she'd deflowered herself on but it was too difficult to reconcile that image with the image of this very alive man. Every bit as alive as the one whose fingertips were giving her so much pleasure at the moment.

She closed her eyes and nodded in response to his question. "Yes, but I want to know what you feel like inside me first." Her words seemed so quiet to her own ears she was worried Eben hadn't heard her at first.

"Mmm…" Eben murmured against her ear. "You have no idea how much I want that. Why don't you turn around so we can give him a show until you're ready for him again?"

Camille let him shift her around so her back rested against his chest and her legs were draped over his. He spread his own legs, forcing hers further apart and slid his hands back down over her breasts and between her thighs. Cool air hit her hot, swollen pussy when he parted her lips for Roka.

"Touch yourself for him, baby," Eben murmured gruffly in her ear.

She gripped one of Eben's arms to steady herself and slipped her other hand down between her legs. Her over-sensitized flesh pulsed under her touch. Eben's strong shoulder behind her caught her head when she tilted it back, sighing under her own caress. She watched Roka from beneath her lowered eyelids, still acutely aware of the press of Eben's cock against her backside.

Roka stood expectantly, a look of blatant hunger in his eyes while his attention focused on her fingers. She slipped them down in an inverted vee, grazing the sides of her clit and squeezing just enough to send a pleasant zing of sensation through her.

Eben's fingertips dug into her hips, urging her to rise.

It was happening now, after all this time. She was going to have him. Maybe it was only a brief taste, but it was a start. She stood, still straddling his hips, her clit throbbing in anticipation.

"Fuck, you have a perfect ass. I could get lost in it."

He gripped each of her ass cheeks in his broad hands and squeezed, spreading her apart. Teasing fingertips trailed gently down the crease, barely brushing the pucker of sensitive flesh. Even that light touch was enough to cause her to gasp in surprise.

"Don't worry, baby, that's for later. Right now I'm on a mission."

He spread her slick, swollen lips with one thumb and forefinger. She heard his breathing quicken when he began to rub the hot tip of his cock against her.

"Does that feel good?" he asked breathlessly.

She realized she'd forgotten to breathe and choked out, "Uh huh."

"Then let me in. All you have to do is ...Oh, yeah, just like that. *Fuck.*"

She abruptly lowered herself onto him, secretly delighted by the strangled sound he made and the way his fingertips dug painfully into her hips. As new as this was to her, she thought Eben's cock might just be magical. She could *feel* him inside her. Even the subtle twitch of his hips made her moan in pleasure to feel the head of his cock rubbing some deep, unexplored spot.

Eben laughed. "You like that, baby? I can do that all night."

His hands gripped her ass. With another slow surge of his hips she began to question her sanity.

She raised her eyes back up to look at Roka. The scene felt surreal, even more than her dreams of Eben, and she wondered if she might just wake up after it was all over and find herself back in the jungle, alone in her tent having to listen to the sounds of Eben and Erika going at it mere feet away.

He urged her hips up and down, guiding her on his cock

"Keep touching yourself. Stroke your pretty pussy for him." Eben's low murmur against her ear made her quiver.

Roka's gaze swept up and down her body, lingering on her nipples until they tightened up as though he were touching them. She only became hotter under Roka's gaze when the large man began stalking toward her, his heavy cock bobbing with each step.

He loomed above her, larger than she imagined he could be. She craned her neck to meet his eyes, but they were too busy taking in every inch of her. His scrutiny made her feel suddenly very exposed. More than that, she felt owned by that all-encompassing look of his. The sensation was alien, yet strangely liberating. It was as though no worry would ever be solely her own to bear again because she belonged to him.

Issa's words came back to her then, and for the first time everything clicked into place. *I may regret letting the Guardian have you both*, the dragon-woman had said. That meant Eben belonged to Roka, too. She wasn't sure if she should be so thrilled by the idea, but to be desired by something so magnificent couldn't be a bad thing, could it? And that Roka wanted them both as a couple made her strong desire for Eben seem even more appropriate.

Roka exhaled, emitting tendrils of white smoke that descended down around her shoulders and fell across her breasts in a luminous veil. The soft caress of his breath sent a thrill through every cell it came into contact with.

She sighed and relaxed back against Eben, halting their motions and just enjoying the thick pressure of his cock resting deep within her. His arms moved up to embrace her around her torso, both hands cupping her breasts, raising them up as though they were an offering.

The huge dragon-man knelt before her and flicked his forked tongue out, tickling at her hard, pink nipples. He bent his head lower, as though he were about to lay his cheek against her thigh, but paused. The close proximity of him to the place where she and Eben were joined caused a shiver of anticipatory tension to course through her. What was he doing, poised like that, with his face hovering inches from her? He closed his eyes and his nostrils flared with a deep inhalation. His lips parted and pulled back ever so slightly from pure white teeth as he drew in more air through nose and mouth. She had the distinct impression that he was breathing her in, as if she were some ethereal being he could simply consume that way.

While his head remained bent, she trailed her fingertips along the smooth, curved protrusions of the horns that rested along the contour of his skull. A tremor ran through his muscled torso. Another gust of pale breath fell from his lips like fog and coiled between her thighs. The wispy tendrils made her pussy tingle and she arched into the sensation. Her clit pulsed with need. Eben moaned softly behind her and his hips twitched, pressing his cock deeper into her.

Roka inhaled again, pulling the tendrils of smoke back into him with one long pull of his lungs. The expansion of his chest made him seem even larger. He tilted his head back up and opened his eyes. His pupils were wide and black, but ringed in a circle of speckled silver that glowed.

His low, resonant voice brimmed with lust. "I must have you both. Your mingled scents are too delicious to sample separately. Find your nirvana together, and then you are mine."

He bent his head deeper between her thighs, pressing cool lips against her overheated flesh. His strange tongue slipped out and slicked over her clit, teased and swirled just long enough to leave her poised on the razor's edge of orgasm, then slid down. In a long sweep, he parted her with his tongue, following the length of her wet slit and beyond. A second later Eben moaned behind her. His hips bucked so hard if she hadn't been impaled on his cock, she might have been dislodged from his lap.

Roka gripped her hips to steady her. Then he lifted her, slowly raising her up along Eben's cock. She let him control the rise and fall, following the fascinated roving of his eyes as he watched Eben's cock sink deep into her. Roka raised her up again, his eyes still focused tightly on where they were joined. He bent his head and his long, beautiful tongue went back to work with fervent intent, but she was beyond holding back. With another swipe of his tongue against her throbbing clit, the barrier against her orgasm fell away and she plunged into the abyss.

Eben let out an incoherent cry. After one violent thrust up into her, she felt his climax flood her with pulsing heat. His arms wrapped around her and pulled her back against him tightly while his hips continued moving for a few more strokes.

Her own sweet finale was only just subsiding when she finally opened her eyes to look down. Roka's white hair and majestic horns were all she saw. His tongue still teased alternately between her pussy lips and over the delicate, pink sack of Eben's balls.

Roka stood and reached out a hand to her. It was such an incongruous gesture after what he'd just done she wasn't quite sure how to respond, but after a second she reached up and laid her palm on his. In a swift motion he pulled her to him, wrapped an arm around her waist and lifted her up as though she weighed nothing.

Hot, smooth lips found hers, and his tongue demanded entry. The flavor on him made her moan. Salty-sweet and just a little spicy, like some exotic cocktail. Was that what she and Eben tasted like?

His cock pressed hard against her hip, and with both hands, he lifted her just high enough for it to slip between her legs, the shaft brushing against her still tingling and swollen pussy lips. She wrapped her thighs around his waist, clutching him to her tightly with both arms and legs. The pressure of his cock against her aching flesh reminded her of the intimate moment right before she'd slipped down onto him earlier, but this time he was the one in control. He turned them around and sat beside Eben on the stone altar.

"You know what to do, my love," he growled. "Find your nirvana again on my shaft. Give yourself to me. Prove you are mine and I will prove I am yours."

The buzz from her orgasm had her too dizzy with residual lust, so she only nodded. She braced both hands on his thick shoulders and pressed her hips down. The sensation this time was exquisite and painless, the stretch of her pussy in response to his thickness more like a deep massage that would leave her as pliant as putty afterward. He was only slightly larger than Eben in this form, and with the mix of both her own and Eben's juices saturating her pussy, fucking him now felt like sinking down onto a pole of softest silk.

"That's good," he whispered, white smoke escaping from his mouth and nose with each panting breath. "Now fuck me like you did before."

Her hips knew precisely what to do in spite of a mind muddled with the sensation and the hypnotic scent of whatever magic permeated his strange breath. She gazed into his eyes, lost in their dark pools until he turned away. She followed his eyes to where Eben still sat watching them avidly.

Eben's hand gripped his own cock loosely but he didn't stroke it. When he met Roka's eyes, a spark of desire flashed through his own.

"Give yourself to me again, lover," Roka said. Every syllable he spoke vibrated through Camille, sending trickles of pleasure to her core. "Issa relinquished you, and you gave me your nirvana only a moment ago to seal the bargain, but it will be a sweeter bargain still if I can have both your gifts at the same time I reach my nirvana. It will be an even sweeter gift for the Queen that way, too."

Without a word, Eben moved to kneel on the altar beside Roka and let the larger man pull him into a deep kiss. Watching them both made Camille feel wonderfully lascivious. And so much more so when Roka's free hand reached between Eben's thighs and gripped his thick cock. Eben groaned against the dragon's lips and shifted closer, closing the short distance between them. He raised one foot, resting it flat on the surface of the altar and pressed his other thigh close to hers where it hugged Roka's hip. When Roka released him from the kiss, Eben turned to meet her eyes. His face was flushed and his lips swollen. She accepted his mouth greedily when he bent to kiss her.

At first, she was uncertain how to process the liberation of giving in to both men. She only knew she wanted to do more than be a passive participant. Blindly, she raised her hand the short distance to trace curious fingertips down over Eben's taut stomach. She reached his hips and pulled away from their kiss to watch in fascination as Roka pumped a hand along the length of Eben's cock.

With a hesitant touch, she ran her fingers over the back of Roka's knuckles, feeling his flexing grip. Roka released Eben long enough to urge her small hand around Eben's shaft, then closed his own hand back over hers and squeezed.

"Oh, baby, that's so good," Eben groaned.

She closed her eyes, lost in the steady, deep thrust of Roka's cock inside her and the hot, hard length of Eben's cock pressing against her palm.

Then their touches began. Two velvety tongues teased and nipped at her breasts; lips wrapped around both nipples and sucked. Roka's hand still gripped her hip on one side, so large it nearly covered one ass cheek to guide her up and down on him.

When Eben jerked against her, she knew something had changed and she opened her eyes. His shoulders were hunched, his blond head bent against her shoulder and he let out a series of desperate, incoherent grunts. He seemed to be pressing even further into them both, though the three of them were already so close there wasn't far for him to go.

She saw the reason for his reaction a second later when she spied movement behind Roka. A thick, shape extended along the surface of the altar; the shimmering silvery-white scales resembled the tail he'd had as a statue. It flexed and Eben moaned. She followed the contour of it in a daze. The thick, tapering length of it circled around behind Eben and she realized with a deep thrill of curious arousal that the tip of Roka's tail was now slowly fucking into Eben's ass. And he seemed to like it.

"Oh!" she exclaimed and stared wide-eyed at Roka.

He grinned back at her. "Would it make you fuck me harder if I did it to you, my love? I only have one tail, but perhaps I can improvise for your sake."

If she could have blushed harder, she would have, but he didn't give her a chance to answer. Before she could react, he'd slipped one thick finger of his free hand further between her thighs from behind, soaked it in her flowing juices, and pressed at her tight little asshole. She arched against his chest with a surprised cry, causing Eben to glance up in surprise.

"What is it, baby?" he managed to blurt out. Without answering, she gripped Eben behind the neck and kissed him again, hard and insistent. When Roka's finger passed beyond the sensitive barrier of her anus, she shoved her tongue deep into Eben's mouth. Their moans and pants mingled and they clung to Roka, who set the rhythm. Her pussy clenched hard at the surprising pleasure of the dragon's finger deep in her ass. She'd said she wanted to do dirty things, but wondered if even Eben could have conceived of something quite like this.

Roka's thrusts grew deeper and harsher. Waves of pleasure coursed through her when she met each stroke with a plunge of her hips down onto him.

"Oh, fuck, baby," Eben said. "I love watching you fuck his cock like that. I'm gonna come watching your pussy sliding all over him."

Eben slipped his hand down her back, his fingertips tracing hot fire along the path. His palm cupped and squeezed her ass cheek, then went one step further, teasing a circle around the sensitive skin at the center that was already being slowly penetrated by Roka's finger.

It only took a few caresses and her entire world narrowed into a pinprick of pure pleasure. One pair of lips latched onto her mouth, and another sucked at her nipples again, the sensations coming at her from every direction. A harsh cry erupted from her throat as the tingling throb of climax took hold of her pussy. Her ass clenched tightly around Roka's finger. He plunged it in deep, fucking her with it quickly. Her body seemed to spin out of control. Breathing became almost too difficult.

"Stay with me, my love," Roka's deep voice commanded, his lips brushing against hers. "I'm close."

She was dimly aware of the air shifting around them and the thick weight of Roka's cock growing even larger inside her. Nothing else existed of her body but the coiling mass of sensations that held her lower body captive. The dragon's cock surged into her at the same time Eben let out a long, low groan against her shoulder. The room grew darker as their bodies shuddered and writhed together. Something hot and wet splashed against her stomach. More hot liquid covered her hand where it gripped Eben's cock within the confines of Roka's larger hand.

Roka's low roar escalated around them. It pulsed against her eardrums, extending the sensations higher, so that her skull seemed to resonate with the same pleasure that gripped her body and made her nipples tingle. With another deep, violent thrust, wet, scorching heat filled her pussy.

Instead of the darkness of blacking out, the world became a thick, white fog.

She clung desperately to the two figures, not quite sure now where she ended and they began. The aftershocks of her orgasm gradually subsided, but only after the long, steady pulses of Roka's cock finally ceased inside her.

Finally she let out a long, shaky breath and collapsed against his chest, resting one cheek against him. Eben sat back on his heels, head bowed, sweat-soaked blond hair obscuring his face. His glistening cock rested limp against one thigh.

She looked beyond him but could see nothing but the fog and realized they were cocooned inside Roka's wings. The pair of massive white membranes almost completely encompassed the three of them, embracing them within a chamber filled with the dragon's breath. She inhaled deeply, taking it into her lungs. The more she breathed, the more the tension of their encounter dissipated, leaving her relaxed and euphoric. And still conscious.

"I didn't pass out," she said, smiling at no one in particular.

Roka rumbled softly. His gentle touch skimmed down her spine. "No. My magic prevented it this time. I needed you conscious."

"So you're awake for good now?" she asked, looking into his eyes. His pupils were now narrow slits surrounded by silver irises that gleamed with inner light.

"Yes. And now you both are mine. A dream come true for a dragon to be so blessed upon first awakening. You must help me thank Issa once the ritual is complete. There is one more thing I must do, however."

He shifted her off his lap and urged her to lie flat. Curious, and eager to please, she did so, uncertain what was coming next.

He bent over her hips and his tongue flicked out, tracing a small design just above the golden curls of her pubic hair.

She winced at the sting, but it dissipated quickly once he blew on it with a quick puff of white fog.

He turned to Eben. "Your turn."

Eben met Camille's eyes and shrugged. "It's a pretty tattoo. White, too—you can barely tell it's there unless you were looking for it." He obligingly lay down for Roka and received his own mark.

Camille stared down at the slightly upraised circular mark. Upside-down it didn't look like much, but she could make out the shape of a tiny dragon in embossed white. She wondered if Erika had been given one, too.

At that moment, the lights around the room flared brightly, then dimmed again. She and Eben both glanced around in surprise. She noticed Erika sit up on the other side of the room, attentive to the disturbance.

Propelled into action, Kris began walking toward the door, but none of the dragons made a move to follow.

"What was that?" Eben asked.

"Someone has opened the second door," Roka said. "The next phase has begun. Soon the Twins will be awakened."

SLEEPING DRAGONS

BOOK 3

GEMINI

OPHELIA BELL

The best things come in pairs.

CHAPTER ONE

Dimtri's eyes popped open unbidden and he stared into the dim reaches of the dragon temple above him. He let his eyes and ears acclimate to being awake, ignoring the remnants of the dream he'd been having about his twin brother. *Alex… you should be here, too,* he thought.

This had been their shared dream, finding a place like this. The desire to find evidence that the mythical creatures were real had driven the two brothers through their studies. Now Dimitri was *there*, waking up to the image of exquisitely carved jade dragons that guarded every reach of the massive temple, and the only thing on his mind was the regret that Alex wasn't there to share it with him.

You're here to let that go. To let Alex go, he told himself as he clambered out of his sleeping bag and hunted for the kettle. The nearby fountain splashed and gurgled and Dimitri marveled at the artistry of the carvings that made up their water source while he filled the kettle. The strange stones that filled the firepit they used for cooking were even more fascinating, and yet another detail he could imagine Alex enthusing over. He set the kettle down onto the hot bed of glowing rocks and sat back. Unable to shake thoughts of his brother just yet, he gave in one more time to the memories that played out in the bright embers while he waited for the water to boil so he could make coffee.

***

"Hey, love. I'd like you to meet my brother, Dimitri."

Dimitri put on his brightest, most welcoming smile to greet his twin brother's girlfriend. "Thea. Alex has told me so much about you." *Probably a lot more than you'd be comfortable with*, he thought. Alex's description of her had definitely done her justice, at least.

He reached out his hands to clasp hers affectionately, acutely conscious of her soft skin and the way she filled out the sheer, black blouse she wore. He let his hands linger over hers just a little longer than necessary, ignoring the little voice in his head reminding him that she was taken.

She was petite and curvaceous, with short, curly brown hair. Pixieish was how Alex had described her the week before. "With luscious lips and a cunt that tastes like strawberries." Dimitri agreed that her lips did indeed appear luscious, and his brother was not prone to exaggeration so he trusted the other detail was accurate, too. If he didn't feel just a little desperate for attention after being dumped himself, he'd have been able to deal with the soft allure of a pretty girl. As it was, Thea was a little *too* perfect. Alex had good taste. They both did, but somehow Alex was the better judge of character.

"Wow, Dimitri, you are every bit as handsome as your brother told me," Thea replied with a flirty twinkle in her eye that made Dimitri curse his brother in response. She'd won him over already, and now she was flirting?

Dimitri pulled his hands back and shoved them in his pockets, taking her in surreptitiously while they walked to the bar. As first impressions went, his impression of Thea was good, at least objectively. Not that he could be strictly objective after thinking about her naked. But as long as he ignored his unmistakable attraction to her he could tell that Alex seemed happy, and his brother's happiness meant more to him than anything.

At the bar, the three of them bantered like best friends. After a few drinks Thea decided to make it her singular purpose to find Dimitri a date.

"I don't think my brother's looking for a date tonight, love," Alex told her.

"How do you know?" she asked.

Dimitri was entertained by her contrary tone. His brother had found a live one. Not exactly surprising, but it didn't help him remain objective.

"I know because we share those details with each other." Alex met his eyes and took a drink of his beer. He hadn't been lying, but the truth was the two of them shared everything. There was nothing Dimitri had experienced that Alex didn't know about. At least not yet.

Of course Alex was being cagey on purpose. It was an unspoken rule between the two of them that the secrets they shared with each other weren't meant for the ears of their lovers.

Dimitri was still raw from a recent breakup. His brother knew all the sordid details of it, so it was unexpected that he'd have introduced Dimitri to a new flame so soon, knowing how sensitive he still was. Yet Alex had. So either Alex's relationship with this perfect woman was incredibly serious or something else was going on.

Dimitri took a long swallow of his beer, studying his brother through low-lidded eyes. *What have you got up your sleeve, brother?*

"Well, he looks lonely," Thea said. "And this place is *lousy* with pretty girls. He may not be as gorgeous as *you*, but it can't be that tough to find someone for him." She winked at Dimitri, obviously pleased with her joke. It wasn't the first time Dimitri had heard the joke—he'd even used it himself once or twice. Dimitri shared an amused glance with his brother, his mirror image, aside from their clothes, while Thea glanced around the room.

That first night set the tone for their interactions. Every Friday Dimitri would leave his tiny graduate assistant's office on campus, walk to the next wing to his brother's similar office, and they'd drive to meet Thea. Their destination was almost always the same comfortable little pub in the neighborhood where she lived.

Thea seemed to love hunting down girls for Dimitri, but after that first night it became clear it was just for show. Whether it was out of respect for him or because she started feeling some sense of possessiveness toward him, he couldn't be sure. She'd gotten into the habit of hooking her arms through both his and his brother's, and walking between them down the street. Dimitri thought she enjoyed some of the envious looks she'd get from other women, bookended by him and his brother as she was. One pretty little pixie flanked by two Adonises was probably the trifecta of attractiveness. He almost wished he could be on the outside looking in, because the truth was nowhere near as interesting as what other people probably imagined.

Buzzed from her third drink, Thea laid a hand on Dimitri's arm. "Dimitri, it's been a month. Alex won't share no matter how much I beg. I think it's time you tell me exactly *what* this girl did to you. You've gotta get back on the horse, sweetie!"

"Thea…" Alex began, but Dimitri cut him off.

"No, it's fine. She's right—I should talk about it." He turned and met Thea's eager gaze. "Well, first of all it wasn't a girl."

Thea's eyes grew wide and she shot Alex a curious look before saying, "Oh God, why didn't you say something? I feel so dumb trying to hook you up with a girl. I'll switch focus, I have lousy gaydar, though…*clearly*."

Dimitri laughed. "No, please. I don't need any help finding a date, and I actually *do* like girls, too. I'm just too busy focusing on my dissertation right now, I don't need the distraction." He took a deep breath and a long swallow of his beer, then let the rest of the story out in a rush just to get it over with. "That, and the person I'm getting over was my mentor so my life's about ten times as complicated as it needs to be." At least his mentor had prudently opted to take a sabbatical while the whole debacle blew over.

Dimitri was still nursing the painful humiliation of the disastrous affair. It never should have started, but it had. The ending had been epic and emotional. He was just grateful he had Alex to bolster his mood in the aftermath. And now that he'd told Thea, he found he was glad someone else was there to shoulder the burden. She reached out and gently squeezed his hand, then adroitly changed the subject. And that was that, at least he thought so.

Around midnight the three of them left, slightly the worse for wear after running into a group of other friends from the anthropology department where he and his brother were both finishing their masters degrees. Thea took up her customary spot between them and they headed haphazardly down the sidewalk toward her brownstone a few blocks away.

At her front steps he started to bid them both farewell and carry on alone back to the loft he shared with his brother. The place was depressingly lonely lately, so he'd most likely end up at the seedy dive bar nearby and close it down before going home to pass out.

Dimitri went in to hug Thea goodnight like always. Before he could react, her lips pressed against his, hot and sweet, and oh so welcome. His brain responded sluggishly at first, but other parts of him were much quicker on the uptake. His hands shifted down her back and pulled her closer before his actions registered.

"Thea, I…I think you got a little confused there," he said when he finally regained control and let go of her. "Alex is behind you. Honest mistake I guess." His stomach lurched when he met Alex's shocked gaze. His brother's look quickly faded, replaced by amused understanding. What the hell was Alex up to? What were they both up to?

"Nope," Thea said. "Not confused at all. Come inside with us, sweetie. Don't go home alone. Alex said you'd just go drink yourself silly anyway."

"Alex, what the fuck is going on?" Dimitri asked his brother. It was incredibly uncharacteristic for his twin to hide something like this.

"I would've warned you, but she wanted it to be spontaneous. Are you coming in or not?"

"You're telling me you planned this?" he asked, staring between them both, incredulous.

Thea appeared flushed and wide-eyed, but determined. "It was my idea, Dimitri. If you're not comfortable that's okay. Just come inside and at least talk about it, alright?"

He followed, not quite certain what he should expect. The kiss had confused him as much as it had turned him on, and incited a whole slew of questions. But there was no talking. Once through her door, she grabbed his hand and pulled him against her again. She kicked off her shoes and stood on bare tiptoes to reach him. The kiss was sweeter this time, now that he was expecting it, but he still had the strangest sense that he was trespassing somehow. He pulled away again, glancing at Alex for direction and to wordlessly confirm that he really wasn't crossing any lines.

"It's okay," Thea whispered. "Alex, tell him it's okay. Tell him I want you both. It's as much for me as it is for you, Dimitri."

The exchange between the three of them was surreal. She kept her eyes locked on Dimitri's while talking to his brother.

Alex never said a single word. Instead, he led them both to the bedroom and paused by the bed, Thea facing him. He gave her a lust-filled, hungry look and captured her lips fiercely in his. The couple seemed to emanate desire and it only made Dimitri more uncertain what his role really was, particularly when Alex met his eyes over Thea's smaller figure. Dimitri didn't think he'd ever seen his brother look quite so lost to his libido, but then this was an aspect of their lives they'd never shared before.

"You sure you're okay with this?" Dimitri's throat constricted.

"Yeah…yeah I am." Blue eyes stared back at him, the mirror image of his own, but filled with a certainty Dimitri couldn't have managed even if he tried. His life had been one botched relationship after another for the last couple years, the latest just the cherry on top. Could he subsist on his brother's convictions?

He was still asking himself that question when Thea turned and leaned up on tiptoe to kiss him again. He closed his eyes and wrapped his arms around her, letting her press herself against him and tease her tongue deeper. She pulled away long enough to let Alex pull her shirt off over her head and unfasten her bra from behind. Her breasts were creamy and plump, tipped by hard, pink nipples. The urge to bend and suck them nearly overwhelmed him, but Dimitri was focused on getting her naked first.

Dimitri knelt and unfastened her jeans. He grazed his palms down her sides, pushing the denim down her hips along with the lacy panties she wore. Her narrow waist flared dramatically to her wide hips. His hands kept sliding down over her creamy thighs, the soft warmth making his palms tingle. She stood perfectly still while he explored skin as perfect and flawless as alabaster. He heard a sharp intake of breath when he grazed his fingertips along the juncture of her hip and pelvis, tracing the perfect little triangle of coarse, dark hair, trimmed to a point just above the cleft of her pussy. He glanced up and met her eyes, low-lidded and bright with desire. His eyes traveled beyond her face to his brother's blue-eyed stare, the wordless suggestion as clear to Dimitri as if his twin had spoken.

He leaned closer and captured the tip of one full breast between his teeth, pulling it between his lips and sucking until she moaned. With a gentle nudge from her, he stood again and enveloped her in his arms. Every lush curve of her seemed to brush against his arms, rub against his chest. She tugged at his t-shirt and they parted long enough for him to tear it off over his head while she hastily unbuckled his pants. Then she was on him again, kissing and moaning against his lips. His cock throbbed against the soft skin of her belly, the steady pulse reflecting the pounding of his heart. Christ, he wanted her so much. He wanted to be buried inside her deep enough to lose himself. All those nights of talking with her and his brother came crashing back, of admiring her wit and beauty and finding some vicarious pleasure in seeing his brother so content while ignoring his own attraction. Had he held himself back from wanting her for the entire month?

He happily gave in now. Whether he was in love with her or just the idea of a good solid fuck was beyond his capacity to decide.

His eyes fluttered open long enough to see Alex behind her, naked now and brushing his lips down her neck. Dimitri heard his brother whisper in Thea's ear, "Tell us what you want us to do, love. This is your fantasy."

So that's what this was about. Alex had found a girl he wanted to please badly enough to share. Or maybe it had happened before but this was the first time Dimitri hadn't been spoken for. How the hell was this going to work with the two of them? He'd imagined threesomes before, but those fantasies had always involved indiscriminate sharing of bodies and pleasure. Never had he imagined his brother as the third party. *Focus on her*, he told himself. That was easy enough because she was all over him.

"Lay down on the bed," she said, sending a heated glance at Alex. He obeyed, resting back against her pillows. She turned, darting a coquettish look over her shoulder at Dimitri and gesturing for him to follow. Dimitri's eyes focused on her plump, round ass when she crawled up the bed to his brother. She paused between Alex's legs and dipped her head, slowly taking his cock into her mouth. Alex let out a groan of pleasure and met Dimitri's eyes with a pleased smile. Dimitri knew that look, or at least the inspiration for it, because he'd had it himself on countless occasions. His own cock twitched sympathetically.

Her glistening pussy seemed to lure him in, the bare, lips glistening and slightly parted. *Strawberries*, he thought. His mouth watered and the thought spurred him into motion. He knelt behind her and leaned down, spreading her open for a taste. She moaned around his brother's cock when his tongue slipped into the slick heat. Maybe not strawberries, but she did taste amazing. She made a cute little squeak when he invaded her creamy, wet pussy with two fingers and began fucking into her.

Her head bobbed diligently on Alex's cock. Dimitri watched, easily imagining what her mouth would feel like on him. He and his brother rarely needed words to understand each other. They had never really needed to talk, growing up, somehow reading each other easily through expressions. The intensity of his brother's look wasn't exactly explicit, but it was enough. *Do more,* it said.

Dimitri let his eyes travel over Thea's body. Her plump breasts brushed against his brother's thighs while she worked his cock. He reached a hand down and cupped one, squeezing the tip gently between thumb and forefinger, then rubbing lightly in slow circles. She let out a muffled moan and her pussy clenched around his fingers.

His gaze followed the curve of her spine down to the cleft of her ass. The pink puckered bud of her asshole seemed bereft of attention, so he grazed his thumb across the delicate skin while still thrusting his fingers deep into her.

She moaned and pushed back into his hand. His brother exhaled suddenly and tilted his head back in pleasure.

Dimitri bent his head and trailed his tongue in a slow circle around the tight little opening. She went completely rigid.

"Sorry," he whispered against one pale cheek of her backside.

It was Alex who answered. "Don't stop, oh God don't stop."

Dimitri wasn't sure whether the words were meant for him or for Thea. She stopped in spite of them, and moved away from Dimitri, leaving him kneeling at the foot of the bed, his fingers glazed with her juices.

What had he been thinking trying something like that so soon? He sat there, cock throbbing, trying to decide if he was desperate enough to just jerk off, or if he should get dressed and leave. But he couldn't take his eyes off her now, and neither could Alex. Dimitri envied his brother for that rapt expression. He'd felt the same thing with lovers before, and he felt exactly that when he watched her now. She spread her thighs and straddled Alex's hips. She gripped his twin in one hand and slid the tip of Alex's cock back and forth between her pussy lips. Dimitri rubbed the tip of his own cock with the fingers still wet from her, in an attempt to feel something close to what Alex must be experiencing.

Alex's eyelids fluttered and he let out a long, low sigh when Thea lowered herself onto his cock. Dimitri couldn't tear his eyes away from where they were joined. His hand instinctively gripped his cock and began stroking while he watched her fuck his brother with slow, undulating motions of her hips. She leaned over to give Alex a long, languid kiss. Turning her head to look over her shoulder at Dimitri, she smiled.

"Fuck me, Dimitri. I know that's what you want, so do it. Please, fuck me."

Dimitri blinked, uncertain at first what she meant. He met Alex's fevered gaze briefly and followed his brother's darted glance to the bedside table. What he saw made him immediately feel like a fool. This was what she wanted with them both.

The scent of strawberries wafted to his nostrils when he popped the lid. He squirted a liberal amount of the clear liquid onto his fingertips. As surreal as the evening had been so far, the intensity with which he was able to focus on this particular task overrode every other worry or fear he had up until then. Nothing drove him but the singular desire to feel her coming apart with his cock fucking deep into her ass while his brother worked her from the beneath.

His slick fingertips swirled delicately around her opening. He pressed his index finger at the center, slowly letting it slide in, enjoying how she quivered and buried her face against Alex's neck. She stopped moving her hips, seeming to anticipate what he would do next. Alex kept pumping slowly up into her pussy.

He and his brother locked eyes briefly, holding the gaze while Alex murmured into Thea's ear. "You like that, love? You like my cock deep inside while Dimitri plays with your ass?"

Dimitri shared a smile with his brother, finally enjoying the endeavor without any uncertainty about the implications. If Alex were this comfortable with the idea, there was no reason he shouldn't be, too. And he was invested in seeing Thea fly to pieces once he and his brother were both fucking her. He pressed a second slick digit into her. She cried out and shot her hands out to either side of Alex's head, gripping hard at the pillows.

"Oh fuck that's good," she gasped. Alex turned his eyes to her face, his expression transforming into hungry need. He accepted her rough kiss and reached down to squeeze both her ass cheeks, spreading her wider for Dimitri.

"Now," Alex said.

Dimitri coated his cock with the slick scent of strawberries. Thea whimpered against Alex's lips, then let out a harsh groan when Dimitri pressed his cock against her tight barrier. Alex had slowed his own pace down, only moving with a slow thrust every few seconds. Dimitri's arms quivered with the effort of holding himself poised over her, but he had to go slow.

"Do it!" she commanded through gritted teeth. "Oh God, fuck me. *Please.*" Her last word came out as a desperate sob against Alex's shoulder.

Her asshole clenched once around the head of his cock, then relaxed. He slipped in by increments, the tight friction around his cock creating heat like a furnace that coursed through him. He was dimly aware of his own harsh grunts when he finally began fucking her in earnest.

Alex's cock pounded into her again in a frenzy from beneath. Her head thrashed and her hands clawed at the sheets. A long, sobbing moan escaped and her entire body shuddered beneath Dimitri. Her ass clenched tightly around his cock and he abruptly sank into her and stopped, hilt deep, unable to stand it any longer. The pressure of his brother's cock pressed and throbbed beyond the barrier between them. Alex cried out. Or was it Dimitri crying out himself? His throat ached from his own harsh gasps. He panted in time with the surge of his orgasm, the hot stream of his cum shooting deep into her.

When they regained their breath she slipped from between them. She paused long enough to press a kiss against his lips before she disappeared into her bathroom. Dimitri sat back on his heels, dazed and buzzed, though he wasn't quite sure whether it was the remnants of alcohol in his system or from *her*. Thinking perhaps he should leave, he glanced around for his clothes and made a move to get up.

"You'd be an asshole to leave after that," his brother said in a low voice.

Dimitri gave him a questioning look.

"I know you're used to us keeping this part of our lives separate, but it obviously isn't working out for you. Face it, our lives are better when we're both invested in something together. Besides, I'm pretty sure she likes you."

"You think?" Dimitri asked, finally finding the breath to respond.

CHAPTER TWO

"You alright, man?"

Corey's concerned words pulled Dimitri out of the depths of his memories. He'd managed to make a pot of coffee, but now sat in a canvas camp chair ignoring his steaming cup while he stared at the oddly glowing fireplace.

"I'm…yeah, I guess. Being here in this temple feels strange. I always expected if I ever made it to a place like this my brother would be with me."

"You two studied together, right?" Corey asked.

"Yep. He was in Erika's program, but just missed having her for a TA, I guess."

They'd done more than just study together. After that first night with Thea, the sharing of interests even extended to their sex lives. The overlap seemed completely natural once they started, and Thea was more than happy to accommodate both of them. Dimitri had even gone so far as to consider himself content—maybe even truly happy—after six months had passed with the three of them completely inseparable. She fit so well into their lives it was hard to imagine a time when she hadn't been a part of it.

But like his life tended to do, it all fell apart. The red glow of the strange embers in the fireplace became the flashing lights of an ambulance in Dimitri's memory; the waning heat of his mug became the diminishing warmth as his brother's life bled away in the mangled car they were both trapped in. He supposed he should be grateful that Thea hadn't been with them. The aftermath had left his soul as mangled and useless as the heap of metal the emergency crew had pulled him out of. They'd probably tested fate and lost, trying to share Thea's love.

"What would he have said about the dragons, do you think?" Corey asked.

Dimitri took a deep breath and finally sipped at his tepid coffee. "Dragons…" He let out a low chuckle, glad for an excuse to picture the happier image of his brother's enthusiasm over this find. "He'd have loved the dragons. Been totally on board with this whole fantasy world we've discovered down here."

He swallowed his coffee down in a series of quick gulps and poured another cup.

"Where is everyone?" he asked, realizing that most of the sleeping bags were empty. All but Hallie's. She still lay snoring softly like the heavy sleeper she was. Must be nice to sleep with such a clear conscience.

He wondered what it was that had pulled Corey out of sleep. His older friend wasn't exactly the sharing type, so he had no idea what made the man tick. Dimitri had only shared the details of his own life in an effort to try to purge the memories, yet they still haunted him regularly.

That sharing, though, on his part, on many of their parts, had brought the team closer. They were almost a family now, if not quite the one he'd loved and lost. Everyone seemed to bear some kind of burden, spoken or unspoken. Still, knowing he wasn't alone in carrying such pain was a comfort.

"Not sure, but I'm about to go look. Want to join me?" Corey picked up one of his small digital video cameras and set off around the corner. Dimitri followed, happy for the distraction.

Walking through the center of the cavernous main room of the dragon temple, Dimitri thought the place seemed more brightly lit than it had when they'd first arrived. The glowing braziers behind the throne at the far end of the room pulsed in a slow rhythm that he found almost hypnotic.

"Did you ever figure out how the lights work?" he asked.

Corey paused by the throne and glanced around with a concerned look on his face. He shook his head. "Beats the shit outa me. It's driving me nuts that I can't figure it out, though. I was hoping to get Eben's help cracking one open but he's disappeared along with Erika and Camille. Kris is MIA, too."

Dimitri chuckled. "Are you sure you want to go looking? I'll give you three guesses what he and Erika are up to and honestly I don't blame them. Maybe Kris and Camille found a dark corner somewhere, too. If I had a willing partner you can bet that's what I'd be doing right now. A find like this definitely warrants a celebratory fuck."

Corey stooped down and picked something up off the polished jade floor in front of him. He shot Dimitri a critical look. "You guys are probably the most oversexed group of people I've ever had the pleasure of working with, you know that? Except for Camille maybe."

"Sometimes you just need human contact," Dimitri said. "Helps you feel a little less alone in the world."

Corey's expression turned sympathetic. "Yeah, sorry, man. I understand that need, but it's never really worked for me. I need more than just a warm, willing body. I'd rather be alone than screwing a woman I don't feel a deep connection with."

"It's alright. Being here just brought back some old memories. I woke up horny as hell, and all I could think about was that first night Alex and I were both with Thea."

"See, that's not something I could ever see myself doing, either," Corey said. "I guess I'm not the sharing type."

"I didn't think I was either, but it made so much sense once we'd started. I think we were both amazed we hadn't done it before. But I suppose Thea was a special girl. It probably wouldn't have worked with anyone other than her." It had worked, though. Before too long he was as head over heels for her as his brother was. The strangest thing about their relationship was the fact that neither he nor his brother had any reservations about the other's hold on Thea's feelings. And she never once played favorites, which seemed odd to Dimitri since she'd been with Alex first. She became the fulcrum he and Alex balanced their lives upon. Except that after Alex's death suddenly they'd lost their counterbalance and had ultimately spun off in different directions. He'd left finally, after a heart-wrenching argument in which it became apparent she couldn't stand seeing him, being reminded every day of what they'd both lost.

"Check this out," Corey said, handing Dimitri a notebook, the top page halfway filled with Camille's tiny, meticulous handwriting. Dimitri flipped back a few pages and read.

"What the hell?" He stared down at the characters carved into the floor around the base of the throne. "Do you think they're crazy enough to try doing this…this *ritual?*"

"Knowing Erika, yeah," Corey said. "Looks like someone managed to open one of the doors back there. Let's go find them."

Dimitri flipped to the next page and read, enthralled by the very idea that this was even possible. Six phases to the ritual, Camille's translation said. Six members of their group, not counting their guide. *Alex, you would have been all over this.* He noted one of Camille's tiny notes in the margin that said, "What if dragons are real?!" in one spot. When he reached the last page, he found an underlined section of text in a language he didn't understand, with another note written in English off to the side, "No wonder we're all so worked up in here. It's by design. It takes *nirvana* to wake one up. Nirvana equals orgasms?"

He tossed the notebook back down where Camille had left it and jogged to catch up with Corey. His mind processed the possibilities presented in Camille's notes. The other man was probably too pragmatic to believe it, but Dimitri had a surge of hopeful excitement. This just confirmed what he and his brother had speculated. He'd accepted Erika's invitation to join the expedition for the novelty more than anything, but now it seemed there were facets to this place that were beyond his wildest dreams.

The giant pair of carved jade doors loomed in front of him, one pushed open just far enough to allow a person to pass through. Corey, ever the diligent cameraman, hit the on switch and began recording as he went.

"You first," Corey said, gesturing for Dimitri to enter.

The wide hallway curved around, mimicking the rear arc of the dais the throne sat upon in the main chamber. Five large doors were spaced at intervals along the apex of the arc, the central door much larger than the other four.

The door closest to them stood open, and from the sounds that emanated from inside Dimitri had the oddest sense that he was walking onto the set of a porn movie.

He glanced back at Corey, gave his friend a smirk and opened his mouth to say, "I told you so." "Except the moment he turned, he found himself close enough to get a first peek into the room itself. The smirk disappeared and the words caught in his throat. He stopped dead in his tracks, his jaw dropping open at the completely unexpected tableau that greeted him.

"What is it?" Corey asked, looking up from the digital display on the back of the camera.

"See for yourself," Dimitri said.

He felt a little wrong watching them, but found it difficult to tear his eyes away. They were tangled up in groups of three. He recognized Camille and Eben in one trio. Their companion was a magnificent man with pale skin, long white hair and horns.

Camille straddled his lap, riding on the man's cock like she was born to fuck him in spite of the shy confession of her virginity that Dimitri had pried out of her the week before. Eben knelt beside the couple, locked into a passionate kiss with the man.

Dimitri's eyebrows shot up at this scene. He'd always suspected Eben's more universal sexual tendencies, but this was the first confirmation he'd had.

Across the room a similar scene played out, with Erika and two other unfamiliar figures, both with vibrant sheens to their skin and similar curved protrusions on their heads. Who the hell were these people? *Creatures…Dragons…*He could almost hear Alex's voice rejoicing in his mind when the scope of what they had discovered down here occurred to him.

Erika lay languid across the lap of a red-haired man while a violet-horned woman knelt between her legs, attending to her. Dimitri watched, fascinated, while they changed places. Erika went down on the other woman while the red man positioned himself behind Erika.

In a previous life Dimitri might have announced himself and asked to be included, but now he just stood enthralled. Alex would have loved the opportunity to be a part of this. The only thought in Dimitri's mind was that this was only one room out of dozens. He wanted his own dragon.

He turned to express this thought to Corey but shut his mouth before the words could sneak out. Corey stood completely rigid and not at all entertained by the scene. His jaw flexed, no doubt grinding his teeth hard enough to lose a layer of enamel…the man was too tense in general.

The sounds in the room escalated. Then before their eyes, the three exotic newcomers shifted almost in unison, as if they had some shared cue when they orgasmed. Suddenly the previously human-looking figures became mythical, beautiful things with wings flaring wide and elongated faces spouting colored smoke and resonant cries of pleasure. Red and white and lavender. Dimitri found it difficult to stop watching until Corey cursed and walked away, leaving Dimitri staring wide-eyed. He thought the dragons would be bigger, but that didn't mean they were any less impressive.

He wanted to be a part of this ritual so badly the wanting made him numb to the hard throb between his thighs. Logically it made no sense, but his compulsion spurred him on and he went with it, moving to the next door in the row. The closed door stood there, the shining gold surface of it glowing at him with subtle, tantalizing pulses of light.

The door. Camille's notes had detailed the importance of these particular doors. Each one represented a new phase of the ritual. Each one required a unique personality to open it and her notes speculated that their group had the perfect combination to see the ritual through.

He paused and stared at the thing. Tried to be analytic about it. From an anthropological standpoint, it was a curiosity. Dragon worship wasn't unheard of, but what culture was so beast-centric to depict humans in coitus with reptiles? *Dragons, just like Alex and I always believed.* The thought sent a thrill through him, but he tried to process the information objectively anyway. In the Western world it would've been seen as Satan worship, no doubt. But in the context of what he'd witnessed a moment ago he believed there had to be more to it than mere worship.

They'd looked human at first. Super-human, really, but still recognizable and articulate creatures. The red-haired one was particularly vocal and there was no mistaking how much he'd been enjoying giving it to Erika for all he was worth. And she was every bit as vocal back to him. Fuck, had that been a turn-on.

But the more he stared at the golden image carved into the door, the less it mattered. He stepped closer and raised a hand to trace the figure of one of the two dragons that flanked the human. When his fingertips came into contact with the surface, a jolt of pure, electrical pleasure shot through him.

"Are you crazy?" Corey asked. Dimitri jerked back from the door as though he'd been caught with his hand in a cookie jar.

"I'm going in," he said.

"The hell you are." Corey gripped him by the shoulder. Dimitri pulled away, frustration churning in his stomach, beginning to condense in a hot ball of spite at being held back. Before he could retaliate another figure joined them.

"Let him go in," Kris said in a soft, measured voice. "He's meant to open that door. You see the twins there?" Kris pointed at the raised figures on the door's golden surface.

Corey gave the door a cursory glance. "I call bullshit," he said. "You slipped some drug in our dinner last night. Now we're all hallucinating."

Kris shook his head. "I won't deny this is a powerful place, but all I've done is help guide you all to where you already belong. Dimitri belongs inside that room."

"What happens once I go in?" Dimitri asked.

"You'll have a choice to make. One twin or the other. When you give your nirvana to him or her, and the dragon returns the favor, you will be bonded to that dragon. The power of your union will help to fill the Queen's well. Then, when the time comes, she will awaken and call the rest of the brood to the skies."

"And then what? They take over the world?" Corey asked in a bitter tone.

"No. It's a symbiotic relationship dragons have with humans. Your kind is rarely aware of us. Only those bonded to us know."

"What the fuck do you mean *us*? Are you one of them?"

Kris smiled and nodded. "I'm a pure blood. I'm the conduit through which they will feed all their collected power to the Queen." He turned to look at Corey. "You should prepare yourself, my friend. There are only two of you left, after Dimitri, and you're the only one suitable to be the Queen's mate."

"Let me guess…she likes to bite off the heads of men after she's done with us, right?"

"You know, Corey," Dimitri interjected, "I liked you at first, but now you're just being an obstinate asshole."

"You're the delusional one. I don't know what Kris did to us, but I don't believe this magical dragon bullshit."

"Fine. You go on not believing it. I'm going to see for myself."

CHAPTER THREE

Five hundred years might seem like a long time to sleep. To Aurin, it was maybe a little too short. Her consciousness aroused for the first time in half a millennium and her first thought was to hope it would go away and leave her be. Let her sleep and fall back into the endless dream of flying—of spreading her wings and casting her large shadow across the earth for days without fatigue or hunger. She could happily fly forever. But the vibrations in the air around her conveyed the fact that it was time. A second later her brother's thoughts invaded her mind, echoing her own.

"It's time, Sister."

"Yes, Aurik. I sense it. Now we wait."

"It won't be long. Humans are impatient creatures."

The velvet blanket of darkness still covered them. Until their part of the ritual began she was still blind and paralyzed. She recalled the ritual to send them all to sleep. Each new generation of their race was sent into a magical stasis to mature while the prior generation lived out their long lives among humans. Five hundred years had passed in the blink of an eye. With a surge of sadness she understood that their awakening meant the last of the prior generation had finally been committed to the skies for eternity. A dragon's death was rare enough that it made the awakening bittersweet to know that she and the other members of the new generation would be cast into the world soon, with only the memories of their parents' teachings to guide them.

Her brother was close enough to touch. They'd been frozen like statues, back-to-back with scant inches between them. Frozen in their human forms as the ritual dictated. Only the guardians and the Shadow were allowed to keep their dragon forms in sleep. Their defenders had to be ready to protect them. The other members of the dragon court slept in their human forms, as did the dozens of other dragons that slumbered within the sanctuary of the temple along with her. Her brother didn't mind it so much, but it made her itch.

"They're taking too long," she griped.

"They'll take as long as they need to. Issa will know when to urge them on, though. We're second."

"Hmm...I wonder what he'll be like. Remember mother telling us how her first chosen had no idea what to do with her? He was a Sultan, even. She said he was terrified when she changed. I hate coercing men into sex, even if they do love it. Sometimes they're so needy afterward."

"It may be a woman who comes in. Whoever it is, they will have to choose between us. You know this."

She seethed inwardly at being reminded of the strict laws they had to adhere to, one of which was that no human should have dominance over two dragons. Except whoever awakened them would be *their* property, not the other way around. Added to that was the even more distressing law that dictated dragons must travel alone until the first of the new brood was born. Too many dragons sharing a border could cause conflict. The old council feared their competitive, greedy natures would result in wars. In spite of her certainty that she and Aurik would be well behaved, she wondered if the laws would even allow them to stay together.

"I'd rather share with you than be parted. I don't want you to have to go find your own mate alone."

"And what a hopeless search that would be, too. Women bore me. I'll make you a promise, Sister. If it is a man and we both take to him, we make a pact to let him wake us both, and we share. If it is a woman, I'll make do with her, but vow that I will stay as near to you as possible until you find your human mate."

"But will the Queen even allow it?"

"Every cycle presents new complications, Sister, resulting in new laws. Maybe we can make the argument and be heard. Patience."

Bolstered by her brother's certainty that sharing the man who awakened them would be possible, she turned her mind to contemplation of what he might be like. Different than the human men she'd known before sleeping, she hoped.

"Do you hear that?" Aurik asked, eagerness obvious in his voice.

She trained her ears to the sounds outside. Voices spoke beyond their door.

One insistent, accented voice said, "It's my choice, Corey. I believe it. You saw the others with your own eyes."

A gruffer voice replied, "Dimitri, there's no proof. You're a *scientist.* You know better."

"No proof? They fucking *changed right in front of you.* Dragons! If you can't believe your eyes, what can you believe?"

The other voice grumbled, "I believe we've been drugged and the rest of you are too in love with Erika's fantasy to see the truth. It's all one big hallucination."

"Fine, you believe that if you want, but I have blue balls from hell right now so I'm willing to do just about anything to fix that."

"Just find a dark corner. I'll look the other way."

"Christ, Corey! Don't you think I've tried that? Something's *different* about this place. You go find a dark corner and try it, why don't you."

"What are blue balls?" Aurin asked her brother.

"I can only guess, but I suspect he's sexually frustrated."

The air released in a sudden rush when the door opened, breaking the seal of the room they'd been contained in. If she'd been able to move, her skin would have quivered in response to the gust. She could smell *him*, at least. Male musk and sweat and an underlying sweetness that she recognized as goat milk. But the aroma was subtle, like he'd been fed on it as a child. He smelled of the old world she was accustomed to. Was this really the time? Surely it couldn't have been five hundred years already if the man who came to wake them smelled so familiar.

"Do you smell him?" she asked her brother.

"Yes, Sister. If I weren't already hard as polished jade, I would be now."

She couldn't laugh or roll her eyes at her brother, but knew exactly what he meant. She was aroused by this new man's scent.

For the first time she cursed the darkness that surrounded her. They could hear and smell …they could communicate silently with each other as always. But they couldn't see or touch or taste anything.

A few seconds later she realized that was no longer true. As is soft footsteps approached, the closer he came the more her hard jade skin began to tingle, until it felt alive for the first time in centuries. He paused close enough for the heat radiating off his body to warm her. The temperature change in such close proximity sent invisible shivers down her skin and the alluring scent of him grew even stronger. Oh, sweet Mother, she wished she could see him.

The slow caress of a warm finger down her naked arm was enough to send her shattering to pieces if she really were only polished jade and not a living thing inside a prison.

"Oh."

"Did he touch you, too?"

"Yes."

Then the most astounding thing happened. He started talking in a low, smooth voice. At first she didn't understand the words as she had the ones he'd spoken earlier, but within a second or two she caught up to the nuances and her mind filled in the rest. He spoke Greek, but a dialect far removed from the last time she'd heard it spoken. His cadence and inflections teased at her ears. When he finally stopped talking she wished he would begin again.

"I wish I knew your names. You are too beautiful for words. I don't quite know what I'm supposed to do, but it seems like such an intimate thing that I shouldn't just start trying to fuck you." He laughed, the sound tickling her ears. "Like that's even possible...I mean, you're *statues*. But you're really more than that, aren't you? Corey doesn't believe in this supernatural nonsense. Neither do I, really, but evidence is evidence. And I don't feel drugged. Fuck, you are both so beautiful."

He paused and traced a finger down her cheek. She could have wept from the tender contact if she'd been able to. But the sensation was stark and jarring against stone skin that had been numb for centuries. She could *feel* him now.

"I want to wake you up," he continued. "But I have no idea how. Camille's notes say I need to give one of you my nirvana. Is she right about the sexual aspect of it? Is that why you're both naked and ready? Well, at least one of you is ready."

She heard a frustrated huff expel from his mouth, and a warm gust of air brushed past her face. His breath smelled of curry and dragon magic.

"In fairy tales, it works with just a kiss, maybe that's enough."

She heard nothing but his heartbeat as close as he was, and the brush of skin against stone somewhere behind her.

"He's kissing you, isn't he?" she asked.

"Oh yes. Sweet he is, Sister." Her brother's voice sounded elated.

"Damn you."

But she didn't carry her envy for long because a moment later the same warm lips pressed against her rigid, unresponsive ones. If any kiss could have awakened a sleeping princess, his would have done the trick. But she was no princess, nor was her brother. It took more than a kiss for them. Still, she strained within her prison to respond to the sweet, soft press of his lips. The warmth of his flesh left her tingling even deeper when he pulled away with a sigh.

"Not enough, huh? I guess this is a different fairy tale."

She heard soft swishing sounds. His movement pushed wafts of his scent to her nose. She guessed he was undressing, and oh how she wished she could see him. A man with a scent like that and lips that kissed so well *must* be lovely to look upon.

"I should tell you both something before I wake you up. I don't know if you can even hear me…but I need to say this anyway. Kris said I had to choose between you. But there's no way in hell I can do that. I don't know how this…ritual works, but he's told me enough. I know deep inside that you two are going to save my life. That's why I'm doing this in spite of my logic telling me it's crazy. If you *do* wake up after this then I'll know the truth. If you don't then I guess I just hope I've found some peace to move on."

Something warm pressed against the rigid curve of her breast. His fingertips brushed around the heavy swell, curling up to trace the outline of her nipple. She felt every single increment of the contact as though each cell of her being were sending its own cries of gratitude at the contact to her soul.

Another part of her reacted to the contact, too, and it felt so real it ached. The tight bundle of nerves between her thighs felt like it contracted and she wished she could touch it to see if it were awake. She needed to know whether they were just phantom sensations of wetness or if they were real. The sensation magnified when his warm touch grazed the tip of her other breast.

But he stopped touching her. She sensed him moving, facing away toward her brother. She wanted to yell out but wasn't yet able to speak. She could only listen to the brief sounds that her hyper-sensitive hearing picked up. Sounds like she'd heard when he touched her, skin on stone, caressing in adoration.

"Yes, he is the one," Aurik said in a languid voice a moment later. *"I almost regret my offer to share, but I will."*

"What did he do to you?"

"Enough to let me know."

CHAPTER FOUR

Dimitri let his hand skitter off the end of the golden statue's erect cock. The warmth of it still tingled on his skin, a subtle signal to him that there was more to these statues than Corey believed. And these two…they were posed so perfectly. Back-to-back, identical aside from their obvious genders. The translucent gold of the jade they were made from shimmered in the flickering lights, enticing him to touch them both more. And he would, because he couldn't resist. The few soft caresses he'd given them earlier had only incited deeper cravings. Cravings that didn't help the aching in his balls while he stared at the two of them. To choose would be impossible. He had to find a way to awaken them both.

"You are two halves of a whole. That's why I have to wake you up together. You see, I was like you. A twin. But I lost my other half last year. And I…" His breath caught in his throat and he paused to stare into the female's stone eyes, imagining she could see him and was looking back with understanding. "I lost myself after my brother died. Ever since, I've been carrying around this dark emptiness that's slowly eating me alive." The only times he'd managed to come close to finding peace after Alex's death and Thea's withdrawal were the random, pointless hookups he'd made late at night with near strangers. They proved ultimately too fleeting and empty of meaning.

Standing beside these two figures, for the first time since that first night with Thea and Alex, his life felt pregnant with possibility. If he could awaken two creatures like these beautiful dragons, find that apex of peace together, he might just be okay. Even if it were only one encounter, he believed he could leave here closer to whole than when he arrived.

His hands kept steadily trailing over the surface of their jade skin. Up the male's arms, down his lean, sculpted chest, then switching his attention to the female's sweeping swell of breasts, the heft of which he could feel in his palm even though they were made of rigid mounds of stone tipped with hard little peaks. He experimentally bent his head to one, teasing the smart tip with his tongue. The texture of it was so close to real it caused a tingle to travel down his spine, and his balls tightened. He was sure he could hear a sigh from somewhere in the room, but when he looked at her placid face nothing had changed.

Both were nearly the same height as him, and slender but well-built. They were completely nude, with long, wavy tresses carved from the same jade, draping in perfect thick tendrils over their shoulders. The male also had the hint of a goatee decorating his angular face.

He circled them, touching by increments as he went, marveling at the warm, smooth texture of their skin. He paused in front of the male once and leaned in for a kiss. The lips felt smooth and he could almost imagine how pliant and inviting they'd be were the man alive. His tongue tingled when he grazed it lightly in the crease between, over the barely visible hint of teeth. He let his hand slide down the front of the figure's torso and come to rest on the rigid cock that jutted from between the golden thighs. It felt warmer now. He must be imagining it…it must be warmth from his nearness permeating the stone. Still, it felt so close to life-like, rendered in minute detail from the sparse texture of carved thatch at the base to the tiny ridges of veins and the slight upward curve. The entire magnificent arc capped by the most delicious looking head, slightly tapered from the thicker shaft.

He stroked it in one long, languid motion, gripping his own cock in his fist at the same time. His living flesh jerked against his palm and a tiny moan escaped his lips.

"Fuck. I'd love to be sandwiched between the two of you. You're just facing the wrong way right now. So what do you think I should do?"

He slipped back around to face the female and rested his lips against hers now, letting them linger a little longer while his hands traced the curve of her waist and his fingertips trailed up to her breasts. He made tight little circles around her nipples imagining she were alive and responsive.

All he could think was to touch them. Make love to them as best he could, considering they were mute, solid forms, frozen and beautiful.

He began by falling to his knees before her and pressing his mouth into the intricately carved folds between her jade thighs.

CHAPTER FIVE

"*Oh, sweet Mother…*" Aurin exclaimed.

"*Tell me, Sister. Don't hide or I'll be very jealous. What is he doing?*"

"*Licking me. And he has such a lovely tongue, too.*"

"*That he does. That kiss. I can still taste it. So sweet. And he kissed me first.*"

"*Brother, when he wakes us I'm going to punch you.*"

Aurik's chuckle vibrated through her mind. "*You might be too busy stroking his cock to worry about payback. How does his tongue feel, Sister? Am I going to like feeling it on my cock?*"

The tongue in question licked between her thighs with a kind of abandon, like she were made of hard rock candy that might melt and not solid stone. The sensations his steady flicks and swirls produced certainly made her feel like melting. Hundreds of years it had been since she'd had a tongue between her thighs. But she knew how the ritual was supposed to work. He had to make a sacrifice to them. His nirvana. If he exhausted himself with his selflessness, that would *not* serve their purposes.

He let out an audible, rumbling groan and she felt his head shift lower, his tongue sinking deeper.

"Oh! Something's happening. Is this supposed to happen?"

"What? Tell me, Sister!"

"I'm…I don't know. I feel like I'm coming alive. My cunt is, at least. But he hasn't sacrificed his nirvana to us yet."

"You've got his tongue in your little dragon snatch and you're complaining?"

"No, you imbecile. You know we won't wake up until he gives it to us."

Her brother began to answer but she grew distracted by the growing heat between her thighs. Something was *definitely* going on down there. The man's steadily moving tongue was splayed across her clit that felt way too alive for how frozen the rest of her was.

"Oh Christ, you're …you're *wet* and soft, and …oh shit," he said.

She wanted to scream out, "And what?" and then grab his head and push it back against her. But she couldn't do that. All she could do was itch inside her prison wishing he would get on with pleasuring himself instead of her so she could break out and throw herself on him. Except she didn't want him to *stop* pleasuring her, either. She might come. Would it count, she wondered? Would she even be able to? Oh, sweet Mother, she'd love to find out.

"I…oh shit. Am I allowed to do it first? Is it possible?"

"He's that good, huh? Damn you, Sister. I thought for certain that he'd pick me first."

The string of expletives on her lips fell short when the tongue between her legs was supplemented by a pair of fingers slipping silk-like into the tight crevice of her pussy. They didn't just slide in, though. They pushed against her now very alive pussy walls and he teased at the insides of her while murmuring pleased little sounds against her clit. Sounds like, "Yeah, that's it. My magic fingers just broke your spell, huh?" But the steady finger fucking and gentle tweaking of her swollen nub made her a little deaf to the rest.

"He's in me. Oh. Oh. How…how is it possi- uh."

Her brother had the nerve to giggle over her reaction. She'd have happily breathed fire on him if that were still allowed. She might still do it anyway after she were free. Damn the rules.

"Are you gonna come, Sister? Stuck in this prison?"

She might just do it. That tongue of his was so talented and insistent. She could even feel the pliancy of her pussy under his touch. What would happen if she did come, most of her body trapped in this rigid form?

What he did next solved the problem.

"I'm going to fuck you now, if that's okay. You feel like you're enjoying what I did anyway. I'm no geologist like Eben, but I'm pretty sure rocks don't normally get that soft and wet when you lick them."

"You bitch," her brother's voice intoned in her mind. Like she cared. Her pussy was awake. More than awake, it felt like her entire existence rested right between her thighs in that bundle of swollen, throbbing flesh that had clearly come to life before the

rest of her and that he was still stroking and licking. And now he was standing up and pressing the hot tip of his cock to it.

If she could have yelled out she would have.

"Yes, just fuck me!"

"You couldn't help yourself, could you, Sister?"

"Oh, but he feels so good. He's going too slow."

"Describe it to me, please?"

"Oh , Brother, he is thick and so, so sweet. He is so sweet, Brother. This one, if we share him, we must treasure him."

Her brother's chuckles of amusement in her mind faded into the background with the thrust of the human man's cock into her needy pussy.

"Oh, sweet Jesus you feel amazing. Tight and hot," the man said, his warm breath leaving tangible condensation on her jaw. His low, desperate groan resounded in her ears. One of his hands warmed her ass cheek where he held it to gain leverage while he fucked up into her. His other arm reached past her, however.

"Ah, that's nice," her brother intoned from behind her.

"Oh, is he …?" She was unable to finish her question amid the steady push of the man's cock into her.

"His hand…fingers are…oh yes that is very, very nice."

"I described for you, Brother. Your turn. Tell me!"

"Your description was lacking, ah…but the man's not shy. And not inexperienced. Ohh, God."

She'd have felt a bit giddy hearing her brother's normally collected demeanor so rattled, except that her own was pretty rattled, too. Her pussy felt too thick and full of him. She couldn't make a sound but her mind was busy crying out with every dirty curse she could think of.

"Sister, you just made an unholy noise in my head, what happened?"

"Ah. Shut up."

The truth was that she couldn't even think straight enough to answer. It wasn't enough that the man's beautiful aroma kept sinking into her nostrils, but his perfect cock kept sinking into her pussy, too. And to top it off, her clit had apparently fully melted and the steady rub of his pelvis against it sent jolts of pleasure through her from head to toe. Her ears tingled from the soft little guttural noises he made that bordered on dirty language. Then she realized they *were* dirty words. But the dirty words weren't only about her, they were about her brother, too.

"Fuck, your pussy's so tight, and Christ your brother's ass wants me so bad. I wish there were two of me so I could fuck you both."

The statement startled her.

"Brother?"

"You told me to shut up," he responded smugly. *"Yes…parts of me are a bit more flexible than they were before. The parts he touches. Remind me why we agreed to sleep back-to-back?"*

"The Queen said we had to. He's not supposed to wake us both, but he's going to anyway, isn't he? Yeah, that's nice and I think he might be about to come. Tell me, Brother, does he still have a finger in your backside?"

"Two. And when I'm awake again I'm definitely returning the favor."

"He's decided I need one, too. Like his perfect cock wasn't enough."

"What, a finger in your ass?"

"Oh yes. Oh, sweet Mother, yes."

"Sister, you know I get first crack once we're awake now right? It's only fair if you get him fucking you now and all I get is a couple fingers, not even a cock-grab."

"Uh-huh, fine." That was all she could lurch out between the thrusts, then the man's harsh cries made her ears vibrate, the sensation a refreshing change from all the silence of the past centuries. To hear the passionate cries of a man was one of the things she'd missed most. Warm heat spread between her thighs. She wished she'd been awake enough to come with him, but there would be time for that soon. Very soon.

An odd popping sounded in her ears as if pressure released, then the world fell out beneath her. The human man's voice echoed around her and with another solid thrust his seed heated her dormant womb. Everything melted into electric clarity. The cool air shocked her skin, the light burned her eyes. But she could *see* the light now, and she could see his lovely face, flushed and exultant after his orgasm.

Wide, blue eyes framed by long, golden lashes stared back at her in amazement.

She wanted to throw him down and fuck him until she reached her own climax, but he was so pretty and shocked to see her eyes blink open, she knew she had to at least give him something. She unfurled her wings first, reveling in the pleasant stretch of long unused muscles. She caught the air with them and wrapped her legs around his hips, careful to avoid letting him slip out of her.

"Don't worry, love. You're mine now. I won't hurt you." She dipped her head to his collarbone and let her animus tongue flick out to mark his skin, worrying that if she waited she'd miss her chance.

"Sister," a deep voice spoke from beside her as her brother's lithe figure moved around behind the man. "Don't forget to share."

CHAPTER SIX

Events bled into themselves after Dimitri came inside the statue's incongruously soft, wet pussy. Two figures rotated around him. He was still standing, his cock solidly sunk inside the woman, but now her legs were wrapped around his hips and she had *wings*. His body tingled with the buzz of pleasure. He'd only hoped for one brief moment of pleasure with one of them. Now that it was done, it hit him that no, this was barely scratching the surface.

Her lips were definitely not light on his own when she kissed him. It was the kiss that finally made him stumble and kneel on the ground, shaky from the orgasm.

"I did it," he mumbled to no one.

"You *did*," a male voice murmured in his ear. A pair of lips brushed against his shoulder, sending delicious tingles through him.

"My sister marked you already, it's my turn. Formality, you understand."

Dimitri cupped the girl's ass and squeezed. The other figure knelt beside him and a strong hand gripped his chin, gently urging him to turn his head. Soft lips fringed with coarse blond hair met his, the man's velvety tongue insistent as he delved between Dimitri's lips. The lips grazed his jaw and lower, until they pressed against his collarbone just opposite where the girl had branded him a second ago.

In the blink of an eye, the figure poised above him wasn't a man, but a golden dragon, forked tongue flicking out and gliding over Dimitri's bare chest.

"You're smaller than I thought," Dimitri murmured in a daze.

The dragon rumbled and a puff of gilded smoke erupted from his nostrils. He leaned forward and flicked his tongue in a pattern on Dimitri's collarbone opposite where the female had made her mark earlier. Another bright sting seared his skin, but the pain faded quickly with a gold breath from the dragon. *This means we're bonded*, he thought. The understanding unburdened him of a great weight for the first time in a year.

"You don't want to see me at full-size," the dragon said. "We like this size. It's manageable. Full size is good for flight and not much else."

"Show me anyway, if it's no trouble," Dimitri said, fascinated to know everything he could learn about these amazing creatures.

"Show him, Aurik." The warm figure of the female shifted to a slightly less intimate position on his lap, but still wrapped herself around him possessively. "My brother is very big. You'll like him," she whispered into Dimitri's ear.

He's big in a lot of ways I like, Dimitri mused, but was still eager to see the dragon. "I'd like to see you, too," he whispered to the girl. He'd learned her brother's name so far, but not hers.

"My name is Aurin," she said as if reading his mind. "What do we call you?"

"Dimitri."

She gave him a sweet, glowing smile. "I'd love to change for you, Dimitri. Anything you like." She pulled away and joined her brother.

Aurik had a wicked expression on his face when she approached him and the scene had the feel of a standoff, the two of them a few paces apart and facing each other. Dimitri sat up to watch.

She slowed and flexed her muscles.

"Biggest wins, Brother?"

"No. He wants to see our natural forms. Honesty, Sister."

She sighed. "Right, okay." She turned to face Dimitri who stared goggle eyed.

The air shifted around him and suddenly two large beasts shared the room with him.

He stood up abruptly.

"Jesus you guys are gorgeous."

Aurik was immense—he took up half the room. He stretched his wings and knocked a vase off a pedestal, then quickly drew them back against his sides. Dimitri walked closer, slid a palm over the dragon's scaled knee. The texture felt like velvet, which was unexpected.

"You guys have fur?"

"Not fur," Aurik said in a rumbling voice. "Just the surface of our scales. Defensive filaments. We're impervious to damage in these forms."

"Oh. It feels nice, though." Dimitri couldn't stop touching it, as soft as it was. He let his hand trail further up Aurik's large thigh. The dragon settled back and a sigh of gold smoke washed over Dimitri.

Curious, he kept stroking further. The taut muscle of the dragon's thigh flexed and his immense cock twitched and pulsed before Dimitri's gaze. It had been nearly two years since he'd been intimate to any significant degree with another man. Each time he tried, he would see his brother's face the last time they had made love to Thea. It often seemed strange to him that he had no qualms about looking in his brother's eyes with Thea's sensuous figure and sounds of pleasure as a buffer between them. But the second she was gone he hadn't been able to touch another man. It just felt wrong without a woman between them. Without Thea.

Now he wanted nothing more than to touch this creature and to be touched by him. He reached out a tentative hand and stroked up the length of the dragon's cock. No velvet armor adorned the beautiful shaft. It was entirely hot, golden skin, the length of Dimitri's arm.

"You can stop me, but I admit I'm curious. Is this as big as you get?" Dimitri asked.

"Not quite, but there's not enough room in here. Particularly not when you're touching me like that." The response was guttural and definitely aroused. “I think you’re making Aurin a little jealous.”

Dimitri became aware of the other dragon in the room. She raised a ridged brow at him over one golden eye. A plume of shimmering smoke rose from her graceful snout.

“You wanted us both,” she said. “Now that you’ve got us, what are you going to do, Dimitri?”

He looked back and forth between them.

“Ah…do you get off better in this form?”

The siblings exchanged a sardonic look. Aurik answered. “Our form doesn’t matter. We change to accommodate our partners.”

“Oh, good. As much as I’d love to experience a full-sized dragon cock, you’d probably kill me in the process. I need you *both* and my size seems more manageable.”

“Wise plan,” Aurik said, his form shimmering to resume a human size and shape.

Aurin seemed reluctant to change.

He stepped toward her where she sat on her haunches a few paces away. She was easily the size of an SUV, but more eager for his touch. He could tell by the short, gusting breaths she let out when he approached her. He remembered that he’d been the only one to come so far.

He reached up a hand to her head.

“You don’t need to pet me, but I do like it,” she said with humor in her voice.

“Maybe I’ll just pet you here,” he said. He stroked his palms down her large thighs that were spread before him. The same velvety texture of her golden scales teased at his skin. So soft. Christ he'd never touched anything as soft, not even human skin. It made him wonder what her pussy felt like.

He let his hands keep moving, enjoying the quiver of her muscles under his palms. She liked his touch and the evidence was very apparent the closer he got to her pussy.

A sweep of a tongue grazed his shoulders and he looked up in question.

"Just wanted you to know you're on the right track."

He nodded and moved forward, his eyes on the tight seam of scaled flesh between her thighs. He knew something wonderful waited beyond, and couldn't wait to discover it.

He reached out a tentative hand to graze her slit. All he could see was the faint seam in the center, but it gleamed with wetness. He raised his knuckles to his nose to smell her, then licked, watching her dragon eyes react. A low growl rumbled in her throat and her tongue lashed out.

"You're a tease," she rumbled. "I like it."

"Open up your dragon pussy, baby, let me see what I can do with it."

"It doesn't work that way. You've got to have a cock big enough. But dragons rarely mate with each other anymore, so that's why we change shape most of the time. We're accustomed to being smaller."

"You'd like a big cock that can fill that dragon pussy wouldn't you?"

"No…I want you. I can change my size at will, so I can accommodate any size that would fulfill me."

"Oh? Can you get even bigger?"

A hesitant rumble rose from her chest and she glanced behind him at Aurik. After a second she nodded her large head slightly. The air warmed around him and she stretched her wings. Her large body bunched and tensed, her scales shimmering and stretching.

The space she occupied forced him to move back several steps. He bumped into a warm body behind him and was immediately enveloped in a pair of thick arms.

"You like big? She's almost as beautiful as I am at her full size," Aurik whispered in his ear. She kept growing until she nearly filled the room and her head bumped against the lip of the deep skylight above them. He stared up at her angular head, highlighted from behind by a dark square of night sky and stars.

"You're bigger?" Dimitri asked, marveling at the immense creature before him. He'd never seen anything so beautiful. Her gold scales gleamed and sparkled in the low lights. She could barely stretch her wings in the room even as large as it was. He could have fit five of his childhood homes inside this room alone, and she seemed to occupy every inch of it. Not just with her beautiful dragonesque bulk, but with her presence. She still eyed him with curious amusement, waiting for him to render judgment for her change.

"I'm bigger, yes," Aurik said, emphasizing his words by pulling Dimitri's hips back against his very large and very erect cock.

Dimitri's thick arousal pulsed at the heat of the other man behind him. Aurik's fingertips dug into Dimitri's hips and pulled more deliberately forcing Dimitri's ass cheeks apart so the thick length of his cock pressed between them. Christ it had been so long since he'd had a proper fuck, but tasting Aurin had incited a deep longing for feminine flesh against his mouth as much as he wanted the solid thrust of a cock deep in his ass. Jesus, did it have to be so fucking complicated with him? Nobody had pleased him enough since Alex's death. He'd only sought out the most mindless of encounters, chased that brief pinpoint of pleasure, then left without looking back. For the first time since that day he finally had the desire to find something deeper that might last.

"Be gentle with him, Brother. He looks uncertain." The resonant voice and gust of sweet breath over his skin made him look up at Aurin's majestic form again. Her wings were folded along her back and she'd settled down, remaining in her dragon form. She looked relaxed, but attentive.

"He hasn't objected yet, Sister. But I will take care. Dimitri, your bond to us is more than just a mark on your skin. It means we are obligated to see to your needs, too."

That was an understatement. The care Aurik was currently taking involved a steady, sure stroke of his cock between Dimitri's ass cheeks. No hint of expected penetration at all, but enough friction to make Dimitri want to beg. When he was about to do just that, Aurik's large hands slid over both his hip and gripped his cock in one hand, his balls gently in the other.

"Sister, do you want to have a taste?"

Dimitri opened his heavy eyelids, his heart suddenly pounding in anticipation. That was something he'd never in a million years imagined.

Aurin puffed another cloud of golden smoke from her nostrils and her heavy voice reverberated through the room. "I was going to say no at first, but he looks like he'd like me to. Would you like this big tongue of mine to lick those dainty little balls of yours, sweet thing?"

Dimitri felt as though he might come again at the mere idea and he stared down at his cock as though it were Judas.

Aurik's thumbs slipped up his length slightly, aiming his pointed tip closer to the dragon mouth that had lowered and hovered closer, forked tongue flicking out.

"Oh, God yes," Dimitri said when Aurin's hot tongue met the underside of his cock. She traced the length of him in a slow, wet caress that sent him right back to that razor edge of intense pleasure he'd felt while fucking her, just before he came. The twin forks of a tongue that large were apparently incredibly versatile. He lost control of his legs and gripped onto her horns. Now he was spread across her face, but her tongue kept flicking across his cock and balls.

"That's good. Perfect, really," Aurik said from behind him.

Dimitri felt his ass cheeks part. By dragon tongue or fingertips he wasn't sure, but it was definitely a tongue that slipped between a second later to tease at his tight asshole.

"Oh fuck!"

"He does have a sweet ass, Sister," Aurik said.

Dimitri clutched hard at Aurin's horns and closed his eyes, enjoying the warmth of her soft scales beneath his body. Aurik's very hot, wet tongue teased at his sensitive asshole, delving deeper with delicate thrusts while Aurik spread him apart with a solid grip on each cheek. Aurin's large tongue still lapped with languid licks, each one sending him farther and farther from his grip on sanity.

Dimitri panted, anticipating the moment of clarity just before an orgasm that he always loved.

Dimitri whispered a few words, having no idea if either of them would hear, "I've never felt this close to another human before. I want you both like you couldn't believe."

"That's very good," Aurik said just as he pressed the head of his cock hard against Dimitri's slick ass and pushed it home with an agonizingly delicious thrust.

CHAPTER SEVEN

Aurin could smell Dimitri's lust, but the way his warm weight was sprawled across her head she couldn't do much besides dart her tongue out and tease at his cock. He tasted so good, yet she refrained because it was Aurik's turn right now. As frustrating as it was that her brother got first crack, she still loved being Dimitri's anchor.

She lowered her head slightly at a harsh cry from him and a harder grasp on her horns. Aurik was fucking him well.

Good move, sister, bend him over more. Lick him. Suck him if you can.

Oh, that was a new one. Participating in more than an observational role in her brother's escapades? Or he in hers, she guessed…They were a team, after all, but this was the first time he'd ever invited more direct involvement.

She flicked her tongue out, searching. She knew his legs were spread across her snout, but couldn't see where everything was. First she found Aurik's legs and darted her tongue back in to recalibrate. She had no interest in accidentally tasting her brother.

When she slipped her tongue out again it was with more focus. Close to her mouth and up. Ah, there he was. Smooth sack hanging just below her nose, and a very tasty cock riding between the ridges of her nostrils.

She looped her tongue around his very impressive shaft and pulled, moving her head up minutely at the same time.

His cock slipped right between her lips, rubbing against the front of her teeth.

"Oh Jesus. Oh that's nice."

He hadn't let go of her horns and still stood there getting steadily fucked from behind by her brother, but he had a very odd look, like he'd noticed a missing piece in the scenario but it hadn't quite caught up to him.

"No, baby, I want to make you feel good, too," he finally said.

She took his meaning immediately. The changing was a chore, and sapped her energy, but it was always smooth enough. Condensing and transferring energy was all it took. Anything leftover sat in her well for emergencies. In her true form she could draw from the earth, but in this form she could only draw from the residual energy left behind after the change. It rarely mattered in these situations, so she was happy to give him what he asked for. He wanted to fuck her. He *wanted* her. That on its own made her want him even more.

His pretty face was already flushed when she shrank back down to her human form. Aurik's hands gripped his hips so tightly she could see the indentations of her brother's fingertips in Dimitri's tanned flesh.

She lay down, beckoning to him.

Aurik released him, slipping out of his ass with a sigh. Dimitri knelt between her thighs.

"You were beautiful like that," he said, sliding his hands up her thighs in a motion that mirrored what he'd done when she'd shown him her true form. She liked being smaller than human men during sex, though, because they could touch so much more of her. "You still are beautiful, and this way I get to taste your pretty pussy again."

She tilted her head back and let him push her thighs wider. When his hands reached the apex of their journey she felt his thumbs graze over her wet lips and spread them apart. She expected a solid thrust into her, but instead she got a tongue. A slick, agile lick began at her tight asshole and continued through the flooded channel between her pussy lips. There was a reason she loved being human. There were so many more little parts to be touched, and human fingers were so small and adept, equipped to tease.

He circled his tongue lightly around her clit. The wet heat of his mouth against her drove her wild. After a second he paused and looked back behind him.

Irritated at the interruption she followed his gaze to see her brother standing and watching, steadily stroking his own cock.

Before Dimitri could speak, she said, "He wants you to fuck him, Brother. Why are you just standing there with your silly prick in your hand?"

Aurik blinked at her and dropped his hand.

"I didn't want to interfere," he said.

"Well, get used to interfering. We're keeping him, and we're sharing him."

Aurik knelt behind Dimitri and ran a large hand down his back. Dimitri's blue eyes closed and his entire body quivered at the contact. Aurin smiled at the look of pure bliss on Dimitri's face when her brother bent down and flicked his forked tongue out to swirl around and around between their pretty human's ass cheeks. Dimitri sank his head down to rest against her belly, leaving his ass high in the air, spread and ready for Aurik and whatever he had to give. So trusting, so eager. Yet so attentive when he flicked his tongue out and began teasing at her wet and hungry cunt again. She lost interest in what her brother was doing, too enthralled by the very talented tongue working between her thighs. He held her pussy lips apart and drew her between his lips, sucking the sweet little bundle of flesh until she began to shake. Then he stopping and licked gently, teasing and drawing it out.

"Will you turn around?" he asked in a hoarse whisper. "I want to fuck you, but…" He glanced over his shoulder at Aurik whose hand was lost somewhere between Dimitri's ass cheeks, busy enough to make the poor man flush and squirm.

Aurin smiled, understanding. He couldn't compromise the very pleasurable position he was in just now by laying on top of her.

"One condition," she said. She enjoyed the drugged look of acquiescence he had on his face.

"Whatever he's doing to you, if you like it, I want you to do it to me. I want to know what you like."

His thick, hard cock lurched between his thighs. She wasn't sure if it was what she'd asked or something her brother did that caused it, but she didn't care. She wanted him fucking her in whatever way he chose to do it.

She turned around to rest on her hands and knees and thrust her ass back against him, urging him to follow through.

"What's he doing to you, baby? Show me."

A desperate groan met her ears and he gripped both her hips with his hands, pushing her forward slightly. She closed her eyes, waiting to find out what he would do next. Strong fingertips sunk into the flesh of her ass and spread her cheeks wide. A hot gust of air hit her puckered asshole, making it tighten and tingle just before his hot tongue probed and swirled.

"Oh, is that what he's doing to you right now? Do you like that?" she asked, only to receive a muffled response accompanied by another puff of hot air against her ass followed by a low groan. He pulled away for a second, then resumed with fervor, squeezing her ass harder and thrusting his tongue past her tight barrier. The sensation wasn't unwelcome but still made her gasp in surprised pleasure.

She stretched an arm back behind her, threading the fingers of her hand through his hair and urging him to keep going with a gentle push. She didn't remember having a lover quite so eager or versatile. Or so sweetly curious about her nature. It warmed her to her core to feel such acceptance as opposed to the cautious fear she'd experienced during the time before she'd slept. There was, of course, something even more warming about having a talented tongue thrusting into her ass that made the whole situation even more delicious. Her pussy was ripe and dripping with juices now, so thick with arousal it felt like a hard knot of flesh between her thighs, but she was patient.

Her patience was rewarded a second later when he shifted a skittering palm up her side and cupped her breast, tweaking her nipple hard enough to make her cry out, but the sharp bite of pain was tempered by his tongue slipping down between her thighs and thrusting into her wet snatch, teasing at her swollen clit, then moving back to resume licking at her ass.

She no longer cared whether he was mirroring what her brother was doing to him. Not that her brother could've been doing *that* anyway. Nor thrusting a pair of fingers deep into her pussy while his tongue swirled around her tight, puckered asshole. Dimitri still seemed to be trying to honor her request, though. Every few minutes he'd pause and switch, tonguing her ass one second, then biting her ass cheeks, then stroking her clit. Then the pair of fingers he'd been fucking her soaking pussy with slid up and prodded tentatively at her tight opening. When she pushed back he moaned and let them slide in.

"Oh God you're tight," he murmured.

"Are his fingers in your ass, too? Tell me, baby. Do you like that?"

"Uh huh. Oh fuck it feels nice. It all feels so fucking amazing. I want to fuck your ass so hard you scream. Can I fuck you now or do I have to wait for him?"

She bit her lower lip hard, trying to resist an overeager response. She might just fall in love with this lovely human man.

So considerate, but so eager. She should make him wait just a little, but oh, did she want exactly what he did.

"You may fuck me, but fuck my wet cunt first. Make sure my juices are coating you well enough before you fuck me my tight netherhole."

"But I'm too big, I think. I don't want to hurt you."

Her heart swelled just a little more at that.

"No, sweet thing, you won't hurt me. I *want* that thick cock inside me. The lubrication is to make it better for you. Go on, fuck my pussy with it."

He obeyed, pressing the tip against her and sliding in. Oh, sweet Mother did he feel good, so hot and hard. Once he was solidly seated deep inside, he even gave a hard little push, just to be sure. But that might have been a result of whatever her brother was doing back there, judging from the harsh grunt that had accompanied it.

He gripped her hips and began fucking, resuming the fingering of her ass with one hand while he moved. Soon she became lost, the pleasure of his cock rubbing against all the sensitive places inside her, sending a myriad of tiny jolts straight to her brain. The sheer pleasure made the room all fuzzy.

He let out a deep groan and paused, his cock pulsing against her pussy walls. His fingers departed from her ass and he slipped out of her pussy, sliding his slick, swollen tip between her ass cheeks and pushing. She pushed back, urging him deeper, relaxing against his steady pressure until his thick length stretched the ring of tight muscle and penetrated her fully. They both sighed when he slid deep in. Another little lurch drove him even deeper and he grunted again. He leaned across her back much the way he'd prostrated himself over her head when Aurik had been fucking him earlier, but this time she knew she would get to come finally. And she was very close.

"Aurik," Dimitri gasped in a harsh whisper. "Oh fuck, yeah. Fuck my ass like that."

She had the same sentiment, but was too far gone to articulate it. Now that he was spread across her back with his hands slipping alternately across her breasts and between her thighs nothing else mattered.

He found her clit somehow in the midst of his own grunts and desperate rutting into her backside. All it took was a steady little rub against the hypersensitive bundle, coupled with a tweak of one nipple and she might as well have been flying again, for the first time in centuries. Yet flying had never felt quite *that* good.

CHAPTER EIGHT

Dimitri regained consciousness amid a tangle of limbs and long golden hair. If there was ever a Heaven he was sure he'd died and ended up there. He lay on his side, one tousled golden head rested against his dead left arm. He looked down expecting to see Aurin, but the incongruous press of soft breasts into his back confused him. No, that was Aurik with his cheek and drooling mouth plastered against Dimitri's skin. Dimitri smiled at the undignified presence, so far removed from the regal dragon he'd seen earlier.

He glanced down past Aurik's head to where the dragon's hand clutched his cock in a loose grip. He felt his flesh tingle and grow taut under Aurik's hand. Before they'd collapsed into a blissful, exhausted sleep he remembered the two dragons laying claim to different body parts of his.

"I want his tongue," Aurin had said.

"Then I want his cock," Aurik replied.

"I want all of you both, all the time," Dimitri interjected. He grinned to himself remembering the stunned expressions they'd given him.

"You can't own us," Aurin said.

"No? Then you can't own me, either. But if you want to, I'll gladly sign a contract, but there's no divvying up of body parts, alright? It makes me feel like you want to slaughter me for meat."

They'd both looked contrite and apologized, reassuring him that they had no intention of eating him. They only intended to fuck him. Then Aurin had given him a wicked little smile and caressed the medallion-shaped tattoo she'd etched into his collarbone. He'd already forgotten about the tattoo along with the matching one Aurik had given him. Brands were what they were, really. They did own him. Body and soul. And the knowledge was frankly transcendent. He no longer felt like he was drifting, lost in the ether without Thea's love or his brother's balance to give his life weight.

The slack hand around his cock tightened and he gasped. Looking down, he saw Aurik's goateed face gazing up at him with suggestive yellow eyes.

"You feel ready again," Aurik observed. The dragon shifted lower, his muscular figure sliding down Dimitri's thigh. He ran his lips along the length of Dimitri's cock, the journey fascinating Dimitri almost as much as the sensation of smooth, warm lips against his cock. Butterflies. Oh fuck that was what he was thinking? He tilted his head back with a groan while the butterflies flitted around his cock. Then Aurik flicked his velvety forked tongue over the tip and Dimitri was reminded of the truth. Dragon tongue. As if butterflies were better? He needed better fantasies.

"Oh, that's nice. What else can you do with that tongue?"

The figure behind him stirred and Aurin slipped her arm around to caress his chest.

"Hmm, I have a tongue too. What do you want, sweet thing?"

His insides melted at the sight of Aurin's sleepy look. Her golden eyes looked expectantly at him from puffy lids visible through a fringe of tangled blond hair.

"You want to make me feel good?"

"Yeah," she said, her voice sexily hoarse in a way that made his cock twitch under Aurik's tongue. God, could he ask for what he wanted? Hell, he'd try it. All she could do was say no, right?

"Do to me what your brother did before."

Her eyes lit up and that was the thing that sent him over completely. There was nothing he wouldn't do for these two if he had to. Especially not now, with her tongue torturing his ass enough to make him shove his cock deep into Aurik's throat.

No. He was pretty solidly in love with the both of them. Aurin's tongue in his ass had a little to do with it. Any girl willing to do *that* on a first date was a keeper. And Aurik had done it first. More than that, he finally felt balanced again, but in a weird way maybe his life had nothing to do with balance anymore. Maybe with them he was the fulcrum. The realization let him relax and give in. He came hard in Aurik's mouth with Aurin still shoving her tongue into his ass.

Released from the burden of grief, now he had a new burden. He looked back and forth between the two dragons.

They'd just pleasured him, but were obviously eager for a return favor, which he would give them both.

But just as he reached for Aurin and had his hand about her thigh everything went utterly dark.

Nothing moved, not even the three of them. All Dimitri heard was a whisper of movement. Aurin and Aurik moved away from him leaving him cold and alone.

He heard soft words nearby. "The Shadow's door is open."

"Aurin, is that you?"

The girl's warm flesh slipped into his arms in the dark.

"I'm here," she said, caressing his cheek to comfort him.

"Who's the Shadow?" he asked.

"He's our brother," they said in unison.

"You don't sound excited about that. I'm guessing this means someone…" he paused, remembering what Kris had said to Corey before he'd opened the door. If Corey was meant for the Queen that left one member of their party unaccounted for. "This means Hallie just opened the door. Is she safe with this… Shadow person?"

"Oh, he won't hurt her," Aurin said.

"No," Aurik said. "But I hope she likes dragons with dark moods."

"I take it he's not a glowing, golden beauty like you two?"

Aurin shuddered. "Kol is the exact opposite of us. The only dragon who rebelled against the slumber, so the council made him our keeper."

"And that means what?"

Aurik answered. "It means he's been awake the entire time, his Shadow patrolling the temple for five centuries keeping watch over us. He's probably gone crazy by now."

"It would drive me crazy," Aurin said.

"Do we need to go?" Dimitri asked. Aurin's soft cheek rubbed against his chest when she shook her head. Glowing golden breath erupted from Aurik to the other side of him, casting the three of them in a warm glow for a moment until it dissipated.

"It'll be dark until your friend has completed that phase," Aurik said. "We just need to wait it out, then we go join the others for the next phase."

"Hmm," Dimitri hummed and pulled Aurin tighter. "I heard something about a well that needs filling. How can I help?"

Aurin's lips pressed against his in the dark. Limbs moved around him but he couldn't be sure who was where at first. He felt weightless in the pitch black of the room, drifting off like a lost mote on the breeze. Then her hot wetness sank down onto his hard cock and the muscled length of another hard body slid down beside him. His hand reached out, aimlessly searching until Aurik's hips shifted and his cock pressed up against Dimitri's fingers.

"Thank you," he said softly, unable to find other words to express his gratitude more fully than that, but resolving to return the favor in any way he could until their shared darkness dissipated.

SLEEPING DRAGONS

BOOK 4

SHADOWS

OPHELIA BELL

Even love has a dark side.

CHAPTER ONE

Darkness was a perpetual irritation, particularly for a creature like Kol. He was not only trapped in it, he was a part of it. For centuries he'd lived without light. The darkness of the temple he lived in was incidental compared to the inky black of the mood he'd wallowed in since the day the exit doors had slid closed, trapping him and his multitude of brethren inside to sleep for half a millennium.

He'd lost count of the days since the light had gone out, but guessed it had to be close to the five centuries the dragons' cycle of sleep should last. He could have done the math but didn't care to. What purpose would it serve to mark time in such a place? Particularly when you were the only one awake.

That wasn't precisely true. They could all be conscious if they chose to be, but aside from himself and the Guardians, the others had a choice in their static jade forms to sleep through the centuries. For the first week he'd heard the others in his mind, speaking in subdued voices. Gradually the voices had grown fewer and fewer as they'd succumbed to sleep, until only his twin siblings had been awake, trying to bolster his mood as always. *We love you, Kol. We know it's an honor to be chosen for your job. We'd do it in a heartbeat.*

Finishing each other's sentences, Aurin and Aurik were as oblivious to Kol's demons as they were to their own strange and shifting symmetry. The two of them reminded him of a gyroscope. As long as their balance of power exchange remained, he believed the Earth probably still maintained its axis. If Aurin and Aurik ever faltered, then Kol would worry about the fate of dragonkind.

In spite of their sentiments, they never would have been chosen for his job. The job of Shadow was only for a black dragon like him. Brilliant gold as the twins were, they were better suited for uplifting humanity than skulking around in the dark.

Skulking was something he was good at, and had been even before doing it for five hundred years. Technically, he *was* asleep. At least his body was. But his magic, unique to black dragons, allowed him to manifest through his breath. While his physical body slept on, frozen in black jade, the shadow of his breath coalesced into a smaller, human form and lurked about the temple like a ghost, ensuring the security of all who slept within.

Tedious, monotonous, dreary, boring—he could think of so many other terms to describe his job. Dragon law dictated that a Shadow watch over the brood each cycle, and he'd been chosen for this one. Though he was not precisely *chosen* so much as compelled. True, he was probably the best candidate for the position, but traditionally potential Shadows were given a choice because of the psychological strain it took. He was the first one who'd been compelled to do it as a penalty for poor behavior.

He chuckled to himself at that. Speak out against the council's outdated ideals and get shoved in a dark prison. Granted, he'd have been here anyway, but at least he could have slept through the whole ordeal and let one of the others like him do the job.

He'd undeniably broken the rules, as archaic as they were. *Willfully* broken the rules, the council had said when he stood before them on the eve of his sentence. As if the heart knew anything beyond what made it beat.

Generations had passed since. The lover he'd accepted the sentence for was long dead, but the certainty didn't help quell the excitement that welled in him knowing how close they were to the end of their confinement. What would he find on the outside? Dragon lore only spoke of vast changes in each cycle, but they were an infinitely adaptable race. Would he look for her? Her descendants? He suddenly wished fervently that he'd had the foresight to mate with her before they'd been parted. He'd already broken one rule by falling in love with her, why not one more by getting her with child? Oh, would *that* have left the council in a bind considering the child wouldn't have been born until after the temple was sealed. But he hadn't left anything behind but regret and a now dead lover.

It happened sometimes. Young dragons breaking the rules prior to their slumber. The marked mates often died of sorrow if the dragon had no elder family to take them in. Any children of such a union would be taken and raised by the council, but would grow up nameless, forbidden from acquiring treasure. They would spend their lives in service to the council and tended to die young, only living out roughly half of a dragon's multiple-century life span. Slavery and grief were the last things Kol wanted for a mate and child of his own. His lover may have grieved him, but at least he'd left her with the freedom to move on.

Eveline.

Even thinking the name after the centuries without her brought back the memories of their time together. The loss twisted painfully in his chest, as sharp as a blade. The discomfort was enough to make him pause in his mindless patrol of the temple corridors. Sleep would be nice right now. Sleep would have been nice for the last five hundred years, but it wasn't for him. And he didn't want to be the one who slept on the job, even if it were a possibility. Hah.

At least he had the Guardians for company during his daily patrols. They were the second defense if their temple were ever prematurely breached, so they existed in a more aroused state of wakefulness than the rest. Kol chuckled at *that* thought. *All* of them were asleep in an *aroused* state, even his massive slumbering form in the room beside the Queen's sported its own huge erection. They had to be ready when the awakening ritual began. The Guardians were just the most visible. He often wondered what they would look like if the temple were ever actually attacked and they were forced into action. White dragons with massive erections might distract even the most determined grave robber.

The thought made him laugh.

"How goes it, Roka?" he asked, pausing on his rounds in front of his closest friend of the Guardians.

"You tease me with your voice, Shadow. If I had breath, we could have a proper duel and see who triumphed." The voice permeated Kol's mind rather than the air between him and the rigid white statue he stood before. Kol still reached out a hand and rested it on Roka's shoulder.

Kol laughed. "If you had breath you know mine would overtake yours in a second."

"We'll see who gathers the most treasure when we awaken. I'll wager I get more, even as a guardian."

"I'll wager you do, too, friend. I don't see the allure in treasure. Not even humans, as pretty and vibrant as they are."

"You deserve more after this cycle. You deserve concubines."

"I do, do I? You know that the Court is already entitled to a multitude of partners if we choose, right?"

Kol smirked at the silence his friend responded with.

"Then why don't you seem happy about that prospect?"

Mother of all…Roka did always ask the most irritating questions.

"I just want one woman. One sweet morsel to savor for the next few decades after this temple is finally opened. Someone whose world I can change enough to see in her eyes how much I mean to her and her alone."

"But you're not a collector? It's our nature. I want at least two. At least I know what I would do with two. More than that might be…complicated."

Kol laughed. "Yes, more than two becomes problematic. All I want to collect is the touch of her skin, the silky dew between her thighs, the little sounds she makes that lets me know my touch is affecting her."

He wandered away from the conversation with his fingertips tingling as though they'd already touched hot skin, memories of Eveline playing over and over in his mind.

CHAPTER TWO

The sweet dark of sleep was a hard commodity to retain. Hallie questioned her own sanity every morning when the camp awakened and she was forced to rise with the rest. She wasn't a morning person, but apparently she was outnumbered. And since she was trying her best to conform to the ideals of the expeditionary type, she rose, too. Or she tried to, anyway.

It was still fucking dark in their jungle camp, but the entire group had been edgy all night knowing the next leg of their trek would likely take them to their final destination.

She opened her eyes and glared at the edge of her sleeping bag, resisting rising for just a few more moments. Five minutes… she could squeeze in five more minutes of sleep if she tried really hard. She clenched her eyes shut, trying to bring back the delicious dream she'd been having about Kris. In the dream he'd had a massive erection and was about to shove it in her.

Something tickled her cheek and she swept her palm over it. The tickle came back a second later, an irritating distraction from her hopeful dreams. She smacked her hand on her cheek smartly, wishing whatever it was would go away.

The tickle returned, accompanied by a throaty giggle.

"Camille, you're in for it," she murmured gruffly against her sleeping bag.

A hard sigh sounded behind her. "I'm sorry. You said you wanted help waking up, so I thought I'd try this. It was fun until you started sounding bitchy."

"Don't take it personally. I'm always bitchy at this time of day. At least if I'm awake."

She rolled over and smiled sleepily at her blonde friend.

"Did he take the bait?" she asked.

Camille scowled. "No. I messed it up. He just…" She flushed brightly and bit her lower lip hard enough to make it shine bright red. Her discomfort made Hallie reach out to comfort her.

"Sweetie, don't do that…Eben loves you, I know it."

Camille looked like she was about to cry. "So why…?" Her lip quivered before she could get another word out.

"Just focus on work for now, alright? He'll come around, I promise."

She felt like a fraud spouting useless advice to the girl. Camille was brilliant and beautiful, in a weirdly delicate way, but completely ill-equipped to deal with a crush on a guy. At least Hallie hadn't been lying about Eben's feelings. That was one detail she'd bet her life on if she had to, considering how she'd seen Eben watching Camille every day since the expedition had begun. He'd cast furtive glances at the pretty linguist, then look away and spend the next hour or so with a broody crease between his eyebrows. Hallie wasn't the least bit surprised, either. Camille possessed the perfect combination of sensuality and innocence that could drive men mad. At least one man.

Hallie felt like a fraud in a lot of other ways, too. Mostly because she *was* a fraud. She didn't know archeology from a hole in the wall, yet she'd convinced Erika somehow that she belonged with them. It wasn't as if she'd been dead weight during their expedition, at least. If anything she'd been more valuable than the others during the rugged trek. It helped growing up in the wilderness of Canada. Tropical hazards were different, but her constitution could handle them.

And they were very far away from the bullshit she'd left behind, which was the biggest plus. No one would even think to look for her here, least of all the asshole she'd conceived this entire crazy plan to escape. Still, every day the easy camaraderie of the others left her feeling like an outsider. She'd lied to join them and kept lying to cover up her lack of experience. She'd only done the bare minimum of research prior to applying for the assistantship required to join the expedition. She'd learned how to manipulate potential bosses years ago. Be pretty and clean, drop all the right words, show the right level of confidence. Her past few jobs were acquired under the same pretense, which was a requirement when you had things to hide.

This one had been a little different. She'd only had two days to set it up. Posing as an esoteric scholar should have been easy but it had proven to be the most stressful interview of her life. Ultimately she'd given up on the exhaustive planning she usually employed and just threw on jeans and a t-shirt, studied her notes on the subject in question, and headed out the door. She was likely dead either way it went, so why stress over details?

Somehow, it had worked.

Erika hadn't even glanced at Hallie's fabricated curriculum vitae. She'd met Hallie in a tiny cafe west of campus. They'd exchanged pleasantries, then Erika had completely ignored the folder of papers she had in front of her and proceeded to grill Hallie on her personal history.

It had been a shock, but Hallie had answered honestly, at least until Erika got to the college questions. The best lies always held a kernel of truth. In the end, the woman she sold to Erika was an intelligent girl restricted by her upbringing and rising up from nothing. It wasn't very far from the truth. She'd always wanted to be that woman, but poor decisions had gotten in her way.

When their interview concluded, Erika had stuck out her hand and pulled her into a tight hug. Flabbergasted at the quick acceptance, Hallie had hugged back. She nodded and murmured a thank you when Erika expressed how she couldn't wait to see her the next day when their flight to Indonesia departed.

CHAPTER THREE

Kol's skin itched. He would give anything to be free of his stone prison and able to stretch his corporeal limbs. To dive into the pool that occupied the center of his chamber and soak in the warmth of the water, wash away five hundred years of regret that he hadn't done more to keep the woman he loved. Eveline's face had faded from his memory. All he had left were fragments of her that came to him in dreams—the softness of her skin, the heat of her breath, the earthy scent of her sex.

Perhaps Roka was right. Maybe he should have avoided focusing so intently on one human. Most dragons avoided favoritism among their treasure, choosing instead to distribute their attention evenly among many humans. There were no limits, according to dragon law. Dragons could possess as much treasure as they were capable of attracting to themselves. His distant predecessors had boasted throngs of loyal subjects, but over the generations, dragons had gradually grown more focused, choosing to reserve their attention for a few very loyal humans. He was the first one who had ever balked at tradition so much that he'd chosen one woman outside his parents' collection, which had been his first mistake.

Young dragons were often encouraged to appreciate their family's treasures, but Kol's tastes were not quite what his parents or the council would have liked him to have. The twins were the same. He supposed it wasn't so much the singularity of his choice that caused the council to punish him, but that he'd never marked her. But how did you mar such a beautiful, perfect creature as she was?

The idea of humans like Eveline as mere possessions left a bad taste in his mouth. When the doors to the temple opened he would be expected yet again to collect treasure. He was under no delusions what that really meant. Humans were status symbols to dragons. The more he possessed, the more respect he received. It didn't help that the urge was innate. He had *wanted* to mark Eveline so many times, yet rejected his own nature in exchange for knowing she was with him of her own volition. Until the council had found out and destroyed his perfect life.

Loving her wasn't the crime. Showing her his nature yet leaving her unmarked was. The magic of the mark made humans intensely loyal and incapable of betrayal. But to Kol there was far more power in gaining the trust and loyalty of a human without resorting to magic.

So they'd forced him to do nothing *but* resort to magic for the last five hundred years. Manifesting his human form with his breath on a daily basis still hadn't changed his opinion on marking humans, but it had made him appreciate the magic he was capable of more than he had before. Not quite solid, without considerable focus and effort his breath could still affect his environment in subtle ways. He could open doors with it, but most often merely wisped between the cracks. He could sense the smooth texture of the walls that held him in, the cool jade tiles of the floor beneath his shadowy tread. He couldn't dive into the water of his pool, but he could cast ripples across its surface.

And when the surface doors finally opened, he could sense the change in pressure causing every molecule of his breath to vibrate, the sensation transferring instantaneously to his true form, frozen in jade. For the first time in half a millennium, his perpetually erect cock throbbed in anticipation.

He sent his shadow to the surface where he lingered in the darkness, watching the seven humans trickle in, each one marveling at the interior of the temple as they began to explore it.

He watched their leader intently at first. She wasn't the most beautiful of the women, but she exuded power he had rarely encountered in human women. This century might prove very interesting if other women were like her. She easily subjugated the male who followed close behind her, and he didn't seem the least bit put down by her dismissiveness. He only had eyes for the prettiest female among them—a petite and round-bottomed blonde. A tasty morsel by any stretch. The man had good taste.

The others followed down the long staircase, oblivious to his presence blended into the shadows. The third woman's scent reached him before he saw her, tickling at his nostrils like the soft down of aromatic feathers. Sweet and pungent, like the scent of the earth right after a rainstorm. With cautious steps, she came down the staircase, brushing past him so closely he could feel her heat and sense the rising arousal that the magic of the temple incited in all the humans who entered it.

The familiar and unwelcome instinct to possess rose so suddenly it made him dizzy. He moved behind her and leaned closer, reaching one ethereal hand up to trace the line of her neck. Skin still damp from the heat of the jungle met his touch. He let his eyes follow the path of his fingers down to her shoulder blade, then across to the front, chasing the path of a tiny bead of sweat as it traveled along the crest of her collarbone.

He stood behind her looking down at that tiny droplet of moisture, poised in the arc of bone and skin that pointed down between her breasts. His ghostly fingertip still rested at the edge of it, the rest of his hand splayed to avoid touching her skin, though he would love to feel the warmth of her against his palm.

Overcome by a sudden thirst, he licked his lips. The droplet quivered then skidded across tanned skin and pores, lower, lower, Kol's eyes following it all the way. What he wouldn't give to be that orb of wetness traveling between her breasts, only to be absorbed at the end of the journey. Or perhaps lapped up by some lucky man. One of the other travelers maybe?

He inhaled deeply, hoping to impress the aroma of her into his memory alongside the scent of the only other woman he'd ever thought he'd want. He couldn't deny the pull from this one, though.

Some force against Kol's back caused his his shadowy form to dissipate like a warm, insistent breeze diluting a bank of fog.

He reformed to the side of the stairway and glared at the large, male figure who followed the young woman. Dark eyes stared straight back at him with unmistakable recognition.

"You can see me?" Kol asked, sending the thought out with intent to the man. The man didn't reply but only nodded quickly. He shifted his attention to the woman when she turned in response to his proximity.

"What is it, Kris?" she asked.

"Thought I saw a bug, but it's gone now," he said with a twitch of his lips. "Must've caught a ride from outside."

"Ugh, I'll be done with bugs after this trip. You don't think there are any inside, do you?"

The man named Kris chuckled. "Not sealed up the way this place is. Legend says that dragons tended to repel most other living things, including insects. Humans tend to be more like moths to a flame for them, though." He darted his eyes pointedly in the direction of Kol's shadow.

"Who's the moth and who's the flame?" Kol heard in a pointed tone in his mind.

"You really believe this stuff, don't you?" she asked.

"I believe it because it's the truth," Kris said matter-of-factly.

"I know, I know. Your *destiny* was to guide us here. Erika's bought into it, too. Me…I'll believe it when I see it, I guess."

The man's identity became clear to Kol with those words, and the effect Kris had on Kol's incorporeal form made more sense. This group was without a doubt the chosen few who would awaken them. It really was finally happening. Today would be his last day trapped here.

"You're the Catalyst, aren't you?" Kol asked. He moved back to walk beside Kris, now more conscious of the barrier of magic that cocooned the man, preventing Kol from moving closer. He kept his eyes on the back of the woman's neck as they walked, watching yet another bead of sweat trace her skin and wishing he could follow its path, dart his long forked tongue out to taste it.

"Yes. But you're the Shadow. Didn't expect to be greeted at the door like this. It's an honor." The man's thoughts reverberated in Kol's mind. He had the blood, too. Otherwise he'd never have been able to communicate that way.

"I'm more than ready to get the ritual started. One more day and we'll all be free, thanks to the seven of you."

"I'll have them itching to get going after supper tonight. Trust me, friend, I'm as ready as you are." Kris reached between his thighs, adjusting himself in emphasis.

"I don't envy you the waiting, but I understand. It's been five centuries since I last touched a woman. Please tell me what that one's name is. I have to mark her."

Kris laughed. *"I've heard of you. The accounts of your little rebellion are a cautionary tale at the monastery where I was raised. Refused to properly mark your lover after showing her what you were. I believed in your argument, when I learned of it. Now you talk like your principles have changed. Did the punishment sink in?"*

"No, but it's the only way to complete the ritual. If they're going to force it on me, I must be sure she's willing when I have to do it."

"That may be tricky. She's a bit of a rebel, too. Her name is Hallie, but she isn't who she pretends to be. Good luck to you."

***

Kol kept to the shadows for the rest of the evening, but never let his eyes wander too far from Hallie. Watching the magic's gradual effect on her kept him enthralled. She savored the dinner Kris cooked them like it was a sensuous treat, eyes closed with every bite, tongue darting out to lick her full lips and make sure she didn't miss a single shred of flavor. Kol could smell the dragon magic that infused the meal from the fresh temple water Kris had used to cook it.

Kris did his job well after the meal was over, encouraging their leader and her human lover to begin the ritual and nudging the others in the right direction when the time came. The man was subtle, but effective. The first couple went willingly, followed shortly by the pretty blonde with the plump bottom. The others stayed in their camp and tried to sleep for a few hours, but the heightened excitement left them tossing and turning, except for Hallie who seemed to sleep soundly.

Then the young Greek man with the deep sadness left, along with the most skeptical member of the group—a man they called Corey, who seemed to grow angrier the more aroused he became.

That left Hallie, curled up in her bedroll in a shadowy alcove away from the glowing fire pit. Kol only watched at first, his mind drifting to memories of the last time he'd been with Eveline. His old lover had awakened one morning and found him watching her, much like he watched Hallie now.

"You have the look of a very patient cat waiting for the chase," Eveline had said. "You could have had me in your jaws a hundred times while I slept, helpless."

"I prefer knowing that you're choosing not to run when I decide to take you." He slipped down beside her warm curves, cupped one breast and pressed lips and tongue to the juncture at her neck and shoulder.

She nestled back against him and tilted her head to grant better access to her skin. "I would never run from you. Not even in my dreams. I was dreaming of you just like this, you know."

"Hmm, like this?" he asked, moving one hand lower and teasing the downy thicket between her thighs. Dewy wetness clung to her fringe. He slid his fingertips a little deeper into the heat of her, enjoying the soft sigh she emitted when he found her swollen bud already slick with her juices.

"Yes. Just once I'd like to wake up to you already inside me. To believe we'd never been parted even during sleep."

Pleasing Eveline had always been paramount, but he'd never gotten the opportunity to fulfill her request. The council had learned of his misbehavior and had sent him immediately to the temple. He hadn't even been allowed to see Eveline one last time.

This could be his chance for redemption. To do things differently. But the ritual was already underway and the one he believed he was meant for was here sleeping.

Hallie rolled onto her side and kicked her covers off, displaying long, tanned legs that led up to the curve of wide hips hugged by dark fabric. She seemed to have an affinity for black. Most of the garments he'd watched her strip off earlier had been varying shades of black. She hadn't been modest around her teammates, either. The only one with a shred of modesty had been the pretty blonde, and the only overtly sexual interaction among the group had been between the leader and her lover.

It must be a very different world for men and women to be so uninhibited with each other. The other men had looked at Hallie appreciatively, but with a surprising level of respect. Dragons looked at each other the same way, but in his experience, human men rarely treated human women like equals.

Now Hallie lay nearly naked aside from her small, black undergarments. The sleeveless top she wore had ridden up to expose her belly. Her thighs shifted against each other, sending a hint of her arousal to him.

Sweet Mother, he needed to touch her again. He needed her to wake up and come to him soon. To open his chamber and awaken his body so he could mark her and complete his phase of the ritual. *No,* he thought. *So she can learn the truth and make the choice. I refuse to do it unless she is willing. Damn the others.* But he knew he owed it to his brethren to try. His disagreement had been with the Council, not the other dragons trapped in the temple with him. So he would try. And the first step was to plan his silent seduction while she slept.

CHAPTER FOUR

The whisper of her lover's breath had always been enough to send Hallie into fits of desire. She responded especially well, when still fuzzy and languid from sleep, to the light touch of him caressing her skin, tracing the curve of her body from shoulder to hip and down over her thigh, while his hot breath tickled the back of her neck.

A soft sigh escaped her lips as those very sensations roused her just enough for her body to respond, yet not quite awakening her fully. A large, warm hand slipped beneath the fabric of her tank top and fingertips teased at the underside of one breast, barely grazing the edge of her nipple.

"Yes," she whispered, pressing back against his hot arousal by reflex.

A deep, appreciative rumble vibrated against her back. His lips grazed the nape of her neck, sending a vivid tingle down her spine and between her legs.

His light caresses continued, slipping down her stomach, past her navel and beneath the waistband of her panties. Her hips twitched at the slide of gentle, probing fingertips exploring between the eager folds of her pussy. She moaned and quivered, pressing harder back against his rigid, naked length.

He gripped the crotch of her panties and tugged them hard to the side. She cried out with harsh joy when he pressed two fingers into her, then slid them out again. He teased her with a few soft strokes against her throbbing clit before he plunged his fingers deep into her wet cunt.

The dreamlike state Hallie had been in during the whole experience began to fall away with each deep plunge of his fingers into her needy pussy, her ecstasy so pure and present it could only be real and not a figment of her unconscious mind.

Confusion gripped her, wrenching her stomach into a quick, tight knot. Her eyes flew open. But what she thought was a dream didn't dissipate, nor did the pleasure of it, in spite of her mild panic.

In the span of a second her mind and body warred with each other, the urge to fling herself away from the unexpected attention at odds with the incredible, mind-blowing pleasure of it. Her desire won out and she surrendered, closing her eyes and pushing back against him with more fervent thrusts of her own, clenching her muscles tighter around the heavy weight of the fingers plunging into her.

It could be any of the four men, she thought. And would she care if it were? But Jesus Fucking Christ, whoever it was, he was giving her the best finger fuck of her life.

His lips pressed against her shoulder, grazing up along the curve of her neck until they brushed against her ear. Hot breath gusted out, carrying with it a word she didn't understand.

Is it Kris? It must be Kris.

She had heard Kris speak in Thai a few times, and remembered the look he'd given her when he picked up her empty bowl after dinner. The thought made her smile in delight. She was sure he'd followed Erika to have a quick tryst in one of the dragon temple's dark corridors, but clearly he'd come back frustrated enough to crawl into her sleeping bag and have his way with her. It was even better than the fantasy she'd had of him during dinner. It made her even more eager to fuck him back as enthusiastically as she could.

Not even caring if she might wake the others, she cried out, "Oh, yes! Fuck me. Make me come!"

The fingertips between her thighs rubbed in even more delicious tormenting circles against her clit. God, she was close.

He murmured something else in her ear she didn't understand, but if she didn't know better the tone of his voice seemed to hold regret. Then without another sound or breath, the sensations dissipated entirely, leaving her abruptly untouched and frustrated as hell with a sopping wet and aching pussy.

She rolled over and yelled out. "Hey! Where the fuck did you go? Come back! You asshole, I wasn't even…I was so *close!*"

The sound of a thump and a curse carried across from the other side of the campsite and she twisted back around to see where it had come from.

"Corey?"

"Yeah, sorry. I…uh…didn't mean to bother you." He glanced at her and quickly averted his eyes, resuming whatever work he was doing.

She blinked at him in surprise, completely and utterly confused by his presence now. He was fully clothed. Maybe a little flushed but mostly he looked irritated. There was no way it could've been him.

"Did you see Kris just now?" she asked.

Without looking at her he nodded. "A little bit ago, back in the corridor behind the throne. He's still there as far as I know. Why?"

"No, right here…ah…*with me* I mean. Like not more than a minute ago."

He finally looked up and stared point blank at her as if she had gone completely mad. His jaw clenched and his lips pursed into a harsh line.

"Not you, too. Shit, Hallie. But I guess from that little performance you just put on I shouldn't be surprised, should I?"

"Me too, what? Corey, someone was just about to fuck my brains out. Not two minutes ago. If it wasn't *you,* I'd really like to know who it was."

"Well, aside from the obvious, um…*evidence* that you nearly had your brains fucked out, considering you've lost your goddamn mind, there was nobody here. Everyone's off on the other side of the temple being crazy over there. And would you mind putting yourself back together just a little bit? Your… ah…" He gestured vaguely at her torso. "Your stuff's all kind of on display. Makes it a little tough to get any work done."

She glanced down at herself and realized for the first time that her top was still pushed up above her breasts and her panties weren't on quite straight, still shoved aside to offer a plain view of her glistening labia. Yet Corey seemed so utterly *nonchalant* about it. He just turned back to banging on whatever it was he was holding in his hand, intent on his project. His thick forearm flexed and his knuckles whitened in a hard grip around the heavy hammer he held in his hand, banging it on the oblong shape with an unexpected level of ferocity coming from him.

She found her clothes draped over her gear where she'd left them and dressed.

"What the hell are you beating on?" she asked, padding barefoot over to him.

"This fucking…light bulb. Or whatever it is. I need to know how it works."

"It looks like a rock now," she said. "Let me see."

She reached for it. After another ineffectual bang that made his hammer bounce off he cursed and handed it to her.

"This is the weird rock Erika saved from the entrance. You think she wants you to beat on it like that?"

"It's not *just* a rock. Look at this." He took it from her and leaned over to jab it down into the glowing fire pit beside him. The pale embers inside the pit had surprised them all when they'd found it. They behaved like coal, but never disintegrated into ash, retaining their integrity after being lit multiple times with no apparent change. Erika had just brushed it off. The rest of them seemed to shrug and go on with business. If Erika was fine with it, they should be, too, right?

Hallie watched the small oblong shape as it began to glow after being plunged into the gravel of the fire pit. No ash lay inside it, only a level layer of small stones that constantly glowed and emitted heat. They'd discovered the night before that the temperature grew hotter closer to the center, and Kris had gauged his cooking by proximity to the middle of the fire pit.

The thought of Kris made her doubt her sanity after the weirdly vivid dream, if what Corey said was true. It had been so real. Jesus, her pussy was still pulsing and wet from it now. She should have changed her panties, but with Corey right there it might have been a little too conspicuous. Why she felt the need to hide from him she didn't know. He was just so willfully oblivious of everything that went on around him, but she was pretty sure it all sunk in.

No, maybe he wasn't oblivious. He was just very good at hiding his reactions.

But tonight he seemed agitated, leaning against the edge of the fire pit Kris had cooked their dinner over. Corey braced one hand on the edge and reached with the other to the stone he'd shoved tapered end first into the coals.

"See this?" he said, yanking the small stone bulb out of the fire pit. "It's glowing now. After what, thirty seconds in there? It only took a second for it to light up when we opened the door at the surface. I want to know how the fuck these things work. What powers them? What the hell are they made out of?"

"So take it with us back to a lab and look at it under a microscope. We're coming back here, you know. We just need artifacts. We don't need to prove anything while we're here. Corey..." She rested a tentative hand on his shoulder and was gratified that he didn't flinch away. "This is the find of a lifetime. Just go with it. Don't over think it yet."

CHAPTER FIVE

Hallie's palm tingled when it came into contact with the warmth of Corey's body through the threadbare fabric. Corey tensed and the cotton of his t-shirt tightened over the bunched muscles of his shoulder. It was crazy that Hallie noticed that single movement, but her entire body responded to it. The push of him against her hand was like a kinetic jolt that jarred straight through her palm to her clit. As much as her principles had steered her clear before, she was definitely attracted to him. What harm would it do, really? She just needed a good fuck, after all. Especially after that...dream she'd just had. They could move on afterward.

"Like all the other men you've moved on from?" the bitchy little voice inside her head said. It only gave her a moment's pause, rationalizing that maybe she wouldn't have to move on from him if she just gave him a chance. Except that she'd thrown caution to the wind with the last guy and look where it had gotten her—on the run and loaded with so much regret she could fill a swimming pool. Did Corey even want to be saddled with her mistakes? She

doubted it. But right now she was desperate enough to test the waters.

She slid her hand over his shoulder and down his arm. His thick forearm clenched tighter and she stared, mesmerized at the play of his tight muscles beneath her palm and the heat of his skin under hers. His head turned slowly to watch the movement of her hand from the corner of his eye, like he was just waiting patiently for it to happen.

Focused on the shadows his muscles cast she was acutely aware of the change in light just behind her. The shadows darkened and a foreign yet very familiar presence pressed against her back. Hands gripped her hips and she jerked her head to look over her shoulder but saw only darkened air, the breath of a shadow. She released Corey abruptly when a hand gripped her jaw and pulled her head back. She couldn't see who held her, and Corey only stood mutely as if nothing had happened beyond her having second thoughts.

The shadow's voice reverberated in a deep whisper in her ear. "*You are mine,*" it rumbled.

She tried to stifle the whimper when he released her and disappeared again.

"You having second thoughts about molesting me?" Corey asked, turning around and staring at her.

"I'm sorry about that. I've been kinda not really myself tonight."

He raised one dark eyebrow. "You mean you don't normally beg out loud to an empty room to fuck you?"

She opened her mouth to answer, then closed it again, not quite sure what she'd say. She was still aroused and confused from the strange, ethereal intruder.

And as frank and uncensored as Corey had been in the month that they'd known each other, he'd never once come across as a lecherous asshole. It was a refreshing change from the men she was used to. Honesty deserved honesty, didn't it?

"No, Corey. I don't do that. I only do that when I'm actually being teased into oblivion. It felt so real but I can't explain it, and even if I could you probably wouldn't believe me anyway."

He settled back on the edge of the fire pit and crossed his arms, the glowing stone apparently forgotten.

"Try me. I doubt you could one-up the crazy shit I've seen tonight."

"Oh?" She glanced around, remembering what he'd said about the rest of the team. "What happened to them?"

"It's a long story. Tell me yours first."

A brush of air against her back made her shiver. The breath on her neck felt like a promise and her nipples pricked beneath her flimsy cotton tank top. *"Tell him the truth,"* the whisper said.

She released the air she'd been holding in her lungs in a soft gasp when a shadowy touch grazed across her nipple. She glanced down and only saw a darkening of air, but it definitely felt like a real hand.

"You can't see?" she asked Corey.

"See what?"

"He's here now," she said. "He…drove me mad before. And he's *still* teasing me now."

Corey's eyes followed hers down to her breasts. The voice in her ear whispered, *"You like the way he looks at you."*

All she could see was the faint shadow of a hand as it slid down, long, translucent fingers sweeping over her breast. Every little graze of finger across her nipple made her quiver. His breath was dry and hot against her neck. She couldn't resist his urgent embrace, but she didn't really want to. Having Corey's eyes on her just made it all more intense. She hesitated and sensed the touch on her body pause.

"You want him to see you undone, don't you?" The voice sounded a little incredulous. An entertained chuckle sounded in her ear. *"Well, then let's give him a show."*

"Yes!" she gasped.

"Hallie?" Corey's voice was rough and uncertain. "It's all in your head, girl. Just let it go."

She whimpered when the fingertips lingering over her breasts decided to tease and pinch at her nipples.

"N-no. Oh God, this isn't in my head."

"You have that right, lover. I'm not in your head, though I would like to be."

"Why are you doing this to me?" she asked out loud. Corey's eyes widened in confusion, but it was the shadow who responded.

"Because you want me to. Because I was meant to. Because you are mine."

The shadow behind her felt as warm and substantial as a real man, yet apparently she was the only one who could sense his presence. He was strong and insistent, his lips hot on her neck and jaw. She tilted her head to give him better access.

Corey stayed glued to his spot, watching. A sheen of sweat gleamed on his brow and upper lip and the front of his cargo shorts looked like it might rip open under the pressure of his erection. It wasn't nice of her to enjoy that part, but she did. He was the man she'd been most attracted to during their expedition, but she was smart enough to figure out that she'd never measure up to what he wanted. Watching him struggle with the urge to fuck her now, while a hollow enjoyment, still gave her some validation.

She vaguely realized how uncharitable she was being to Corey, though. He was the polar opposite of the man she'd left behind. Her ex had been polite and respectful, and a liar to the core.

Corey was brash and rude most days, but honest to a fault.

So she'd gravitated to him only to realize that he was even better behaved up close. The polite dismissals. Oh so polite. And respectful. Fuck the man for not wanting to dominate and violate her.

It had been over a year, but David's confession of love still twisted like a knife in her gut. Worse than that, his pursuit when he'd learned of her pregnancy had driven her to the ends of the earth to escape him. The child wasn't meant to be. She'd begun this Hail Mary of a trip broken hearted and desperate, denying her misdirected love for the man she'd left behind and the baby she'd lost

"You are mine," the shadow had said, but something wasn't right about the way he'd said it. She was too familiar with the tone of voice of a man who meant words just like that. The shadow's words lacked conviction. Was this just some supernatural prank? Lies were her forte and this—man or creature or whatever he was—was a very bad liar.

But he'd struck a chord. The small lie he told was twisted up with the truth. She wanted him to touch her, that was the truth. And he believed he was meant to. She could twist the belief around to her advantage.

"Yes. I want you, but you can't own me. No man can own me, you bastard. If you want me it's on my terms, you got that? Now if you're going to fuck me in front of my friend, which I would *dearly* love for you to do, stop being a little pussy and show yourself."

Corey stared at her, incredulous. She grinned back in response. He seemed transfixed by the unfastening of Hallie's shorts through no power of her own. It felt like hot, urgent fingers trying to get her naked. This…*shadow*…wanted her, whoever he was. All she knew was that he'd teased her nearly to orgasm before and was back. Maybe this time he'd finish the job.

"I'm not going to fuck you. I just want to watch you torture him a little bit," the voice said.

"Why?" Hallie asked.

"Because you want it. I can feel how much you want it. What did he do to you?"

It probably was terrible of her to resent Corey's lack of interest, but she certainly had his attention now. Corey watched her with avid concentration. Her shadow's fingers gripped her breast with one hand and the other teased again with expert care between her exposed pussy lips, rubbing her slick clit enough to make her eyes roll back in her head.

Oh, Christ. She opened her eyes to see Corey watching, his hand pressing hard against his crotch like he could keep the monster in check with enough effort. And as much as she would love to have him involved, having the hot hands of this stranger on her felt so good.

"Nothing. That's the problem. Is that so bad?"

"Kiss him."

She didn't have an obsession, did she? Maybe so, considering her blatant lie to Erika about why she'd never made a move on Corey. She had a bad habit of falling in love with men who were emotionally inaccessible. It wasn't casual sex if you were in love, right? Corey was the first man she'd been infatuated with in that way who hadn't gravitated to her like a moth to a flame. It just made her want him more, but professional courtesy dictated she maintain a boundary between them.

Now she had to breach that boundary to prove that it didn't matter anymore.

Corey still sat on the raised edge of the fire pit, his gaze fevered as he watched her. She adjusted her clothes, feeling just a little too exposed for a simple kiss, then moved to kneel between his spread legs. His arms stayed braced on the stone ledge he sat on, and he just stared at her. God, she wanted to reach out and stroke the bulge in his shorts, but didn't dare.

He stared back at her with a mixture of hunger and conflict. In that split second he reminded her of one of her older brothers. Even before kissing him she knew how it would go, but she needed to do it anyway.

His eyes were wide and curious, his brows raised in expectation. He must have known what she was doing, but he hadn't objected yet.

"Corey," she said in a voice rough with need. "I've wanted you since we met, but you've been…reserved."

"Sorry, I…have some issues I guess," he said.

She splayed her fingers wide on his thighs and moved closer. He smelled nice, even after their sweaty day and haphazard bathing ritual. She was still dirty from the trek, too, she realized. But the aroma of the jungle on him just aroused her further. She didn't like his passivity, though. He just sat there, watching, while she moved in. She pressed her lips against his throat and flicked out her tongue across the lightly stubbled skin, drawing away the salty taste of sweat.

"He wants me to kiss you," she confessed.

"Ah, right. So I get tortured to fulfill the fantasy of an invisible man, is that it?" He let out a defeated laugh.

"I guess we both do. So kiss me."

"Kiss you, huh?" he asked in a quavering voice. "That's what *he* wants?"

"It's what I want."

"Fuck," Corey muttered and gripped the sides of her head in his hands. He pressed his lips hard against hers. Hard enough to hurt, but the second his tongue plunged into her mouth she didn't care anymore. Holy fucking Christ was he a good kisser.

When she finally pulled away, breathless and elated, the look in his eyes destroyed her mood entirely.

Hallie sighed. "You want something different, don't you?"

He looked so dejected she couldn't help but reach out to him. He leaned his head into her palm when she stroked his hair.

"Yeah. I love you, Hallie…more like…like…"

"Like a sister?"

His shoulders sagged. "Yeah. I admit I'm spun up enough to nail you right now, but I would feel incredibly dirty if I did. I'd never forgive myself."

Another hand roamed down her side from behind and she shivered from the touch. Corey seemed to notice the change and his brow furrowed.

"Is he still here? Tell me if you're okay, Hallie. I'll figure out some way to make him go away."

"I will never harm you as he seems to think I might, but if you want me to show myself you have to come to me."

"No. I like what he does. I want to go to him, Corey. I know it sounds crazy. I don't even know how to find him, but he's somewhere in here."

"I get it," Corey said. "I've been out of my mind with the need for sex since dinner with no suitable prospects in sight. No offense. Are you sure you want to do this?"

"No offense taken. And yes. Yes, I'm sure."

Corey nodded and turned back to the table where he'd left the odd stone among his other gear. He picked up one of his cameras and flicked on the power.

"What're you going to do with that?" Hallie asked, pointing at the stone.

"Giving up. I'm a tech. I'm not a scientist like you guys. I just don't buy into this dragon thing, though. Erika's like the crazy cult leader and I feel like I need to be the voice of reason since nobody else is doing it. But I'm outnumbered. Starting to think if all the *scientists* believe this BS then maybe there's something to it. Hell, if you believe it…maybe 'voice of reason' is not my true calling after all."

"You've always been that haven't you?" she asked, suddenly seeing a piece of him she'd never seen before, and liking it.

"I guess. Not that anyone ever listens to me. I'm the successful member of my family, but everyone around me still acts like morons in spite of all the advice I give them. And it's not like I just volunteer it. They fucking *ask for it* and then brush it off. Why the fuck should I bother?"

She didn't have the heart to tell him she wasn't even technically a scientist—not even a fraud of one. The resumé that had gotten her onto the expedition showed her credentials as a Ph.D. in ancient Eastern religious cults. But she figured she may as well play the part if it made Corey more comfortable.

"Why don't you believe it if there's evidence to the contrary?"

"You've heard of Jim Jones, right? Let's just say at first I believed there was something in the Kool-Aid."

"And now?"

Corey nodded at the camera and tilted it toward her so the small screen was visible.

"Pretty sure the cameras can't drink Kool-Aid," he said.

CHAPTER SIX

Kol was oblivious to the sounds coming from the other chambers when he retreated to his own, slipping beneath the door with an effort of will. He felt like a fraud, pretending to be the domineering, demanding lover. She'd seen right through him. He *could* be that way. He loved the heady rush he got when he was in control and his lover did as he asked, but it never began until she asked for it to begin with.

He believed Hallie would ask for it. She *was* the one who would see him clear of this prison once and for all, but the waiting in these last crucial moments was even more tortuous than the last five hundred years. He hid inside the huge, rigid prison of his body. The massive black dragon the council had insisted he become before the temple was locked down and they were all frozen in their assigned chambers. His true form. But the truth was, he'd long since begun to hate himself for his shape. The urge for dominance was overwhelming after living that way, even in stasis. And in spite of it, he still hadn't been able to convince *her* of his need to possess her.

The door finally opened, but he kept silent, waiting to see what she would do. Two figures slipped in. One stood within the dim light of the entrance, the second moved in from behind to stand in a dark corner.

"Did she come willingly? You didn't force her, did you?"

"Yes, Shadow. She found me and asked me to explain the ritual in detail. She is here by her own choice." Kris answered out loud, causing Hallie to jerk in surprise.

"Where is he, Kris? I can't see a goddamn thing in here." But Kris didn't answer. Kol knew it was up to him now, and up to Hallie to make a decision.

He sent his breath past her to push the door closed with a soft thud. After all these years cursing the darkness, somehow he felt too exposed even with the tiny amount of light that had come through that door.

Hallie's heartbeat seemed the loudest thing in the room. She seemed to be holding her breath. He manifested his shadow into his chosen form in front of her.

"Follow my voice," he said.

"Can't you turn on a light or light a torch or something. You said you'd show yourself to me if I came. Why can't I see you?"

She still hadn't moved from her spot.

"Hallie, you can trust me. I can see you fine. I won't let you fall. Come toward my voice."

She barked out a harsh laugh that betrayed her lack of conviction in his words. "Trust you? I know better than to trust a man who believes he can *own* me. Did you actually believe that would work? Tell me, did it work on Erika? Camille? Did those dragons convince the women they should be their slaves? I highly doubt it. I know them. They'd never give in, any more than I would."

He winced at her misunderstanding of the situation. The other women had given in, as had the men, but they hadn't known the truth beforehand, either.

"Wake me first, please. Then I will tell you everything."

"Tell me just one thing now, alright? Can I leave this temple without doing what you want me to do?"

"No. The doors above are closed. They won't open again until the ritual is complete."

"Well, okay then." She took a soft footstep toward him, then another. "As long as I'm trapped, you might as well finish what you started earlier."

The determination in her voice was unexpected. She was going to go through with it, willing or not. This wasn't how it was supposed to go. She had to want him to wake up and mark her and not just because she was trapped if she didn't.

"It's true that if you don't wake me you can't leave, but someone else will come. Another team will crack open those doors. It's inevitable. The rewards are too great for most humans to resist. Like your friends. They understand because the other dragons are…" he paused, hating what he was about to say. He released a heavy breath through his nostrils. "They're better at this part of attracting humans than I am."

"What was that?" she asked in surprise, jerking her head slightly to one side. "I saw a light somewhere behind you. Do that again!"

The breath he'd just exhaled had not come from this form, which didn't breathe so much as sense, because it *was* his breath. When he'd let out that long sigh, the breath had come from his static form in the back of the room, on the far end of the pool. He emitted another breath and watched the dark light of it illuminate his long, shiny snout and brows, and the horned crown of his head where it rested in slumber along the pair of huge foreclaws. Rather than let the breath recede into his lungs again, he let it continue, pushing the magic residue back over his sleeping body until it settled on the entire surface of his skin leaving him glowing as though in phantom moonlight.

"Is that you?" Hallie asked, awe-struck. She walked faster toward him. Too fast in the darkness.

"Wait, stop!" he called out, nearly too late to keep her stepping headlong into the pool.

"What? I can't believe you think you're worse at attracting humans. Can you see how beautiful you are? And that stunt you pulled earlier. Very forward way to seduce a woman, sneaking into her dreams like that. But you know what? It worked on me."

"I didn't…what do you mean it worked?"

"Listen, dummy, I disagree with your approach but that doesn't mean I didn't absolutely love what you were doing. I'm doing this because I *choose* to. Because I want to. Consider me an adventurous spirit. And because whatever *magic* is in the air—water—whatever—in this temple is making me the horniest I've ever been in my life. And trust me, that's saying something."

"Sweet Mother, I don't know if I'm ready for women in this century," Kol muttered.

"So, you'll adapt." He could hear the smile in her voice and relief washed over him. "Now tell me why you made me stop."

"You're about to get very wet if you don't."

She let out a throaty little laugh. "I thought that was the plan. Get me hot and bothered, then have your way with me? It's a little late for that."

Kol smiled to himself. She had a point, and she also had a wicked sense of humor. The idea that he could have a woman so self-assured that might still willingly submit to him thrilled him. And he thought he might just play along a little bit to see how she responded.

"Well," he said, lowering his voice, "You should take off your clothes before you take another step."

CHAPTER SEVEN

Hallie's heartbeat raced in spite of her cocksure attitude. Strange as it was, getting naked in the dark wasn't exactly her style. She liked having everything out in the open, knowing what to expect, and being able to trust her lovers implicitly.

But it wasn't her lover that had betrayed her, was it? David had been perfect until she'd run from him. A perfect life. A perfect lover. Rich and beautiful. But a man who insisted she follow his rules. She'd been on board for love. Until shit happened.

How, she still wasn't sure. She'd gotten pregnant in spite of taking precautions. Intolerant of mistakes, David had blamed it all on her. So she'd left.

Somewhere down the road he apparently had second thoughts. When he learned she planned to keep the baby, he came after her. She'd never seen how brutal he could be until he was.

She'd seen the signs before. But the level of illumination in a room didn't matter at all when you had blinders on.

Now here she was, standing in the dark, listening to a perfect stranger—someone not even *human*—ask her to trust him enough to take off her clothes. And like a fool, she was going to.

She squatted down and reached out a tentative hand before her, searching. The surface of the water was barely six inches in front of her, and warm. He hadn't lied about that, but he *had* lied.

"Why did you lie to me?" she asked, pulling her tank top off over her head. "If you want me to trust you so badly, tell me that."

He remained quiet, she guessed he was trying to figure out what lie he had told. Oh, God, she hoped there weren't more than the one. When he spoke, his voice seemed a little more distant than before, like he'd retreated to the far end of the room.

"I think I wanted to believe it, to believe I could make you mine simply by commanding it. I'm not as good as the others at making humans believe what I tell them."

"I believed everything else you told me. Was any of that a lie?"

"No."

She stood and shimmied out of her shorts and panties in the dark, then pulled the clip out of her hair, letting the silky waves fall to her shoulders.

"Are you going in with me?"

"I can't. Not yet, anyway. Just follow my voice."

"Did you consider just, you know...*asking*? Unless you mean you don't really want me in the first place, in which case, why bother?"

Hallie fumbled back down in the dark to grip the edge of the pool. She sat on the smooth stone and slipped her feet into the warm water. The residual ache from her journey immediately began to dissipate from her sore calves. She slipped the rest of the way into the warm depths, her feet coming to rest on the floor of the pool with the water just covering her breasts. She stood there, staring into the blackness and hoping to catch just a glimpse of him or anything that would let her know where to go. All she had so far was the hard stone at her back and the warm water surrounding her.

Her heart raced at the unknown, but so far nothing about this entire encounter had felt the least bit sinister. In spite of the utter lack of visibility, she had the strongest impression of a man trapped and lonely, and very reluctant to ask for what he really needed.

But she decided she wanted *him*, not this shadowy manifestation he'd been communicating with, and she understood from Kris's explanation that there was only one way to get to him. She took a deep breath, positioned herself in the direction she believed he rested, then threw caution to the wind.

She stretched out her arms and dove beneath the water, eyes closed and aiming forward as surely as if the pool had been lit and she could see the markers on the opposite wall. She only had the sense of the distance from the soft glow on the sleeping dragon at the far end. Her Shadow had to be there somewhere, too.

The smooth stone of the pool's wall met her fingertips and she grabbed on and stood, grateful that the pool seemed to have a uniform depth. She definitely didn't feel like treading water.

His massive, sleeping shape rested peacefully a few feet from the edge of the pool. She hoisted herself out. Her nipples immediately prickled slightly in the cooler air and gooseflesh rose on her skin.

She sat for a moment at the edge of the pool catching her breath. In spite of the stillness around her, she could feel the pulse of life from the large, static form behind her. That was *him*. She cut her eyes to the side and caught a glimpse of a massive thigh and claw. To the other side she saw a resting snout, the graceful introduction to a head the size of one of the black leather seats in David's Maserati. But prettier and still glowing faintly with the ethereal light he'd cast on its surface. God, he had *horns*. Big, coiling things that shot out from his brows.

"This is you?"

"It is."

"I just have to be in contact right?" she asked in a whisper, sure he was close enough to hear.

"Yes." The rough voice was right against her ear. "Just touch me, I'll do the rest." She could sense the warmth of his body nearby, but he still had yet to touch her again.

"I can make myself come, if you don't want to do it."

The sensation of soft fingertips grazed over her hip and down her ass. "I want you. When you wake me up, I'll want you even more."

"I want you, too," she whispered. "I just haven't decided yet whether I can trust you. Call it an overabundance of caution."

"What is it you need me to say?"

Too many different things sprang into her mind at once, but none of them had any bearing on what really worried her. She dug her fingernails into the smooth scales of the large, jade shape in front of her. A hesitant touch grazed her shoulder and she leaned into it. The warm shape of him gave slightly, like sinking into a hammock, then grew even more solid. Heavy arms wrapped around her and held her.

"Oh, God, if you even knew. I need you to tell me you'll never betray me. I'm afraid of falling in love and you never returning it. If you believe we belong together, I need assurance that you mean it. And if…" What she had on the tip of her tongue was the hardest thing to admit, but it was the reason she had run to begin with, and kept running. "If we *do* belong together, I want a family. But under no circumstances otherwise will I ever let myself get pregnant again."

"Again? You have a child already?"

"No," she whispered. "I wasn't ready when it happened before. He was a good man, but the idea of my pregnancy changed him. I betrayed his trust, but he betrayed mine. He chased me, threatened me."

Her Shadow's voice sounded gritty with anger and he held her tighter. "You didn't fight him?"

"I *trusted* him. It was his child, too. But soon I was just the vessel for the baby and his feelings for me didn't matter."

Hallie turned in the invisible arms and looked imploringly into the shadows before her, wishing she knew where his face was.

"Up here," he said. Warm fingertips touched her chin, tilting her head up higher.

"I wish I could see you," she said.

"How's this?" The air shifted slightly in front of her, and the faintest outline of a face shimmered, then disappeared, but it lingered long enough for her to see the concerned press of a pair of lovely lips and furrowed brows in a strong, open, and honest face.

"Better," she said with a small smile.

"What did you do after that?" he asked.

"The only think I could think of. I ran. I thought I'd left him behind. Then he found me. So I ran again. But he *kept coming*. Accused me of robbing him of love and family. He offered money. Insisted I come back and be a family, but I couldn't have a child with *him*. Not after what he'd turned into."

"And the child?"

"I miscarried. After that, I wanted to get as far away from it as possible. But I found Erika, and the others. And now you."

His arms shifted, one large hand caressing the small of her back. Warm lips pressed against her forehead.

"I will never betray you, I will love you forever, and if we didn't belong together, another woman would be standing here in my arms right now. Also, it's against my nature to lie to someone I love."

Something in his voice carried a hint of despair.

"You're not talking about me when you say that, are you?"

"I'm talking about you, and one other who I lost. It was a long time ago. She's gone now."

Hallie didn't miss the hint of equivocation in his voice. She pinched his naked, ethereal backside hard enough for her fingers to meet through his foggy flesh. He jerked against her.

"Ow!"

"You are a lousy liar, or at least terrible at hiding things you'd rather not say. Spill it or I'm diving back in that pool and leaving. I don't care if I end up rotting away in some dark corner. You want me, you tell me everything."

"Sweet Mother. Alright! I was in love with a human woman before I came here. I broke the rules and lost her."

"So dragons have rules, huh? Which one did you break?"

"The one that said we must mark a human if they find out our true nature. It guarantees their loyalty, among other things." The sulky tone made her wonder a few things.

"How old are you?"

"Five hundred and twenty five."

"And you've been stuck here for all but twenty five of those years. No wonder you're such a broody mess. Five hundred years and you still haven't gotten over her."

"It isn't about *her*. You don't understand, it means I have to mark *you*. They took her away because I failed to do what was expected...*required*. But I *hate* that rule."

"So you have to mark me, so what? I saw the others get marked in Corey's video. That didn't look so bad. Looked pretty damn hot, if you ask me."

"This man you were running from, did he ever give you anything…permanent?"

"Just the determination to avoid assholes who want to treat me like a vessel for their offspring."

"That's what it would signify if I do it. You would be branded like livestock. Except it would be more than that. It would tie you to me like a contract."

"Oh," she said, realizing suddenly two things. First, that his cock had just gotten epically stiffer against her stomach at the talk of marking her, and second, that his words were exactly counter to the signals his invisible body was throwing off.

"You want it, deep down. So where's the conflict?"

His forehead rested on her shoulder and he groaned. "I don't believe in treating humans like …breeding stock. But yes, it's instinctual. I have to fight the urge."

Was she crazy that the idea turned her on incredibly?

"Come here," she said. She backed up, pulling him with her until the wall of the stone dragon behind her hit the flesh of her ass. She reached up and tangled her fingers into the short hair at the back of his neck, pulling him into a kiss. He sank against her, as hard and solid as flesh now, his tongue delving deeper at her invitation. He tasted faintly of juniper and something a little salty. Would he have the same flavor in his true form? Oh, God, did she want to find out how he tasted—every inch of him.

"Sweet Mother, women are confusing now," he said when she came up for breath.

"How in the world do you have short hair after five hundred years?" She raked her fingernails along his scalp when he bent to her breast, sucking deftly on one nipple, flicking it delicately with his tongue and pulling at it with his lips.

"Dragon magic," he whispered, brushing lips against her other nipple and pushing one hand down between her thighs. "You're even wetter than you were before. How are you so wet?"

"Dragon magic," she said with a gasp when he thrust a pair of fingers deep inside. "What else can you do with it besides make me beg you to fuck me? Oh, God, whatever you're doing, do it harder."

He laughed against her nipple. "Give it to me, love, so I can have you for real. Give me your Nirvana."

He relentlessly fucked her with both fingers. He found her sweet spot and now rubbed at it while he thumbed her clit. She reached for his cock, the beautiful thick length that she'd wished for when he woke her up earlier. She wanted him to fuck her now, but knew this little taste was just an appetizer. Soon she'd have the genuine article, not a facsimile.

The mountain of dragon flesh behind her began to quiver when her orgasm began. The pleasure rocketed through her so hard she wasn't sure if it was the earth moving under her feet or if she'd merely lost balance from the effect of him. Soon it became clear he was no longer holding her up from the front, his fingers were no longer sunk deep in her pussy, but something altogether bigger had gripped her from behind, then lifted her, cradling her gently in a pair of massive talons.

A massive, shiny black head peered down at her, tilted to one side. As her spasms subsided, she abstractly thought that if David ever found her again, he might be in danger of being eaten.

"That's it, Hallie," her dragon's deep voice reverberated off the walls in the room. "I'm going to fuck you so hard we wake the entire temple without the Queen's help. But first, please tell me you want my mark. Tell me you'll have me."

The desperation in his tone contradicted the majestic ebony beast that held her. In that moment she understood it wouldn't be she who was bound to him, but the other way around. He would be in thrall to her. She was as sure of it as she was that she would never have to run from him.

"Do it now, but first tell me who you are. I need to know the *name* of the dragon I'm essentially marrying."

CHAPTER EIGHT

S*he said yes!*" Kol vibrated with the excitement of her answer, unable to resist sending the thought out to all the others who could hear. Now he would be able to have her without betraying his brethren, forcing them into another long sleep.

"*I heard her, Shadow,*" Kris sent the thought from somewhere in the darkness at the other end of the room. "*Don't leave me hanging, finish the final step. It's MY turn next.*"

"*Let me savor this moment. I know you're eager, but trust me, I think we'll both want time to recover so we can enjoy being a part of the Nexus. As will the others. And you can't begin without all of us.*"

"Kol," he said, regaining his senses and gazing down at the beautiful woman in his arms. "My name is Kol. This may sting a bit."

Hallie arched her back, thrusting her breasts up to him. Kol nuzzled them with his long snout and she laughed. "That tickles."

"Sorry, I'm not used to staying in this form for very long. The world has always been a little too small for me."

With a long, forked black tongue, he traced the pattern of the mark between her breasts: a medallion-shaped crest with a coiled dragon within—black to represent his color. She hissed in response to the sting and he quickly exhaled a steamy breath to soothe her skin. The magic of their bond wasn't instant, but within the span of a heartbeat his craving for possession dissipated, replaced only with the need to pleasure her.

Unable to resist the allure of her twin, pink-tipped mounds he darted his tongue out to taste her.

She sighed and arched further, grabbing onto him and pressing her mouth against the side of his, her breast closer to his tongue.

"Go lower," she whispered.

He complied, flicking his tongue along the smooth skin of her stomach. Her hips twitched and she spread her legs for him when he reached the fringed mound of her sex. Slowly and delicately he parted her slick lips with the forked tip of his tongue. She tasted of earth and rain and sky. He delved deeper, tasting, teasing, enjoying how her juices flowed over his tongue the deeper he went.

A low, contented purr rose up through his chest. She was his now, and her surrender to him tasted even sweeter than the creamy dew between her thighs. Her orgasm took her more slowly that time, washing through her over several seconds and leaving her limp and languid in his talons. Kol relished the clench of her muscles around his tongue, letting it linger inside her a moment before withdrawing and licking his lips.

She winced and shifted within his loose clutch.

"I can change if this is uncomfortable for you," he rumbled.

"Don't you dare. Now that I've had a taste of what dragon magic is good for, you're showing me all the tricks."

"I've never made love to a woman like this. I think I would hurt you."

"What good is such a beautiful shape if you don't use it? I'm sure we can improvise."

Kol blinked at her. He couldn't possibly…he glanced down at the massive ebony erection between his scaled thighs, easily the size of one of his arms in his human shape. He remembered how tight she had been around his fingers and tongue. It didn't matter how juicy her sweet pussy was, there was no way he'd fit. Sweet Mother, he wanted to be inside her, but to abuse her perfect pussy that way was unthinkable. There had to be a way to please her without hurting her.

"As you wish," he said finally. "But we're going slow and we're doing it my way."

Eveline had asked him for one thing at the end, and he had failed her. He wouldn't let Hallie be disappointed.

He shifted into his human form, leaving only his wings still manifested, twin extensions of his wide shoulders. He carried her to the pool, then stepped off the edge, still holding her cradled in his arms. Before his feet could hit the water, he extended both wings and hovered, lowering them slowly into the warm, dark pool until his feet rested on the bottom. He let his wings fade back into his shoulder blades.

"Stretch out," he whispered when Hallie's body broke the surface of the water. "I'll support your weight."

Hallie obeyed, stretching out across the surface with her arms above her head.

"That's it. Arms out. Feel the warmth. Let it sink into you. You swam too quickly to find me earlier, the soak would have done you good."

"Let me guess, dragon magic has healing properties?" she asked

"Among other things, yes."

Kol kept one hand beneath the center of her back, then moved the other over her. She tensed when the additional support disappeared. He quickly bent his head and kissed her, a long, languid press of lips sliding across lips, tongue thrusting between until she relaxed again.

"Stay with me," he said.

"It feels like I'm weightless," she said. "But I can feel your heat. And your cock keeps rubbing against my hip."

"I know," he growled. "I'll have it inside you soon enough. Can you feel this?"

He caressed the underside of her breast, tracing fingertips around and around until they converged on her nipple. She sighed, growing even more pliant under his touch. The scent of her arousal grew stronger with each caress and he inhaled. Eveline had smelled like this and he had always loved drawing the aroma out of her along with the sweet sounds she made. He gave Hallie's nipple a light pinch and enjoyed her sharp intake of breath and the way her chest began to rise and fall more quickly.

He shifted his hand to the other breast, repeating the action while he bent to wrap his lips around the first. The skin of her areola puckered against his tongue.

"Yes," she whispered. "Oh yes."

"Shh. Quiet now. Just let yourself feel me."

She nodded slightly and her mouth opened with a soft little gasp when his fingertips trailed lower, past her navel, and slipped between her pussy lips. Her bud pulsed under his touch, already swollen and ready again, but it would have to wait. He slipped two fingers between her lips and sank them into her, deeper than before. The magic that infused the water provided lubrication to supplement her own fluids. Her hips raised up to meet each slow thrust of his fingers and her slick muscles tightened around them.

Kol continued sucking and teasing her breasts with his mouth and gradually added another finger to her wet depths. Then another. Soon he had four fingers in.

"Tell me if you want me to stop."

She shook her head. "No. I want to feel you. All of you."

His cock throbbed hot against the soft swell of her backside. She could take him as he was in his human form, but not his true size. His siblings had always experimented with their sizes, the twins in constant competition with who could manifest bigger than the other. Preferring his human form he'd never quite mastered the middle-ranges. It was either his human form, or his dragon form, no in between.

He had an idea of how to find a suitable middle ground with Hallie. With her marked now, he hoped it would work.

"I'm going to add another now. Promise me you'll tell me if I'm hurting you."

"How…how many?" she panted.

He swallowed hard as he gently pressed, adding his thumb to the tight, wet sheathe of her. Beads of sweat trickled down his temples. Her pussy clamped like a vise around his hand.

"Relax. Take a deep breath and relax. Hallie, I don't want to hurt you."

"You're not h-hurting. Oh, God, Kol. That feels too good."

When she relaxed again, he pushed a little deeper and murmured in her ear, "What feels good? This?" He twisted his hand so that the knuckle of his thumb rubbed against her sweet spot, then slowly began to close his fingers into a fist. She bucked violently, splashing water and gripping his arm tightly with one hand.

"Oh God, yes!"

His closed fist pushed, rubbed, and pushed incrementally deeper. Soon, he'd reached her limit and pulled back out. The walls of her pussy clenched and released around him. Hallie's head fell back and she moaned incoherently when he pushed his hand back into her to the wrist.

He found it hard to draw breath now, watching her come undone under his careful attention. Her pussy clenched around his hand, but she took it without complaint. On the contrary, she had grown even wetter.

It seemed that not a drop of blood was left in his head to keep him sane—it had all rushed to his pulsing groin, his thick shaft eager to be inside that hot, velvet chamber and feel her milk him until he came.

Hallie cried out, low and rough. He kissed her and held tight with his free hand while she came.

He carefully pulled his hand out of her and spun her on the surface the water so that her legs were on either side of his hips. "I think you're ready. Promise me you will speak if anything hurts."

She gave him a feverish, low-lidded look and nodded. The flush of her glowed in the darkness, but she seemed to see him, too, and stared in rapt appreciation.

"You know you glow in the dark a little bit?" she said. "Can I see more of you?"

"It's just my sweat and breath. I can make them do things. Like this." He tilted his head back and exhaled deeply. The breath luminesced in a cloud above them both, before settling over his skin, leaving a sheen that she could see.

She surged up in the water, wrapped her legs tightly around his waist and gripped his shoulders.

"You're beautiful," she said and pressed her lips hungrily against his.

He gripped her hips, guiding her pussy down over his stiff and, for the moment, still human-sized cock. He could have come from the single stroke, as long as it had been since the last time, but knew he had to make this last, for her. They'd have other chances for other fun afterward. A lifetime of other chances.

"Oh, baby, that's it. Now get bigger. Show me that beautiful dragon again," she said.

He took a deep breath, gathering the magic into him. The process of shifting was gradual, the transformation occurring over several seconds. His cock grew along with the rest of him, pressing tighter and tighter against the walls of her pussy. At the same time, he began fucking her, surging up into her slick, inviting channel.

As he grew, she took him. Every thick, swelling inch of him thrust into her. He was too lost in ecstasy to realize that he'd done it. He'd fully shifted and she hadn't said to stop. Now, she was moaning and writhing hard against him, her legs splayed wide across his scaled hips, working herself on him. Her pussy muscles clenched and released while she gripped his shoulders, riding him and meeting the surging rhythm of his thrusts.

He clutched her hips in his taloned claws and bent his head to sweep the forked tip of his tongue around her nipples, both at once. With slow, careful effort, he lifted her up his length, then let her sink back down. The tight, wet friction sent tremors of pleasure through him, all the way to the tip of his tail.

Haunches braced beneath him, he leaned forward, laying her down along the surface of the water. She gazed up at him, face constricted in desperate tension, but she relaxed and let her arms fall back to float in the water above her head. With one gentle talon, he lifted each of her legs, pulling them up to rest her ankles against his wide, black-scaled chest.

"Give me your Nirvana again, Hallie. I want to feel it surge into me when I give you mine."

"Y-you can feel it?" she asked breathily.

He resumed the slow, push-pull of his hips against hers and looked down to where they were joined. Her pussy was stretched impossibly around the thick, black girth of his shaft. Her pretty little clit throbbed bright pink in contrast. He dipped his snout and snaked out his tongue to tease at the tiny bundle. Her tangy juices tingled on his tongue. He licked again and she arched her back. The tighter clench of her pussy muscles and the sudden slackness of her legs spreading just a little wider signaled she was close.

"Give it to me *now*," he growled, swirling his tongue around her clit and slamming hard into her. The hot friction drove him wild. He couldn't hold back a second longer, but it seemed neither could she.

She yelled and thrashed in the water. He held her torso to keep her head above the surface. Wet ripples flowed over her breasts and stomach, lapping at her skin with the undulations of her body while she came. Her pussy pulled relentlessly at his cock, urging the hot stream of cum that flowed into her. A loud roar escaped his throat as he came and his balls constricted, sending every last drop into her willing depths.

She fell limp in his grasp, gasping for breath when it was over. Worried, he quickly shifted back to his preferred shape and lifted her, sliding his half-hard cock out of her. He extended his wings and lifted them both out of the water, landing at the edge of the pool.

Stooping, he began to lay her down, but the hard floor of his chamber wouldn't do for her. With the power of a thought and a heavy exhale, a large, black bed formed in the spot where he'd lain asleep for five hundred years waiting for her to find him. He laid her gently on its soft surface, then climbed on behind her and tucked her into his arms.

"Women in this century are surprising, and wonderful," he said, caressing her temple with his lips.

"No," Hallie murmured. "Just this woman, and you'd better not forget it."

CHAPTER NINE

Hallie woke a little later to the sensation of a warm, flesh-and-blood body beneath her cheek. She opened her eyes and glanced around in surprise. The chamber was awash in a warm glow from sconces like the others in the temple.

She looked at Kol's sleeping face for the first time without the shade of darkness or invisibility between them. His fine features were startling. She didn't usually go for pretty boys, preferring… well, large and *swarthy*, if she had to put a name to it. But she decided he was a far cry from unappealing, and he did have the *large* part down, even when he wasn't in his dragon form.

His black eyebrows, twitched in his sleep, perhaps from a dream of her. His skin was very fair, almost translucent, but his hair was jet black and, at the moment, sticking out in every direction.

Full, pink lips parted when she grazed her fingertips over them. This was the mouth that had started it all—its wide bow shape was very kissable. She traced fingertips over the line of his jaw, down over his neck and shoulder, across hairless, angular planes of chest and abs. Strange, she'd had the sense of a kind of velveteen texture over his scales when he was in his dragon form and she could feel the same thing now, but couldn't see it. Whatever it was, it tingled like soft down against her palm when she moved her hand lower. She paused at the swath of black fabric covering the rising erection that rested in a long, thick shape beneath his navel.

Hallie gently tugged the sheet off, baring him to her entirely from head to hips.

God, he was as magnificent like this as he was shifted. His cock twitched under her light touch, fully awake and aroused even while Kol still slept. The sight of him caused a pleasant, aching heat to grow between her thighs. Experimentally, she clenched her vaginal muscles tight, testing for pain, but there was nothing aside from a comfortable soreness.

She raised up slowly and quietly, straddled his hips, and lowered herself down the thick length of him, enjoying the pleasant friction of that first stroke.

With the third stroke he finally roused enough to push back, though it may have just been a reflex. His brow creased in confusion and his hands slid up to her thighs.

"Hmm, you just take what pleases you, don't you?" he murmured, finally opening his eyes.

"I have this little mark that says I can, at least from you," she said.

"You could never take from me, Hallie. All I am, I give you freely." He shoved his cock harder into her for emphasis, then sat up, wrapping his arms around her.

Eyes as dark as night gazed into hers while she took him in. Did he even have pupils? She leaned closer and saw that yes, there was the barest hint of variegation in his iris, but it nearly disappeared when his pupils widened in response to the clench of her pussy around him.

His hands slid down her back to grip her ass and she shifted to wrap her legs around his hips. In movements that mimicked his water-borne fucking before they slept, he tilted her, laying her flat on the bed. The angle let him sink deeper and she sighed in pleasure at the way even his human cock could reach all the best parts of her just fine. But she was an adventurous spirit, she had to know how it felt to fuck a dragon.

This time she came only with the deep strokes of his cock rubbing against her slick walls and the whispers of endearment in her ear. Dirty endearments, like, "I loved the way your sweet pussy tasted when you came on my tongue. I love the taste of your Nirvana when you give it to me. It tastes like power. It feeds me."

The pulse of his orgasm, hot inside her sent her beyond the edge and farther.

Her sensibilities kicked in when the pleasure subsided and she pulled away abruptly, that cold, "Oh shit" feeling sinking into her. She'd let him come inside her. Could dragons and humans even crossbreed? She shifted and sat at the edge of the bed, dipped her fingers between her thighs and brought back cream-covered fingertips. The heady scent of the two of their juices mixed made her a little dizzy and undeniable lust welled up in her again, but she'd already been a fool once. This she needed to know, and now. *More like yesterday*, she thought, but she'd been too overcome with the powerful pull of lust to think straight.

"Kol," she said in a quavering voice.

"What is it?" he said, immediately by her side with a comforting hand at her back.

"Can…you get me pregnant?"

She stared straight at him, watched concern mix with confusion and a kind of pleased curiosity. "If you want me to, I will, but it isn't possible in the temple."

She shook her head, confused. "No, I mean *dragons and humans*. Can we…you know…have babies. Christ, I can't believe I was so stupid not to even *ask* before. I brought condoms but nobody's done any screwing during this trip besides Erika and Eben. I haven't been on the pill in months."

His brows drew together. "You don't want to get pregnant?"

"Will you just answer the goddamn question?"

"Yes! That's what we do. It's the whole point of the ritual, to find suitable mates for the purpose of, well, *mating*. But…" His face relaxed and he lowered his head and sighed. "This is about the man who chased you. The baby you weren't prepared to have …or to lose."

Hallie couldn't respond, her throat already too knotted up with frustration and incomprehension.

"Hallie, there is no such thing as an unwanted, unexpected dragon child. We breed when we are ready." He touched the black emblem etched above her heart. "Your mark ensures that even if I wanted it, if you weren't ready, it wouldn't happen. And even if we *both* wanted it right now, it isn't possible for a dragon child to be conceived within the temple. It prevents inbreeding in the last days before we sleep."

"Why us, though?"

Kol sighed. "It's a long story. Centuries long, really. We used to be hunted, feared. Our numbers dwindled so we had to take steps to ensure our race survived. Hence the ritual. But those of us that remained were too close by blood. Humans are the only race on Earth worthy of mating with."

Hallie stood and walked away, needing a second to process the information. She slipped back into the warmth of the pool and dipped her head under water.

She could have everything with him. More than that, she could have her life back. And a child someday, too. His child, but only if she was ready. Lungs hungry for air, she breached the surface again and inhaled.

Kol crouched at the edge watching. "It's a lot to digest in a few hours, I know, but this is only the beginning, Hallie. It is my only dream in life to make you happy. And only you."

He slipped into the water and pulled her into his arms.

"Good," she said and let him kiss her.

While they embraced, a slew of excited, chattering voices washed into the room and they turned. The entire crowd of their friends traipsed in through the doors and began diving into the other end of the pool.

"What the hell?" Hallie said, irritated at their interruption.

Camille swam up to them, eyes wide and mouth open in an excited smile. "Wow, Hallie. He's pretty. Not as pretty as Roka, but he looks right for you."

"What are you guys doing?" Hallie asked.

"Roka said the best place to bathe was in here, and since the phase was over and the doors unlocked, we just came right in. Gotta get ready for Kris's big performance. He's so, so excited. We just wanted to wash a bit of grime off first. It's gonna get very, *very* dirty in there. I can't wait!"

Kol chuckled when Camille swam away and was promptly lifted up and kissed soundly by a large, white-haired man who Hallie assumed must be the one called Roka. Roka passed her into Eben's arms, who then diligently and carefully began rinsing her from head to toe. After a moment it looked less like washing and more like fondling.

"Don't be mad," Kol said. "They're excited. The next phase will be a sight to see, and we all have to be there."

A throat cleared from the edge of the pool and Hallie looked up. Corey gave her a tentative wave. "Hey," he said with a sideways smile, then his brow quickly furrowed in concern. "You alright? I admit I heard…sounds that worried me." His eyes shifted uncertainly to Kol.

Her face relaxed, pleased that he'd thought to ask. "Yes, I'm better than alright. Corey, this is Kol."

Corey reached down and shook Kol's hand amiably.

"I've decided to take him home with me after we're done here," she added.

Corey's eyebrows raised. "Oh? I didn't think you had a home, being on the run and all."

Hallie blinked and stared at him, open-mouthed.

He grinned. "You think we didn't all know from the beginning? Erika still insisted you were right for the team even though you were outright lying to us. That woman has the strangest instincts, but I've known her a long time and learned not to second-guess her."

"Even about all this stupid *dragon stuff?*" Hallie asked pointedly.

He shrugged. "I'm still on the fence about it. Too much indiscriminate sex, as far as I'm concerned. And I'm still not sure where the hell I fit in considering all of you have paired up."

"There are only two dragons unaccounted for," Kol interjected. "Issa just left with Kris, and I don't see her mark on anyone. She's probably preparing him for the next phase."

"Who's the other one?" Hallie asked.

Kol stared at them both like they were imbeciles. "The other one is the Queen."

SLEEPING DRAGONS

BOOK 5

NEXUS

OPHELIA BELL

All paths lead to pleasure.

CHAPTER ONE

Isolation can affect a man in many ways. He can either feel apart from his world, merely looking in from the outside, or by contrast he may feel at the very center of it with events revolving around him and beginning to coalesce. Kris had been at the edge looking in for his entire life, but the balance in focus was about to shift.

He had no recollection of his own mother's touch. His mother—the last living dragon of the prior cycle—had died not long after his birth. He hadn't even been old enough to feed himself. Only two of the monks at the monastery where he was born could accomplish the task. It wasn't until he was a teenager that he learned those two men were different from all the others. They were dragons, like his mother, but they had taken a vow never to manifest their true forms in an effort for spiritual enlightenment.

They became his caregivers, then later his teachers. He learned the marks on his body had been given to him by his mother when he was just a newborn. The large dragon shape that graced his torso and the dark inked scales on his thighs looked as fresh and vibrant as the first day, even twenty-five years later.

The significance of his status became apparent very early on. His teachers maintained their distance from him, their proximity only dictated by the type of lesson required. Early lessons could be taught from a few feet away. Later in his youth, their combat lessons required closer instruction, yet they were always careful to avoid contact. On the rare but inevitable occasion when they did accidentally touch him the experience was never pleasant—the sensation akin to the time he'd grievously burned his palm on the kitchen stove. The other monks who lived at the monastery never touched him.

In spite of the experience, touch became something he craved, even if it was merely the casual touches that the monks he lived with shared between each other. He'd always experienced some pleasure and comfort from his own touch, but it wasn't until he was twelve years old that the light stroke of his hand on his stiff prick became a substitute for what he believed he was missing. The slide of his palm against his hardened flesh could be a balm to his worries, but it never lasted.

Kris knew there had to be something transcendent that happened beyond the end of the touching. He would stroke himself for longer minutes each night, the pleasure escalating more each time. He *felt* like there was some threshold he should cross as a result but never could quite get there, like the door was perpetually locked to him. His caregivers never overtly discouraged it, but Kris soon discovered unpleasant side effects. He always ended up cranky and out of sorts once he finally gave up out of frustration.

Eventually his teachers explained that his unique situation prevented him from finding satisfaction and that by learning the discipline they and the other monks had to teach he would be able to endure the frustration—maybe even find some peace from it. They also explained that when the time came he *would* get to experience that Nirvana, and that it would be the most soul-defining experience of his life.

Kris dutifully threw himself into his training, the understanding of what his teachers explained as his destiny driving him forward.

While the monks of the monastery were decidedly celibate, his two teachers only pretended to be. It was a surprising discovery to learn that what his teachers, Zak and Darius, truly abstained from was not sex at all.

Late one night Kris found himself unable to sleep, waking up with an irritating erection. Such occasions became easier to deal with the older he got. At eighteen he'd learned that a long walk around the stone paths of the compound would usually allow his mind to calm and focus on other things besides the vividly erotic dreams that came to him while he slept. He always woke craving touch, but knowing if he gave in to the temptation, he'd only be left frustrated.

When he padded on slippered feet around the corner of the bath house that night, he was surprised to see the soft glow coming from within and murmured voices carrying through the window. It was uncommon for anyone who wasn't sitting in meditation to be awake at that hour.

He paused at the edge of the window, remaining in shadows. Moist, aromatic air drifted out, the scent of lemongrass tickling his nostrils. Through the steamy air within, he could see the two men, naked in the bath and wrapped in a tender embrace. His teachers never touched in public. They were as polite, quiet, and reflective as any of the human monks, but that night Kris witnessed the truth of their relationship.

His own erection returned when Darius, the older of the two, climbed out of the stone bath and sat on the edge of the small, rectangular pool. Zak came closer, combing fingers through wet hair, and rested his hands on his lover's naked thighs on either side of his large erection. They kissed, Darius gripping Zak's jaw and tilting his head back with both hands.

Kris was first overcome by irrational envy. To feel the lips of another person on his own, to feel such tender, intimate emotion was something he dreamed about, but had never known in life. He almost turned and stalked off, but couldn't quite bring himself to stop watching.

Zak's hand had slipped in and gripped Darius's cock by the base and slowly and surely stroked it while they kissed.

Darius murmured a soft affirmation and leaned back. He tilted his hips upward for the other man. Zack slipped his mouth over the tip of his lover's shaft and engulfed him between his lips while continuing to stroke with his hand. Kris knew the steady build of pressure well. He could feel it now because his own hand had unconsciously slipped beneath the waist of his pants and begun stroking and squeezing his cock. He knew better, but couldn't help himself.

Darius panted and moaned, raising one hand to the side of Zak's head, encouraging him to quicken his tempo. Within a moment the man's torso tensed and his hips thrust hard into his lover's grip. Kris paused his futile stroking and watched, wide-eyed at the transformation that went through his teacher, one he'd aspired to but never yet achieved—the intense concentration followed by an explosive release and then languid satiation while Zak licked his lips and smiled like a smug cat polishing off its kill. "My turn," Zak said.

Kris's erection throbbed almost painfully. He abruptly stopped stroking and turned to go back to his room to suffer in solitude. It took days for him to recover from his own self abuse. When he finally did, he'd confessed what he'd witnessed to his teachers and asked why they weren't celibate like the other monks.

"Dragons follow different laws," Darius told him, and proceeded to explain the exchange of power that occurred during that moment of sexual release; it was that energy that allowed the two dragons to maintain their human forms. "Your time will come."

Kris begrudgingly accepted his teacher's explanation, but steered clear of the bath house during his evening walks after that.

Soon his training was finished, and his teachers told him it was time. His teachers explained that once his journey was complete he would return to the monastery for one final task, but that after that his life would be his to live, free and unburdened with the restrictions of his youth. He gathered his things and left the monastery for the last time, uncertain but excited about what the future would hold. The solemn responsibility of his role occupied his mind less than the thrill of discovering what lay in store for him afterward.

In a Singapore hostel after a year of traveling he had the first dream. A beautiful woman with sleek auburn hair and a fierce expression appeared, accompanied by a group of other young, attractive people. "Show me your secret," the woman said to him in the dream just before kneeling down to pleasure him with her mouth. He woke drenched in sweat and panting, his cock hard and hypersensitive, but he believed the dream was a sign that he was closer to the end.

A week later he found the six explorers in a small bar near the hostel. It had to be them, he decided, but sat quietly at the bar trying to listen to their conversation, waiting to see what would happen next.

One of the women from the group approached the bar and sat beside him. She wore cargo shorts that displayed long, tanned legs. Her expression caused a jolt of recognition to shoot through him. He knew her from his dreams.

In what seemed a desperate plea, she asked the bartender in Mandarin if he knew where she could find a jungle guide. The sullen man merely eyed her chest and made a rude comment about finding a tour guide somewhere else.

"Well, fuck me for having tits," the woman muttered.

"I can take you there," Kris said in a low tone when the bartender was out of earshot.

The woman turned an eager look on him and Kris was struck by her determination. "Do you know the place? They call it *Keseronokan Kuil.*"

Kris smiled to himself. *Pleasure Temple.* Of course they called it that.

He'd never been inside the place but his teachers had told him what lay within. He knew of the ritual to awaken their brethren and his part in it. Knowing the power of the temple had been the focus of his training for the last few years before he left the monastery.

Kris had spent five years of his youth training in the jungle that surrounded the place the woman spoke of, which was merely a legend to most of the natives. His teachers had taken him to the edge of the surrounding jungle, given him supplies, and told him when he found the temple his teachers would find him. It took him a month the first time. Then two weeks when they made him take the second trip, even though every path he'd followed before seemed to have been destroyed—consumed by the jungle entirely. Those five years of his training were mostly spent learning the outlying landscape and the different points of access to the temple itself. His teachers would always send him to it by different paths.

Like the hidden temple was the pole to his tether, soon he would always feel himself drawn to it, being led back to it even if that weren't his original destination. It finally got to the point where he could find the place in his sleep, and he had one night.

He'd woken up with his hands resting against hard stone and an even harder pressure throbbing between his thighs, uncertain why he was there and with no recollection of having made the journey.

Now he would finally begin his last journey into that jungle.

"It would be my pleasure," he said to the woman with a wide grin.

"Terrific! I'm Erika, the leader of this motley crew." She tilted her head to the large table where the others sat. Three men and two other women, all young and attractive, watched eagerly.

"Kris," he said, ignoring Erika's proffered hand, but waving amiably at the others who all smiled and waved back.

Once the trek began, he was unprepared for the shock of being exposed to the brash attitudes of the Westerners who had hired him. He remained on the periphery of the group, and they tended to give him space, which was expected, but he often found himself in conversation with them and found he enjoyed their camaraderie.

He was particularly fascinated by the level of sexual energy they all possessed—something he rarely encountered growing up, but that he could sense from them as prevalent as the sounds of the jungle.

Only two of them seemed to be giving in to it. Erika, the group's leader, and Eben, the older of the two blond men in the group. Erika seemed to be the instigator on the nights when the pair coupled. The rest of the group would head into their own tents rather than sit and have to communally bear witness to the sounds coming from the tent the couple shared that night. Some nights Kris might even hear furtive sounds from the others as they each saw to their own needs in the dark, the noises of the jungle obscuring the noises from all but Kris who had learned to discern the sounds of carnal pleasure from the cacophony of the wildness that surrounded them.

Kris understood the frustration of being witness to a pair of lovers, doubly so having no outlet himself. In the seven years since the night he'd first seen his teachers together, he'd learned better mental discipline, so he was able to appreciate the dynamics of the party he now served as guide to without becoming overly aroused. Not even the very graphic noises coming from Erika's tent in the evening bothered him, nor did the generally uninhibited behavior of most of them.

Whenever they reached a suitable bathing spot, women and men both stripped to nothing and dove in, with the exception of the pretty blonde, Camille, who preferred to wait until the men were gone before tentatively slipping into the water in her very demure underthings.

Kris also preferred to bathe alone, choosing the early mornings to take advantage of the cooler water that would help slake the burn of carnal need that had he'd been afflicted with most of his life. After regaining control of his libido, he always felt revived and even more excited to lead them closer. He didn't dwell much on what might lay at the end of his journey, preferring to focus on the task at hand. Instead, he let his subconscious revel in the gradual approach and play out his fantasies while he slept.

One such morning, he'd finished bathing and lay naked, drying in the morning sun on a large stone near the pool they'd found the evening before.

The sound of soft splashing reached his ears and he opened his eyes to see a single figure, partially obscured by a mossy outcropping several yards away. He raised up on his elbows and watched while the dark-haired Hallie dove beneath the water and came up again, water sluicing over her very naked breasts. Heat flushed his cheeks and he swiftly averted his eyes, but the image of the sleek globes, wet and tipped with hard, pink peaks had already burned itself into his brain. He gave in and looked again, too tempted not to.

Kris tried to decide if he should announce himself, but before he could, Hallie swiped her hands over her face and opened her eyes.

"Oh, shit! Sorry, Kris. I …ah …didn't …" She stammered and then broke out into an embarrassed laugh.

"I can go," he said, but made no move to get up. Hallie swam a little closer, taking him in. He glanced down his torso, relieved to see his cock was mostly behaving, in spite of how enticing her glistening breasts appeared in the morning light.

"Wow," she said. "That's a big one. I'm impressed."

His eyes shot back up. She stood a few feet away, her lips quirked in a sideways smile. "I meant your tattoo," she said, filling in his stunned silence.

Of course she meant his tattoo, but a different part of him responded to the mistaken compliment.

"Though the rest of you is impressive, too," she said. Her gaze swept over him again, lingering at his groin.

"Thank you," he said, choosing to ignore the throb of his hard-on in favor of studying her reactions. This was the first time he'd been naked and aroused in a woman's presence. It wasn't like he could do anything about it, but what would she do? Would she keep her distance the way every other human he encountered seemed to?

"You should come back in for a bit," she said, her voice a low purr that reminded Kris of how his teachers occasionally spoke to each other when they thought he wasn't listening. Once he'd discovered their relationship, that tone had always been a signal for Kris to leave the two men alone.

Oh what he wouldn't give to be able to accept her invitation and see it through to her desired conclusion.

Pushing aside the internal regret, he replied innocently, "But I just dried off. Maybe you should get out and join me here. The sun feels nice."

Hallie seemed to ponder his suggestion and started toward the rock he reclined on. A few feet away from him, her determination faltered and a cloudy look passed across her face.

She raised both hands and buried her face in them. "What the fuck am I doing?" she asked in a muffled voice behind her palms. "I'm sorry, Kris. I can't."

"Can't what? Get out of the water?"

"No, I can do that. Just not to do what I was *about* to."

"Which would be…?" He continued playing dumb, even though he knew precisely what she'd been considering because that was what had gone through his own mind, too, in vivid detail. He quickly quashed the thoughts before they caused more trouble than they already had.

With that, the palpable tension wilted and Hallie sighed. She swam the last few feet to the rock and hoisted herself up beside him, close enough that the cooler temperature of the water radiating off her skin was tangible to his heightened senses. She stayed just far enough to avoid touching him outright.

"Something completely inappropriate and unprofessional. That's what I was about to do. Jump your boner …er…*bones*. Sheesh, I'm a mess." She glanced sidelong at his lap. "You don't look much better, come to that."

"If I ignore it, it'll go away," he said, sitting up and giving his stiff prick an irritated look.

"True enough," she said. "If only all of life's little annoyances worked that way." After a contemplative pause, she changed the subject. "So, Mr. Jungle Guide, how soon until we reach this fancy dragon burial ground or whatever it is?"

"It's a temple, not a grave. The dragons there are very much alive."

"Ah. These dragons Erika's so hot for. Don't tell me *you* buy into her crazy ideas."

"Not exactly." Kris had taken the measure of the group's leader and realized that in spite of Erika's adherence to science, she was very much an acolyte of dragon lore. Her ideas about what to expect were only half correct, however. She definitely wasn't expecting the ritual he was diligently leading them to. He hoped he'd be able to convince her of its value once inside the temple.

"Not exactly...You don't believe her? Or...Please do explain, because us *sane* people are a little outnumbered at the moment."

"Do you believe in destiny, Hallie?"

Hallie didn't answer for several beats and Kris looked over at her. Her expression had grown even darker and she rested one hand lightly over her abdomen. In a shaky voice she said, "If you had asked me that a year ago I'd have said no, but now? Yeah, I think I do a little bit."

"Good, because tomorrow we're all going to meet our destinies. All seven of us."

CHAPTER TWO

Like all dragons, Issa believed everything happened for a reason. So when Eben, the lovely human man who'd awoken her, made her stop midway through servicing him, she considered it a sign.

Roka had humbly apologized for the interruption, and continued doing so for the entire intermission while Eben and Camille intimately conferred. She only felt the merest pinprick of regret that she hadn't yet marked the man, but the more she watched him with the golden-haired virgin—*former virgin*, she corrected herself, giving Roka an appraising glance—the more convinced she was that this was the natural order of things.

"They belong together, and she belongs to you, my friend," she said to Roka.

Her large, white-haired friend nodded at her from across the room, replying with a thought. "*Don't let our Shadow hear you speak that way of* belonging. *Besides, the woman will be the one with two mates, not I. Perhaps my first child will have a human brother.*"

"Or sister," Issa replied.

"Or sister. If that's the case I will name her Issansaelethessis."

In truth she was relieved. Eben, seemed the sort who could adjust to sharing. But Issa had always admired the Shadow for his principles. It might be against her nature, but the idea of only having a single mate to please appealed to her very much.

"Issa," Geva said in his deep, comforting voice when she approached the red dragon and his new mate. Her trouble-maker of a friend had always managed to bolster her mood, but their antics during their youth were centuries behind them. Still, she could allow herself some pleasure until she decided what to do next.

The human woman, Erika, sat up from Geva's embrace and extended a hand. Issa clasped it and greeted the woman. The pretty auburn-haired woman was still flushed pink from Geva's attention, but her eyes were bright and alert. She looked ready for anything, a good quality in a leader. And a mate. Geva hadn't wasted time marking her.

Issa's red-maned friend lounged smugly against the sloping side of the wide bench where he reclined with his lover. His eyes trailed down Issa's length in that familiar way he had that was just suggestive enough to make her wonder if it was an invitation or a promise. She felt the violet sheen she liked to keep on her skin ripple and intensify in response to his eyes.

It was the woman who spoke, however. "Join us, please," Erika said, her voice a rough purr. Oh, she was definitely ready for more. Issa's mouth watered at the prospect of another human's Nirvana. Eben had given her just enough of a taste to leave her wanting more.

"Do you mind?" she asked Geva, already sure she knew the answer.

"If I recall, I am still in your debt for before," he replied. *"If not for your intervention, the Council would have banished me from the Court for what I did. Being chained to your bed for five hundred years wasn't so bad, especially not considering what I got to wake up to."*

"Promise me you won't try to incite any orgies in the street again. As fun as they are, it confuses the humans and the Council hates the backlash."

"I didn't show myself. I just breathed a little life into an otherwise desultory last day before my exile."

"You guys are having an entire conversation in your heads right now, I bet. Anything I should know?" Erika asked, sitting up straighter.

Geva chuckled and leaned up to nuzzle at Erika's neck. "Just letting Issa know I don't mind sharing as long as you don't, love. Can she have a little taste?"

Erika's eyelids lowered slightly when she gazed up at Issa. "Only if I can taste back."

Issa smiled and met Geva's eyes. "She is perfect for you, Geva. How much has she given you so far?"

"Hmm, half a dozen with no signs of flagging. The next one's all yours."

Erika leaned back against Geva's chest and he tilted her head back enough to lower his mouth onto hers.

Issa knelt on the bench between Erika's thighs, urging them further apart while she slid her palms down the silky length to the human woman's core.

Erika's lips still glistened wetly with her own juices, mixed with the familiar scent of Geva's heady spunk. This would be a banquet. Geva's large hands slid around Erika's chest to cup both breasts and thumb her nipples while he watched Issa. Issa smiled up at him from between Erika's thighs and Geva grinned back, nodding and urging her to continue. He'd always expressed how he enjoyed watching Issa with a woman as much as he'd enjoyed doing the deed himself, or doing *her* himself.

Issa let her longer Animus tongue slip out for a taste. The twin forks slipped along the creases of Erika's pussy, gathering juices to pull back into her mouth. Issa closed her eyes, savoring the flavor and enjoying the rough moan that came from the human.

Before she could dip her head for a deeper taste she felt a prickle at the back of her neck. Glancing back over her shoulder, she saw the guide standing in the shadows, watching intently. *The Catalyst*, she corrected herself.

She turned back to her task. As her lips fastened on the sweet human cunt before her, she sent a thought back to her observer.

"Kris, do you like the view?" She spread her legs a little wider and with her free hand reached between them. Her fingertips slid between her own slick, swollen pussy lips and pushed them apart to give him a better view.

"How does she taste, describe it to me." His answer exploded urgently into her mind. He'd interacted with these humans for a time already, Issa realized. Did he have some connection to this one?

Issa delved deeper, pressing an arm down across Erika's hips to hold her still. *"She tastes like ripe pomegranate coated in rich chocolate and sprinkled with sea salt and pepper flakes. Sweet Mother I haven't tasted anything so good in five hundred years."*

"Spicy? Is that from her or him, do you think?"

"Oh, the spicy is most definitely from Geva. Do you like spicy? If so I will be sure to tell him to let you have a taste during the penultimate phase."

"I plan on tasting everyone, trust me. Especially the juicy delicacy I can see between your thighs right now. Touch yourself again for me."

Issa dipped her fingers deeper into her own cunt while thrusting her tongue into Erika's hard enough to make the woman squirm and buck.

"Your pussy is the most beautiful color." Kris's voice sounded awestruck in her mind and Issa had to remind herself how inexperienced he was. Still a dragon, but innocent of the sensual delights dragons would normally have partaken of by his age.

Deciding to give him more of a show, she spread her legs a little wider and thrust her ass higher in the air. The thought of breaking in a new dragon thrilled her, particularly one with as much potential as he had. The way he managed to stay unnoticed in the shadows for so long spoke of the incredible magic that protected him. But once that energy was tapped and he realized his true power, she could only imagine the heights he could bring her to.

Issa resolved that he would learn everything she had to teach him during the next few hours while he waited for his turn. Then she would be the first to reap the rewards, and to give him everything she had to give. But that meant she needed to gather more of the humans' Nirvana first.

Erika cried out under the steady lick of Issa's forked purple tongue. Unlike the juices coating Erika's sweet pussy, her Nirvana lacked flavor. Instead, it had the essence of a cool night wind when it coursed through Issa, leaving her hyperaware of the room around her, and of Kris's eyes on her in particular. The pulse of Erika's orgasm washed over Issa's tongue , sending the flood of power straight between her thighs.

Issa's clit pulsed and her juices flowed thickly over her fingers when she came. She resisted the urge to clench her thighs around her hand and ride the wave of her orgasm, instead spreading herself even wider for her audience.

Kris didn't speak to her again, but Issa could sense an impression of his thoughts, little bits of appreciation for each motion she made. He liked it when she leaned up and kissed Erika deeply, followed by Geva. He grew tense with anticipation when she moved back across the room to the other trio of lovers, who had parted while they rested, and encouraged them into another round.

Roka was only too willing to allow her to take their Nirvana as a thank-you for letting him mark Eben, too.

She performed the same tongue-tricks against Camille's pussy, relaying the combination of flavors back to Kris while Eben fucked her again and Camille took Roka's cock in her virgin mouth for the first time.

Each rush of their energy infused her more, until she craved a high mountain on which to shift and fly.

"I'm giving this all to you very soon. Will you be ready?" she asked Kris.

She glanced back to where he'd been standing before, but he was gone. A moment later his voice sounded in her mind. *"I have work to do. Come watch with me when you're full."*

CHAPTER THREE

Issa and the other two dragons all glowed with the Nirvana they'd channeled from the humans by the time Kris sensed the next phase beginning. As much as he would like to, he didn't have the time or the constitution to watch her continue. He had to get to the Twins' chamber door. And above all, he had to survive the ritual long enough to make it to his own chamber before imploding from desire.

His powers of observation began to falter for the first time when Issa joined him shortly in the Twins' chamber. His task, his purpose, was to witness the awakening of each dragon, to watch each phase of the ritual from its beginning until each potential mate was marked and thus bonded to a dragon.

The task Issa didn't know about was his responsibility to report to his teachers and then the Council when it was all over to let them know if the ritual had proceeded smoothly. Objectivity was one of the things his teachers had impressed on him as being paramount. He'd done just fine until one rogue, lavender dragon gave away her mate, then soaked up every spare drop of Nirvana the humans chose to give her.

Once she was beside him, the power radiating out of her and her intoxicating aroma filling his nostrils, he really wanted to urge the others to move along with their fun.

Dragon law had been his most common lesson in the monastery, and the details of it were etched into his mind. The most prominent one was that dragons were required to mate with humans to preserve their fertility and prevent inbreeding. There were too few of them born in each generation to risk it. The imperative to reproduce was what drove the dragons' instincts, and also what drove the Council to make the laws it did. Though the infighting that would occur with too many dragons alive in each generation was probably equally undesirable. It was a double-edged sword and the laws they followed were designed to maintain the strict balance.

Yet he was drawn to Issa with a kind of urgency that he hadn't felt from any of the human women he'd traveled with, in spite of spending several weeks with them. From Hallie's honesty during their shared mornings bathing, to Erika's frustrated display earlier that evening, then Camille's very enthusiastic sacrifice of her own virginity.

Issa still outshone them all in some unfathomable way.

After the ritual, Kris would be an unbonded dragon, free if he chose to be. Free to find his own human mate. *Human mate*, he thought. Not dragon, which was what Issa and he both were.

Lost in his tangled ruminations, he was only half aware of both of the twins marking Dimitri. Damnit. That couldn't be good. But Kris was only a guide, not an enforcer. He had neither the ability nor the inclination to intervene.

"Is that supposed to happen?" Issa asked when the trio before them continued their tryst.

"Not exactly, but you weren't supposed to give Eben away, either."

"I guess that means I'm not supposed to be in here watching this all unfold with you. Should I leave? I can go wait patiently by the doors until it's all over."

He turned to look at her, suddenly bored with the tableau of sex that he couldn't participate in. He wanted them all, but Issa had already given him the best preview. The image of her violet folds spread open before him lingered even as he observed the two golden dragons and their new lover. Issa's nearness comforted him even as he found himself dwelling on what she might feel like to touch.

"No. I'm weary of watching, but it's easier with you beside me."

Her lips curled into a pleased smile.

They watched the others, Kris finding himself more aroused by Issa's nearness than the acts of pleasure playing out between the trio in front of him.

"I knew your parents," Issa said after a few moments. The comment seemed completely incongruous when he'd just been contemplating doing to her some of the things Dimitri was currently doing to the lovely, golden Aurin, right in front of her brother.

Issa studied him for a long moment until he started to feel a little uncomfortable, then turned back to watch the twins and their new plaything, a brighter smile gracing her pretty face, probably entertained by his speechlessness.

As if inviting more conversation, she continued. *"My father was the Virgin's Guardian in the last cycle. He wasn't born a Court dragon like the others' parents. Or like your parents."*

It hadn't occurred to Kris that Issa might have known who his parents were. He'd never even known them himself. *"My mother was the last Catalyst, so I'm not sure if that counts as a Court dragon. My father wasn't, though."* His teachers rarely mentioned his father, only that he was a Red with no status. *"I never knew them…"* he said, trailing off as the understanding dawned on him. His father was a Red. Not a human…a dragon.

"I did. They were nice. Racha can tell you more about them when this is all over."

"Racha?" Kris asked, blankly.

"Yes," Issa said, her tone holding a smile. *"The Queen. Your sister."*

The revelation stunned him. His teachers had never told him that detail, or even explained his parentage to him aside from sharing his father's identity. He briefly panicked, wondering if he'd failed in his studies somehow, but no. He'd only glossed over it when it was taught to him because they'd never emphasized the details. He'd never connected himself to those abstract roles.

The Catalyst and the Queen shall be pure-born siblings, meaning their parents were always a bonded pair of dragons, the only two in a generation allowed to co-breed, though they had the option of breeding with humans, too, if they chose. Kris had always written off that detail as one that wouldn't apply to him when he was younger, as inevitable as his own isolation felt.

When the twins and Dimitri finally dozed off, he and Issa left the room to wait by the doorway to the next chamber. He only sensed the Shadow's breath drift by and seep beneath the door. Hallie followed not long after, hesitant but grateful for his and Issa's presence when she opened the door.

Issa left his side there, heading back to the first chamber to check on the others and make sure they followed with little delay once the Shadow's phase was complete.

After stepping inside and a brief exchange to make sure the two were headed in the right direction, Kris stepped back into the darkness to observe, as always. He appreciated the darkness of this chamber, deciding to close his eyes and focus his energy into mental preparation for the ordeal ahead of him. The lack of sight caused his other senses to become keener, but he didn't need powerful hearing to understand the tone of the interaction unfolding inside this room. The lovers had to know he was still there, but he felt like even more of an intruder hearing Kol and Hallie's emotional exchange than he had in the other chambers. Yet he understood.

What a complicated world they lived in, with such arbitrary rules. He supposed things might change during this cycle, but it was up to the Council to decide. Kris resolved to voice his honest opinion, however. He and Issa may not have anything to worry about, but the twins might run into problems. Kris was just grateful that Hallie had ultimately decided to accept Kol's mark. Still, he didn't relish the prospect of running interference for any of them with the Council. He would have to be honest and try to convince them that way.

He opened his eyes when the voices changed from intimate conversation to even more intimate sighs and moans. This was he part he was truly meant to observe, so he watched, his eyes adjusting easily to see through the darkness.

In spite of being dulled to the image of two people coupling in a myriad of configurations, the interaction between Kol and Hallie fascinated Kris. It wasn't how their bodies connected that kept him interested, however, but the way they never broke the intent gaze they shared. It incited a much deeper longing in him—one that overwhelmed the already dull ache between his legs that he'd endured for hours.

The phase was long complete, the room now illuminated in a warm glow, yet he still watched them sleep contentedly, unwilling to leave just yet. When they did rouse and make love again, he made sure to stay in the shadows, marveling at the intensity of their coupling. Soon Issa was by his side again, followed by the others, who quickly dove into the large pool in the center of the room.

"It's time," Issa whispered. She reached for Kris's hand and he flinched back instinctively.

Issa stared at him like he'd just slapped her. "You're going to need to touch us all to finish this."

Kris pursed his lips and nodded. "I know. Let's just get into the chamber first. I'll be ready once we're finally inside."

CHAPTER FOUR

Issa stood back and let Kris go past, careful to keep her distance. Out in the corridor he paused before the colorful door, staring at the raised scene carved into its surface—it didn't look like a single man so much as some other creature with many heads and tails.

She wanted to say something encouraging, give him a warm caress for comfort, but she'd felt the static push of his magic even in the small gesture of trying to take his hand earlier. It had been an unusual, tingling sensation, but not entirely unpleasant at first. More like the first plunge of cold feet into a hot bath—something she knew would require acclimating to before it began to feel good.

Kris's eyes closed and his shoulders rose and fell with a series of deep, meditative breaths. Issa watched while he stripped, first pulling his dark shirt over his head. He swiped the fingers of both hands back through his shiny black hair, then traced part of the outline of the huge dragon tattoo that coiled around his torso. The image seemed to glow as though imbued with its own power, separate from Kris. He hooked thumbs into the waist of his simple drawstring pants, pushed them down, and stepped out of them.

When he placed his palms against the door, he closed his eyes again. With a slight effort, he pushed and the doors swung open.

It wasn't a chamber that the doors revealed, however, but a narrow staircase leading down. Without a word or a look back to Issa, Kris descended. Lights in the walls of the staircase sprang to life in advance of his passage.

Issa followed a few paces behind. The staircase turned once, then continued, opening shortly into a small, sunken chamber. The circular room must have been beneath the Queen's chamber. In the center of the chamber was a low, round, and oddly shaped altar carved into smooth undulating waves. It was made of the same enchanted stone as the temple that had been her bed for the last five hundred years, carved from exquisite white jade that luminesced with faint energy. Kris would add his own to it soon, and hers would be fed to it through him.

She watched him enter the room, her heart pounding at the monumental moment she was sharing with him. He was the Catalyst—the one Dragon who held the key to awakening the rest of the brood. She'd learned of the Catalysts and their mates. The longest-lived dragons were always mated to a Catalyst. Perhaps they lived so long because of the bond. And Catlysts always bonded other dragons, but only ones the Council deemed worthy.

Issa had had her eye on him for more than one reason, but his appeal had overshot her ambition with his first word to her.

Now, she ached to have his hands on her, his thick cock inside her, certain that the experience would be more than memorable, in spite of his inexperience.

Beyond the center, the room was divided into five equal segments of varying colors of smooth jade, radiating from the center upward in a series of widening tiers. There wasn't a hard corner in the place, not even the edges of the tiers, which were all beveled as smooth as the column and the altar. Issa was reminded of the eddies of air currents she would catch when she first learned to fly as a young dragon centuries before. The memory caused a pulse of the energy that made her ache. She needed to give the collected power to Kris, and soon. But first he had to let her touch him.

Still ignoring her, Kris stepped carefully down the tiers into the center of the chamber, then stepped up onto the altar. The room grew brighter with a glow that emanated from every surface, particularly in the center where Kris stood. He crouched down, running his hands across the contours of the altar, which glowed a little brighter for a moment under his touch before fading out again.

In the very center of the altar his hand circled around a deep, bowl-shaped impression, then slipped into it, drawing back fingers that glistened with clear, oily liquid. From the back of the room she caught the spicy aroma of concentrated dragon essence, potent enough to make her core heat up even more than the sight of Kris's naked, crouching form.

While Issa watched, the clench of his jaw tightened and he acquired the look of someone bracing himself for something unpleasant.

"It won't hurt," she said gently, finally walking the rest of the way into the room and sitting on the edge of the altar a few feet from where he still crouched in the center.

"It always hurts eventually."

"This time will be different. You watched all the others together. Did they look like they were in pain? I hold inside me a volume of what they felt. Let me give it to you so you can understand. Trust me, you will love it once it begins." She tried to reach out to him again, but he moved away, sitting on one of the higher sections of the altar and watching her. This was going to be harder than she thought.

"Alright," she said and moved to the opposite side of the altar, reclining against another of the contoured backrests that faced the center. She kept her legs together, hands at her sides. "I don't have to touch you. So why don't you try to touch me first, instead?"

"Issa. All I can think about is touching you. I just don't know where to begin."

She nodded and reached into the well of essence in the center, drawing out a bit of it on her fingertips. "Start like this." She raised her fingertips to one breast and traced a glistening circle around one nipple. The peak of flesh tingled and hardened under her touch.

Kris slid toward her and knelt beside her a few inches away. His brows drew together and he clenched his fists. "It hurts even being this close. Doesn't it hurt you, too?"

"I feel heat, but the longer you stay this close, the nicer it feels. Have you never touched another?"

"My teachers stayed far unless training demanded it. Then it was always…uncomfortable. The humans I lived with never tried to touch me. Sometimes I thought they might, but something always changed their minds without my even trying to tell them so."

Issa ached at the idea of the beautiful man never having felt the touch of a lover. His eyes seemed so expectant now, and so determined at the same time. She had the sense that he would do this even if it hurt him, and it might, but she would be here until it played out one way or the other. Whether she had to comfort him or fuck him were only two sides to the same coin for her.

"Stay there." She held her hand out, palm out halfway between them. "Place your hand against mine."

Kris raised one fist and slowly unfurled it, stretching his hand out flat in front of hers. His breathing quickened as he moved it closer and a sheen of sweat broke out on his upper lip. As his hand came incrementally closer to hers, her hand tingled with energy and a soft glow appeared in the gap between their palms. Issa sensed her well of energy seeking to escape into Kris, but without her release of it through orgasm, it would have to wait.

"Close your eyes," Issa said. Kris obeyed. Without the visual indication of their proximity, the draw of her energy seemed to take over. Without any effort on her part, his hand moved the remaining distance between them.

Kris let out a gasp when his palm met hers, fingertips to fingertips.

"You're soft," he whispered. He looked at their hands in fascination when she spread her fingers slightly, allowing his to twine between and clutch her hand. "I feel like I might break you. Does that hurt?"

Issa smiled. "You can't hurt me. Does it still hurt to touch?"

"No…it feels warm. Comforting," he said with a note of wonder.

Without releasing her hand, he raised his other hand and tentatively brought it to the side of her face. With the barest, tickling touch he traced the line of her cheek, continuing with his fingertips down her neck and over her shoulder, down the length of her arm, and up past her elbow to the wrist of the hand that gripped his own. He traced the entire path backward to her shoulder.

Issa's breathing became rapid, her heart pounding with each slight touch. Kris's eyes followed his touch and Issa watched his expression transform with each new discovery: the pliant silk of her lips, the wet texture of her tongue when she darted it out to taste the tip of his thumb. He pressed and caressed and sometimes pinched just a little while he explored.

"I'm made like you," she whispered.

"I know," he said. "But I already know what I feel like. You feel much nicer. Does Erika feel like this? The other women?"

Issa smiled and nodded. "They're all just a little different, but mostly the same. Dragons feel different from humans, too. You'll see."

"How?" he asked.

With a tiny surge of energy she let her scales show, her skin growing a brighter lavender and shimmering in the ambient glow of the altar beneath them.

Kris swept the flat of his palm along her arm. "You feel the same as before."

"Yes. Humans are a little smoother—softer. That's all."

He grew bolder with his touch, brushing both palms down her chest and around the sides of her breasts. He cupped them both, pushed them together, then released them, watching with fascination while they sprang back to their natural shape.

"I think women are a lot softer," he murmured.

"We are, yes." She sighed softly when he cupped her breasts again and dipped his head to taste each pert nipple. After several seconds of him doing laps around her nipples, during which Issa thought she'd lose her mind, he raised his head and pressed his mouth against hers.

The kiss was clumsy at first, the simple press of lips on lips, until she took control. She gripped the back of his head, tangling her fingers through his silky hair, urging him to tilt his head. He moved his lips experimentally, pulling at hers, darting his tongue out to run it along her lower lip. Issa let her tongue slip out to meet his and parted her lips a little more, inviting him in. He pressed his lips tighter against hers, the vibration of his harsh moan sinking into her mouth along with his slick tongue.

Without thinking, she spread her thighs and Kris moved between them. The scorching heat of his erection brushed along her inner thigh.

Kris's body went rigid in response to the contact and he pulled back from their kiss, hands gripping her shoulders tightly. He stared between them, panting from desire. His cock twitched against her thigh, just to the side of the deep lavender of her glistening pussy lips.

"Does it feel good yet?" Issa asked, her voice rough with need.

A lock of dark hair fell across Kris's forehead with his brisk nod. He looked back into her eyes, his gaze feverish. Then he pulled back and shook his head, grimacing.

"I have to wait. It's too soon. But Sweet Mother, I want to be inside you. Deep inside."

"Too soon?" she asked, confused. The energy she had gathered from the humans boiled inside her. Her entire body felt like it was pulsing with the need for release and he was *here.*

"We have to wait for the others. I can't begin until they're all here. The chamber might destroy me if there isn't another to give me their power soon after I take yours."

Issa caught a glimpse of movement over Kris's shoulder at the entrance. Geva stepped softly into the room, large and naked and more aroused than Issa had ever seen him. He looked just as hypersaturated with energy as she felt, his red eyes glowing. He reached behind himself and pulled Erika forward, then bent to scoop her up into his arms while he whispered something in his new mate's ear.

His entrance couldn't have been better timed, and she shot a quick thought to him to that effect.

"You don't have to wait any longer," she said to Kris. "They're coming now."

Kris looked back down between them, concentrating on her core. He gripped his hard length in one fist and centered it between her folds, letting out a stuttering breath when his tip brushed against Issa's swollen clit.

The buzz of his energy sent tingling currents through her. All of that would be given to the Queen along with her own abundant supply very soon.

With the tip of his cock seated just barely at her entrance he slipped both palms down her inner thighs and spread her lips apart, exposing her throbbing clit. He rubbed one thumb over it in a tight circle, sending a rush of heat through her entire body.

"Does that feel good?" he asked gruffly.

Issa could only nod and twitch her hips, aching for him to sink into her fully. He hissed in response to her motion over his cock, eyes closing and head bowing while he concentrated.

He sank in slowly and Issa watched the enjoyment grow with each incremental push until he filled her completely. And fill her he did, the soft velvet of his cock sliding so perfectly against the slick walls of her until he had his hips tightly settled against her thighs and ass.

She wrapped her legs around him and tilted up to meet his next thrust, accepting his kiss and the push of his tongue between her lips. Sweet Mother, he tasted like flying through an electrical storm, and it was good.

Kris kept one hand between them, rubbing rhythmically at her clit.

"Just fuck me," she silently said, too breathless to vocalize.

"Issa," he murmured. "I can't…you feel too good."

Issa could only make more inarticulate sounds of enjoyment to encourage him. He couldn't seem to stop touching her while he fucked her. With each rhythmic pistoning of his cock into her, his hands roamed, sliding over her breasts, down her sides, gripping her ass and squeezing. He slid both large hands up her thighs and pushed them wide, exposing her to him again. Each thrust grew more violent, more desperate.

"You have something to give me. Give it now," he commanded, rubbing at her engorged clit again until the energy overwhelmed the dam of her self-control. She came hard in a collapsing flood, thrusting her chest up, head back and voice crying out into the air above her.

The depleted sensation was almost instantaneous, the energy leaving her in a series of pulsing rushes. When she opened her eyes to look at him, the previously inky marks on his torso glowed bright white. He shuddered against her, his face contorting with his own soul-gripping climax. He bent his head against her shoulder and pressed his hands into the stone of the altar at her back.

The stone underneath his touch glowed blinding white and radiated out as though flowing from Issa to Kris and into the stone behind them. The air in the room crackled with the power as it pulsed from his fingertips at the same time his hot cum shot deep inside her.

Issa lay back against the warm stone of the altar. Kris lay atop her, his hands now both fixed against the stone. She could still feel the transfer of power like a steady stream until the pressure of its presence dissipated and she was left empty. Kris relaxed with his head on her shoulder, his body covering hers heavily. She stroked his hair and adjusted their position slightly, grateful for the supporting contour of the altar's curvature that allowed her to still see the rest of the room.

Geva came forward while Kris still knelt between her thighs, cock still embedded deep inside her. Erika followed, an eager look on her face.

"Our turn," Geva said.

CHAPTER FIVE

Kris closed his eyes and smiled. Issa had been so right. The aftermath left him buzzed and hungry for more. Too hungry, and a little weak, but he didn't want to part from her just yet.

"No," he said when she tried to get up. He gripped her hips tightly, preventing her from separating from him. His cock was still hard. He moved it in a slow stroke inside her slick depths. She sighed in response and relaxed, raising her legs back up and encircling his hips. The silken brush of her skin against his sent tremors of pleasure through him. It was even better than he could have imagined. He would fuck her forever if he could.

"I gave you everything," she said in protest. "I don't think I can come like that again."

A pair of figures approached, the large, red Geva slipped onto the altar behind him, reclining in the spot Kris had occupied earlier. Erika settled in a curved, seat-like depression by Issa's head.

"I'm a little jealous," Erika said. "Does he feel good?"

"Very good," Issa said. "You can find out if he'd only let me go."

"Why would you want that beautiful man to ever stop fucking you?" Erika asked, giving Kris a hungry look.

Geva's heat permeated the skin of Kris's back, the red dragon's breath hot against his neck. "Her well is dry," Geva said to Erika. "Why don't you fill her up again, my love. You said you liked her tongue between your thighs before. Give her more of your juicy quim to taste so she can keep him for a little longer. While you do that, I'll fill *him* up."

Kris closed his eyes at the hard throb of his cock when Geva's lips brushed against his neck with those words. The male dragon's hand slid over Kris's right ass cheek, already slick with the essence from the small well. Now Kris understood exactly what that liquid was intended for.

As uncertain as he was what to expect, he shook with excitement at the prospect of new pleasures to experience. Issa's glorious pussy squeezed down on his cock and he opened his eyes. His lover's face was now obscured by a pair of wide hips, a pussy he'd craved seeing for weeks poised above her lavender lips and her tongue already darting out to taste it. His eyes roamed up Erika's torso to her breasts that were gripped in each hand. She tweaked her nipples and smiled.

"Am I allowed to touch you now?" Erika asked while she rocked her hips over Issa's face.

Before Kris could answer, a warm hand at his back urged him to bend forward. He instinctively grabbed onto Erika's thighs to steady himself while a pair of hands squeezed his ass and spread his cheeks apart.

"I guess that answers that. Be gentle with him," Erika said over Kris's head.

"Aren't I always gentle, love?" Geva's deep voice replied.

"Until I ask you not to be," she replied in a suggestive tone.

A slick touch teased at Kris's tight opening. He squeezed Erika's thighs tighter, wanting to fuck harder into Issa at the same time he really wanted Geva to do just a little more to his ass.

Issa clamped down on his cock with her pussy just reinforcing how trapped he was between them.

He couldn't move or else he'd lose one of these sensations, and he wanted to feel all of them.

He closed his eyes again, becoming lost in the sensations. Erika's hands clutched the sides of his face, pressing a stiff nipple against his lips. He sucked, grateful for the command to action.

Geva pressed deeper with a gentle, probing touch. Issa's hips urgently rose up against him, pulling at his cock, but he still couldn't move with the tight grip Geva had on his hips.

He concentrated on Erika, sucking each stiff nipple into his mouth, rolling it against his tongue. Her entire torso undulated while she rocked her body over Issa's mouth.

"Oh God, that's it, shove that tongue deep," Erika gasped.

Kris opened his eyes and looked down. He might not be able to do anything, but he could still use his eyes, and what he saw was beautiful. Erika's clit was pink and wet over Issa's lips, Issa's purple tongue flicking at it, then disappearing.

Erika grabbed Kris's hand and shoved it between her thighs. "Rub me there, Kris. Make me come. She's hungry. God that tongue goes deeper than most men's cocks."

He knew hunger, he ached for more energy, more magic. He could already feel his power being depleted, drawing away from him into the altar. The walls of the room were pulsing with it, the shifting glow traveling outward and rising up the tiers into the walls and the ceiling above him.

Erika's wet heat coated his fingertips as he rubbed her throbbing clit. The motion of Geva's fingers against his ass mimicked his own fingers, pressing circles against aching flesh. The dragon behind him had a reservoir of energy filled to brimming, ready to give it to him.

Kris relaxed, pulled out of Issa's pussy just enough to signal his willingness to Geva, then pushed back into Issa with a hard thrust.

"That's it," Geva sad roughly against his ear. The red dragon thrust a slick finger past Kris's clenching barrier. Kris tightened then relaxed and pushed back again.

The squeeze of Issa's pussy urged him on, so he repeated the motion. With each push back, Geva fucked into him with his finger, then added another.

Just when Kris thought he couldn't take more from behind, Erika cried out and pulled at his head, crashing her lips against his while she came. She slid to the side in a boneless heap, smiling, then leaned up to kiss Issa in gratitude.

"You just worry about fucking and getting fucked, Kris. I'll take care of her," Erika said.

Kris nodded and closed his eyes, letting Geva control the rest. The stretch of fingers in his ass disappeared, only to be replaced by something thicker and hotter. He managed to remain poised on both arms above Issa, conscious still of her silken thighs sliding against his sides and her hips rhythmically thrusting up against him. Erika was busy with one hand between the lavender dragon's thigh's and the other at her breast.

Kris groaned at the deep thrust of the cock as it pushed into his ass, stretching him almost painfully, but it was a pleasurable pain he could handle—not the soul-crushing ache of futile, misspent desire he'd always felt before today. Once deep inside him, Geva gripped Kris's hips. The red dragon pushed Kris forward and off his own cock, the pressure causing him to sink deep into Issa, then Geva pulled Kris back until his cock slid deep in, hips nestled against Kris's ass.

The heavy pressure of Geva's length deep inside and slick friction from both sides of him were so intense his body felt on fire from the pleasure. His eyes locked onto Issa's and never left them, unable to articulate even a thought but he knew she understood. They were together now, the clench of her around him as much a signal of her feelings as the impression in his mind of how she felt.

Issa came again, her hips smacking hard up against Kris, the brief surge of energy Erika had given Issa rushing into him. The walls of the room brightened as it flowed through.

Geva growled in his ear and pushed him forward so that he sprawled inelegantly over Issa's body. She held him tight, letting her pussy clench and release around his still hard, pulsing cock. The sensation of being filled to the brink of overflowing triggered the first of the waves.

It all came crashing over with a harsh yell from Geva and a solid thrust that pushed Kris over the edge once again. Issa quivered underneath him, holding him tighter while he came. The fiery pulse of Geva's considerable well of energy coursed through him. It was hotter, more vibrant and shocking than Issa's had been, and a residue seemed to remain behind after it sank into the altar, leaving Kris tingling from head to toe.

Geva carefully slid out of him and Kris extracted himself from Issa. The red dragon smiled and wiped sweat from his brow. His chest heaved and he bent, breathless, surprising Kris with a deep kiss.

Kris collapsed beside Issa, pulling her close and finding comfort with his face nestled against her breasts.

"That was only the beginning, love," she whispered in his ear.

"I know. I just want to hold you for a second."

She shifted out from under him. "There will be plenty of time for that after, trust me."

Kris grasped at her as she moved away, the absence of her touch suddenly as painful as the initial presence of it had been. He didn't want her to leave, was about to mindlessly follow when a pair of soft, feminine arms wrapped around him from behind and hands trailed down his chest.

CHAPTER SIX

Camille saw the anguished look in Kris's eyes when Issa pulled away. She remembered that first departure when the lovemaking had ended between herself, Eben, and Roka and the two men left her alone briefly. Then Issa had appeared and urged them all back together. She could give Kris the contact she knew he craved, so she did, reaching around to embrace him from behind.

"We're all here for you, Kris," she said, cheek pressed against his back. "We won't let you go until it's over. Roka has a gift for you now. A little of me, a little of Eben. But you already got a taste of us all from Issa, didn't you?"

It seemed to be enough. Kris paused and sank back on his heels, bowing his head. He reached behind to squeeze her hip affectionately. His hand lingered and after a second the touch became more exploratory. His other arm reached behind, both hands stretching back to squeeze her ass.

"You do feel a little different from Issa. So did Erika," he said in a wondering tone, turning in her arms.

"Oh?" she asked, smiling up at him. He was so much taller than her, and so dark and exotic compared to the other men. She'd always admired his looks, but had never felt as strong a connection with him as she had with Eben. "How are we different?"

Kris's eyes traveled from her face down her neck and lingered at her breasts. His hands followed, tracing the sloping curve and cupping both weighty mounds gently in his palms.

"You're bigger in some places, smaller in others. Your skin is just as soft. It feels good to touch."

She inhaled a sharp gasp when his thumbs brushed across her nipples.

"Still sensitive?" he asked.

Camille nodded and reached up. Remembering that this was still his first time, too, she brushed her own thumbs over his nipples. Kris closed his eyes and sighed.

"You like that, too, huh?" she asked. He nodded, his eyes locking back onto hers.

Eben and Roka were both watching intently from the sidelines. Camille could sense their impatience to get on with things, but she'd insisted that she get to choose who did what this time around, and she'd just discovered one of her new favorite dirty little things to do.

"Lie back," she said huskily and pushed both palms against Kris's chest. "I learned something new tonight that I'd like to show you."

Kris obeyed, moving to recline back against the upraised curve of the altar where Issa had been resting earlier while he fucked her. Camille pushed his thighs apart and knelt between them, sliding her palms up his legs, over his muscular stomach and chest, then back down to the thicket of dark hair his large erection jutted out of.

"Sweet Mother," Kris muttered when she took his thick tip into her mouth. Camille marveled at the tangy flavor of him. That must be Issa she tasted—he'd been fucking her for a long time. Camille had wondered what the pretty dragon had tasted like. After Issa had taken such care to make Camille come, Camille had hoped she'd get the chance to return the favor. Giving it to Kris would be just as rewarding.

From the corner of her eye, Roka's massive, pale shape approached, his cock already stiff and loosely gripped in his palm. He stepped up onto the altar and knelt by Kris's head. The white dragon-man was so large that his hips were level with Kris's shoulders where Kris reclined. Just before Camille closed her eyes to take Kris deeper into her mouth, Roka's hand brushed Kris's cheek, urging him to turn his head. Kris shifted slightly, twisting his entire torso just enough to dart his tongue out to taste the tip of Roka's glistening cock.

Camille had learned already from two masters how to pleasure a man with her mouth. She'd insisted they both teach her in detail over the course of the night and they hadn't let her down, so now she believed she could teach Kris.

"Do to him what I do to you," she said.

Kris glanced down at her and nodded. "Okay, but I think I have a pretty good idea already."

Careful to keep her lips over her teeth, she sank her mouth down around Kris's cock so far his tip hit the back of her throat. She glanced up briefly, pleased that he'd done the same to Roka. She gripped his base with one hand, moving the other down to stroke his balls. He whimpered slightly and his hips surged up, thrusting into her mouth. She pulled back, stroking his velvet shaft with her palm as she went. She swirled her tongue around the head of his cock, taking care to tease at the underside just so before engulfing as much of his length as possible again in a long, slow sucking motion.

Behind her, she was dimly aware of Eben's presence. He was taking his time already, probably stroking himself while he watched. Camille's pussy was a hot knot of need between her thighs and getting even hotter the more she sucked. She hoped Eben would hurry up and fuck her, but he apparently had other ideas.

With the briefest of glimpses while she sucked on Kris, she could see Eben working his way from Roka down. Eben gave Roka a long, deep kiss, letting the dragon stroke him while he toyed with Roka's chest and ass. Roka let out a deep rumble of appreciation. Then Eben spent a few moments touching Kris, kissing his neck, sucking his nipples, and urging Kris to give his cock a few strokes, too. Camille almost laughed, but didn't want to lose her concentration, so she kept her eyes closed to block out her lover's antics. Eben seemed to love getting everyone to touch him.

Finally he made it to her, pausing to lay gentle kisses against her shoulder and whisper in her ear, "Take his cock like a pro, babe. I know how good that feels, especially with your pretty mouth wrapped around it. That's right. Suck him. Make him shoot his load all over those gorgeous titties so I can lick it off you."

Camille moaned around Kris's cock, already eager for exactly that to happen. Eben seemed to love coming up with new challenges for her and she was only too happy to follow through. She sucked and stroked Kris a little faster, moaning harder when Eben positioned himself behind her and tongued her ass and pussy over and over until it made her want to scream at him to fuck her and fuck her hard. But she had a task to complete and was loving it too much to stop.

It didn't take long. Soon Eben sank his shaft deep into her in a quick, impatient thrust. He bent over her back from behind, fucking her hard and rubbing her clit.

She emitted a strangled moan around Kris's cock and groped with one hand in front of her. A second later, Roka's large, competent hand found hers. He always knew when she was about to come. Eben was, too, apparently, and he also reached a hand out to clutch hard at Roka.

Camille couldn't help it. She had to breathe. Slipping Kris's cock out of her mouth, she continued stroking him with one hand, rubbing her breasts against him for added friction while she and Eben cried out in unison. Eben slammed into her, his hot cum shooting deep in throbbing spurts. His voice gusted hot and rough against her ear, urging her to keep stroking Kris, whose hips were rhythmically thrusting up against her chest.

Roka's grip tightened on her hand and he groaned. Camille looked up at him, loving to watch his majestic face when he hurtled over the edge. His eyes blazed white and his jaw clenched, then he threw his head back and let out an unholy roar to the ceiling while his hips thrust deep into Kris's mouth. Kris's face contorted and flushed red, but he took it all. Camille watched in fascination as the glorious tattoo that graced his torso lit up. Just then, a wet heat splattered against her chest and she looked down, realizing that she'd still been stroking him the entire time and he was coming hard all over her in streaks of thick white fluid.

Eben withdrew from her and she sat back on her heels, breathless and pleased at how it had gone.

"You're a genius," Eben said into her ear. He reached a hand around her and dipped a finger into the liquid dripping down one of her breasts. He trailed it in a circle around one of her nipples causing her to quiver slightly with pleasure.

"Allow me," a new and entirely feminine voice said from behind them.

Camille craned her head around to see the pretty golden-haired dragon girl, Aurin, move forward and kneel before her.

"I think there's enough to share," Eben said, bending to lick the creamy remnants of Kris's orgasm off one nipple. Aurin followed suit on her other breast while the male twin to the girl moved to the other side of the altar, scooting up close to Kris.

"Can't let you guys have all the fun," Aurik said. He bent his head and kissed Kris soundly, then pulled back and licked his lips. He gave Roka an appraising look and smiled. “So that’s what Guardian tastes like. I always wondered.”

CHAPTER SEVEN

Kris sat up and looked around himself in a daze. His entire body seemed to be vibrating from the rush of power still seeping into the altar beneath him. The room glowed even brighter now. Roka had moved away, taking up a spot behind Camille and merely watching with interest while Eben and the lovely, golden Aurin licked Kris's spunk off Camille's ample bosom.

The round, golden curve of Aurin's backside beckoned. He glanced at Dimitri first and the young, blond man smiled.

"You'll never forget being sandwiched between the two of them, trust me," Dimitri said.

Kris glanced to the side at the still grinning Aurik. "She's ready for you, friend," Aurik said, gesturing to his sister's already wet and glistening pussy. "Dimitri made sure of it. But are you ready for me?"

A deep voice called from nearby, "I made sure of that." Geva smiled in satisfaction as he reclined sleepily with Erika draped over him, watching with fatigue-glazed eyes.

Kris didn't see Issa anywhere and craned his head around looking for her.

"I'm still here," her sweet voice cut through the murmurs of the others and he found her seated out of the way on one of the tiers across the room.

"I'll be with you when you're done with them, I promise. In the meantime, I'm enjoying the show."

Her words gave him the push he needed to continue with greater enthusiasm. Kris rose to his knees and smiled around at the others.

"Alright then, let's fuck."

He gave himself up to the pleasure, finding a rhythm between the others for the first time since it all began. The dragons gave all they had to him, and Erika's team eagerly participated, slipping into the openings where they could be found. Some would pull back for a breather while others came forward.

True to his promise, Kris tasted every one of them, and they tasted him, in turn. Issa's promise held true, too. He loved it. Every second of every touch. Every stroke of a tongue over his skin, every tight squeeze of a slick pussy around his hard length or a thrust of a cock into his ass.

Just when he believed they'd surprised him every way they could, they managed to do it again.

When he thought it was close to ended, he realized there were two he still hadn't touched yet. The tangle of limbs surrounding him slipped away, leaving two figures still at the perimeter of the altar.

Kol looked uncertain, but Hallie tugged at his hand, urging him forward.

"He doesn't want to share," she explained. "But I told him I didn't mind. And look at him—he's about to go nova from all those orgasms he gave me earlier."

Kris sat quietly and nodded, knowing exactly how Kol felt about sharing. He was honestly grateful Issa had opted to eschew participation in the event aside from preparing him for it.

"I don't even have to touch her, Kol. You're the one who needs to surrender to me. It only needs to be the two of us."

Kol's worried frown smoothed a little bit, but didn't disappear entirely. "No, I know, but I want to please her, too. And she wants us both inside her."

Kris furrowed his brow, understanding the other dragon's hesitation. "You and I need to be in intimate contact for me to gather your energy. That won't work with her between us."

"But I won't be," Hallie explained. "I don't want you like that. I think Kol's just a little shy about being in such close quarters with you."

Kris didn't think he'd ever seen a dragon blush the way Kol did. He raised one eyebrow, intrigued at what Hallie proposed. His eyes fell to Kol's erection and contemplated its size, then looked at Hallie's compact form. She was taller than Camille, but narrower through the hips. She seemed to guess his thoughts.

"Trust me, if I can take Kol at his full size, I can handle the both of you at once."

Kris's eyes widened. Women were pliant and flexible, he'd learned during the course of the evening, particularly given enough lubrication, but he'd felt how very *tight* the others were and couldn't imagine being shoved inside Hallie along with something the size of Kol's considerable and impressive unit. Still, the idea held some interest. A *lot*, to be honest. He'd tried every configuration so far, and this was new, but *big* didn't even begin to cover the size of the dragon who stood before him in his human shape. Kol was easily the largest of all the males, even Roka. So big, Kol's deferential behavior toward Hallie seemed incongruous.

He glanced over to where Issa sat. She watched raptly and Kris's cock grew even harder in response to her interest.

"I would love to see what pleasure you get from this," Issa's voice purred in his mind. She leaned back now and began lazily stroking her nipples, one at a time, then flicked her long tongue out and licked one just for his benefit.

"Alright," Kris said, more flushed with arousal for seeing Issa begin to please herself.

He gestured for Kol and Hallie to join him. Hallie seemed to understand exactly what she needed to do, pulling Kol along until he knelt on the altar facing her. She kissed Kol soundly while sliding her hands down between his thighs and stroking his cock into a thick, hard column.

"Lay her down," Kris said. "Taste her, and tell me how she tastes while you do it. I've always wondered."

Hallie reclined in the same spot as the others had and Kol settled between her thighs, raising her feet up to his shoulders while he bent his head and fastened his lips on her pussy. The first thrust of Kol's tongue made her gasp out loud and push her hips up against his lips.

"She tastes like the sky."

"Does she need more lubrication?"

Kol sat back, licking his lips. His eyes were bright with desire when he pulled Hallie up toward him. "No, she's as wet as a monsoon. Touch her, you'll see."

Kol's eyes remained locked on Hallie's and he pulled her down with him as he lay back in the flat section of the altar. Hallie straddled him, letting her wet pussy slide along the length of his cock. Kris watched, fascinated by their interaction, so slow and deliberate. They hadn't parted contact at all while in his presence. Kol reached around to Hallie's backside with both hands and spread her open.

Kris brushed both palms up Hallie's inner thighs, her skin yet another erotic texture for him to experience. She quivered under his touch, her breathing quickening the closer he got to her center. He brushed the fingertips of both hands along the contour of her folds. Her soft fringe of fur was saturated with her juices. Sliding fingertips further in he found a deep well of heat so wet he thought he might drown in her if he didn't have a partner in the experience. She smelled like the jungle after a fresh rain so he wasn't the least bit surprised by Kol's assessment of her flavor. Kris brought one set of fingertips to his mouth and licked, closing his eyes in ecstasy over the taste of her.

He pressed his other fingers a little harder between her thighs, finding her pulsing clit and teasing it until she moaned and bit down on Kol's shoulder. Kris met Kol's hungry gaze over Hallie's shoulder. The Shadow was ready. More than ready from the feel of his twitching erection that rubbed against Kris's knuckles while he fingered Hallie.

Kol rumbled against Hallie's ear, "Are you ready to get fucked, love?"

"Yes!" she gasped, twitching her hips and rubbing harder against Kris's fingers.

"You do the honors," Kol said with a smile to Kris.

Kris shifted closer on his knees, straddling Kol's thighs behind Hallie. He gripped the other man's cock by the base, letting his palm brush across the heavy sac beneath it. Kol growled, his eyes narrowing, but he smiled a little bit, clearly enjoying Hallie's tense anticipation.

Kol urged Hallie to raise her hips far enough for Kris to extract the man's heavy prick and position it at her entrance.

Kris could sense Hallie's need to be filled, visible as it was from the clench of her tight opening before his eyes. Unable to resist, he pressed two fingers against her. They slipped inside the scorching velvet heat of her and his eyes fluttered closed at the tight squeeze of her around his digits. He pulled back out and slicked the coating of moisture along the length of Kol's cock, inciting a rough moan from the other man, then rubbed the remaining slippery fluid over the head of his own engorged shaft.

Kris held Kol's cock steady while he pressed his own against Hallie's eager entrance. He held Kol's gaze when their tips came into contact.

"Now," he sent wordlessly. Kol nodded and tilted his hips up in a slow, even motion at the same time Kris pushed his own inside.

Hallie moaned, her ass quivering under Kris's grip. Kol's full length slid against Kris's cock, deep into the depths of Hallie's pussy, and kept going for a second when Kris had hit his limit. Hallie's muscles clamped down hard on them both, pressing them together in erotic, slippery communion.

With silently shared understanding, the two men began moving in unison, fucking slowly at first. Hallie pushed back, eagerly meeting them. In such tight proximity to Kol, the energy surge built quickly. It seemed the other man began deliberately causing additional friction against Kris's cock by thrusting just a little bit faster and deeper, so they weren't quite a single co-unit fucking Hallie, but two independent shafts sliding against each other, just out of sync.

Hallie cried out in an incoherent curse and buried her face in Kol's neck. The Shadow tilted his head back, letting out his own long, low groan.

Kris closed his eyes when the beginning of the energy surge began. He thrust deep into Hallie, the electric friction of her and Kol together causing blackness to cloud his vision. Kol's large hands gripped Kris's hips, holding him tight and deep while Hallie let out a series of harsh yells. Her climax milked both men into oblivion.

Kris's muscles all seemed rigid as stone for a split second, his concentration focused between his thighs and the rocket of his orgasm surging together with the Shadow's. The throb of the other man's cock pushed Kris even further over the edge than he could imagine until he found himself freefalling through the well of Nirvana that flooded from Kol through him and into the altar.

He was only dimly aware of collapsing to the altar and lying against the warm and brightly glowing stone.

CHAPTER EIGHT

B*rother, we finally meet.*"

Kris opened his eyes to find himself surrounded by warm, glowing light. He had no sense of up or down. None of the others were nearby, nor could he hear evidence of them. All Kris heard was the resonant female voice coming from all around him.

He had no frame of reference for anything aside from his own body, but even that felt somehow unfamiliar. When he looked down at his hands, he instead saw a pair of massive, iridescent talons. He took a step, testing his motion and weight. A heaviness and overwhelming sense of mass enveloped him.

He sat back on his haunches and stretched, feeling new limbs. *Wings?* And more than that, even. He moved his backside and the sensation of yet another limb stretched out behind him. He moved it experimentally and the sleek tip of a tail swept around and hovered before his eyes. Curious, he looked down between his thighs and cocked his head, staring in wonder at the huge, erect cock that jutted up between his scaled thighs.

It shimmered, the light causing its smooth surface to display a myriad of colors.

"Yes, Brother," the voice said with a hint of humor in the tone. *"You have arrived. You have been reborn, in a sense—come into your own. The ritual was a success. I am awake now. You have one final task, however."*

Kris had so many questions for his elusive sibling, but knew they would have to wait until the end of the ritual.

"What is it…Sister?"

"My mate. He should have come to me already, but he hasn't yet. I am still alone in my chamber, waiting. Without a proper mark, I can't sense him, and you know I am forbidden from leaving the temple without a mate."

"Corey…he's been resistant to the idea of the ritual since the start. I will try to convince him."

"You must do better than that, Brother."

"I will."

The light brightened to a blinding degree and he closed his eyes, but just before he did, he caught a glimpse of a brilliant green serpentine shape. The image evoked a distant memory, something that had come to him once in a dream long ago. He grasped at it, tried to hold on, but it slipped away like mist through his talons.

***

In the fog of the aftermath Kris imagined he was weightless, flying through a cloud of glowing, pulsing light, the sounds of ecstatic pleasure filling the air around him. He had the sense of Issa by his side, her gentle voice comforting in his ear.

The sense of place came back to him gradually. He opened his eyes and peered up into a pair of lovely eyes as violet as the dusky sky. He lay on one of the tiers away from the altar, his head cradled in Issa's lap.

Wondering if it had all been a dream, he raised his hand up to stare at it. Human fingers waved in the air in front of him, but with the barest intention his skin tone altered slightly and the hand grew and elongated, sharp claws springing painlessly from the tips.

"You did it," Issa said.

Kris smiled up at her, his chest warming from the hint of pride he heard in her voice.

"You helped."

"No, I just watched. You were *magnificent*."

"You did more than watch, and you know it." He reached up and traced a fingertip down her jaw, letting it trail further, down her chest until he reached the tip of her bare breast. He paused and drew a tight circle around her nipple with it, enjoying the way the purple flesh grew stiff. The earthy scent of her sex reached him a moment later and he realized all the things he'd done with the others, but had yet to do with her. He understood Camille's enthusiasm for the entire experience. Everything was new and wonderful, especially when you'd never been touched before.

Kris shifted on Issa's lap, preparing to push her back and spread her thighs. He craved the taste of her now like he'd wanted nothing else before. He wanted to bury his tongue in her pussy and maybe come up for air in a hundred years. He turned and gripped her thighs, squeezed them, then groaned in frustration.

"What is it?" Issa asked.

"I've got something I need to do first. Don't go anywhere, alright?"

"I've waited five hundred years for you. What's a few more minutes?"

He bent and kissed her. It was an effort not to give in and stay, but he forced himself to turn and leave.

Of course Corey was nowhere in the small chamber, but when Kris glanced up toward the entrance, he saw the tripod with the camera perched on top, focused at the center.

He walked out the door and found Corey seated on one step in the shadows of the staircase, head tilted back and resting against the wall. His eyes were closed, his brow creased intently, his lips curled down in a tight frown. His hands rested in his lap, but when Kris looked more closely he realized Corey wasn't just resting his hands there, he was cupping himself gingerly.

"If it's any consolation, I know exactly how you feel right now."

Corey's head snapped up and his eyes opened. He stared at Kris in surprise.

"I didn't hear you come. Well, actually, I *did* hear you, and all the rest of you *come*. Like, every ten minutes for the past two hours. Jesus you guys are unstoppable. How the fuck do you… *fuck* so much?"

"You could have joined," Kris said. "You'd feel a lot better now if you had."

Corey looked him up and down, appraising. "You seem more relaxed than you have since we met. I always wanted to ask what your deal was, hanging out away from the group when we were in camp. Shit, I think there were only two of us who *wouldn't* have banged you, knowing how the others operate."

"And now there's only one."

Corey held up his hands, palms out, and shook his head. "I'm not fucking banging you, man. I think you've had your fill already. It's bad enough that all of you have been running around naked all night."

With a chuckle, Kris sat across the corridor on the same step and rested his elbows on his knees.

"You're in pain, aren't you?" he asked.

Corey remained quiet, then nodded. "Yeah. Worst blue balls of my fucking life. I tried to stay and film you guys—Erika wanted me to—but fuck if I could watch. There was a second there when that little golden beauty aimed her backside at me I almost fucking lost it."

"So why didn't you? Dimitri strikes me as the sharing type and he has more than enough to go around now."

"Because…I don't *do* that. It's against my nature, I guess. I don't fuck other men's women. I don't fuck other *men*, come to that, no offense…I do see the appeal, but no. Not for me. I guess I'm just not wired like the rest of you. And fuck…Camille surprised the hell out of me. Of all the women in this party, I never expected *Hallie* to be the conservative one where sex was concerned. Jesus, I know way too much about all of you now."

"And being intimately familiar with your friends is a bad thing?"

"Well, no. But it does feel a little…incestuous? I have to ask, those two…the golden ones with Dimitri…they're related, aren't they?"

"Twins."

"See, like that. Incestuous."

"They don't touch each other except platonically. Trust me, I watched every second of their phase with Dimitri. They're more like…" Kris struggled for an appropriate analogy, wishing he'd been allowed to spend more time learning about popular Western culture. "They're a team, I guess. Partners after a common goal. Dimitri was that goal. Technically only one of them was supposed to have him, but they're devious."

"Huh."

Kris glanced at Corey, who seemed to be processing the details. After a second Corey said, "I guess there's someone for everyone, even if it's two people. What about you?"

"What about me?" Kris asked.

"You just had sex with all my friends, man. Right in front of me. First, I think kudos are in order for having that much goddamn stamina, but where do you stand on actual—you know—*relationships*?"

Kris stared into the distance, at a loss for an answer. It had never been a topic of consideration during his training, but he remembered the dynamic between Zak and Darius. Mutual respect, intelligent conversation, caring gestures that were never overt. Once Kris had seen his two teachers behave in a more intimate way their behavior toward each other in public had taken on a different meaning. He realized, with a sudden jolt, that they had loved each other. Probably very deeply. Had their relationship affected him somehow without him even knowing it? All they had explicitly taught him was how to focus, how to fight, how to track, how to be who he was now becoming. He'd once asked them to show him how to do the things they did in private. Darius had looked upset. Zak had merely told him that was something he'd learn on his own when the time came. They were always right.

"Relationships?" Kris finally said. "I have no idea. I only came here with a task to complete. And I just did—mostly. But if what you mean is who do I want to be with? Well, she's been very patient with me so far, but I can't imagine anyone else I'd rather devote the rest of my time to after this."

"The purple one? I saw her with you a couple times. She definitely has the hots for you, that was clear."

"Issa. Her name is Issa."

"Right, sorry. I have the worst people skills sometimes."

Kris laughed. "And you've actually lived with people your whole life. I grew up in a monastery."

Corey sat up abruptly. "Bullshit. After that performance? Tell me it was a monastery where they train you for nothing but sex."

"Issa was the first person who ever touched me." And she'd be the last if he had any control over the situation.

Corey seemed to marvel at that idea. "You two. Wow. I thought that would be the end of it after you guys fucked. Just watching you with her rocked my world. I remember thinking, 'now that's what lovemaking should be like'. Not the fucking part so much, but all the leadup. She was invested in every single second, even though you were being a jackass at first. I…I want to be that for a woman."

"A jackass?"

"Fuck no, man. *Invested.* You turned it around. Then all the others had to get in on the action and it ruined it for me, but there was that sweet few minutes when I was on the edge of my seat, just dying for you to …"

"To what?"

"I don't know, tell her you loved her. That would have been the cherry."

"There's someone for you, you know. You can have that, if you want it."

Corey stared at the ceiling. His face looked troubled, confused. "No," he said. "She's not even human."

"You know who I'm talking about?"

"Kol said something. This…ritual. The Queen? I guess I'm the only one left for her. Talk about leaving dregs. You should have given her Erika first, they'd have hit it off fantastically. But I can't. I just fucking can't."

"You're a better person than you know, and she's not like the others."

"What, she's not a nympho?"

"Ah…No. She's my sister."

That confession seemed to draw Corey back. Kris could tell the man's paradigm was shifting. Kris had interacted with him closely for the last few weeks. He'd probably talked more with Corey than he had with either Dimitri or Eben. The group's tech had been the friendliest, most open male in the group, which had drawn Kris in. Conversation was easy with someone willing to openly share their thoughts the way Corey always did. But opinions could cloud perceptions in the worst way.

"You're one of them," Corey said in an awed tone. "So, let me get this straight…your sister wants a date and you're probably going to kick my ass if I don't show up for it, huh?"

"I won't kick your ass, but I can't guarantee its safety if the rest of these guys find out you didn't show."

Corey's shoulders sagged. It wasn't so much a gesture of disappointment, or even of resignation, but of relief, which struck Kris as odd. Corey smiled at him and nodded, gesturing up the steps. "I guess I've gotta go get ready for a date, then. Wish me luck."

As Kris watched Corey stride up the steps he realized what it was about the man. Corey's sense of honor was what drove him onward, not the desire for sex, or glory. He just needed a purpose to follow through on.

And Kris had all he needed now, too. A new purpose beyond seeing this ritual through to completion. As he walked back down into the chamber he watched Issa. He could already feel her soft skin under his palms, hear her throaty moans in his ear. He wondered whether it was a quirk of dragon nature that made him look forward to immersing himself in a life with her and no one else, even though he knew most dragons tended to collect multiple human mates. But they weren't most dragons, were they?

When he reached her, he sank down on his knees before her. He only rested his hands on her thighs, instead of spreading them wide to pleasure her like he'd intended to do when he left her moments earlier.

"What is it, Kris?" she said, brushing her fingers through his hair.

"I love you. If there's nothing else that I've learned from this, it's that I need to tell it to you as much as I need to show you."

If the Mother was willing, he'd have several lifetimes to do both.

SLEEPING DRAGONS

BOOK 6

ASCEND

OPHELIA BELL

Love will release you.

CHAPTER ONE

Corey stood in the center of the corridor staring at the massive green jade double door. He felt like a fool for deciding to go through with this—*date*—or whatever it was. As much sexual eye candy as he'd witnessed over the last few hours and as frustrated as he was as a result, he'd always considered himself the kind of guy who cared about more substance in his partners.

It had been Kris, finally, who had changed Corey's mind about going through with this. Kris who had made him understand the unique nature of these people their team had awakened. He had a hard time thinking of them as anything other than people, in spite of the fantastic shapes he'd seen them take. He'd drawn a few of his own conclusions, too. Very unscientific conclusions, probably, but he had a feeling Erika or the others might agree with him.

In spite of the very sexual nature of their new friends, each one of them ultimately had seemed human to him in one very particular way. They weren't mindless sex fiends. That realization had come, ironically, in the middle of watching the only orgy Corey thought he could ever stomach. He'd stayed to man the camera for as long as he could endure, but in that span of time he'd seen how attentive and caring each of the dragons had been to his or her lovers.

Corey had been with his share of lovers, all women, but only with one of them had he ever come close to feeling what he'd seen in all the dragons' eyes during the course of that night. It made him ache in a much deeper place than his balls to think he could have that again with a woman. He just hoped this particular woman wouldn't end up finding him wanting after a few months and leave him for a richer man.

Hell, she might hate him from the beginning, but he'd been on plenty bad dates and the world hadn't ended as a result. Shit, he hoped the world *didn't end* if this went badly. He'd seen some of the magic the dragons could do and wondered how much more they were capable of when full-up. *Like Kris shooting fireworks from his fingertips*, Corey thought. If only a normal orgasm could feel *that* good. Just being in the room at that point would've been enough to make Corey's cock hard as a rock, if it hadn't been already.

Corey wiped his damp palms on his pants and took a tentative step forward. Should he knock? Or should he just go in? All it had taken Dimitri was a touch to the doors of that chamber and they'd opened up, like he'd done it with the power of a thought.

"Fuck it," Corey muttered and rapped the knuckles of one hand lightly on the carved jade figure that graced the front of the door. He only had a second to regret which part of the woman's image he'd managed to choose to touch before the doors both swung inward. He hurriedly raked shaky fingers through his hair and wished fervently that he'd had more time to prepare—to bring her flowers or something. As it was, all he was showing up with was a raging hard-on that hadn't subsided in hours. He'd finally just written it off as something he'd have to live with for the time being.

He stood on the threshold, gazing around at the interior of a massive chamber easily the size of the throne room. It was completely lit, and at the far end was a huge bed with four columns of carved jade rising from each corner.

He almost didn't see her, as small as she was relative to the scope of the room and the bed. When he finally realized she was there, seated serenely in the center of the bed, he raised a hand and gave her a tentative wave.

"Ah…Sorry I'm late."

She only nodded and raised a hand to gesture for him to come forward. Once he was a few paces in, she made another slight gesture and the doors swept closed behind him.

Corey's heart pounded as he looked over his shoulder at his only means of escape. But escape from what, exactly? He swallowed his anxiety and turned forward again to take a good look at this *dragon queen* he was somehow so irrationally afraid of. He stepped a few more paces into the room, keeping his eyes on her. She seemed so placid, sitting there, just watching him come to her. Halfway into the room he stopped, deciding that was far enough. If she wanted him, she'd have to meet him the rest of the way.

Now that he was closer he could see her very clearly. His uncertainty replaced by cautious interest in the lovely figure. She was a petite young woman with skin so fair it glowed and thick black curls that fell past her breasts. She had the same Asian features as Kris, though much more lovely and feminine compared to the guide's. Of course, Corey reminded himself, she was Kris's sister. Her bright green eyes watched him take her in. He only made a cursory glance of her body, quickly shifting his eyes back up when he realized she was stark naked.

Of course she's naked, dummy. This is like the dragon nudist colony. Though he supposed dragons might not normally wear clothes when they were being…well…*dragons.*

She frowned and finally spoke. "Do you not find me pleasing to look upon, human?" Her voice sounded light and smooth, and carried easily across the expanse of the room to his ears.

Corey cleared his throat. "Oh, trust me, I find you spectacular."

"Then why won't you come to me?"

Corey stood blinking at her. She sounded genuinely confused by his hesitation, but not in the way he'd have expected someone with the title of "Queen" to sound. She cocked her head in an endearing way, waiting for him to respond.

"I'm not sure what you expect so I'm just being cautious, if that's alright. I'm not in the habit of just jumping into bed with a pretty girl the first time we meet, I don't care how kinky you normally get with your lovers."

"What can I do to appease your reservations?"

Corey took a deep, calming breath through his nose and rubbed the back of his neck. Eyebrows raised slightly, he said, "Well, you *could* start by telling me your name. Then maybe we just talk a little?"

"My name is Racha. And you are Corey. My brother told me of you before you arrived at my door."

"Oh? What did good old Kris have to say?"

"That you are not like the other humans, but I think you are."

"And what makes you think that?"

"You're here, and you want me."

Now *there* was the Queen he'd expected. Her assertion irritated him, which he hated because she wasn't lying. Except it was a hollow want he felt, not the deep abiding need he'd seen in the others' eyes, particularly Kris's just before he'd made love to Issa for the first time.

"Maybe I just don't want you enough," he said.

Racha grew thoughtful. Her gaze slid over his body and paused at his hips before moving back to his eyes.

"Prove you don't. Take off your clothes."

Heat rushed to Corey's face at the command. The hell he'd strip naked. Well, he might have just to prove the point, except being naked in front of her would only prove the opposite.

"I have a better idea. Why don't you put something *on* and we can talk about this like two sane people who…I dunno… actually get to know each other before fucking."

CHAPTER TWO

Racha was fascinated by the human's reluctance to bed her. All the others had participated so enthusiastically. She was brimming with the power the others had fed to her and could taste how willingly the humans had given of themselves. All except for this one. That he'd resisted participating thus far either meant he was physically incapable or he had some other aversion to the act. And the evidence of his body's willingness was as plain as day.

Tired of the vast distance still between them, she gave in and left the comfort of her bed. She'd slept there long enough already. Perhaps it was the bed itself he had a dislike for?

As she approached him, a bright flush rose up his neck and into his cheeks. He kept his eyes averted, first to the floor, then to the side when she stood before him almost close enough to touch.

"Do you prefer males?" she asked, leaning up on tiptoe to whisper the question in his ear. The answer was evident from the swell in the front of his britches, but she enjoyed the irritation on his face nonetheless. It almost got him to look at her again.

His jaw muscles clenched and he shook his head curtly. "I prefer a woman I can talk to, that's all."

"And my naked body is not worthy of words?" She gazed down at herself and slid her hands over her slight curves. The touch felt nice, but not as nice as his hands might feel—his hands that were now clenched tightly by his sides. She began to slowly walk around him. When she paused in the direction his head was turned, she saw his eyes were tightly shut.

"Racha…" he began in a desperate tone. He opened his eyes finally and let his gaze rake down her length. Her nipples prickled tantalizingly when the look lingered on her breasts. His hands relaxed and he raised one up. He gently cupped her jaw and she gasped, surprised at how warm and gentle his touch was against her skin, in contrast to how rough his calloused fingertips felt. "You are worth more than a word or a touch, I'm positive. You might be worth the entire universe, but until I know more about you, this…" He swept his hand in a gesture down the length of her body. "…isn't happening."

She let out a deep sigh, expelling a cloud of thick, iridescent breath that she manipulated into a diaphanous gown to cover her naked body.

"Alright," she said once he'd finally relaxed a bit more now that she had hidden all her best assets. "Let's sit and talk."

She sat cross-legged right where they stood and peered up at him. From a lower angle he appeared even more impressive than before. She'd liked the look of him the second he'd walked through the door, and even found his obstinacy endearing in a way. He was so very different from the male dragons she knew, all bent on their various seductions, eager and willing to devote their unflagging attentions on as many partners as possible. It became a game to most, even the females, to collect multiple lovers just to prove their prowess.

Racha tasted the Nirvana of five of the humans who had entered the temple, and the essence of the dragons who had coaxed it from them. It was power she would not keep, however, for it was the power with which she would awaken the rest of the sleeping brood that occupied the smaller chambers throughout the temple. The human man who sat before her was the key, and he seemed oblivious to the effect holding that power in check was having on her.

She could be patient for a time. She would have to, even though the scent of him had made her almost uncomfortably wet and caused the power she held to pulse insistently in her core, seeking release. Now she watched the play of the muscles beneath the fabric of his shirt when he finally bent to sit across from her, knees bent and his arms resting casually across them. It was a defensive posture, unlike her own. Even though he couldn't physically see her spread labia, the light brush of her gown over her skin made it difficult to forget how aroused she was.

"Tell me what you would like to know," she said. "I am an open book."

CHAPTER THREE

Corey felt like such a lech sitting across from Racha and struggling not to imagine how open her book might be just then. Was it some trick of the air currents in there that he could imagine the lush scent of her sex thick in his nostrils? He was at least grateful that she'd covered up, though her wispy gown left little to the imagination.

Now she sat looking attentively at him, waiting for him to speak to her, to tell her what it was he wanted to know.

He couldn't think of a damn thing to ask. All he kept thinking about was his first date with his ex and how they'd hit it off so spectacularly that they'd ended up in bed forty-five minutes later. He hadn't needed any prompting for conversation with Jill—they'd had too much in common already, including both professional and extracurricular interests. Not to mention there had been that amazing spark of attraction that he'd felt instantly when they shared a joke. He'd always been that easygoing with women. It wasn't until after she'd left him for some corporate executive only a few months later that it became pretty much impossible to carry on a conversation with another woman without instantly comparing her to Jill.

He owed this lovely young woman something.

"I'm gonna go out on a limb here and guess that you have no idea what a 'date' is, do you?" he asked.

She frowned and shook her head. "I admit I will have to reacquaint myself with human conventions, but I'm hoping you'll be the one to show me."

Corey was struck by her unassuming attitude now that they were seated across from each other, on fairly equal ground. He took a fresh look at her, trying to shed the preconception of her as a dragon queen. Her sleek, black curls were a little mussed and one of her gauzy straps had slipped off one shoulder. Her slightly slanted, almond-shaped, green eyes watched with intelligent curiosity, maybe just a little eager for him to move things along.

"We'd be having sex right now if things were going your way, wouldn't we?" he asked softly.

She lowered her dark eyelashes until they brushed the tops of her pink cheeks and nodded. "Yes. You don't understand the effort it takes to wait, but we will wait if it makes it a better experience for you."

"Tell me what it feels like…to be…like you are."

"Like a dragon? Or like the Queen of Dragons?"

He shrugged. "Both, if you want."

"You observed the others, did you not? Being a dragon is like that. Giving pleasure to as many as we can, or to one person many times. It's that energy which sustains us, allows us to do our magic. Even this gown I wear for you required energy. Maintaining this form requires energy, but it is second nature. Some of my energy is innate but not all of it. What my brother gave me does not belong to me, it belongs to the others. I must give it to them soon."

"The others…do you mean this *brood* that Kris mentioned?" Corey couldn't disguise the apprehensive tone in his voice. He still didn't quite know what to think about the idea of a multitude of magical flying, fucking creatures taking over the world as a result of what he might do today.

Racha smiled proudly. "Yes, the brood. They're my children."

"Hang on," he said, shifting backwards a couple inches. "You've gotta have a…a…*mate,* or whatever you call it to have kids, right? How many are there in this brood of yours?"

"Corey, no, they are not my blood children. We are all of the same generation. I've never mated. I've never even played at it like other young dragons do. But as Queen, I am both mentor and caretaker of all of them. I spent my early life training for this honor before I slept.

He relaxed again. "So you're like the CEO or something. Or maybe a cult leader," he muttered.

Racha laughed, the sound low and melodic. "I know of cults. It used to be a cult that we relied on to awaken past generations, but the mates from those groups made poor parents. I had the good fortune to have two dragon parents, but other dragons aren't so blessed. Luckily the imperative to breed is strong enough that most dragons have multiple mates so the dragonlings don't want for adequate role models."

"Right, and a parent dead set on fucking everything in sight is an adequate role model?" He'd seen the male dragons in the group earlier. With the exception of Hallie's Kol, who he'd actually come to respect, he found it hard to stomach how easily the others seemed to be with fucking—well, anyone. He wasn't sure if their tenderness during the act was enough to justify the promiscuity.

There was that laugh again, the sound catching his attention and holding it like his favorite song always did. It sank into his mind, calming him.

"Don't let the ritual give you the wrong impression of how we behave. Yes, sex is one of our key methods of survival, but if you could only conceive perhaps three children in a decade wouldn't you try to take advantage of every opportunity you could?" She cocked her head cutely, but the words still sank in.

"So you're telling me that the whole purpose for this ritual was to knock up all our women?" Corey could hear his voice rising in pitch and was about to run out of the room and force condoms on all the other men if he had to.

"Knock up?" She shook her head and stared at him, uncomprehending.

"Yeah, you know…*Impregnate them.*"

"Oh, Sweet Mother, no! The ritual's sole purpose is to awaken the brood. Impregnation is not possible until we leave the temple. And even then it's not guaranteed for dragons, even if their mates are willing."

"Oh." Corey deflated and the rest of what she'd said finally caught up to him. He did the math. Five hundred years, the dragons had been here. In ten years of what she suggested might be sex every bit as enthusiastic as what he'd just witnessed, they might conceive only *three* children? "Geeze, I'm sorry. How many dragons are there, anyway?"

"Several hundred. Our numbers are strictly monitored. There are never more than a thousand of us in any generation."

"Christ. I'm one of seven kids. I have about a dozen nieces and nephews, too."

Racha's eyes widened at his confession. "How many humans are there now? When we slept there were maybe a few hundred million."

"Ooh, there's a lot more of us now. A *lot* more. More than seven billion last count."

Racha froze and stared at him, her mouth working, but no words came out.

Corey relaxed, the wide-eyed wonder at what was in store for Racha giving him the upper hand for the first time. He might still have an incredible hard-on for the beauty, but seeing her flustered over the idea of how outnumbered she and her brood were at least gave him slight comfort. It didn't make him stop wanting her, though. On the contrary, it made Racha—the Queen of Dragons—even sweeter to him. Suddenly she wasn't this unusual creature who could do magic beyond his imagining, who could very likely command his cock with a twitch of a finger. Now she was just a young woman, embarking on a new life and very much out of her element.

His protector instinct kicked in and he shifted closer to her, reaching for her hands and holding them gently between his.

She twitched in surprise at the sudden contact and he realized it was the first time he'd touched her.

"Shh," he said. "It's really not so bad out there. You guys seem to like having more of us anyway, right?"

She recovered quickly, but didn't remove her hands from his. Her grip tightened around his fingers and a jolt of pleasure shot between his thighs, reminding him of the perpetual hard-on he'd been sporting since the last room.

"Yes, but right now I have you. Will you show me the ways of this new world? I know human nature well enough, but conventions shift. Will you help me, Corey?"

Was it crazy of him to want to say yes? She was just a girl trying to find her way, and she needed his help. With four younger sisters he knew how thankless the task of older brother could be, but also how rewarding. Except he didn't feel particularly fraternal toward this pretty young woman.

He sensed a strength in her that his sisters never had. Something iron-hard and probably razor-tipped that kept him from giving in and trusting her. He was attracted to that glimmer of strength, but wasn't the least bit fooled by her plea.

"No, because I don't trust you." He gave her a pained expression and released her hands gently. He regretting having to disappoint her, but he had to tell her the truth. "I just can't do this. I'm sorry. I'll help if I can, but you'll just have to find someone else to do the deed."

CHAPTER FOUR

Racha stared down at the space between them where their hands had been joined. How was she supposed to make him understand? If what Corey said was true, the modern world she had awoken to was far different from the one she'd fallen asleep in, but that was the least of her concerns.

"I do need you, but not for the reasons you think." Racha reached for Corey, but his hand shot up quickly and gripped her wrist before it reached his cheek.

"No. I've seen your power. I think the only thing you need from me is a good hard fuck and after that we'll be done. Tell me, do you really want me? Or am I just some surrogate prick you can use to escape this prison?"

The strength of his grip startled her at first, but the ferocity of his gaze angered her. "Let go of me! You don't understand!"

"You're a dragon. You have power. Make me understand." His brows drew together shadowing his already dark eyes. Eyes she'd begun to get lost in while they spoke, but which now frightened her.

Frustration beat at her will as she struggled against his strong grasp. How had this man not given in to the magic already like the rest of them? "I can't force you! My magic doesn't work that way."

"I don't care how you do it. If you want me to know how badly you need me, make me understand why." His eyebrows raised in emphasis and he let go of her wrists, leaving them tingling from his touch. She wished she could go back just a few moments to better enjoy the first gentle grasp of his fingers around hers. He was a good man, but not a one to suffer secrets easily.

Racha's chest constricted with a tight, painful feeling she'd never experienced before. She stood up abruptly and walked away a pace, struggling to contain the emotions welling up. Wet droplets trailed down her cheeks and she raised a hand to wipe at one.

She stared at the crystalline orb on her fingertip, not comprehending what it meant but knowing she'd been beaten. There was no recourse. No other alternatives. If he didn't agree to their coupling there was only one thing left to do. The power was already swelling to a breaking point within her. It must be close to dawn.

She sighed shakily and nodded, still refusing to face him. "There is an alternative. The power is persistent. We are each other's slaves right now, the power and I. You would have been the key to our release. If you won't give yourself to me, the power will take its course anyway."

"What do I need to do?"

"Leave. You're safer out of this room."

"No. Tell me what to do. Let me at least help."

She turned on him, her chest tight with rage as much as sorrow. "You want to *help?* What I want more than *anything* is for you to *fuck me.* But it isn't just to release the others. I…I want you."

She wanted him like she couldn't believe—for his strength of will as much as his strong body. A man who had withstood the magic of the temple throughout the entire ritual and held out only to give her a chance at convincing him to give in would have been a perfect mate.

She cursed herself for the lack of effect her words had on him. She'd been so strong as a young dragon. She excelled at her training, was described as persuasive and effective by her teachers and the Council both. Yet this *man* somehow made cracks appear in her foundation that she'd never known existed.

He didn't answer her, just looked away again, his jaw clenching. If he wouldn't have her, and wouldn't leave either, there was only one other option.

"I want you to bind me before it's too late. The power will force me to change and I may not be rational when it takes over. If you insist on staying, you must bind me or I can't promise you'll survive until dawn."

She held her tongue on the last plea she could have given him that may have changed his mind, but to tell him now would only make her seem weak and helpless. She would not end this night by begging.

CHAPTER FIVE

Corey's chest burned, the conflicting emotions warring inside him. Yes, he wanted Racha but that wasn't enough to compromise his principles. In another time, perhaps he might have gone through with it but not now. Not after everything he'd been through with Jill, then the failures with women after her. He was grateful Erika had seemed to see that damaged part of him and steer clear in spite of their attraction. Hallie had tried, but both of them had known it wasn't meant to be.

Racha shot one last beseeching look at him, her bright green eyes brimming with tears, then nodded and turned toward the bed.

Somehow Corey knew the tears were real, and not some ploy to manipulate him into changing his mind. Why did that understanding make him suddenly feel like crying, too? He could do this thing she asked. Bind her to her bed and try to give her some comfort through her ordeal. Company was something he could offer her, at least.

He followed her, watching the sway of her hips and the ripple of her gauzy gown where it draped alluringly over her slight curves. Abstractly he thought a woman more perfect for him probably couldn't exist, at least in terms of features he preferred. Petite and beautiful, with just the right amount of muscle mass relative to soft curves. He could easily picture gripping her round bottom while she rode him and those intense green eyes looking into his, her dark-lashed eyelids fluttering with pleasure while he…

Get her out of your head, man. You don't even know her!

Maybe after he got her through this they could talk more. Maybe something *could* work out for them both. It was just way too soon for him to lose his mind over a woman because of sex. He wanted a clear head when he decided whether or not he could love her.

Her skin seemed to pulse with a luminescent internal glow as she crawled onto the bed and lay down in the center.

Corey had to climb on after her to reach her. He did his best not to look at her while he found the ropes that were already fastened to the green jade columns of the bedposts.

Racha silently raised her arms. When Corey stole a glance at her face, her eyes were closed, her cheeks still streaked with tears.

"How long will this take?" he asked in a gentle voice. The rope slid silkily through his fingers as he secured one of her wrists deftly in a sailor's knot, then moved to tie the other.

"I don't know. I think it happens instantly when the sun rises, but I can feel the power pushing to get free already."

Corey glanced at his watch. Sunrise was only a short while off, by his calculations.

"Should I tie your feet, too?"

"Yes."

"What does it feel like?" he asked while binding her ankles to the other two bedposts.

She let out a soft moan and shimmers of pale light traced up the skin of her feet and legs where Corey held them. The barest texture of greenish scales was visible as the light traveled up her lower legs.

"It feels pleasurable sometimes, but others…" Racha's words halted with a strangled cry and her back arched violently, limbs straining at her bindings. Her free foot kicked away from his grip and Corey barely managed to dodge it before it smacked into his jaw. He gripped her ankle and quickly secured it with the rope.

Corey moved up beside her once the spasms subsided.

Racha lay panting, her chest heaving from the exertion. Her brow shimmered with green-tinged sweat.

"Shh," Corey said. "I'm with you. I won't leave you until it's over, I promise."

Racha gave him a weak smile that disappeared when another ripple of light passed across her skin. Her lips parted and her brow creased as though she were bracing herself for the next painful episode.

The spasm began and she let out a strangled cry. The sound rose in strength, becoming a deafening roar incongruous with the petite form it escaped from.

At a loss for what to do, Corey rested one large hand against her shoulder and squeezed in an effort at comfort. Her skin felt feverish to the touch.

The bed shook and her skin rippled not only with light but with undulating waves of motion.

The barely there slip of a gown she wore faded away like dissipating fog. Translucent green scales replaced it, covering her arms, legs, and torso. Only her creamy-white breasts remained bare and pristine with small, erect pink nipples.

Her body collapsed back against the bed, limp and panting.

Corey slid closer to her and carefully leaned on one elbow so her cheek rested against his chest. With his free hand he brushed sweat-drenched curls off her brow and caressed her temple.

"You'll be alright." Impulsively he bent and pressed his lips against her forehead.

"T-tell Kris that he and Issa have my blessing." She slurred the words out in between harsh pants to regain her breath.

He kept ahold of her through the next series of seizures that wracked her body from head to toe.

"Tell them yourself when this is over" he said gruffly. He was so tense with worry for her he'd entirely forgotten the previously persistent discomfort from hours of aching arousal. In fact, he was pretty sure his cock had gone on vacation.

Her fever grew with each body-wrenching spasm. During the next one, large, coiling green horns emerged from her forehead and tangled up with her curly, sweat-drenched black locks. Her eyes glowed with green fire and a green, forked tongue darted out to lick her dry lips.

Tears streamed unchecked down her cheeks and Corey reached up to brush them away with a thumb.

She shook her head, nearly delirious. "Corey, thank you for staying. You would have been a fine mate. I am sorry."

Her words had the weight of the words of a person in the throes of death. Corey struggled to suppress an irrational panic that solidified like an icy stone in his belly. She hadn't said what would happen, had she?

"Do I need to get Kris? Can someone else help?" He feebly grasped at ideas. Something wasn't right, but she hadn't told him anything. He had been right not to trust her, but for the wrong reasons.

Her green gaze latched onto his, wide and terrified, but also resigned to her fate. Her entire body shook against her restraints.

"The energy will consume me alive like this. But it was…the only other way to give it to them. They must awaken. If I have no release by my mate's touch, the power will still find a way out. It is my burden…and my honor."

"No! There has to be some other way!" Had it really come to this, because of his own ridiculous sense of propriety? What a goddamned hypocrite he was, too. *Yeah, man, when the dragon queen asks you to fuck, you say, "How hard?"*

Racha shook her head. "Too late…" she murmured in a weak voice just before another spasm gripped her body, forcing her head and feet to dig into the bed and her torso to torque violently.

He'd been such a fool not to read the signs. The resignation, her nearly exhausted look when he tied her, the tears. She wasn't such a weak woman to give in to rejection by crying. Her tears had meant something completely different, and the understanding chilled him to the bone.

The light from beneath her skin became nearly blinding, pulsing from every velvet scale. Corey hurriedly stripped and waited for her body to sink back to the bed again.

"God help me," he said. He hoped it wasn't too late for her. She had said she would shift, and the transformation was clearly occurring, but had only gone partway so far if what he'd seen the other dragons do was any indication. Perhaps there was still time if he hurried.

When she relaxed again he wasted no time.

He pressed his mouth to hers, tenderly at first, then harder when a moan escaped her lips and she raised her head to kiss him back. The wet velveteen sensation of her alien tongue filled his mouth. Within only a few seconds he was rock hard again.

He pulled away, breathless, whispering, "I'm sorry. Why didn't you tell me it would kill you?"

Her nipples had become a verdant shade of green, but the color didn't faze him now. Not the way their hard, pebbly texture felt on his tongue.

"Please don't stop," she gasped, her chest now arching up to meet the teasing suck of his mouth on her breasts. Fuck, she tasted amazing. Refreshing to his heated arousal, in spite of how much hotter her skin was under his tongue. He had no time to pause and savor her now, though.

Corey cursed himself for tying her. Had he just known… what would he have done? Bedded her in a more proper way while still resenting the fact of doing it? Taken his selfish time to gain his own pleasure from her body?

Now he had no choice—make her come or watch her die, likely in a brilliant show of fireworks that would rival Kris's.

"Racha, baby. I've got you. I'm going to fuck you now. You'll be okay soon."

He pressed fingers between her spread thighs. The wet heat that he encountered sent his head spinning. She was slick and ready and so hot.

Her bindings made the position less than ideal, but she tilted her hips up into his touch as far as she could. He met her desperate gaze as he moved to lay atop her, holding his weight off her body with one arm while he used the free hand to guide his throbbing tip between her folds.

"Please hurry," she said through green-tinged lips. The telltale surge of illumination began to glow beneath her skin again, beginning at the tips of her horns and running southward.

She is even lovelier like this, he thought as he slid deep inside her with one quick thrust.

Racha's head pressed back against the pillows and she cried out.

She's a virgin, you asshole!

Corey hesitated for a split second until he saw the slight smile on her lips that widened just a bit when he pulled back out slowly. He thrust again, more gently the second time, then again, encouraged by her soft sigh and the press of her naked torso up against him.

His body rejoiced at the sensations of her skin against his, her tight sheathe gripping his cock while he buried it over and over inside her. Yet this wasn't about his pleasure now. While he knew the tricks of many women's bodies, he'd never been with this particular beautiful young woman. She felt more heavenly beneath him than anyone else in memory. Would her body have the same response to him as his did to her?

Sensing her urgency from the intent look on her face, he reached between them and pressed his fingers against the swollen nub between her thighs.

After just a few circular strokes, she cried out and her slick muscles tightened around his cock. The intense squeeze of her overwhelmed him and he struggled not to lose his pumping rhythm before she was ready. It was an effort to hold back, but he didn't to restrain himself for long.

At that moment, she arched her chest into him and let out a harsh, gasping cry. The light within her coalesced into a hot, white ball of ecstasy between them. It grew in brightness and intensity until it encompassed them both.

An electric buzz seemed to pass through Corey. He lost strength in his arms and almost fell atop her. At the last second he reached up and gripped her hands above her bindings, entwining his fingers with hers while they rode the currents of power that rocketed through them, pushing ever outward.

The heat of it reached searing proportions. The resonance of a singing chime filled Corey's head as intense as both their cries. Electric vibrations coursed through his body, from the point where they were joined to every extremity. Visual pulses of light shot out from them both and he could feel each one taking a piece of him with it. He was about to die here with her, from the pleasure of her contact and the explosive release of his soul in one complete and glorious moment. And he had no regrets. Not even this. Especially not this.

Just when he believed the power would tear them both apart, it exploded, the energy rolling out and away from them, surging through the walls of the chamber and making everything it its path glow and pulse with power in rhythm with their own orgasms.

With the departure of all that immense power went the remains of Corey's own energy. Nothing was left behind but two sweating bodies, their panting breaths echoing starkly in the chamber.

Corey struggled for a moment to keep himself up. He had just long enough to look into Racha's eyes to ensure her continued consciousness. He was incapable of speech himself, but hoped his own expression would convey the magnitude of what they had just shared.

When their gazes met, he registered an expression of unrestrained gratitude, before he finally gave in and collapsed, breathless, beside her.

CHAPTER SIX

The exhaustion Racha felt in the aftermath was a welcome respite from the intense pressure of the power that had finally been released. She still wanted more of Corey, however, but knew it might not be possible. He had only done what he had to save her life. She was grateful, and would find some way to reward him, but it wouldn't be in the manner she had always dreamed.

She clenched her eyes shut tightly, struggling to hold back more tears. She'd already cried enough in his presence and refused to now, even though the departure of his thick, hard length from inside her had left her feeling every bit as empty as the absence of the power.

But she was alive, at least. The elated murmur of hundreds of dragon voices reached out to her in diffident gratitude. That was reward enough. It would have to be.

Dimly she became aware of gentle tugging at her wrists, then her ankles. She opened her eyes when Corey was at her feet and watched in open admiration at the flex of his broad shoulders while he untied her, then tossed the bindings across the room in disgust.

He ran large, shaky fingers through thick, tousled brown hair. He looked as beaten down and exhausted as she felt, but seemed to gather himself together with a deep breath. She braced herself for what he would say when he turned to her.

He said nothing, at first. He just turned and knelt between her ankles, raised one foot to his thigh and rubbed the skin gently where the rope had dug into it. It was tender, but the skin wasn't broken and his warm, calloused touch felt nice. It felt even nicer when his large palm slid higher, skimming up her smooth calf.

Racha tried to pull away from his grip and rise, but he held her ankle tight.

"Hey, pretty dragon lady," he said with a smile. "You just stay put a little while, alright?"

"You don't have to. You did what I needed you to do. You can go now."

Corey frowned and picked up her other foot, beginning the slow, delicious massaging again.

"No, I can't. You see, I'm the kind of guy who sticks around. I'm also the kind who pays attention and I've been watching the rest of this crew all night—well, most of them, anyway. One thing I noticed is that at the end of each little *phase*, all of my friends were given a sort of…well…gift."

"I won't mark you if you don't want me to." She knew what she offered was against Dragon Law, but there were always extenuating circumstances during awakenings. Concessions would be made.

Corey shook his head and narrowed his eyes at her. His hands continued their tender caresses, now along the skin above her left knee. His touch sent pleasant tingles straight between her legs. He shifted his hands so that both palms skimmed down her inner thighs.

"If you want me to trust you, Racha, you need to start spilling your secrets. I'm pretty sure those little tattoos the rest of my team got are damn important to you all, or the other dragons wouldn't have wasted so little time doling them out. Tell me what they mean to you and why you didn't give me one."

Racha closed her eyes. Her mind churned over how to tell him. She didn't want to bind a man to her who didn't want her, but she feared he would accept her mark out of some sense of obligation. Just like he'd finally given in and helped her release the power.

She'd survived the awakening. Perhaps the Council would understand if she failed to mark him. They could let Corey find another female more to his liking and send Racha a mate who was willing.

She gasped when his fingertips reached her core and teased along her lips, still wet from their combined juices. He sank his fingers into her slowly, then drew them back out again and teased around her clit in tortuous, slow circles. Even though he'd untied her, she was too mesmerized by his touch to move away.

When he pulled his hand away after a second, her hips raised up on their own, seeking contact.

"Please," she whispered. "I need more of you."

In truth, she was depleted of all but the barest wisp of power now. If he would only bury himself in her again and give her more, perhaps she could think of the right answers.

"More of this?" He leaned down beside her and flicked his tongue over her nipple while his fingers moved back between her thighs, caressing just enough to make her crave more, but not giving it to her.

"Yes, more!"

"Answer my question first. Why didn't you mark me?"

Just when her throbbing need had subsided and she thought she could regain her senses, he began again. He thrust his fingers deeper and teased her clit so expertly she thought she might just lose control. Except he stopped again.

She nearly cried out in frustration until she felt a hot, hard pressure pulse against her hip. Her eyes flew open and she looked at him.

He gazed down at her, a fevered expression on his face. He looked almost haggard with longing.

Experimentally, she shifted her hips slightly so that she rubbed against him.

Corey's eyelids fluttered and fell shut. His hand came to rest on her mound again, fingers gently stroking as before.

"You still want me?" she whispered.

His voice came out in a rough growl. "Like nothing I've wanted in my life." His eyes opened again and he met her gaze.

In those brown depths she saw the truth of his words, and it shattered her. The tears began again, only this time they weren't from sorrow or regret.

She sat up abruptly and captured his mouth with hers.

Corey tried to push her back, a mumbled objection making it to her ears, but she pushed harder, forcing him back against her pillows. He went, pulling her with him.

She kept kissing him, peppering his face, his neck, his chest with more kisses, elated at finally understanding. Once she let him have his breath and had moved down his torso, he let out a low, frustrated grumble.

"You gonna answer my question?"

She only nodded and smiled up at him from between his legs. She would answer all his questions, but first she needed more of him.

His hard shaft was coated with the flavor of them both. She savored every inch when she slipped her mouth over his tip and down, licking and sucking as she went.

"Oh, fuck, baby. You're driving me crazy. Do you…" He seemed intent on saying more, but the rest only came out as a strangled groan when his hips rose up off the bed in a violent jerk.

His orgasm flooded her tongue as sweetly as the power it carried into her with his abating pleasure. The sweet rush of his Nirvana invigorated her, cleared her mind and conscience, and left nothing behind but the exultation of being with him and knowing he was not unwilling as she had believed a few moments earlier.

She crawled back up his body and lay fully atop his panting chest.

He gazed up at her, a perplexed and slightly irritated smile on his face that disappeared as he let out a hearty laugh.

"That was nice. More than nice. But you're not off the hook that easily," he said.

"I am an open book," she said with a grin.

Then she explained everything.

He held her tightly and buried his face against her neck when she stopped talking.

"Are you angry?" she asked.

"God, no. I just…Racha, you could have died before I ever got a chance to learn how good this feels. That thought terrifies me."

He suddenly flipped her over and kissed her roughly. His resurging erection pressed hot and hard against her belly.

She laughed. "What are you doing?"

"Forgive me. I just need to make love to you again. Gotta make extra sure you won't self-destruct."

Racha pushed back against him and sat up when he leaned back on his heels.

"What is it?" he asked.

"There is just one thing I need to do first, if you're willing. Are you?"

CHAPTER SEVEN

A*m I willing to be hers. Marked. Branded. Bonded?* Corey's mind ran through all the things she'd told him the mark meant. She admitted she hadn't told him everything, just what mattered.

He'd always imagined the day he would ask a woman to marry him. He'd get down on one knee, hand her a ring after saying something particularly eloquent that he could never have thought up himself. There might be music playing and champagne. And ideally they'd have been together long enough that he knew all her secrets well enough that there would be no surprises.

This isn't the same thing, by a longshot, he told himself. But somehow it was. Commitment wasn't something he was shy about. Hell, he'd come on this expedition, hadn't he?

Yet every moment of this expedition had been a surprise and Racha was just the cherry on top. Fate was telling him something and maybe, for once, he ought to listen.

Corey looked down at the petite beauty, finally letting himself hear what it was fate wanted for him. He answered her question with a kiss, tongue sliding deep. Every ounce of hesitation or reluctance disappeared with the stroke of her tongue against his.

He spent a second vaguely aware that when they kissed her tongue felt as solid and fleshy as a human tongue. As human as all the rest of her now that the power had ebbed and her skin had regained its normal pink sheen.

Except this is not normal for her. What I saw before is closer to what she is. The idea didn't bother him as much as it might have the day before. On the contrary, it made him want her more.

He held still while she traced her lips down over his jaw and throat, closing his eyes at the silken caress of her lips and tongue. She paused at his chest and pulled back. A gentle fingertip traced a large pattern on his pec just over his left nipple, leaving a tingling sensation behind.

Corey looked down just as she darted her forked tongue out to redraw the same pattern with swift, stinging strokes. The sting didn't bother him any more than any of his other tattoos had. Nor did the understanding of what it meant. She had explained that the glowing magic that infused the mark protected him, and established their bond—one that would not be broken until one of them died.

The gravity of the small ritual hit him when she gazed up into his eyes. Her fingertips dug a little harder into his naked thighs. She seemed to be waiting for his reaction. He didn't feel any different, however. The abiding need to be with her hadn't changed, only now it was accompanied by a sense of permanence. Far from frightening, the feeling was a comfort.

"You're what I've always wanted," he said.

Racha raised up on her knees and wrapped her arms around him. He embraced her and carried her back down to the bed with him. Even the sounds she made were perfect little breathy moans as he explored her body with mouth and hands.

Her fingers tangled in his hair when he lowered his head between her thighs for the first time, tongue flicking out, eager to taste the sweet place his cock had been deeply buried in earlier. She spread her legs wider and tilted her hips up to meet the thrust of his tongue deep into the hot, velvet depths of her. His head buzzed from the tangy flavor and heady aroma of her sex. He had to taste the flood of her climax before he made love to her again.

She writhed and cried out when she came and Corey braced himself for a violent, spectacular surge of energy, but all that happened was exactly what he'd hoped—the drenched folds of her pussy spasmed against his lips, coating them with even more of her sweet flavor. He lapped it up, ignoring the giddy twitches and stuttering breath from her until he'd had his fill.

"Are you ready for more?" he asked, rising up onto his knees and gripping her hips. He tugged her toward him until his hard cock slid against her well-attended pussy. He smiled when her eyes rolled back and she nodded.

With a slow, deliberate thrust, he buried himself deep into her. He fucked her as slowly as he could endure, watching her face with each stroke to gauge where she found the most pleasure. She quickly reached the point of quivering, pent-up need for release again.

"Touch yourself," he said gruffly, pushing her legs a little wider and hooking her thighs over his arms.

She gave him a fleeting smile in acknowledgment before her face drifted back to a mask of pure enjoyment. Her fingers slipped between her thighs and Corey groaned at the way she gripped him at first, squeezing the base of his cock while he pistoned into her.

Her gorgeous, small breasts thrust up when she arched her back in response to the first touch of her fingers on her clit. She rubbed in tight little circles, obviously adept at pleasuring herself, but seemed to lose rhythm the deeper and harder he fucked her.

He sucked first one pert nipple into his mouth until she moaned, then the other. The tight squeeze of her pussy became more than he could endure.

Her hips bucked hard into his. He yelled out her name and bent over her, fucking with an erratic, pumping rhythm while his climax gripped him. The shuddering pull of her muscles surrounded his cock and milked him dry.

The glow that accompanied her climax was subtle at first, then grew brighter, coursing through her in tiny ripples across her skin. He watched, enthralled until it subsided and her eyes opened. She gave him a sleepy smile.

"You're glowing," he said.

"So are you." She gestured at the mark on his chest. He looked down to see that it was, indeed, glowing with a faint, green light.

"Does this happen every time?"

"Now that the ritual is finished, when we please each other like that, we share our energy. You give me your Nirvana and I give back some of my magic. It protects you. It also reminds other dragons that you belong to me."

"Oh?" he asked with a cock of one eyebrow. "And who in their right mind would steal from the Queen? Not that I'd go with anyone else, of course."

"No one would, but the mark will ensure you're treated with the level of respect deserved of the Queen's Consort."

Consort. Corey let the title roll around in his head, not sure how he should feel about it. It sounded a little fancy for a guy raised by a traditional, blue-collar family like he had been. He brushed it off as yet another old convention her kind had that they'd learn to outgrow once they acquainted themselves with the modern world. But if the mark gave him an advantage over other dragons, that was a good thing, right?

A thought occurred to him. "So what's to remind other people…or dragons that you belong to *me*?"

She tilted her chin at his chest again. "That mark means I'm yours. Dragons can bond with many humans, but many of us choose only a few as true mates. Some only choose one—the fewer we choose, the stronger our bond is."

She seemed to grow a little pensive and turned away from him, burying her head in her pillow.

"Well that's good, right? We both got pretty lucky, I think." He lay down beside her and brushed his palm down her back.

"It depends on what the world is like out there now and if you can endure a lifetime with me."

"Hey, what's this talk of enduring? I'm in this for the long haul. The world's mostly pretty great. Confusing as fuck a lot of times, but you're a bright girl, you'll get the hang of it."

She turned back to meet his gaze, her lips pursed. "I'm not concerned about adjusting to your world. It's you adjusting to *our* world that worries me. "

Something niggled at the back of his mind as he attempted to comfort her, though. The whole *lifetime* thing.

"Wait, you've been asleep in here for how long? Five hundred years?"

She nodded solemnly.

"So, when you say 'lifetime' how long are we talking?"

She eyed the mark on his chest again. "My magic…. As long as I share it with you, you will live as long as I do."

Corey narrowed his eyes at her evasive answer. "Spit it out, Racha."

"Another five hundred years, give or take."

He leaned back and stared at the ceiling. "'Give or take,' she says," he muttered. "What about the others?" he asked, looking at her again.

"It works the same for them, though the more mates they collect, the shorter their lifespans. Some consider it worth the sacrifice, others don't."

Corey had never in a million years considered he'd walk away from this expedition with such a confounding gift. But it sounded like she was hedging on something.

"What aren't you telling me?"

"It means we are bound together for the duration. Some mates can't endure it. After the first century they go a little mad. Some commit suicide rather than go on."

"So, we can still die…"

"Yes. Did you think we were immortal?"

"Well, from my perspective it sure seemed that way. But wow…Imagine the things you can see in five hundred years."

Racha grimaced. "My mother told me it was easier living in the monastery. The world was cruel when I was a child, and crueler still during the lifetime before Mother awoke. She always said it never changed much between generations."

Corey tried to recall all he knew of ancient history. Half a millennium ago wasn't precisely the dark ages, but it may as well have been from his perspective. She was going to be overwhelmed by the changes, and he was only too eager to show them all to her and see how she reacted.

"Everything moves a lot quicker now than it did when you were young."

"But you weren't even there, how do you know?"

"Erika and the others can tell you—it's their specialty, not mine. All I know is that in *this* lifetime, two people can speak to each other instantly from opposite sides of the planet, and it takes about a day to travel that far. But humans haven't changed all that much. We still eat and shit and fuck. We fall in love and we make babies and we try to raise them to be like us and fail miserably. My point is, the world is changing faster than even I can comprehend right now, but at the same time it's all the same.

Having centuries to absorb it all could be a lot of fun. Especially with the right person."

Racha smiled at him. "I'm glad it was you who came into my chamber today."

"So am I," he said, laying a kiss upon the swell of her creamy breast.

She rose abruptly and with a breath was pristinely coifed and clad in a much more solid piece of clothing than she'd worn for him earlier. If it were possible, she looked even more stunning.

"Where are you going?" he asked.

"It's time to meet the brood. You should dress. I can hear their eagerness to leave—they are already assembling in the Grand Hall."

Corey grabbed her hand before she could walk away.

"No matter what happens, I'm with you," he said.

"Thank you."

CHAPTER EIGHT

The excitement in the huge hall was infectious. Erika stood near the front of the Queen's dais, as giddy with the mood as the rest of them. She stared around, marveling at all the beautiful figures that filled up the tiers that surrounded them.

"Geva, I had no idea there were so many of you!"

Her lover's arms wrapped around her waist and his lips brushed her ear. "We are all here thanks to you and your friends. I will spend the rest of my life thanking you for your sacrifice."

She snorted out a laugh. "Sacrifice? With that tongue of yours, I promise, the pleasure was *all* mine."

The other members of her team had gathered around, standing before the dais that held the throne. Waiting.

"What do you think is taking them so long?" Hallie whispered.

"I bet they fell in love like I did," Camille said, eyes twinkling. Erika eyed the pretty blonde where she stood flanked by the two beautiful men who couldn't take their hands off her. Even now, Eben was stroking her back and Roka held her hand, pulling it up to his lips and kissing it periodically.

All the dragons had foregone their preferred nudity in favor of garments in every color. Erika admired the man at her side. How sexy would he look in modern clothes if he cleaned up this nice? What he wore now mimicked her own attire of loose-fitting shirt and draw-string linen pants—the cleanest things she had packed for the expedition. Geva had admitted that he could clothe her with his magic but refused to because he'd rather keep her naked.

Kris and Issa stood off to the side, sharing private whispers. Erika nudged Geva in the ribs with her elbow. "Use your fancy mental skills to ask what's taking them so long."

Geva let out a suffering sigh that would normally have provoked a deeper dig into a man's ribs from her, but the smile on his face let Erika know he enjoyed it. He grew quiet for a moment.

"Kris says they're on their way. And…No, I shouldn't say."

"The hell you say. Tell me!"

Geva grinned. "And he says the Queen sounds very happy and satisfied. Your friend Corey performed wonders, it sounds like."

Erika was on the verge of retorting when the doors behind the dais opened, and the pair emerged. Corey looked tired but radiantly happy…happier than she'd ever seen the good-natured tech. On his arm was the loveliest woman Erika had ever seen. Erika gaped for a second before realizing that everyone around her had fallen to their knees and bowed their heads. *Holy shit! Right. I'm in the presence of royalty.*

"What the hell?" Corey whispered, the words just barely audible to Erika's ears when they all knelt.

"Everyone, please stand."

The Queen's voice was strong and light and carried audibly through the room. Erika liked her already.

When all were standing again, the Queen introduced herself.

"I am Rachasara, your Queen, whom most of you already know. This is Corey." She paused to grasp Corey's hand and gaze up at him admiringly. Erika raised an eyebrow. The man did have skills if he'd made her that happy.

The Queen continued. "He tells me the changes between our birth time and this time are very drastic. Our transition may take more time than past generations experienced, but our awakening decree remains unchanged."

Erika heard murmurs of surprise and excitement and turned to look behind her. The Queen continued talking, but Erika was too fascinated—and possibly too exhausted—to focus on her words, instead becoming distracted by the activity of the other dragons. Corey had his camera on, at least, though she expected none of their footage from the last twenty-four hours would ever see the public eye.

Geva's hand clutched her hip, urging her attention back to the front.

The Queen stood before her, arms outstretched. Corey was behind her, rubbing his neck in embarrassment.

"She wanted to meet you first," he said apologetically.

"Of course!" Erika grasped the outstretched hands affectionately. The woman had startling, slanted green eyes and a sweet, heart-shaped face.

"Corey says you are the one to thank for the awakening. I am eternally grateful to you." The Queen cast a sidelong look at Geva who had seemed to recede a bit behind Erika. "Any favor you ask, I will be happy to fulfill. Even for him."

"Um, thank you so much, your highness. I hope we can talk a bit less…formally soon. I have a lot to ask you."

The Queen smiled. "Call me Racha, and I would very much like to talk." She gave Erika's hands another squeeze with her tiny, delicate fingers before moving on to speak affectionately to Kris.

"What the hell was that about?" she asked Geva who had moved back to her side.

"I told you I was a bad boy. She only knows me by reputation, so I didn't take it personally."

"Well, good to know she's forgiven you, I guess."

Geva shrugged, the overtly careless, nonchalant gesture more of an indication of his self-consciousness in the presence of his *liege* than any words could be.

"You feel *bad* about what you did, don't you?" Erika asked.

"Yes," he said, meeting her eyes squarely. "I would give anything to redeem myself. I don't feel worthy of *you* with that hanging on my past."

"Jesus, you fool. That was centuries ago! I don't care! And I get the feeling she's giving you a clean slate, too. So take advantage of it. Be better. Or just be very, very bad with me and me alone." She gave him a wicked grin, enjoying the growl and hungry kiss she got in return.

His erection was pure and present against her hip, but Erika got the sense that right here and now, amid the entire congregation, as it were, was not the place for them to indulge themselves. And the truth was, she very much looked forward to having Geva in her own domain for a change. Maybe tied to her bed in her apartment in Boston. She wondered how well her old bed could withstand the weight of a dragon. Or maybe she'd open up her family's estate again to give them more room and sturdier furnishings.

Her pulse picked up thinking about revisiting the place where she'd grown up. Particularly her father's study where she had first found the glimmer of a clue that a race like Geva's might even exist.

It was done, she realized. The last twenty-four hours had been a whirlwind. Had it really only been that long? Her watch, which she'd recovered from the pile of clothing in the first chamber when she dressed, told her that it was barely even dawn, and they'd arrived just after sunrise the day before.

Now there was a multitude of very much living and breathing dragons milling around the room. The excitement was infectious.

"What happens now?" she asked Geva, but he'd left her side again. She looked around for him, and found him and the other Court dragons standing in the center of the room.

The eight beautiful figures joined hands in a circle and raised their arms above their heads. The air above them began to shimmer. All heads in the room tilted back to observe.

Erika felt hands grip her own from either side, but her companions remained silent, as awed as she was at what was transpiring.

Before their eyes, the huge, round dome of the ceiling glowed orange as though with the breaking dawn. Waves of light hit it from beneath.

In unison, the eight figures walked backward, drawing the circle of light wider and wider until their circle encompassed the entire ceiling. Then they began to shift. Their clothing disappeared and their bodies grew. Colored scales replaced human skin. Horns coiled from graceful, elongated heads. Thick tails extended from the ends of their spines.

A moment later, eight horned heads craned up, breaths swirling together in a twisting cyclone of colorful fog. Erika's skin tingled, whether from the crackling magic in the air or simple exhilaration, she couldn't be sure. Either way, it was a spectacular sight, particularly seeing Geva's breathtaking true shape at full size.

The column of variegated smoke reached the dome and exploded in a burst of light.

When the spots receded from Erika's vision, the view above was of a clear morning sunrise, wisps of clouds still tinged pink but beginning to glow brighter each second.

The entire hall erupted in a flurry of roars and beating wings as the dragons that filled it shifted and ascended. Free for the first time in centuries.

Erika's hands were numb from the tight grips of Hallie and Camille, her vision blurry from the tears that streamed down her face.

"Beautiful," someone murmured, and she was dimly aware it was her own voice.

The others moved away while Erika still gazed up, enraptured at the sight of all those majestic horned, winged creatures taking flight.

"It is time, my love," a deep, resonant voice said.

A gust of warm breath against her neck brought her back to the present. Geva's massive, horned head took up her entire field of vision. He cocked sideways to gaze at her through one eye.

"Time for what?"

"Time to fly. Climb on."

***

Destiny. It had never meant anything to Erika even though it had drawn her to this expedition from the very beginning. That first day in her father's study, finding his sketches of the creatures he was sure existed but none of his colleagues would believe in. It all made sense now. This was where she belonged.

Well, maybe not *here*, in the literal sense. She looked around the austere but comfortable room she and Geva had been given at the monastery the dragons had flown to in their exodus from the temple. The trip had been both spectacular and terrifying, clinging to Geva's back while her team followed suit with the rest of the Court.

They'd finally landed on an island that had to be somewhere in the South China Sea if her sense of direction was still working. A throng of monks prostrated themselves in greeting to all the dragons, this time, not just the Queen and her retinue.

But what happened after they left this place? *Destiny,* her irritating inner voice said again. So, she believed it, and she did kinda give them all the benefit of the doubt. Particularly when one big, red dragon was insistently pulling her into a white-sheeted bed and tearing off the clothes she'd quickly thrown on to meet the Queen. *A bed. Yes, a bed would be good.*

Oh, Jesus, none of that mattered when his cock was fucking her. Dragon fucking *magic*. Followed by the pleasant burn of her tattoo and basking in the glow…a literal glow, she realized. That was new, but somehow not the least bit surprising.

Geva murmured against her sweaty skin. "We may be here for awhile, until each of the dragons is sent home. But if you can endure a wait like this, so can I. I don't really care where we are. I just want to love you for the rest of my natural life."

"Which means dragging me along for the next few centuries?" They'd had the conversation already but Erika still felt overwhelmed by the thought of being held in these arms every night for what seemed like an eternity for her.

"Yes. And others, if they're willing. It doesn't just have to be *me* who you endure. I'm sure we can find someone else equally irritating to distract you."

She laughed, but the prospect encouraged her. She loved him. Christ, it was crazy, but she did. Yet, was it so bad that she couldn't imagine five hundred years fucking one man? But if there were more of them, would she even want to share? Or even be shared?

"Why are you so tense?" he asked, massaging her shoulders. "I'm trying to make love to you but you keep me on the outside. I don't understand."

"No, you don't. Because you're not like us!" She cringed over her outburst. She'd never been quite so tied up in knots over her feelings for a man at the same time as wanting him to fuck her until she ached from head to toe. Again.

"I am more like you than you know. Let me in, sweet Erika."

He nuzzled at her breasts and she opened her legs reflexively because she really, *really* wanted him between them.

"Stop. I need to talk." She gripped his forehead just as he was about to sink his sweet tongue into her pussy. God, what a force of will *that* took.

He sat back and looked at her expectantly.

"Sweetie, you are too perfect for words. When we're done with this conversation I promise you can fuck me any way you'd like to."

Geva grinned wickedly. "So good deeds still garner rewards in this generation?"

"Yes. Yes they do. But I need to figure out how the hell we're going to support your fucking *brood* once we get out there. I can't abide homeless dragons in Boston. And they all seem so…sex starved and destitute. I mean, no offense, but the first place we come to all the residents have taken vows of poverty. Frankly, I worry for the population."

Geva's brows creased and he nodded sagely. Then let out a hearty laugh.

"You're worried we can't support ourselves?"

"Well…yeah?"

He gripped her shoulders and pushed her back against the pillows.

"My love, we are dragons. Riches are our specialty and we have cultivated them for several thousand years. We want for nothing. And neither should you. You will soon see. Yes, the humans who live here want no riches, but that is because it is their mandate to protect *our* interests. Different sects of their order have functioned in this capacity for millennia." He looked around their room with a creased brow. "They've changed since I first visited before sleeping, however. It's much cleaner now."

"So where is 'home' for these dragons? Another halfway house as destitute as this one?" Erika felt a little bad for being so pissy at him. The truth was the first meal they'd been served had been one of the most delicious dishes she'd tasted, and the bed they were in was a far cry from sleeping on hard ground.

"I said you will see. We all are descendents of the most prominent dragon citizens. These men are the keymasters to our treasure, between generations. You had a father, yes? You've spoken of him."

"Yes. I loved my dad."

"When he died, what happened to his treasure?"

She had no idea where he was going with his line of questioning but answered. "It's mine now."

"And what are you doing with it?"

"Well…nothing. I've been away too long to bother. Everything's locked up tight. Waiting for me to come home, I guess…"

She was lying a little bit. Her father's estate wasn't locked up exactly. The staff still lived there and kept it up. When she was stateside she called regularly to talk to the caretaker, Walt. Conversations were as much about her life as they were about the continued smooth running of the estate. Her father had left her enough money to keep it going for at least her lifetime, if not longer. Maybe she had been away too long?

She rolled over and looked up into Geva's eyes. "I get it. You guys all have a legacy. Lucky bunch you are, I have to say. I wonder what happens to orphaned dragons."

Geva's brow creased in confusion. "Orphans. Rare enough, but they happen. They're provided for."

Erika thought he seemed a little uncertain about his answer, but dismissed it. She wanted to ask him more, but got a little distracted by his exquisite tongue finding its way between her thighs yet again.

Yeah, she could deal with that for a few centuries, and who cared about the rest of the world?

Thank you for enjoying Sleeping Dragons.
Please look for the next series:

RISING DRAGONS

BOOK 1: BREATH OF DESTINY

Erika Rosencrans has accomplished her life's dream: proving that dragons exist. Now she only wants to share her life with the amazing red dragon, Geva, and hunt down more lost ancient temples while exploring her dragon lover's vast sexual appetite.

Geva, a member of the dragon queen's Court has two desires: to make Erika happy and to convince the adventurous archaeologist to stay put long enough to bear his child, the singular thing most dragons crave upon leaving hibernation.

They return to Geva's ancestral home, and in the process of exploring his dead mother's journals, Geva and Erika discover a secret his parents kept that could change the lives of all dragons. But in order uncover the details of the secret and get what they both want, the two lovers must compromise.

Read on for an excerpt.

BREATH OF DESTINY

CHAPTER 1

"Are we headed the right way?"

The words reached Geva's ears but he didn't quite hear them. He was too enthralled with the pleasing ivory column of Erika's neck and the slope of skin that led down, down, down, into the low-cut black shift she had donned before they'd left the luxury of the London hotel to brave a gray, windy afternoon.

Dress, she called it a dress, he corrected himself. His memory of dresses was a bit different from what she wore now—he preferred this mere slip of fabric that hugged every curve, cradled her full breasts, and showed an abundance of skin. Especially her glorious legs, tanned and muscular like a dragon woman's legs. Was she even human? He'd wondered it often, but seeing the other women she associated with he had to believe that human women in the current cycle were more attuned to their bodies than they had been when he was born.

He reached out a hand to caress the bare expanse of skin beneath her hem. The sharp smack of her hand made him look at her.

"You made me bring you out today, dummy. Tell me we're going the right way. And you're learning to drive. I can't stand driving on the wrong side of the street."

Chastised, he smiled at her and looked around.

The beasts Erika called *cars* sped down the lanes on either side of them. Gleaming, monolithic towers of glass drifted past, foreign and bizarre as they travelled through the city. Every so often he would recognize some small landmark or symbol on a sign, but other than that, his beloved city had become a stranger to him.

"It all looks different now, but the direction of the sun tells me we're headed in the right direction."

Soon the landscape changed. The bustling city with its alien structures replaced by smaller communities, then rolling green hillsides. The shine of a metropolis was a treasure trove to explore for a dragon like him, but the peace of the countryside let him breathe. He knew precisely where he was now, the landscape as familiar to him as the lush curves of Erika's body. They didn't have far to go.

Soon they approached a wide driveway, flanked by security booths. Erika provided identification to the man inside and they drove through.

The huge building they finally stopped before was one he knew well, inside and out. An imposing fountain in the forecourt spurted water out of a sextet of dragons' mouths into a pool below.

The most familiar was the emblem on the grand, polished sign that hung over the broad entryway. The stylized dragon caused a brief pang of homesickness in him. He didn't even need to read the strong type beside it. "Hayden Capital and Antiquities." He was home.

And yet he couldn't bring himself to get out of the car.

He considered himself the luckiest dragon of his generation, all of whom had slumbered along with him, deep in the depths of that jungle temple, until Erika and her team had completed the ritual to awaken them.

He'd never expected to awaken to such a beautiful, strong, and infuriating woman. One he desired to fuck as much as he desired to argue with her. Their latest argument had been about coming here today. Understandably she was more eager than he was. Everything was a new discovery for her, but finding out about his family's past wasn't going to be a happy moment for him. That his hibernation had ended meant his parents were dead now. Expired at the end of a life he believed he should have been a part of.

Dragon law had kept him away. Forced his generation into hibernation to lengthen their lives and preserve their bloodlines. And now they'd awakened to a vastly different world already inundated with humanity to such a degree that the dragons would be hard pressed to catch up.

The Council's magical restrictions on procreation seemed even more ludicrous now than they had when he was young. He felt it as keenly as his brethren—a kind of itch to get on with it, but with their hands significantly tied. Even though a dragon and his or her mate might both desire a child, wanting was only half the battle. The Council's magic meant it could take decades for a couple to conceive. Geva hadn't shared that detail with Erika, nor did he believe the others had with their mates. Human lives were normally so fleeting relative to a dragon's. There was no sense worrying them with it when they had his longer, dragon's lifespan to work with, his magic prolonging Erika's to match. Longer lives meant more opportunities.

Except the breeding restrictions and enforced hibernation had been instituted during a time when there was a real danger of dragon populations overtaking humans and beginning to view them as breeding stock. That was far from the case now.

Well, maybe not that far, considering Geva just wanted to stay in their hotel room and convince Erika to take his seed. He had no desire to mate with any other woman. But after the first attempt he wasn't sure how to broach the topic again. Apparently "let's make a baby now" wasn't an acceptable incentive to get Erika to agree to try. Even though trying was likely all it would be.

"You're still pissed about the baby thing, aren't you?" Erika asked. She shifted in her seat to face him.

Sweet Mother was she intuitive. "Yes. I don't understand the hesitance. A dragons' offspring are his greatest treasures. And most women want children. I want…" Heat flushed his cheeks and he glanced at her. He wanted more than anything for her to have *his* children. As passionate as they both were, they could produce a strong Red like him, or maybe a Gold. Those were the happiest dragon offspring. But after her response to his initial request, he hesitated. He also hated himself a little bit for being frightened of her. A human woman? Intimidating to *him*?

She brushed a palm down the side of his face and he closed his eyes, savoring her touch.

"Geva, I never wanted kids. I love my work too much. Maybe in a few years. Just not now."

Not now. The words stung but incited a blaze of desire in him that he couldn't explain. He wanted desperately to share his power with her, maybe to show her what their bond meant again and how beautiful it would be to have some tangible product of their union. He should just tell her why it was so important that they start soon, but he felt the need to convince her to want a child first.

With another swipe of her fingers through his hair, she was gone. She stepped out of the car and walked toward the entrance to the huge, stone building with the emblem of his mother emblazoned on its sign.

He watched her for a moment, admiring the flex of her calves and thighs beneath the short, black dress she wore. A gust of wind blew through and plastered the sheer fabric to her body. The visual made him go hard almost instantly. Then her impatient glower back at him made him question his sanity.

He grasped the lever to extricate himself from her vehicle and joined her. He slung an arm around her waist, only too conscious of the warmth of her body radiating through the slim scrap of fabric she'd covered herself with. It even penetrated the thicker wool of the modern, tailored suit he wore, causing his own skin to tingle pleasantly. Women in this cycle would be the death of him.

Erika would be the death of him. His cock twitched in agreement.

The interior of the castle that was his family's home centuries before was not quite the same as he remembered. True, the same pattern of polished marble shone beneath their feet, and the same grand, gilt details graced the walls and high ceilings, but as they climbed the wide, low steps that led from the foyer to the grand hall, the subtle differences became more apparent. The lights were first to capture his attention—the chandeliers that hung at intervals glowed much brighter than they ever had. They were as bright as the magic lights from the Temple he and his brethren had hibernated in for so long—a luxury dragons had to avoid when living among humans, but that humans had apparently caught up with. He wondered if there had been a dragon influencing the creation of these electric lights.

He'd encountered all these things over the last six months since awakening. *Technology* as she referred to it. He took it all in stride. In particular, he was fascinated with the tiny "gadgets" she used for her work and for communication with the others. He loved the sleek shine of them and their compact, symmetrical shapes. When Erika implied that the small object she called a "smartphone" was particularly valuable, his interest piqued, prompting a slew of questions. She finally had to resort to some not entirely unpleasant means to shut him up.

Seeing what he knew now to be surveillance cameras scattered around the place where he had come of age was jarring, however. When they reached the grand hall he stopped in his tracks. The hall was lined with cages, each one with a human standing calmly behind the bars, some having smiling conversations with other humans who stood on the outside. There were gaps midway down each cage where he could see exchanges being made.

"Are they prisoners?" he asked Erika in a low voice.

"No, sweetie. The place is a bank now. A very exclusive one, from the looks of things and how far we had to drive to get here. The cages are for protection. The clerks can come and go. Come on, let's find someone who can help."

Geva let her take him by the hand and lead him to one of the cages. He still marveled at the alien newness of the place in conjunction with its bone-deep familiarity.

"Welcome to Hayden Capital and Antiquities," a chipper male voice said, with only the barest hint of the familiar lilting accent Geva had grown up hearing. He looked away from the bank of huge, flickering screens on one wall that streamed numbers in a steady ribbon, each value he believed represented some form of wealth worth acquiring. He stored the information away to ponder later. Right now he was faced with an attractive, clean-cut young man with a mop of curly blond hair and blue eyes that took him in with a sense of familiarity Geva was unaccustomed to from humans.

"Good morning," Geva said, letting his lips curl into his most charming smile.

The man's eyelids fluttered when the breath carrying Geva's words reached him. His pupils dilated and then his cheeks flushed brightly when his gaze flicked over to Erika. His eyes rested on her face for a split second before sinking lower. The man cleared his throat and tore his eyes from Erika's chest. He was flustered when he met Geva's gaze again, but made a concerted effort at formality, even going so far as to feign haughtiness.

"How may I help you today, sir?" The man's words came out in an almost seductive drawl. Geva hadn't intended his breath to be more than a calming influence. The reaction surprised him.

Erika muttered a curse. "Remember we're here on business," she said in a low tone. He got the sense she was trying to remind herself of that detail as much as him. He'd seen the way her nipples hardened and pushed against the fabric of her dress when the man's gaze rested there. He'd also seen the way the man had licked his lips at the sight of her. This might be a more rewarding outing than he'd thought.

He reached into his jacket pocket and pulled out the small, flat piece of metal that he'd acquired months ago, shortly after joining the world again after his centuries-long hibernation. The object had no intrinsic value. He'd been informed that the embossed figures on its surface were the true key to his legacy. He had expected an actual key to his family's treasures, something he could shove into a lock, just as he accessed Erika's pleasure on a regular basis. Things were very different now than they had been before he slept.

The man in the cage—"Benjamin," the tag pinned to his lapel proclaimed—took the key and studied it curiously. He glanced at Geva with a somewhat eager expression, picked up the nearby handset and placed it against his ear. After a brief exchange, he nodded, replaced the handset and pointed toward the side of the hall.

"Mr. Hayden, please walk to the double-doors. I will escort you down to the vault."

The man left his post and began traversing the open area behind the other cages. Geva turned in the indicated direction with Erika at his side.

"Hayden, huh?" Erika said. "You didn't tell me that was your name on the sign out front. What else don't I know about you?"

"It was a name my mother chose before I slept. The one she began using then. It's what's marked on this." He held his key out to her.

"Sir Gavin Hayden the Fourth," she read. "Gavin's a nice name. It'll take some getting used to, though. Are you royalty? By human standards, I mean."

"Hmm, minor nobility most likely. We used to seek ruling positions over humans, but it became problematic to maintain the relative anonymity we prefer. And please *don't* call me Gavin when we're alone. Mother was just trying to conform. I've grown to like Geva much more."

Erika gestured at the blond clerk who was scouting his way past the other clerks to meet them at the other side of the room. "Mister Helpful over there certainly knew who you were. That's a far stretch from anonymity for someone who's been out of the public eye for several lifetimes."

"It's his job to know who I am. This is my home. He is a bonded servant of my family. Employee is the right term now, I believe."

"Even your employees are marked?"

"Not as such, no. Their bond isn't permanent."

Benjamin stood waiting by the double-doors. Geva watched his eyes rove over both him and Erika and wondered if the young man had been acquainted with Geva's mother to be so eager. His mother had been striking in her human form. She had been a Green, but more passionate and desiring of power than her own parents. His human father had been an ideal mate, a true partner in all things, the way he hoped Erika would be to him.

"My condolences on your mother's passing, sir. She was well loved." The light flush that colored the back of Benjamin's neck betrayed his true feelings.

"You knew Geva—er—Gavin's mother? What was she like?" Erika asked, picking up her pace to walk beside the young man.

"Beautiful, and very generous. God may strike me down for saying this, but I daresay she was better loved than the Queen."

Erika faltered for a second. "Oh, you mean the Queen of England?"

Benjamin gave her a curious look. "What other Queen is there, ma'am?"

Geva smirked at Erika's amused expression, then bent to whisper in her ear. "Mother *was* our Queen, so it stands to reason."

Erika glanced ahead, but Benjamin had outpaced them and was now out of earshot.

"Your hierarchy confuses the hell out of me. How do you decide who's boss?" she murmured back.

"The Council makes the laws. The Queen is their enforcer, chosen by a combination of familial wealth, gender, and color. Racha was the highest-ranking Green female born to our generation, so they cultivated her as our next Queen. It fits her, but no other dragon could have ranked higher, either."

Benjamin turned and led them down a narrower passageway that Geva knew led to the Keep as well as the dungeon beneath the castle. He was eager to see what modern improvements they had made to the rest of the place. Another heavy door lay ahead, this time with a small, silver box set into the wall to the left of it.

"Swipe your key card and place your thumb like so," Benjamin said, demonstrating.

Geva pulled his key out of his pocket and inspected it. One edge was smoother than the other. He slid it through the groove of the metal box, observed the blinking light, then placed his thumb on the shiny glass window at the top of the box. A heavy click sounded from somewhere inside the door and Benjamin moved to let them through.

Geva became more impressed with the measures of security as he went, but kept his interest to himself. Everything he had seen so far represented his inheritance. He had expected his family's wealth to be his when he awoke. Before he slept he had lived with a sense of entitlement that had only gotten him into trouble. His mother had graciously tolerated his transgressions. His father had inflicted him with passionate lectures about being worthy of the legacy. He'd had centuries since then, during his hibernation, to let it all sink in. Now with the memories of his parents haunting him like ghosts as he traveled the halls of his childhood, he was determined to be a son worthy of those memories. And to be a mate worthy of the beautiful woman at his side.

They descended down the narrow, spiral stone steps into the dungeon.

Erika chuckled. "Deja vu. Are there sleeping dragons down below?"

"Not below," Benjamin said, surprising them both. "The living quarters are in the upper floors of this tower. Lord Hayden liked to call the bedroom 'where the dragon sleeps.' I believe that was his term of endearment for her Ladyship."

"Oh, that's sweet," Erika said, shooting Geva a playful look.

Geva smiled back at her, and when he looked away felt the pleasant squeeze of her hand through the trousers covering his ass. He tensed just slightly under the familiar caress, then let out a hiss of breath when her hand ventured further between his legs from behind. The pressure against the back of his balls sent a jolt into his cock, which became instantly rigid. Sweet Mother, the woman was testing him. He'd have taken her right there on the stairs if he wasn't trying to prove to himself he could assume the role of Lord here.

At yet another heavy door, Benjamin paused and waited for Geva to repeat the unlocking procedure. The young man's eyes widened when he caught a glimpse of Geva's groin. Erika's hand still rested against Geva's hip and she had a devious smile on her face. She was using his reactions to test the other man. Geva didn't exactly disapprove but his focus was faltering as a result.

He wasn't sure what to expect on the other side of the door. His memory of the dungeon was of a place filled with dark corners to hide in, and it had very rarely been used to house prisoners. Considering the level of security, he'd predicted they would find a majority of his family's collection. He wasn't wrong, but the elaborate arrangement of every priceless object was far more impressive than he could have imagined.

The doors of each jail cell had been removed, the small alcoves converted into elaborate displays organized by century.

As they stepped silently down the corridor, Erika gripped his hand, her fingers clasped tightly around his. Her breath sped up and Geva caught the sweet, warm scent of her sex. She was only that aromatic when she was ready to be fucked. And *very* ready if the pink glow of her skin indicated anything.

"This is all yours?" she said, her voice sounding like she had trouble finding the breath for words.

"It's ours," he replied, squeezing her hand.

They reached a wide chamber at the end that had an open staircase leading to the deeper dungeons. The chamber was filled with priceless objects from a time even before Geva had been born, and the pieces were arranged in the manner of a large and luxurious boudoir including rugs, cushions, tapestries, armoires, and chairs. A massive wooden bed featured prominently, the headboard taller than Geva.

Erika gasped. "Is that an original Byzantine bed? And in perfect condition, too. Oh, baby!"

She rushed toward it and brushed her hand reverently over the elaborately carved footboard, then up along one of the columns that supported a heavy red velvet canopy.

Geva had never seen the bed before, but then if his parents had always used parts of the dungeon in this manner, it was no wonder.

"Can I?" Erika asked, making as if to climb onto it. "I don't want to break it."

Benjamin nodded. "It is really quite a sturdy piece of furniture. It has easily held her Ladyship, his Lordship, and guests." Geva shot a surprised look at him and Benjamin stammered. "I—I mean her Ladyship and—oh, bugger."

"Exactly how close were you and my parents, Ben?"

"Ah—um—they were lovely, lovely people. Took me in and made me welcome. And—well, your mum—I should say it was quite a blow when they were killed. In the prime of their lives, too. I'll just—go now. Leave you two with the, er, bed."

Geva resisted the mirth that bubbled forth hearing the young man fumble for an explanation

"Do stay," Geva said, not looking at Benjamin, but watching Erika.

She kicked her shoes off and slid onto the bed, her eyelids fluttering as she sank back against the cushions and velvet. She made pleasant little noises of appreciation and looked for all the world like she didn't even need a partner. She watched him in return, turning on one side to face him and slide her hand down over her body as if to smooth her already wrinkle-free dress.

Instead, the tug of her fingers caused the skirt to slide up over her thighs a little higher until Geva could almost catch a glimpse of the lacy underthings she'd put on that morning. A garment so spare as to be almost pointless, aside from his arousal to see her wear it.

Benjamin was even more enthralled by the sight. Geva stepped over to him and slid his hand across the man's shoulders, then bent and murmured in his ear, "Shall we see if it's sturdy enough for us three?"

ABOUT OPHELIA BELL

Ophelia Bell loves a good bad-boy and especially strong women in her stories. Women who aren't apologetic about enjoying sex and bad boys who don't mind being with a woman who's in charge, at least on the surface, because pretty much anything goes in the bedroom.

Ophelia grew up on a rural farm in North Carolina and now lives in Los Angeles with her own tattooed bad-boy husband and four attention-whoring cats.

You can contact her at any of the following locations:

Website: http://opheliabell.com/

Facebook: https://www.facebook.com/OpheliaDragons

Twitter: @OpheliaDragons

Goodreads: https://www.goodreads.com/OpheliaBell